NINJAK

WEAPONEER

MATT KINDT | CLAY MANN | BUTCH GUICE | JUAN JOSÉ RYP

CONTENTS

Collection Cover Art: Lewis LaRosa
with Brian Reber

Associate Editor: Tom Brennan
Editor: Warren Simons

VALIANT.

Peter Cuneo
Chairman

Dinesh Shamdasani
CEO & Chief Creative Officer

Gavin Cuneo
Chief Operating Officer & CFO

Fred Pierce
Publisher

Warren Simons
VP Editor-in-Chief

Walter Black
VP Operations

Hunter Gorinson
Director of Marketing,
Communications & Digital Media

Atom! Freeman
Matthew Klein
Andy Liegl
Sales Managers

Josh Johns
Digital Sales & Special Projects Manager

Travis Escarfullery
Jeff Walker
Production & Design Managers

Alejandro Arbona
Editor

Kyle Andrukiewicz
Tom Brennan
Associate Editors

Peter Stern
Publishing & Operations Manager

Chris Daniels
Marketing Coordinator

Danny Khazem
Operations Coordinator

Ivan Cohen
Collection Editor

Steve Blackwell
Collection Designer

Rian Hughes/Device
Trade Dress & Book Design

Russell Brown
President, Consumer Products,
Promotions and Ad Sales

Jason Kothari
Vice Chairman

MATT KINDT
CLAY MANN
BUTCH GUICE
ULISES ARREOLA
VALIANT
#1
NINJAK

CLASSIFIED

NINJAK SPECIFICATIONS & INSIGHTS

Multi-Tool Battle Belt

5-FUNCTION THROWING DISKS.
Subject displays an uncommonly hard-shell exterior, even for an agent with his experience and training.

POWDERED FLASH-BANG PROJECTILES.
Pressed for information regarding his formative years, agent employs distraction and digression as conversational techniques.

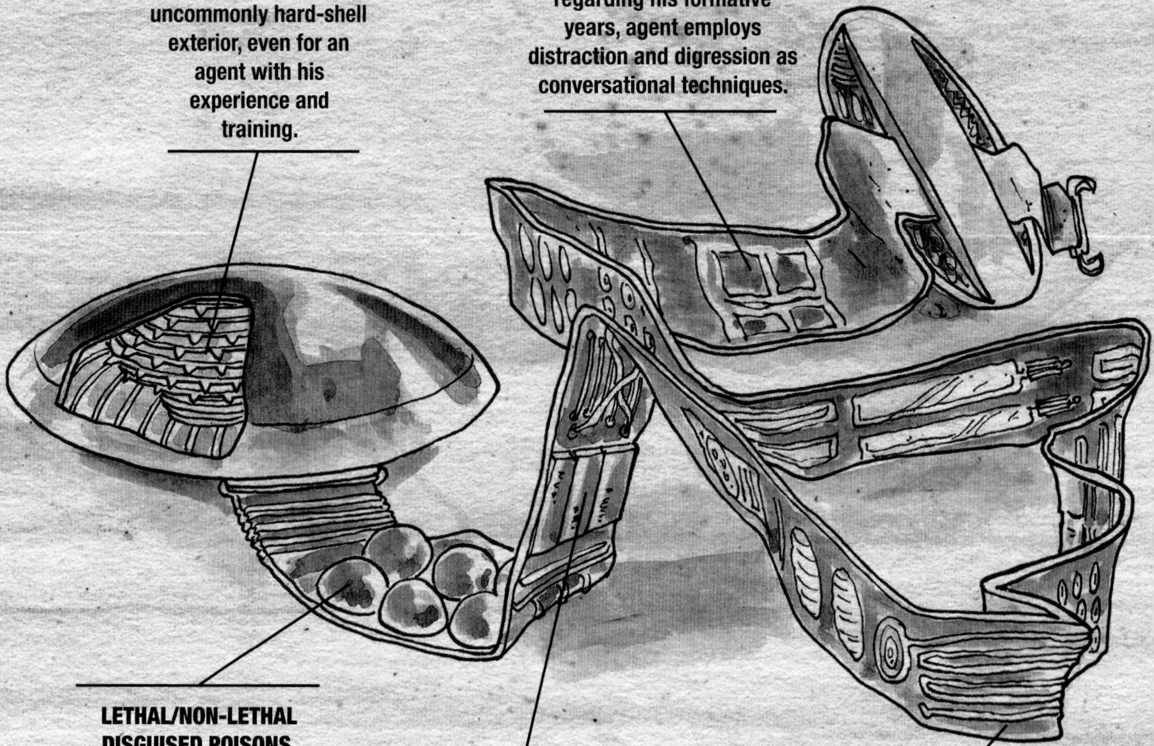

LETHAL/NON-LETHAL DISGUISED POISONS.
His psych evaluation interactions are typical of a subject harboring an unusual or traumatic childhood.

ADHESIVE OVERWATCH MINI-CAMERAS.
Upon further analysis/hypnosis, subject reveals childhood trauma was regularly visited on him by a family caretaker.

HIGH-TENSILE TITANIUM REINFORCED BELT.
Trauma was delivered to the subject via corporal punishment. Often with the primary caretaker's belt. Parents were [redacted].

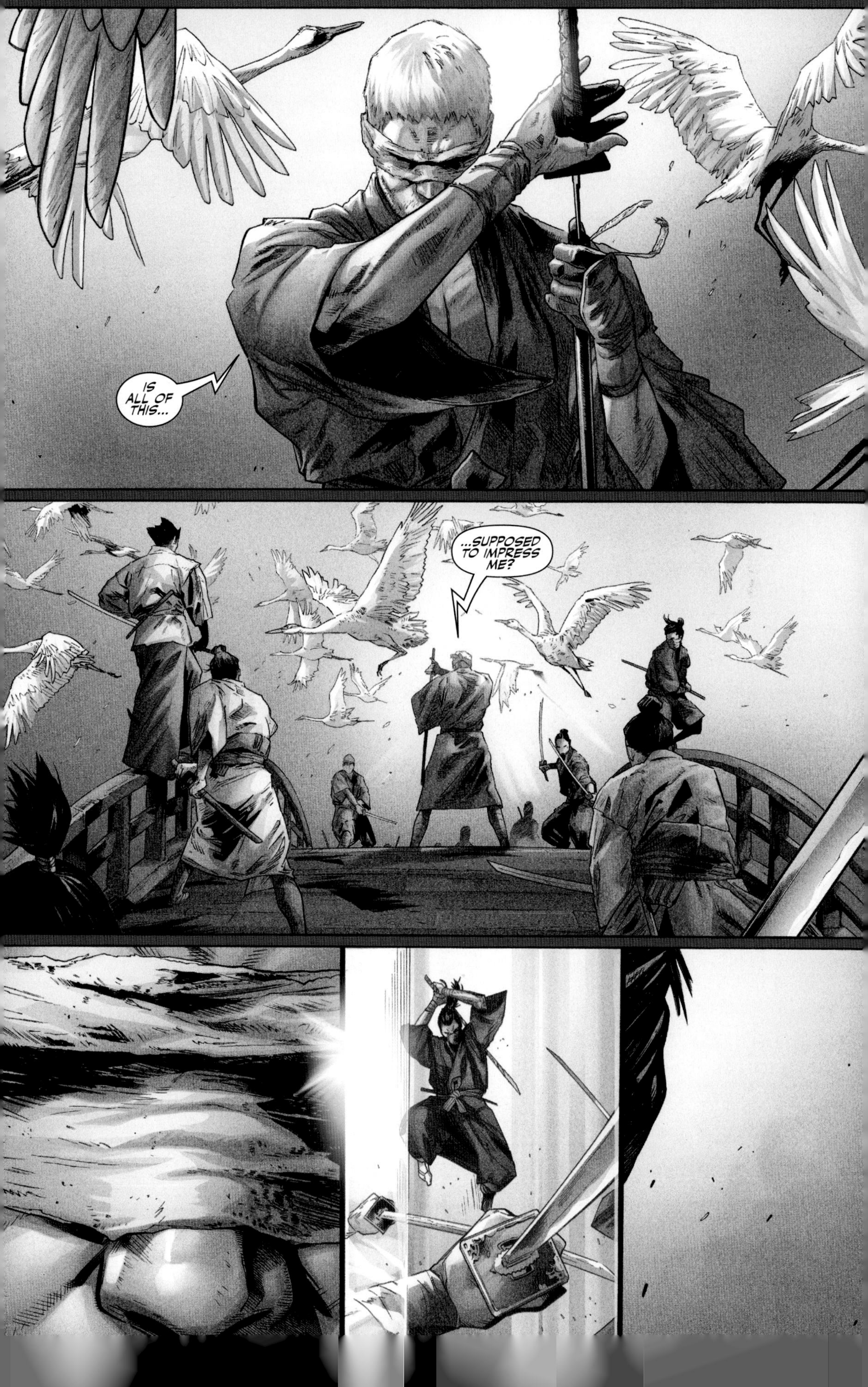
IS ALL OF THIS...
...SUPPOSED TO IMPRESS ME?

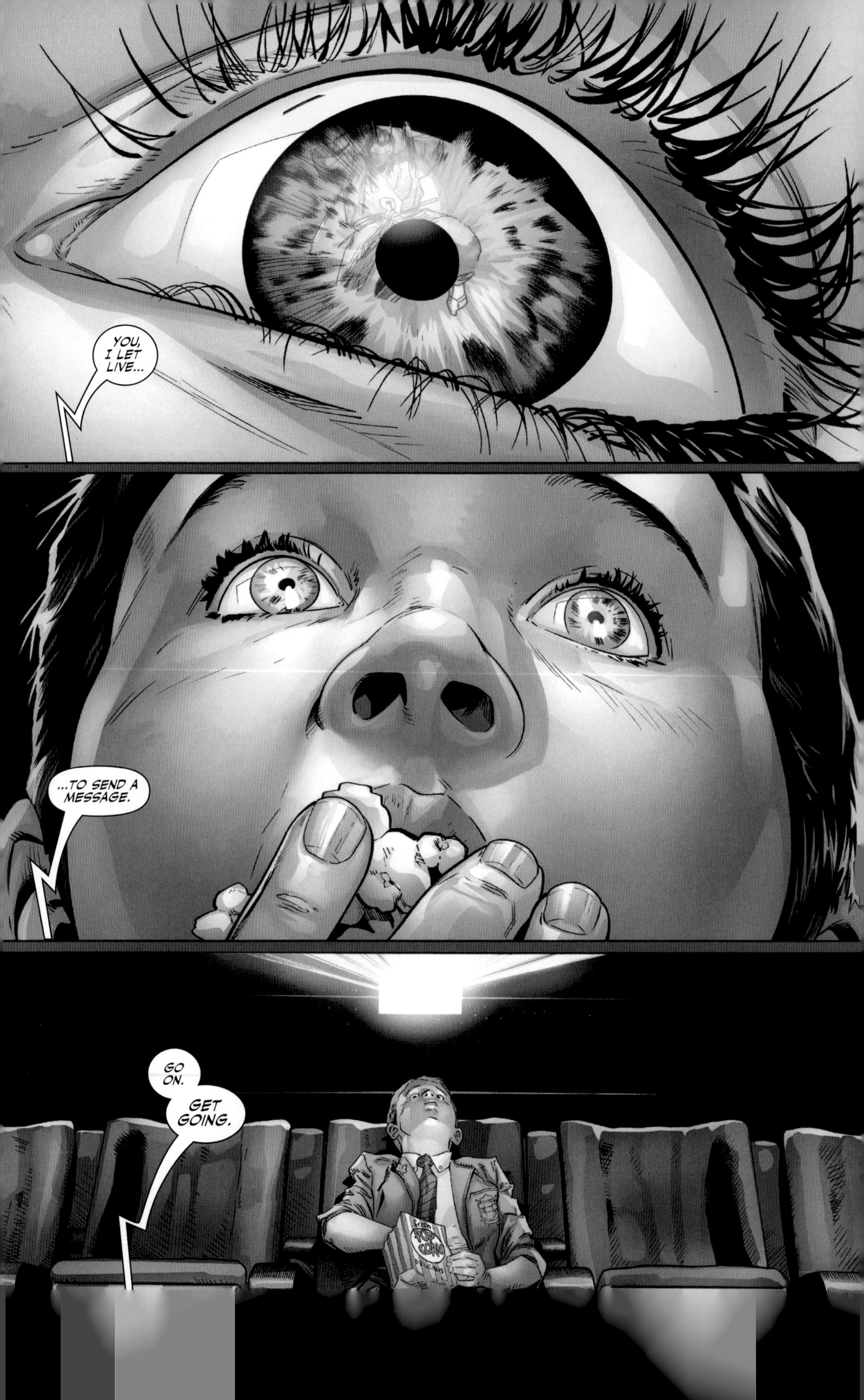
YOU, I LET LIVE...
...TO SEND A MESSAGE.
GO ON.
GET GOING.

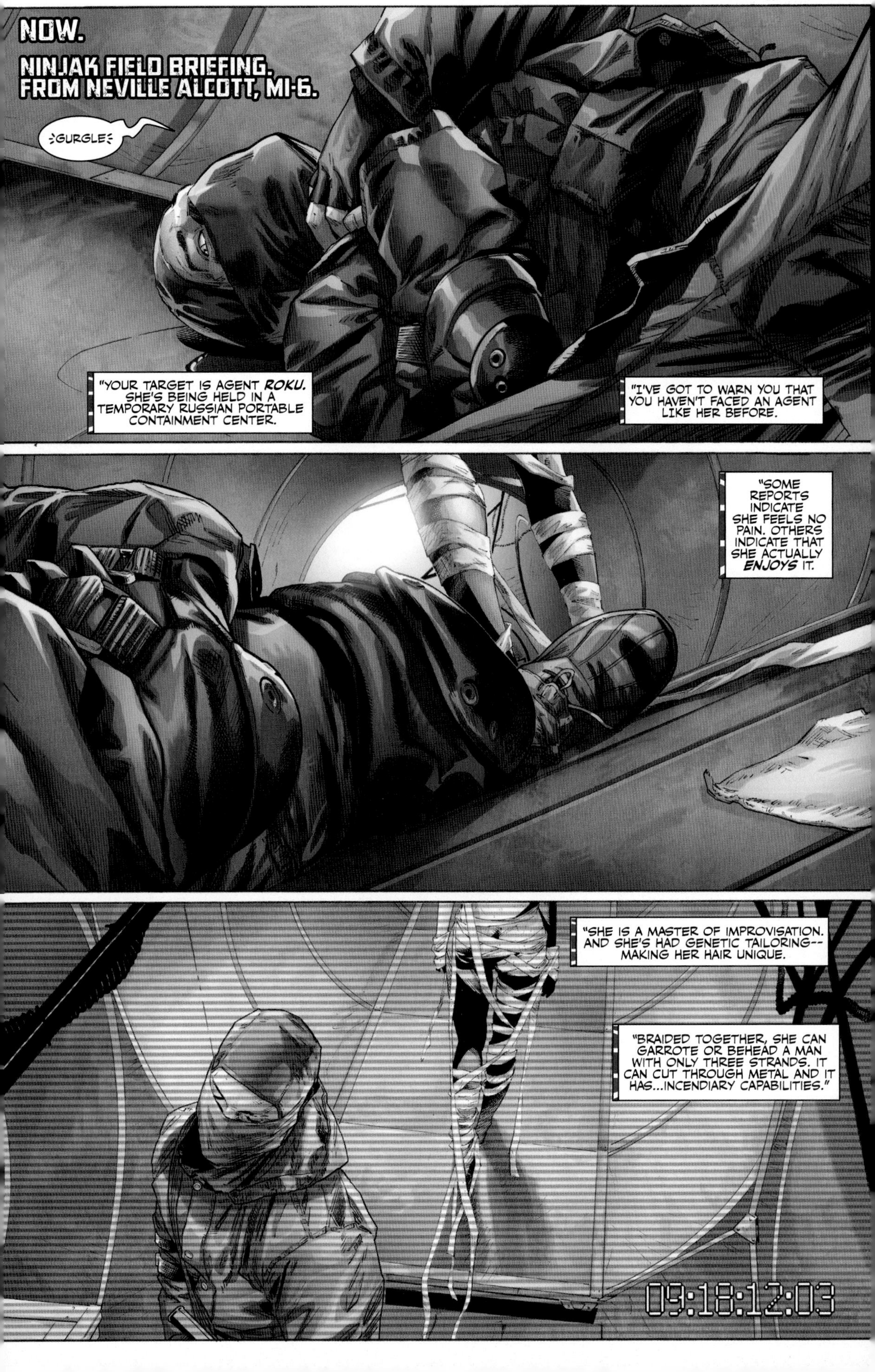
NOW.
NINJAK FIELD BRIEFING. FROM NEVILLE ALCOTT, MI-6.
GURGLE
"YOUR TARGET IS AGENT ROKU. SHE'S BEING HELD IN A TEMPORARY RUSSIAN PORTABLE CONTAINMENT CENTER.
"I'VE GOT TO WARN YOU THAT YOU HAVEN'T FACED AN AGENT LIKE HER BEFORE.
"SOME REPORTS INDICATE SHE FEELS NO PAIN. OTHERS INDICATE THAT SHE ACTUALLY ENJOYS IT.
"SHE IS A MASTER OF IMPROVISATION. AND SHE'S HAD GENETIC TAILORING--MAKING HER HAIR UNIQUE.
"BRAIDED TOGETHER, SHE CAN GARROTE OR BEHEAD A MAN WITH ONLY THREE STRANDS. IT CAN CUT THROUGH METAL AND IT HAS...INCENDIARY CAPABILITIES."
09:18:12:03

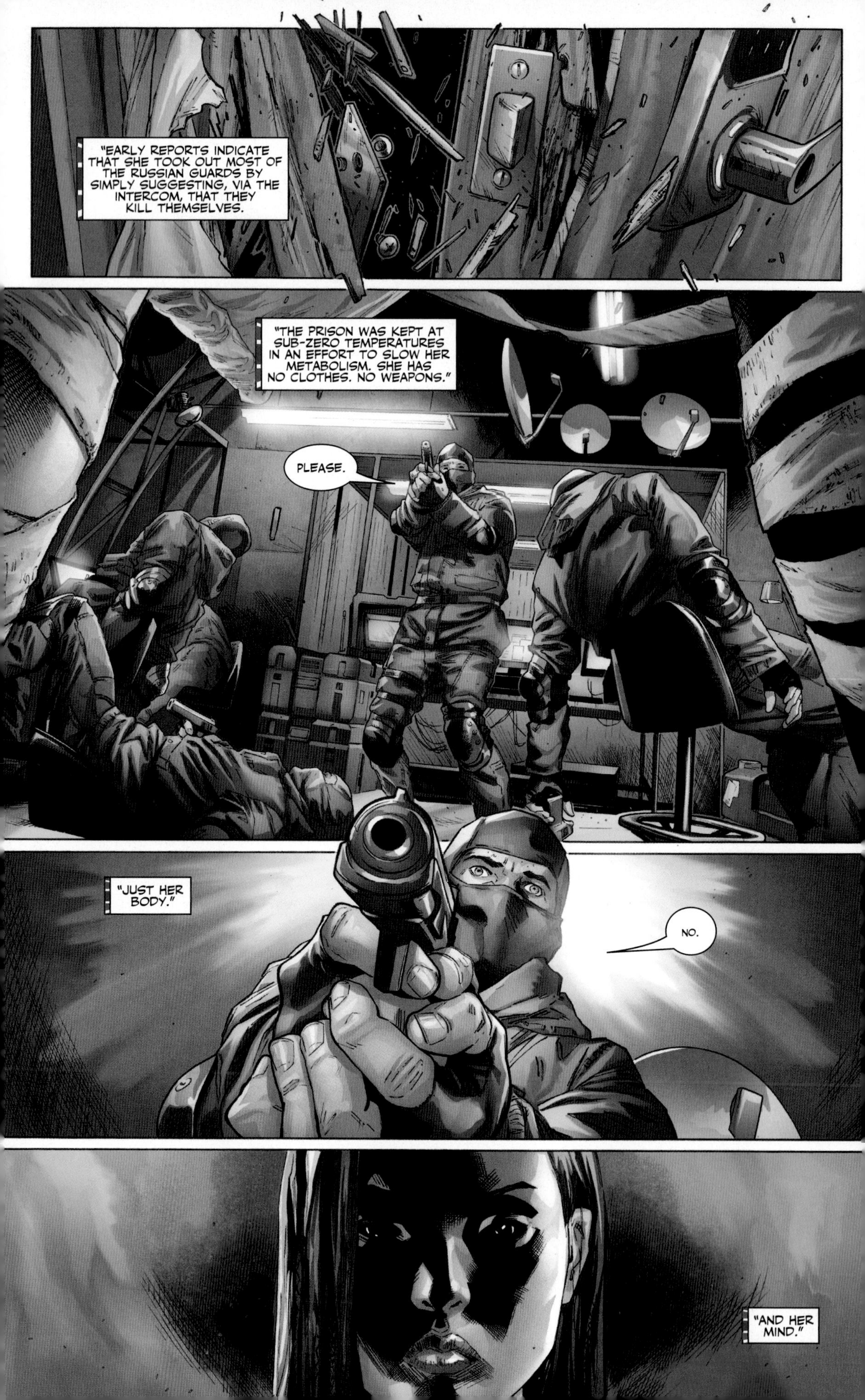
"EARLY REPORTS INDICATE THAT SHE TOOK OUT MOST OF THE RUSSIAN GUARDS BY SIMPLY SUGGESTING, VIA THE INTERCOM, THAT THEY KILL THEMSELVES.
"THE PRISON WAS KEPT AT SUB-ZERO TEMPERATURES IN AN EFFORT TO SLOW HER METABOLISM. SHE HAS NO CLOTHES. NO WEAPONS."
PLEASE.
"JUST HER BODY."
NO.
"AND HER MIND."

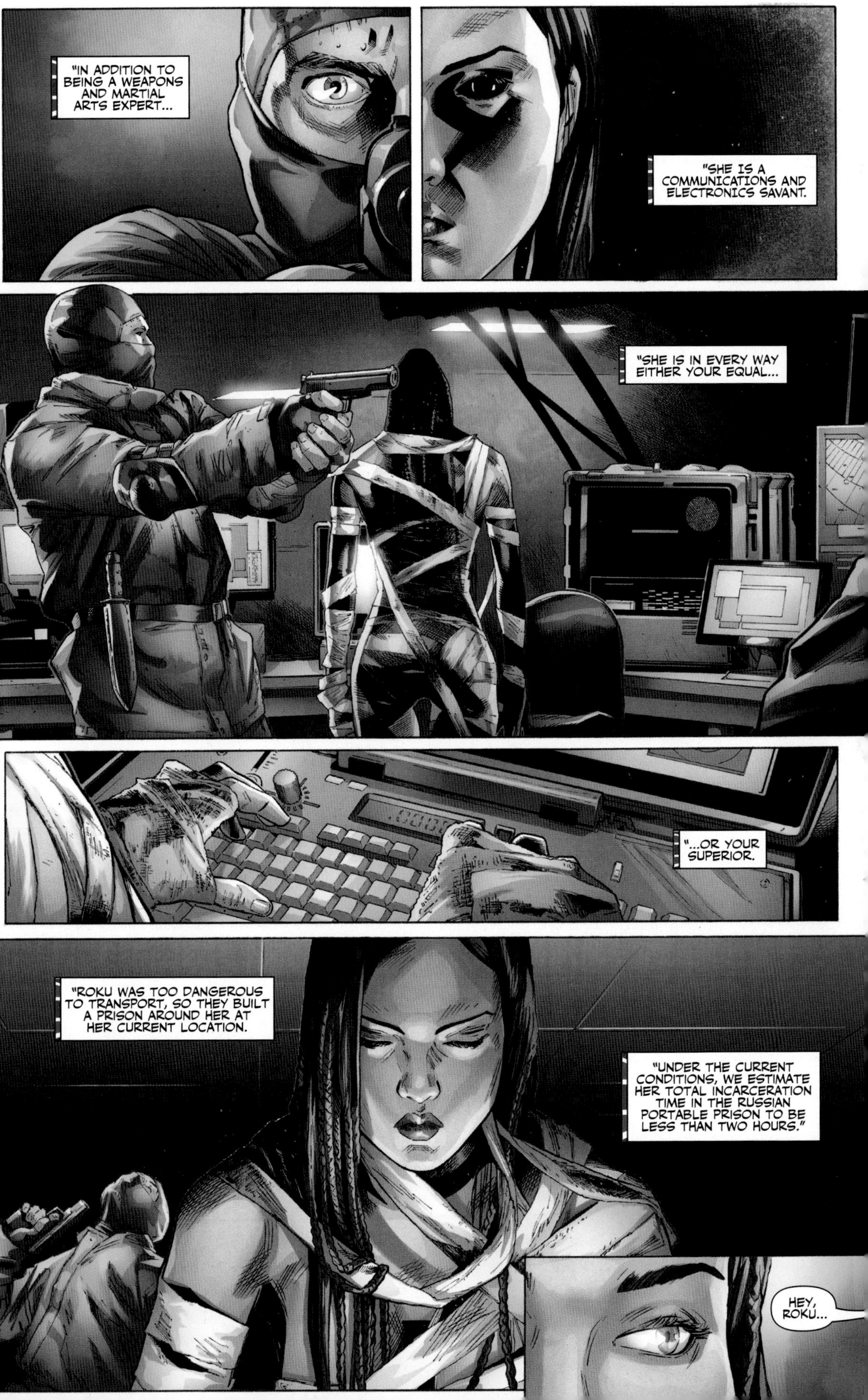
"IN ADDITION TO BEING A WEAPONS AND MARTIAL ARTS EXPERT...
"SHE IS A COMMUNICATIONS AND ELECTRONICS SAVANT.
"SHE IS IN EVERY WAY EITHER YOUR EQUAL...
"...OR YOUR SUPERIOR.
"ROKU WAS TOO DANGEROUS TO TRANSPORT, SO THEY BUILT A PRISON AROUND HER AT HER CURRENT LOCATION.
"UNDER THE CURRENT CONDITIONS, WE ESTIMATE HER TOTAL INCARCERATION TIME IN THE RUSSIAN PORTABLE PRISON TO BE LESS THAN TWO HOURS."
HEY, ROKU...

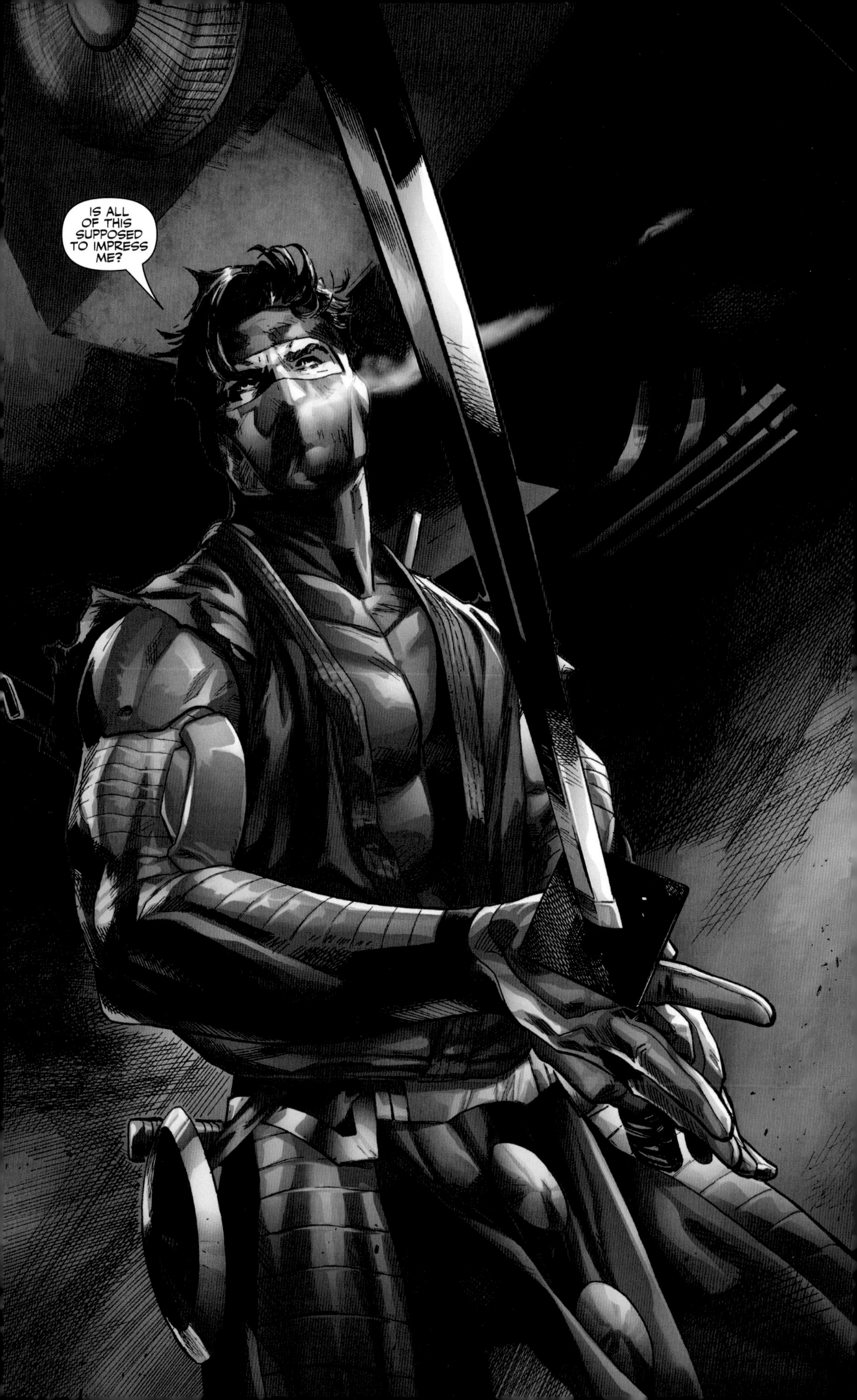
IS ALL OF THIS SUPPOSED TO IMPRESS ME?

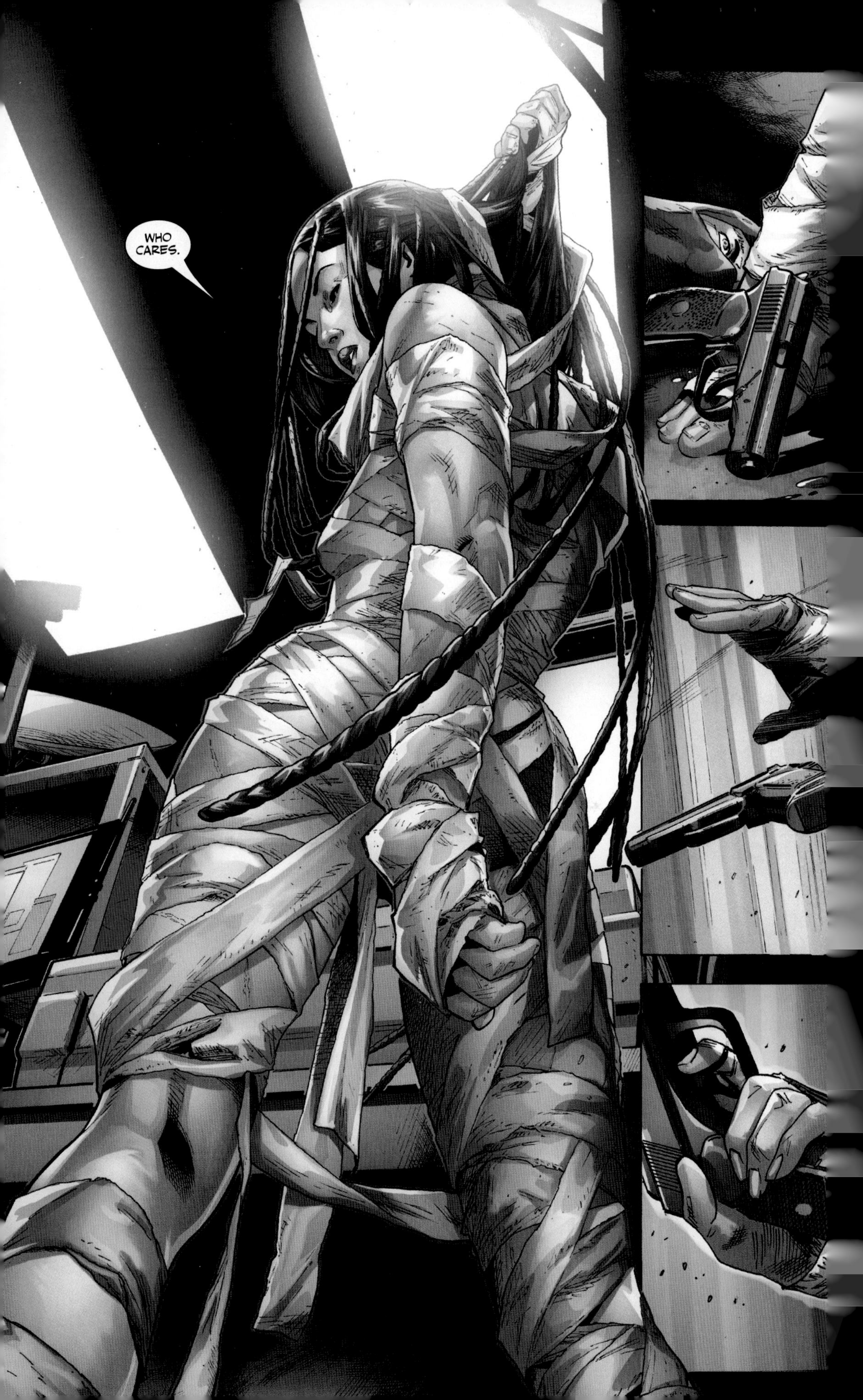
WHO CARES.

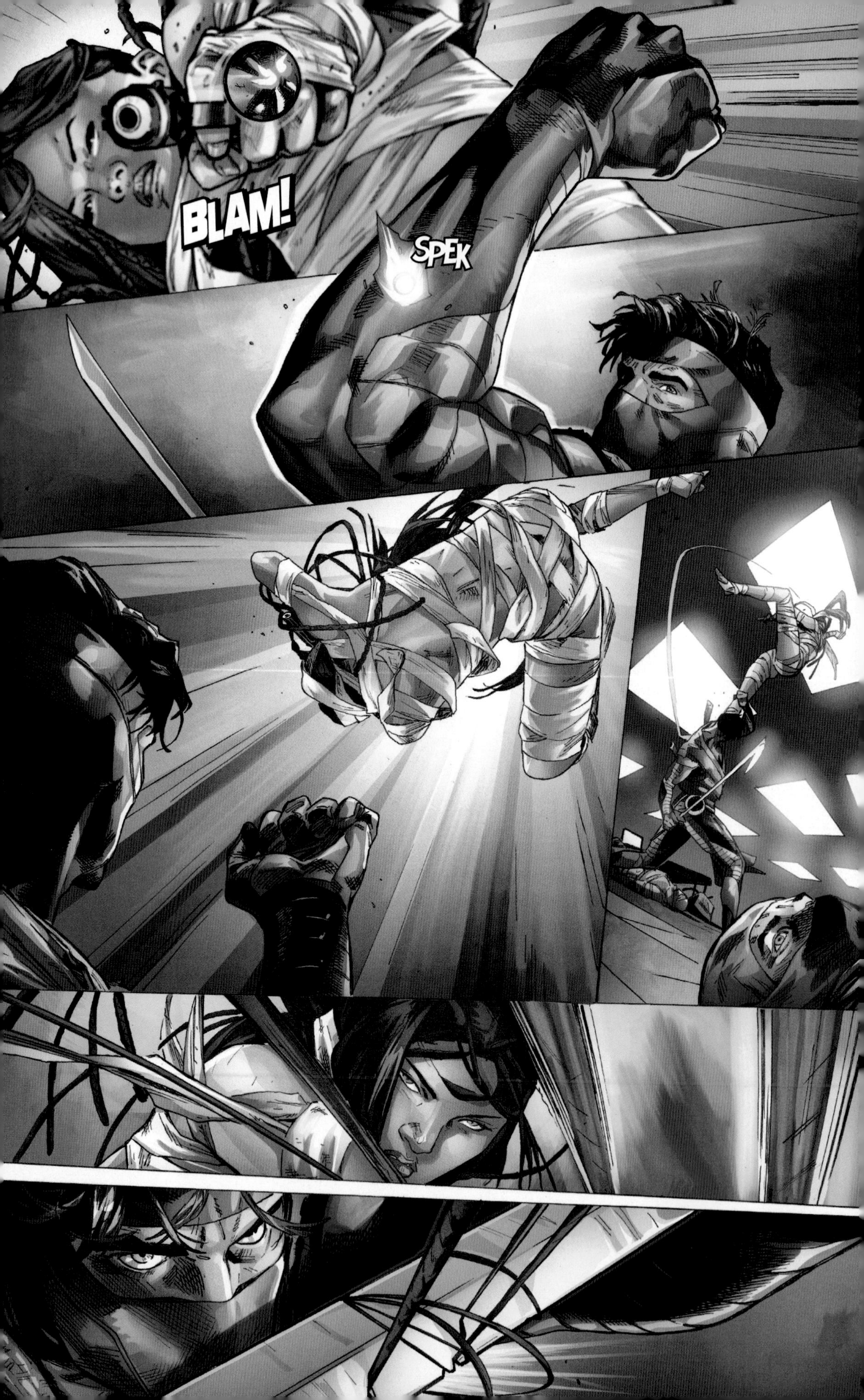
BLAM!
SPEK

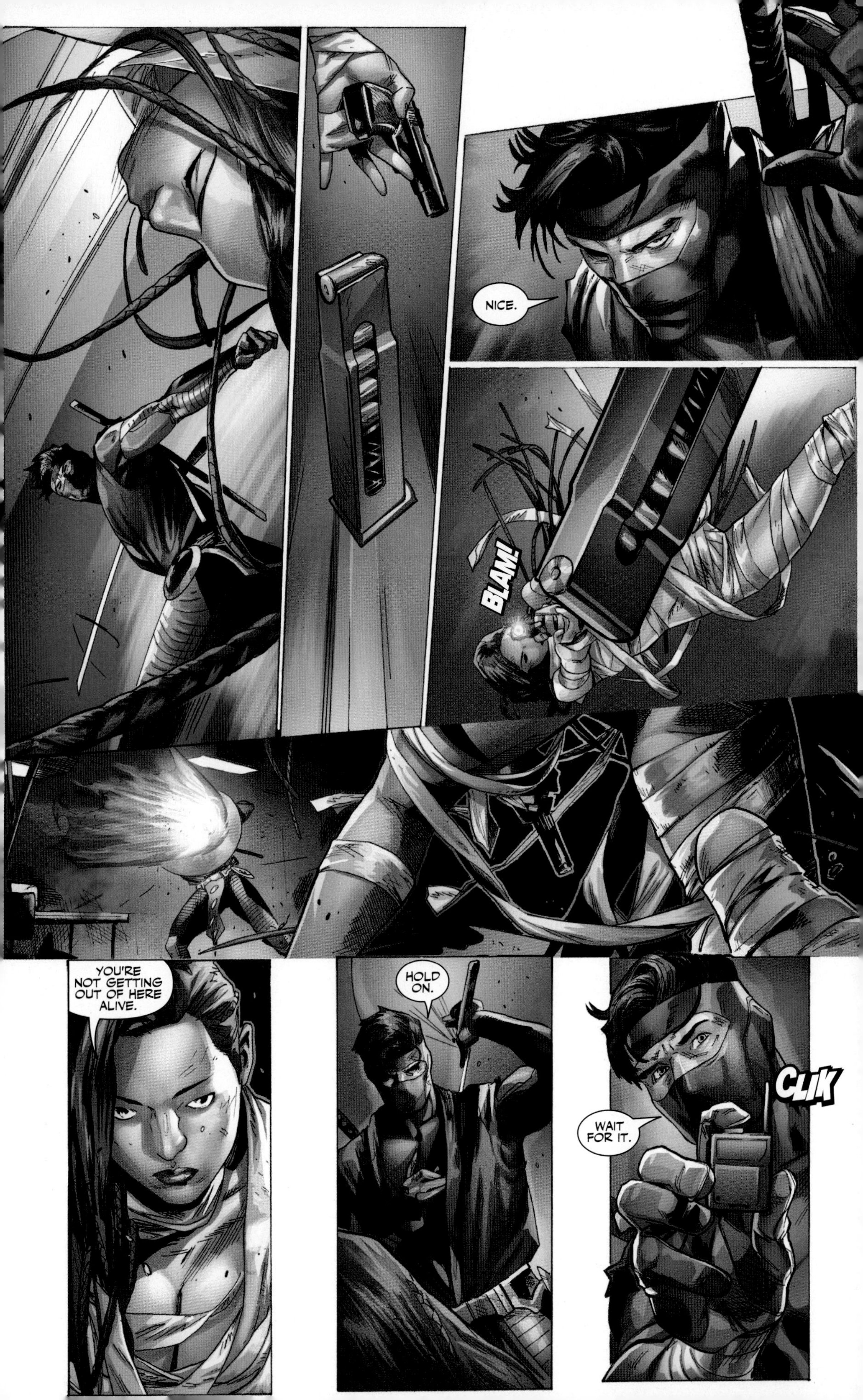
NICE.
BLAM!
YOU'RE NOT GETTING OUT OF HERE ALIVE.
HOLD ON.
CLIK
WAIT FOR IT.

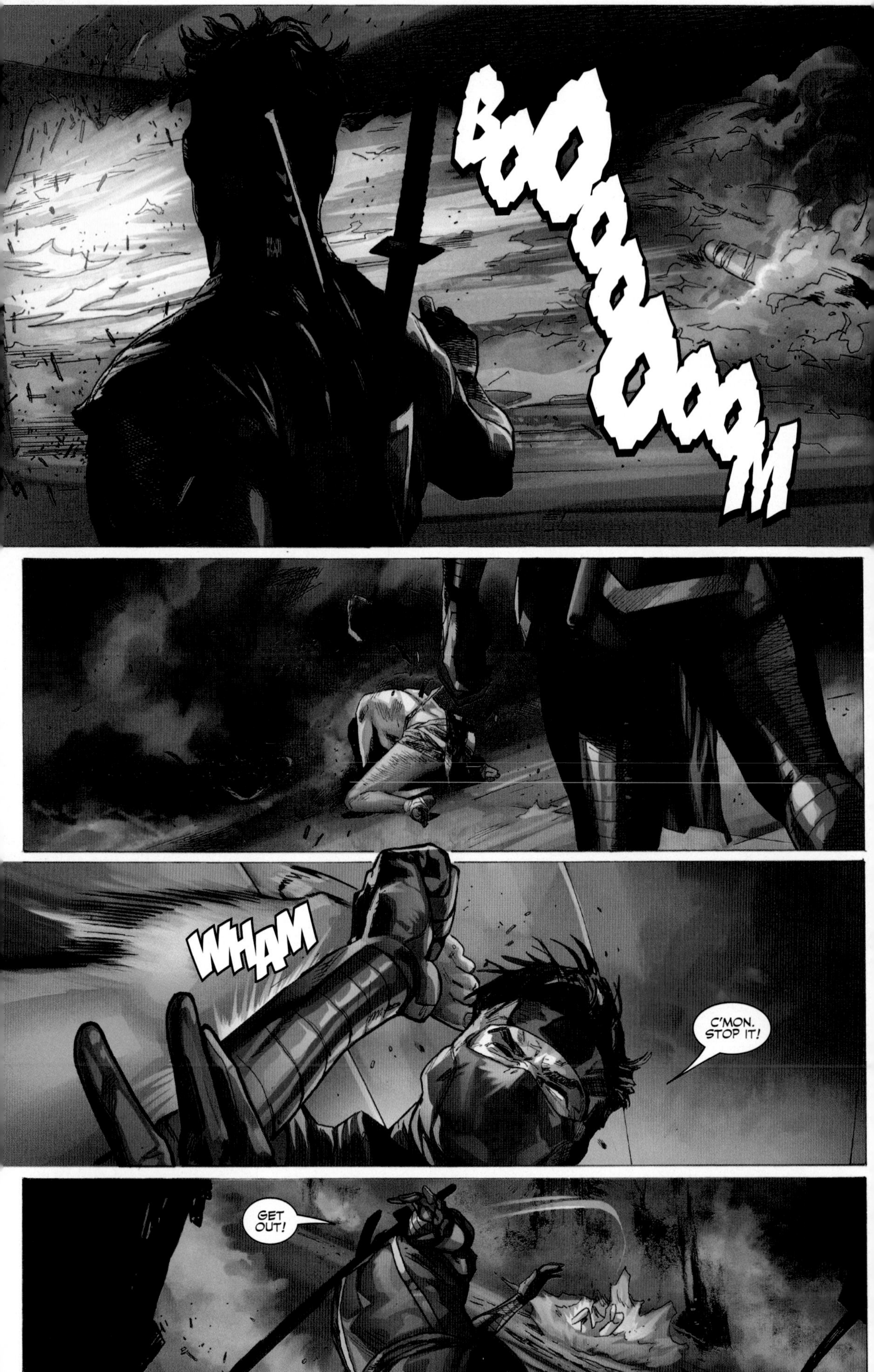
BOOOOOOOOM
WHAM
C'MON. STOP IT!
GET OUT!

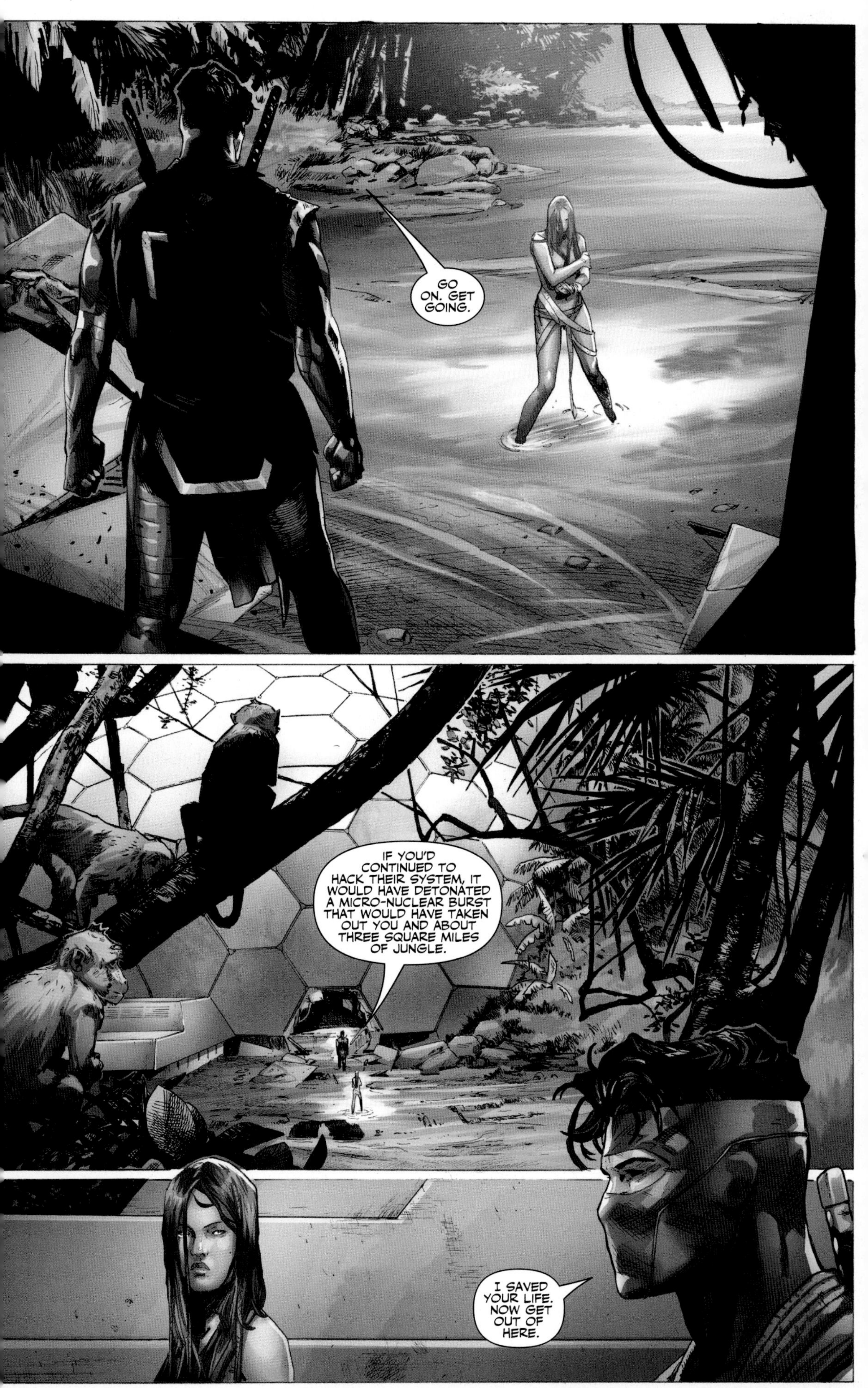
GO ON. GET GOING.
IF YOU'D CONTINUED TO HACK THEIR SYSTEM, IT WOULD HAVE DETONATED A MICRO-NUCLEAR BURST THAT WOULD HAVE TAKEN OUT YOU AND ABOUT THREE SQUARE MILES OF JUNGLE.
I SAVED YOUR LIFE. NOW GET OUT OF HERE.

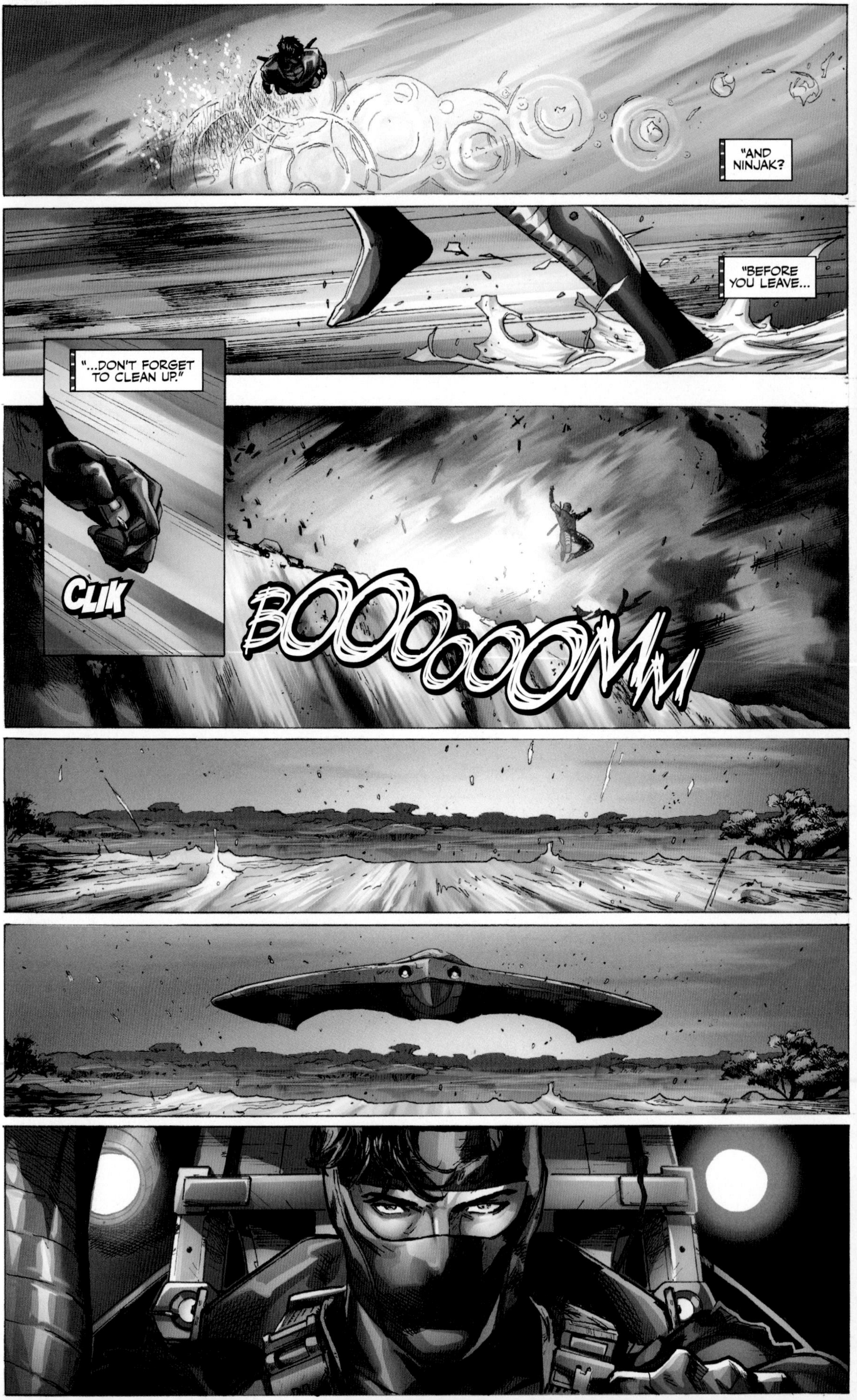
"AND NINJAK?
"BEFORE YOU LEAVE...
"...DON'T FORGET TO CLEAN UP."
CLIK
BOOOoOOOMM

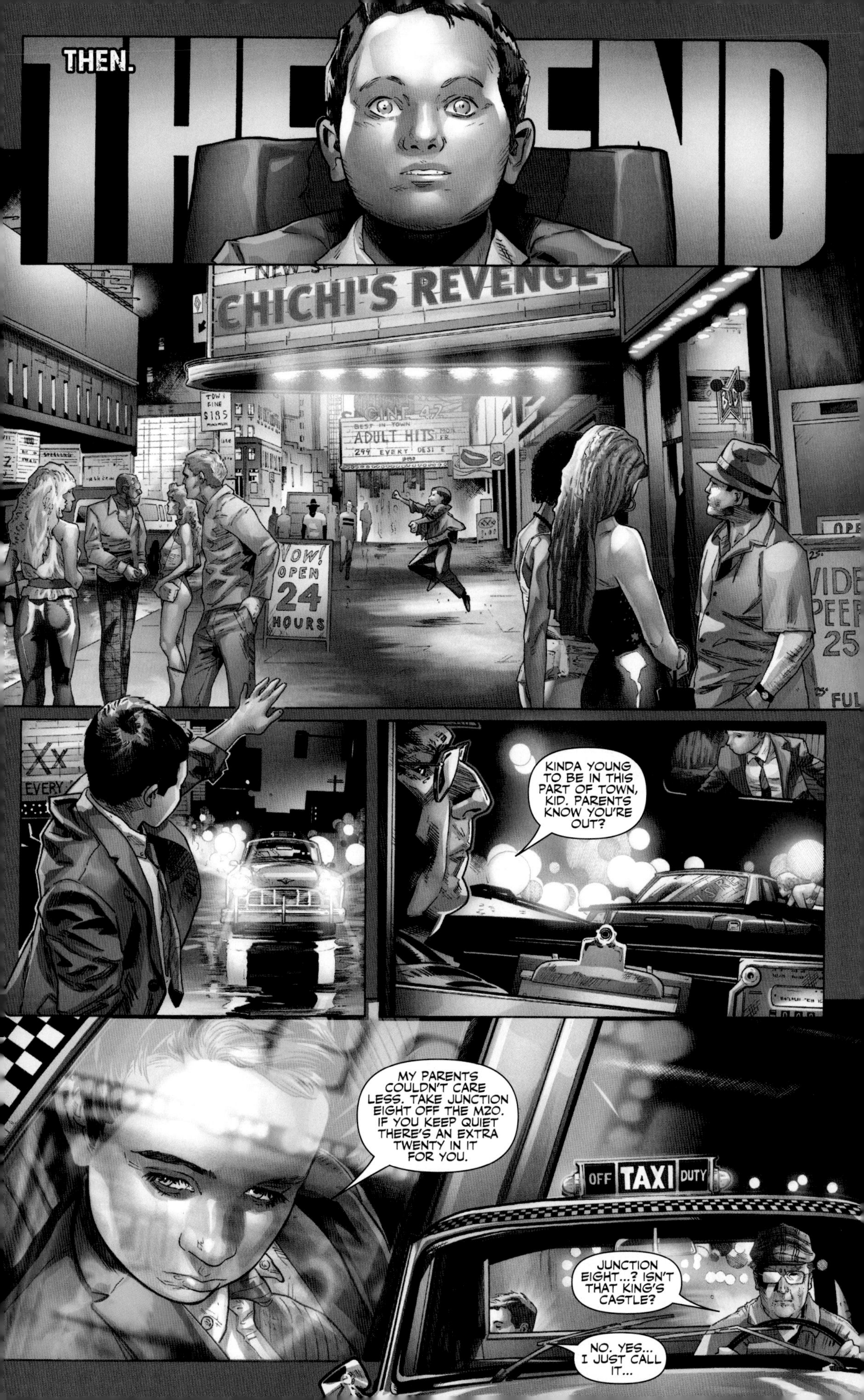
THEN.
THE END
CHICHI'S REVENGE
CINE 42
BEST IN TOWN
ADULT HITS
NOW! OPEN 24 HOURS
VIDEO PEEP 25
KINDA YOUNG TO BE IN THIS PART OF TOWN, KID. PARENTS KNOW YOU'RE OUT?
MY PARENTS COULDN'T CARE LESS. TAKE JUNCTION EIGHT OFF THE M20. IF YOU KEEP QUIET THERE'S AN EXTRA TWENTY IN IT FOR YOU.
OFF TAXI DUTY
JUNCTION EIGHT...? ISN'T THAT KING'S CASTLE?
NO. YES... I JUST CALL IT...

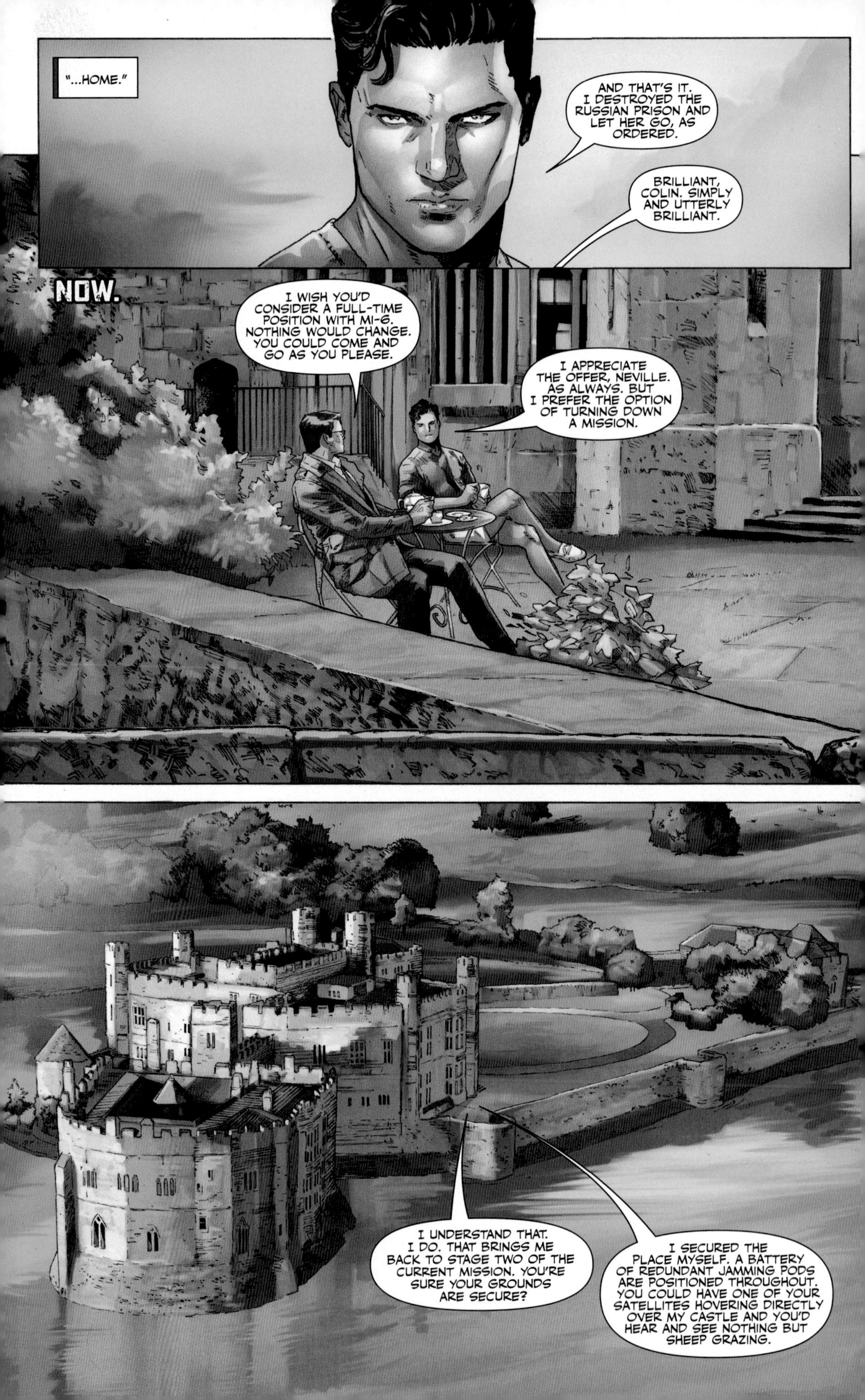
"...HOME."
AND THAT'S IT. I DESTROYED THE RUSSIAN PRISON AND LET HER GO, AS ORDERED.
BRILLIANT, COLIN. SIMPLY AND UTTERLY BRILLIANT.
NOW.
I WISH YOU'D CONSIDER A FULL-TIME POSITION WITH MI-6. NOTHING WOULD CHANGE. YOU COULD COME AND GO AS YOU PLEASE.
I APPRECIATE THE OFFER, NEVILLE. AS ALWAYS. BUT I PREFER THE OPTION OF TURNING DOWN A MISSION.
I UNDERSTAND THAT. I DO. THAT BRINGS ME BACK TO STAGE TWO OF THE CURRENT MISSION. YOU'RE SURE YOUR GROUNDS ARE SECURE?
I SECURED THE PLACE MYSELF. A BATTERY OF REDUNDANT JAMMING PODS ARE POSITIONED THROUGHOUT. YOU COULD HAVE ONE OF YOUR SATELLITES HOVERING DIRECTLY OVER MY CASTLE AND YOU'D HEAR AND SEE NOTHING BUT SHEEP GRAZING.

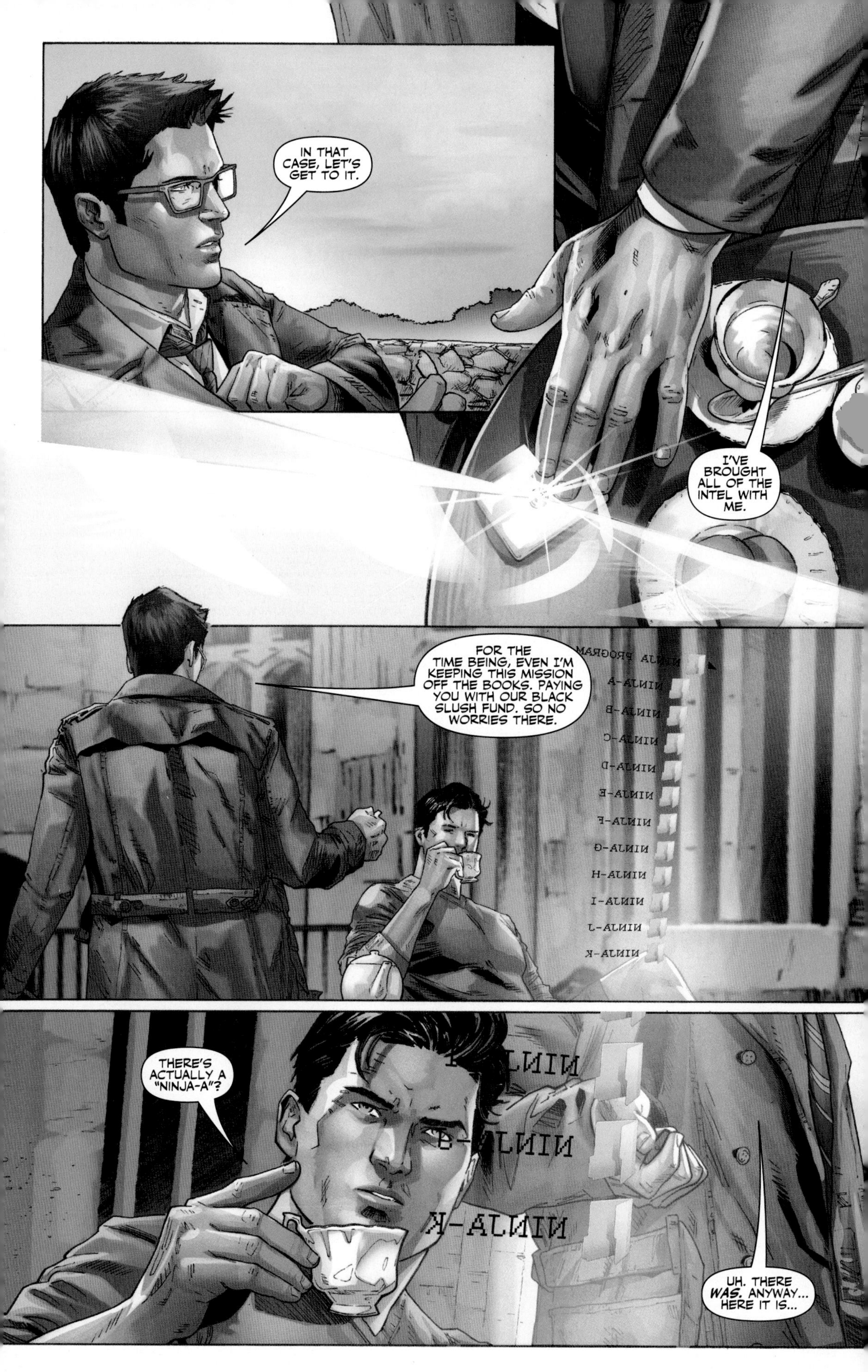
IN THAT CASE, LET'S GET TO IT.
I'VE BROUGHT ALL OF THE INTEL WITH ME.
FOR THE TIME BEING, EVEN I'M KEEPING THIS MISSION OFF THE BOOKS. PAYING YOU WITH OUR BLACK SLUSH FUND. SO NO WORRIES THERE.
NINJA PROGRAM
NINJA-A
NINJA-B
NINJA-C
NINJA-D
NINJA-E
NINJA-F
NINJA-G
NINJA-H
NINJA-I
NINJA-J
NINJA-K
THERE'S ACTUALLY A "NINJA-A"?
UH. THERE *WAS.* ANYWAY... HERE IT IS...

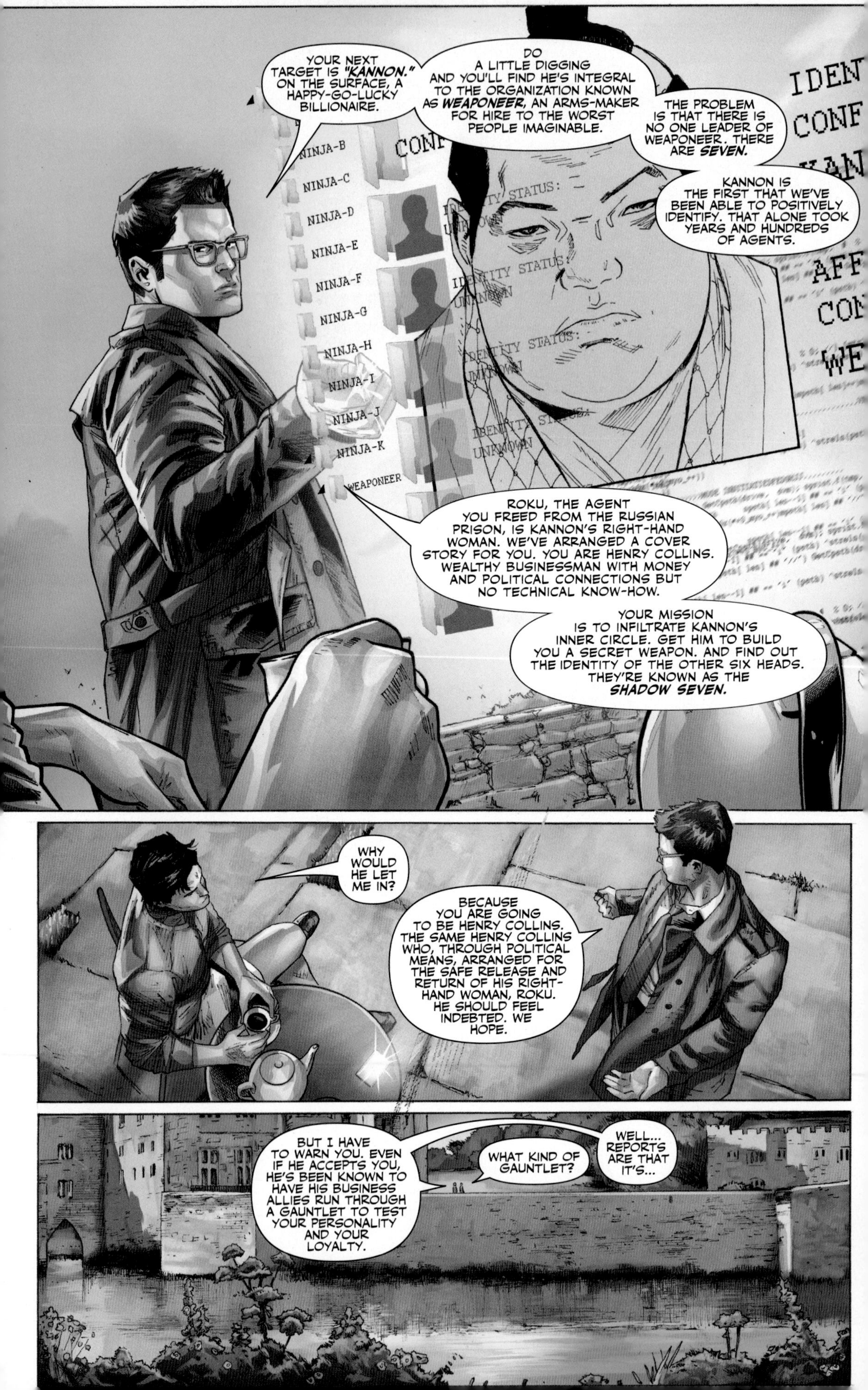
YOUR NEXT TARGET IS "KANNON." ON THE SURFACE, A HAPPY-GO-LUCKY BILLIONAIRE.
DO A LITTLE DIGGING AND YOU'LL FIND HE'S INTEGRAL TO THE ORGANIZATION KNOWN AS WEAPONEER, AN ARMS-MAKER FOR HIRE TO THE WORST PEOPLE IMAGINABLE.
THE PROBLEM IS THAT THERE IS NO ONE LEADER OF WEAPONEER. THERE ARE SEVEN.
KANNON IS THE FIRST THAT WE'VE BEEN ABLE TO POSITIVELY IDENTIFY. THAT ALONE TOOK YEARS AND HUNDREDS OF AGENTS.
NINJA-B
NINJA-C
NINJA-D
NINJA-E
NINJA-F
NINJA-G
NINJA-H
NINJA-I
NINJA-J
NINJA-K
WEAPONEER
ROKU, THE AGENT YOU FREED FROM THE RUSSIAN PRISON, IS KANNON'S RIGHT-HAND WOMAN. WE'VE ARRANGED A COVER STORY FOR YOU. YOU ARE HENRY COLLINS. WEALTHY BUSINESSMAN WITH MONEY AND POLITICAL CONNECTIONS BUT NO TECHNICAL KNOW-HOW.
YOUR MISSION IS TO INFILTRATE KANNON'S INNER CIRCLE. GET HIM TO BUILD YOU A SECRET WEAPON. AND FIND OUT THE IDENTITY OF THE OTHER SIX HEADS. THEY'RE KNOWN AS THE SHADOW SEVEN.
WHY WOULD HE LET ME IN?
BECAUSE YOU ARE GOING TO BE HENRY COLLINS. THE SAME HENRY COLLINS WHO, THROUGH POLITICAL MEANS, ARRANGED FOR THE SAFE RELEASE AND RETURN OF HIS RIGHT-HAND WOMAN, ROKU. HE SHOULD FEEL INDEBTED. WE HOPE.
BUT I HAVE TO WARN YOU. EVEN IF HE ACCEPTS YOU, HE'S BEEN KNOWN TO HAVE HIS BUSINESS ALLIES RUN THROUGH A GAUNTLET TO TEST YOUR PERSONALITY AND YOUR LOYALTY.
WHAT KIND OF GAUNTLET?
WELL... REPORTS ARE THAT IT'S...

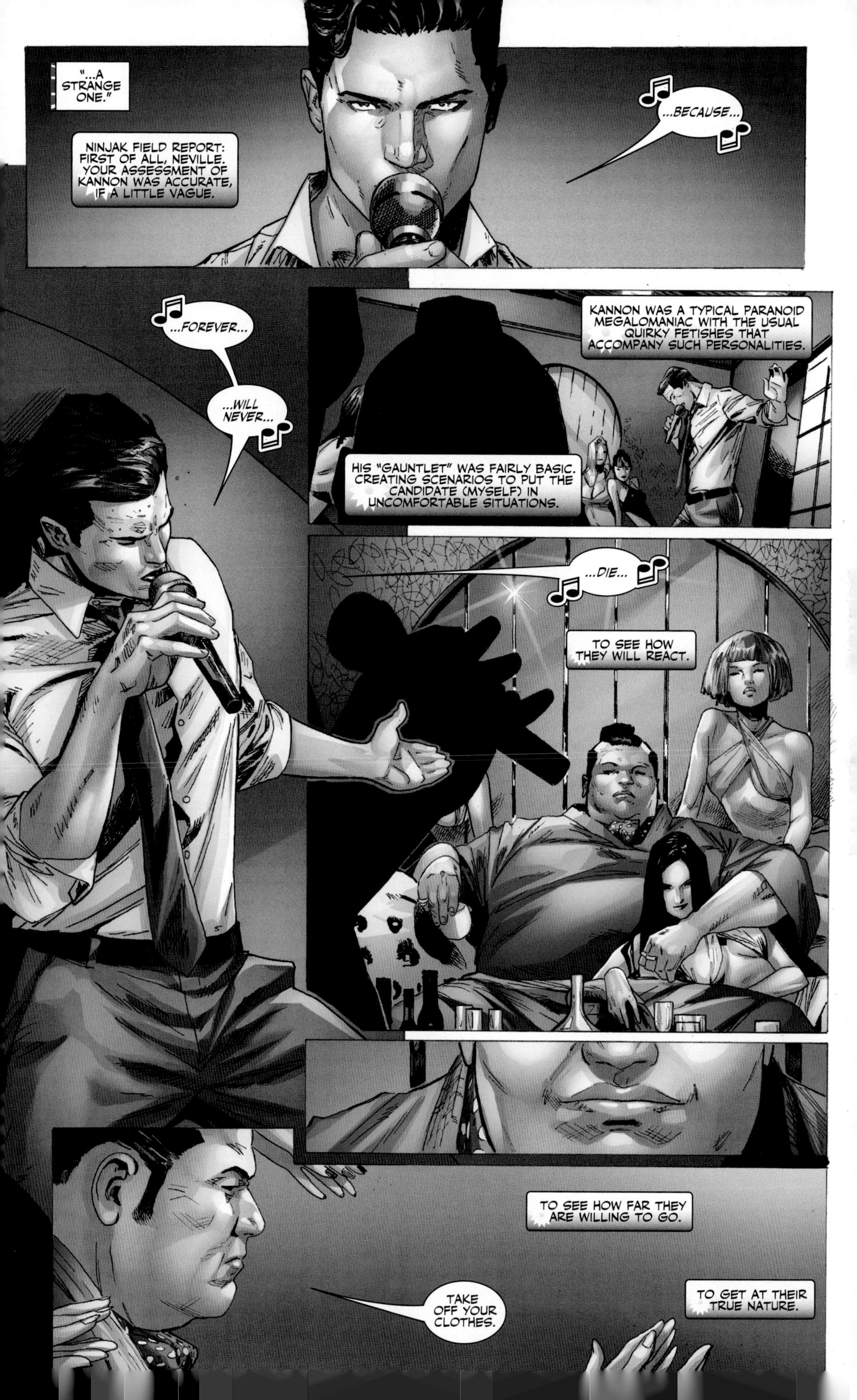
"...A STRANGE ONE."
NINJAK FIELD REPORT: FIRST OF ALL, NEVILLE. YOUR ASSESSMENT OF KANNON WAS ACCURATE, IF A LITTLE VAGUE.
...BECAUSE...
...FOREVER...
...WILL NEVER...
KANNON WAS A TYPICAL PARANOID MEGALOMANIAC WITH THE USUAL QUIRKY FETISHES THAT ACCOMPANY SUCH PERSONALITIES.
HIS "GAUNTLET" WAS FAIRLY BASIC. CREATING SCENARIOS TO PUT THE CANDIDATE (MYSELF) IN UNCOMFORTABLE SITUATIONS.
...DIE...
TO SEE HOW THEY WILL REACT.
TO SEE HOW FAR THEY ARE WILLING TO GO.
TAKE OFF YOUR CLOTHES.
TO GET AT THEIR TRUE NATURE.

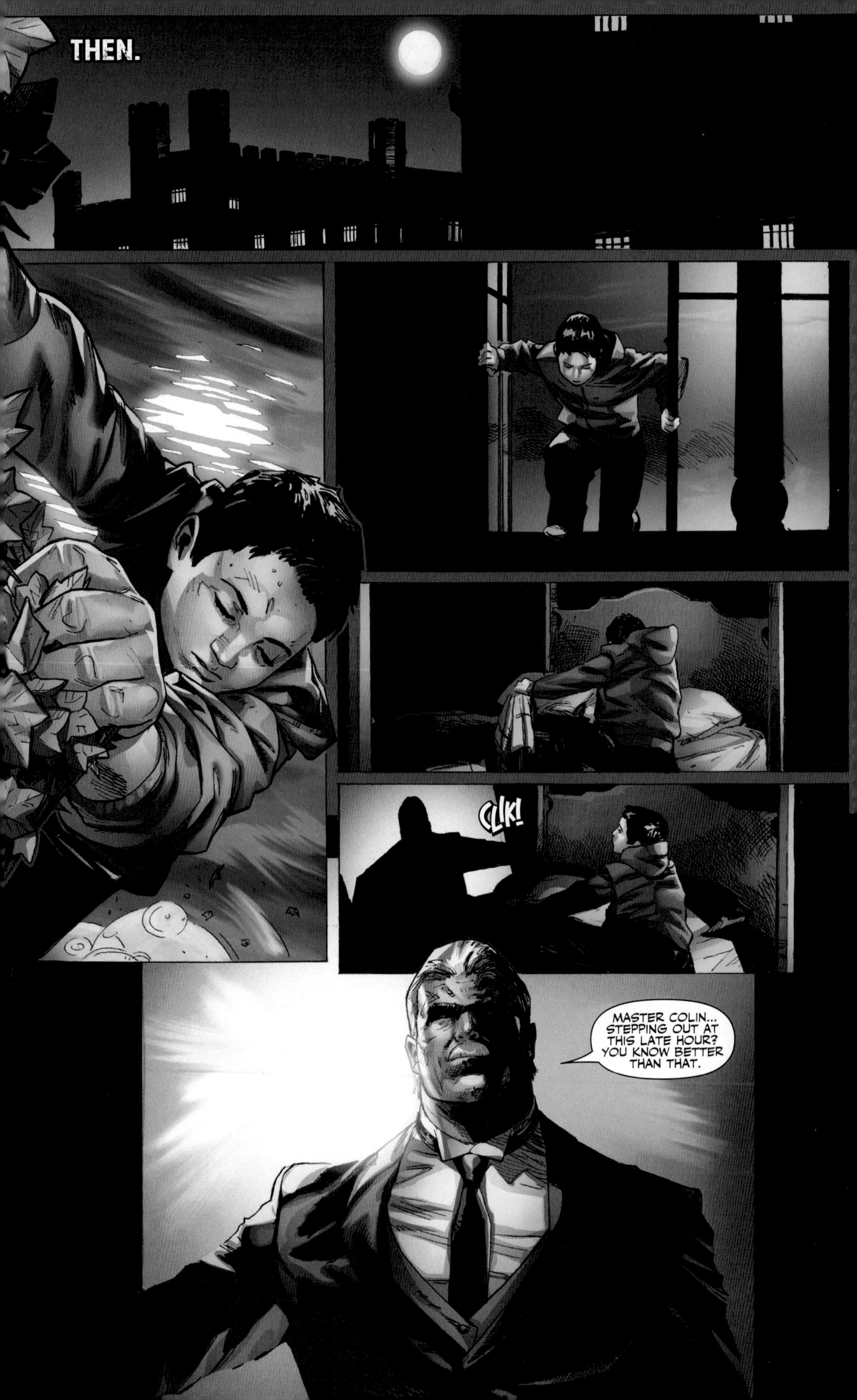
THEN.
CLIK!
MASTER COLIN... STEPPING OUT AT THIS LATE HOUR? YOU KNOW BETTER THAN THAT.

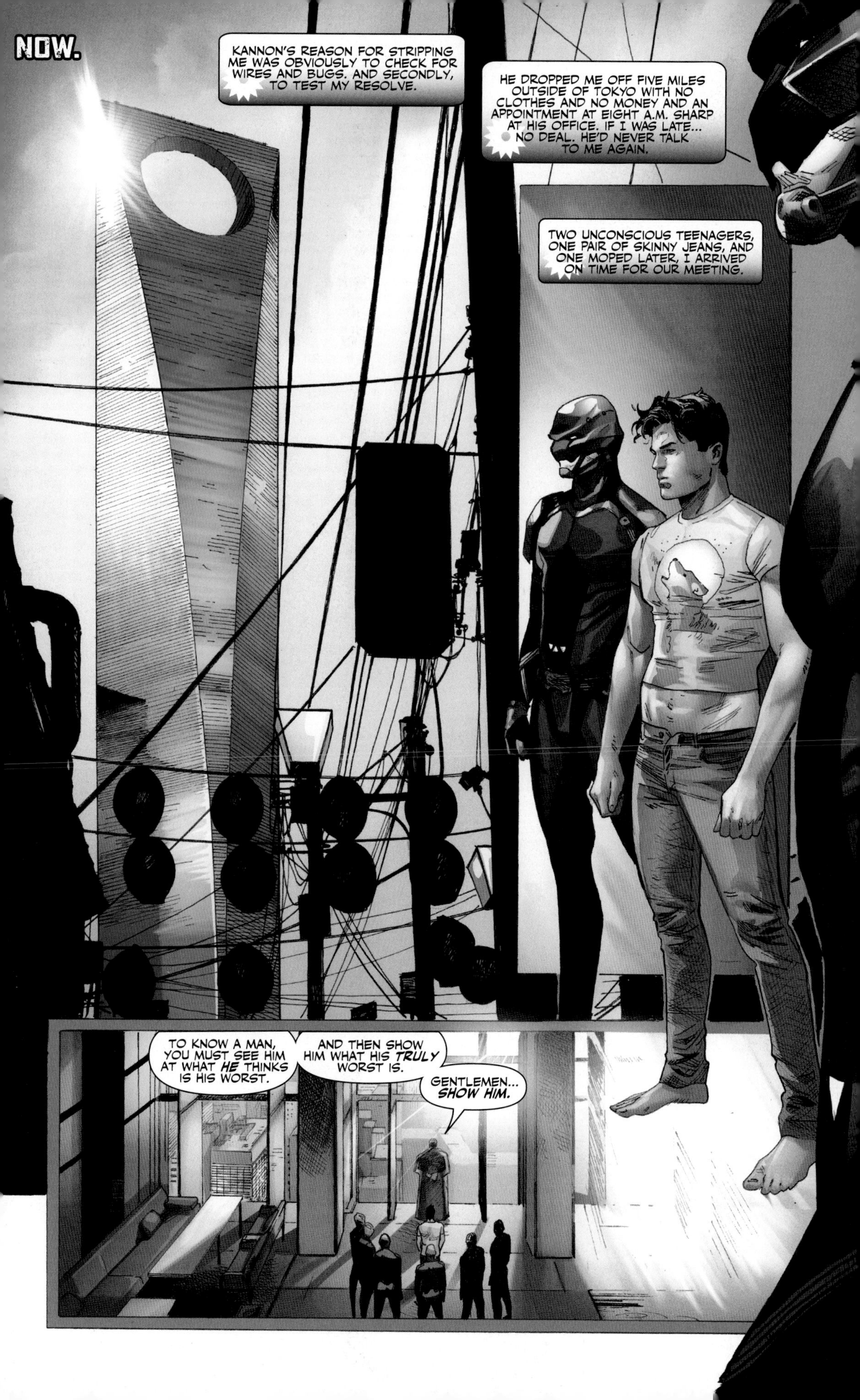
NOW.
KANNON'S REASON FOR STRIPPING ME WAS OBVIOUSLY TO CHECK FOR WIRES AND BUGS. AND SECONDLY, TO TEST MY RESOLVE.
HE DROPPED ME OFF FIVE MILES OUTSIDE OF TOKYO WITH NO CLOTHES AND NO MONEY AND AN APPOINTMENT AT EIGHT A.M. SHARP AT HIS OFFICE. IF I WAS LATE... NO DEAL. HE'D NEVER TALK TO ME AGAIN.
TWO UNCONSCIOUS TEENAGERS, ONE PAIR OF SKINNY JEANS, AND ONE MOPED LATER, I ARRIVED ON TIME FOR OUR MEETING.
TO KNOW A MAN, YOU MUST SEE HIM AT WHAT *HE* THINKS IS HIS WORST.
AND THEN SHOW HIM WHAT HIS *TRULY* WORST IS.
GENTLEMEN... *SHOW HIM.*

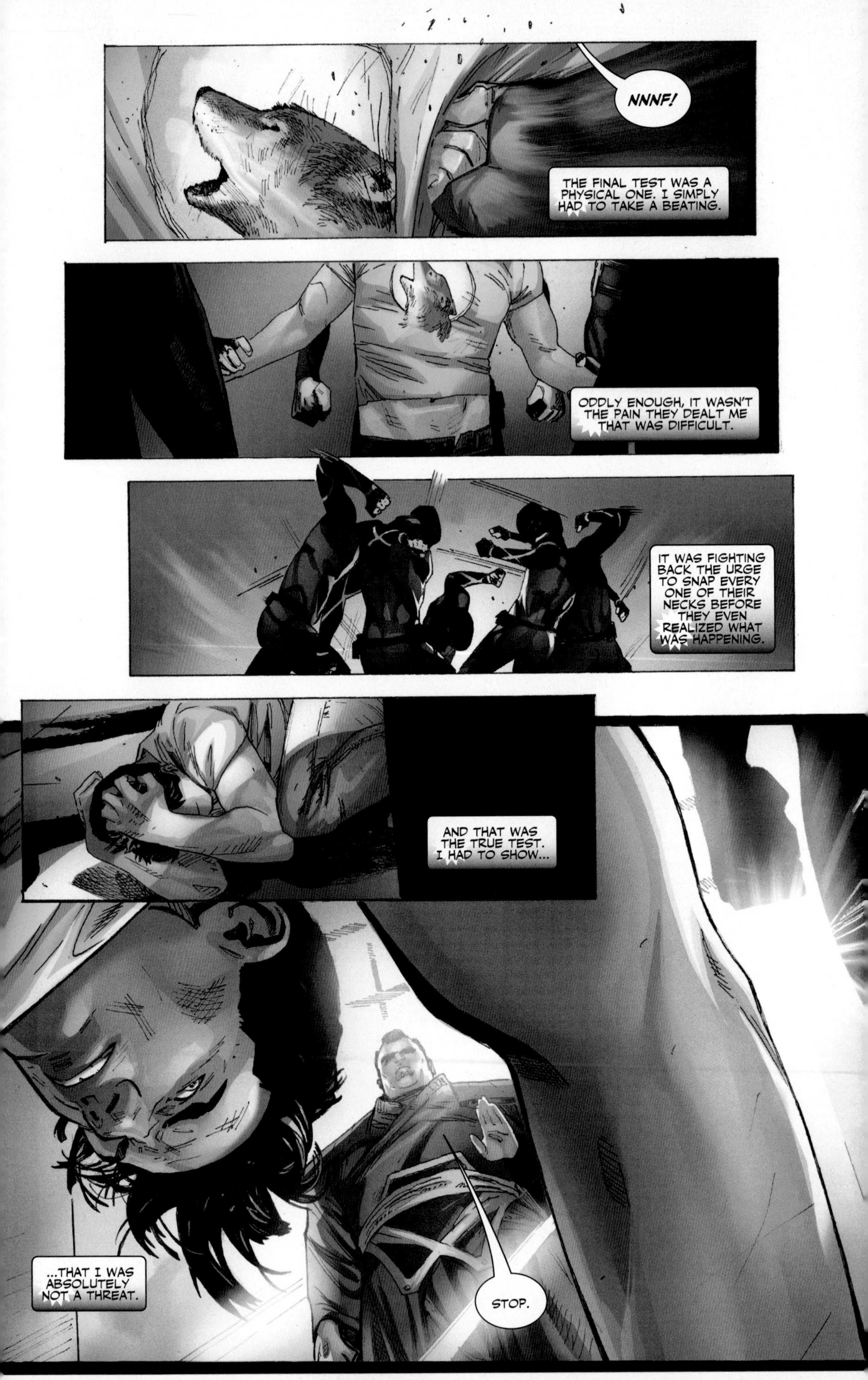
NNNF!
THE FINAL TEST WAS A PHYSICAL ONE. I SIMPLY HAD TO TAKE A BEATING.
ODDLY ENOUGH, IT WASN'T THE PAIN THEY DEALT ME THAT WAS DIFFICULT.
IT WAS FIGHTING BACK THE URGE TO SNAP EVERY ONE OF THEIR NECKS BEFORE THEY EVEN REALIZED WHAT WAS HAPPENING.
AND THAT WAS THE TRUE TEST. I HAD TO SHOW...
...THAT I WAS ABSOLUTELY NOT A THREAT.
STOP.

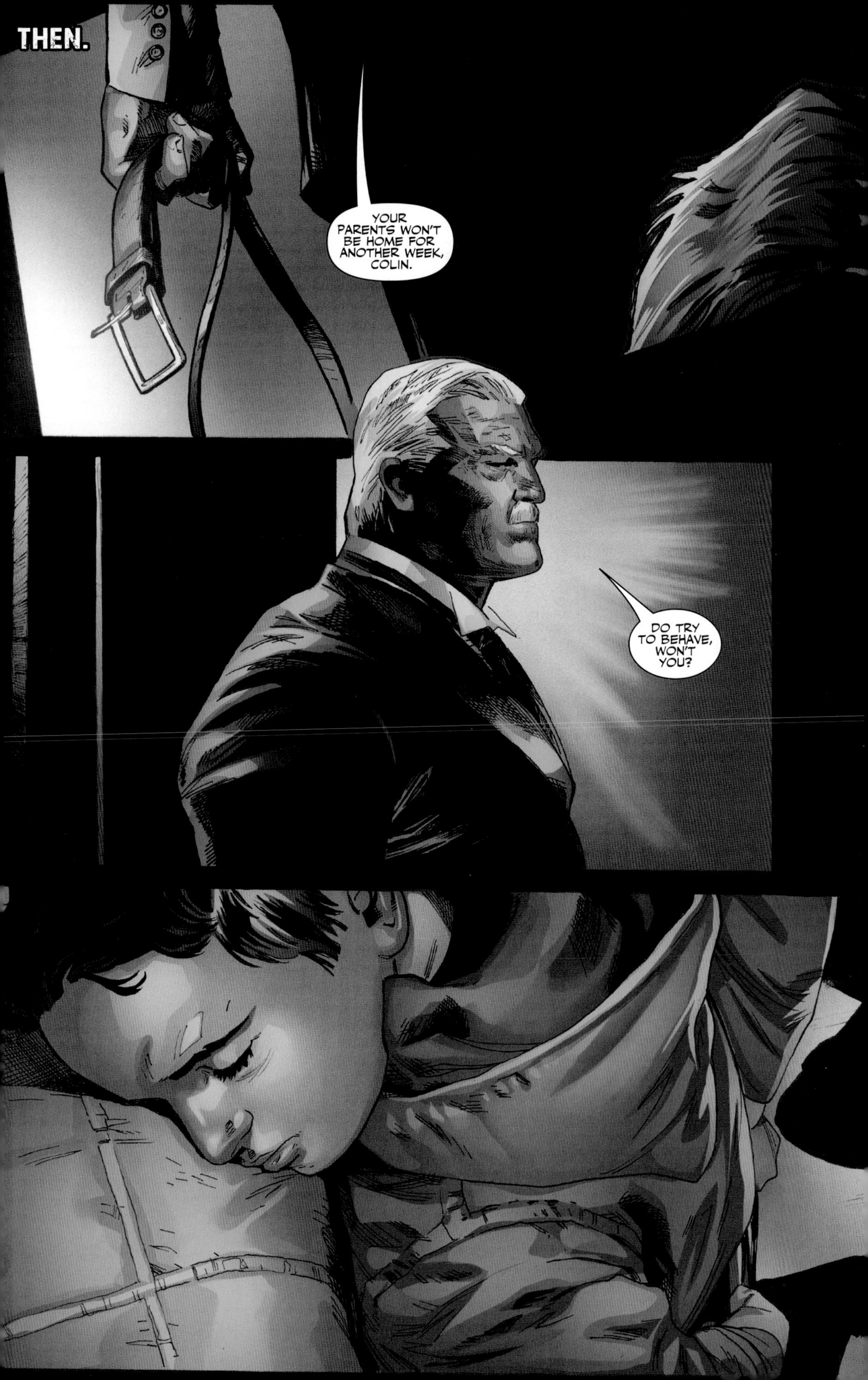
THEN.
YOUR PARENTS WON'T BE HOME FOR ANOTHER WEEK, COLIN.
DO TRY TO BEHAVE, WON'T YOU?

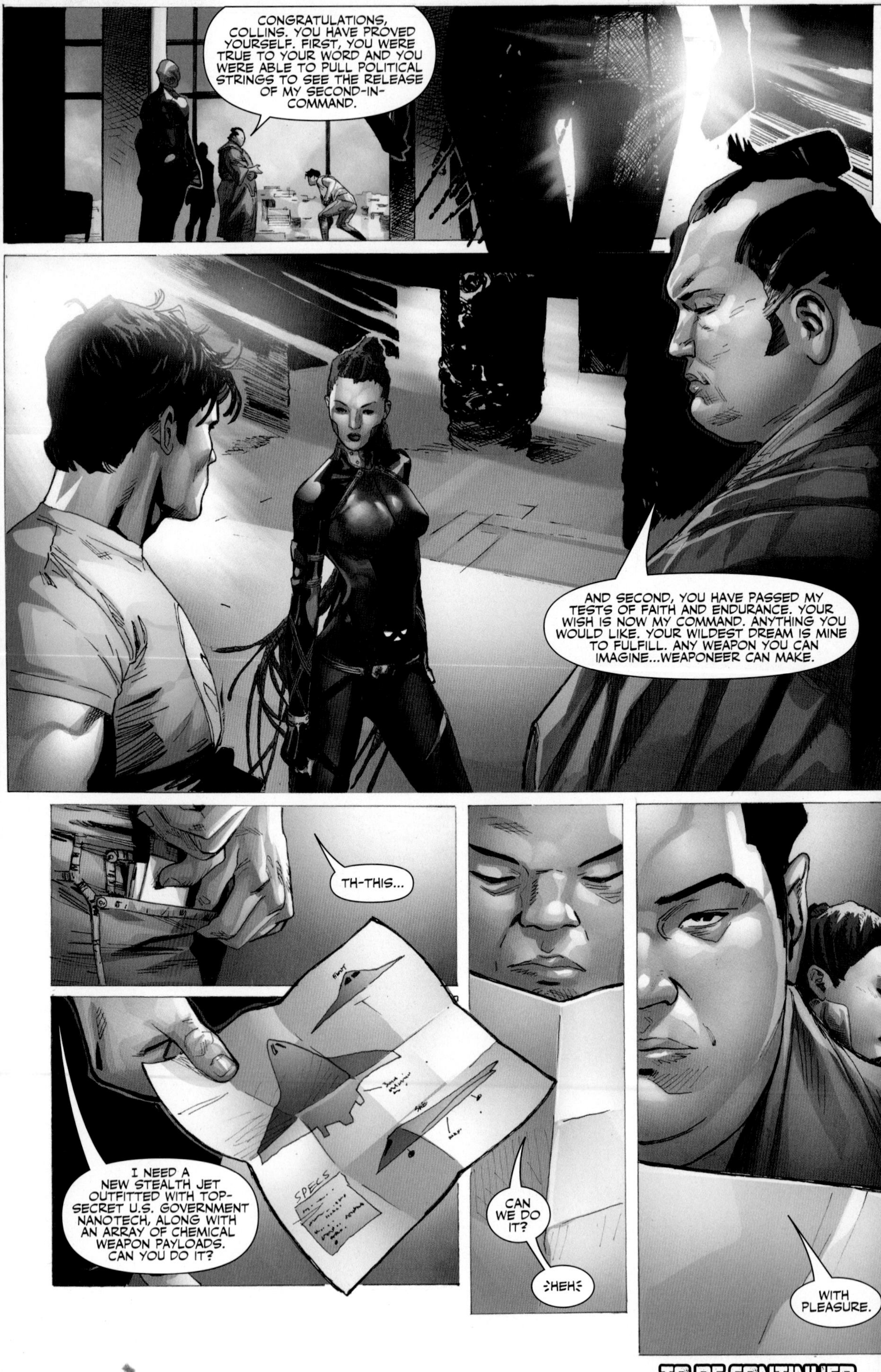
CONGRATULATIONS, COLLINS. YOU HAVE PROVED YOURSELF. FIRST, YOU WERE TRUE TO YOUR WORD AND YOU WERE ABLE TO PULL POLITICAL STRINGS TO SEE THE RELEASE OF MY SECOND-IN-COMMAND.
AND SECOND, YOU HAVE PASSED MY TESTS OF FAITH AND ENDURANCE. YOUR WISH IS NOW MY COMMAND. ANYTHING YOU WOULD LIKE. YOUR WILDEST DREAM IS MINE TO FULFILL. ANY WEAPON YOU CAN IMAGINE...WEAPONEER CAN MAKE.
TH-THIS...
SPECS
I NEED A NEW STEALTH JET OUTFITTED WITH TOP-SECRET U.S. GOVERNMENT NANOTECH, ALONG WITH AN ARRAY OF CHEMICAL WEAPON PAYLOADS. CAN YOU DO IT?
CAN WE DO IT?
HEH
WITH PLEASURE.

TO BE CONTINUED...

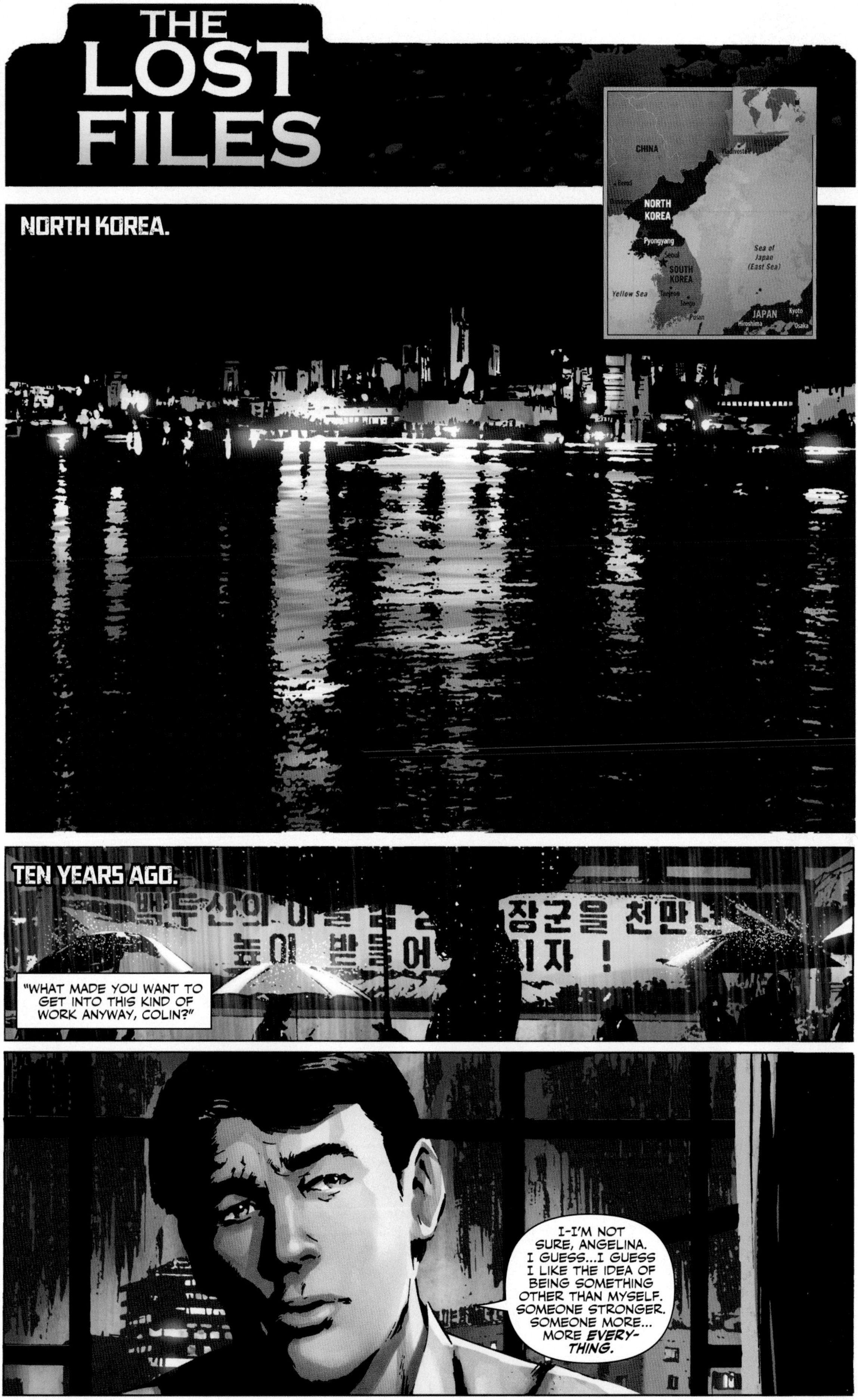
THE LOST FILES
NORTH KOREA.
CHINA
Vladivostok
NORTH KOREA
Pyongyang
Seoul
SOUTH KOREA
Yellow Sea
Sea of Japan (East Sea)
JAPAN
Kyoto
Hiroshima
Osaka
Pusan
TEN YEARS AGO.
"WHAT MADE YOU WANT TO GET INTO THIS KIND OF WORK ANYWAY, COLIN?"
I-I'M NOT SURE, ANGELINA. I GUESS...I GUESS I LIKE THE IDEA OF BEING SOMETHING OTHER THAN MYSELF. SOMEONE STRONGER. SOMEONE MORE... MORE *EVERY-THING.*

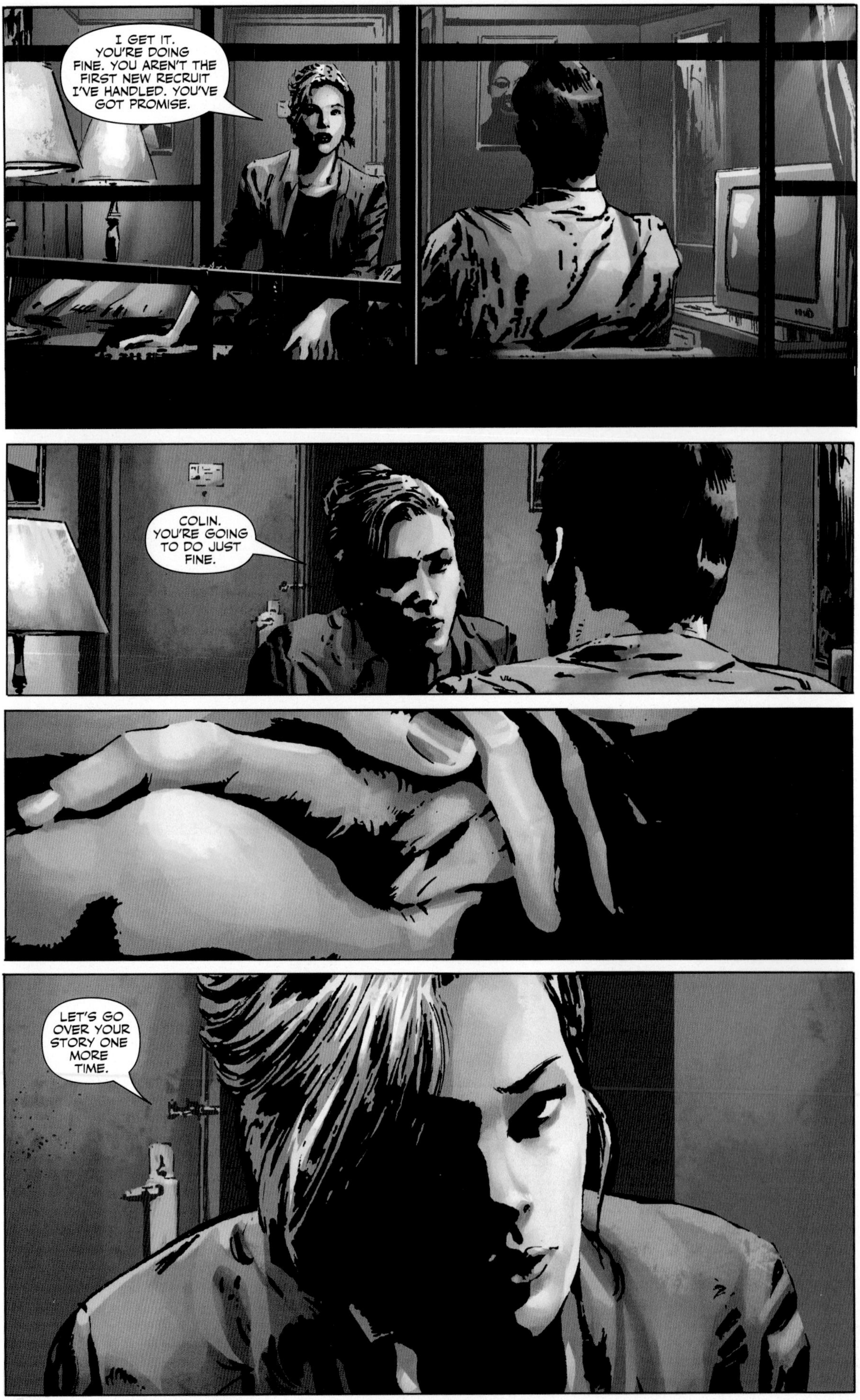
I GET IT. YOU'RE DOING FINE. YOU AREN'T THE FIRST NEW RECRUIT I'VE HANDLED. YOU'VE GOT PROMISE.
COLIN. YOU'RE GOING TO DO JUST FINE.
LET'S GO OVER YOUR STORY ONE MORE TIME.

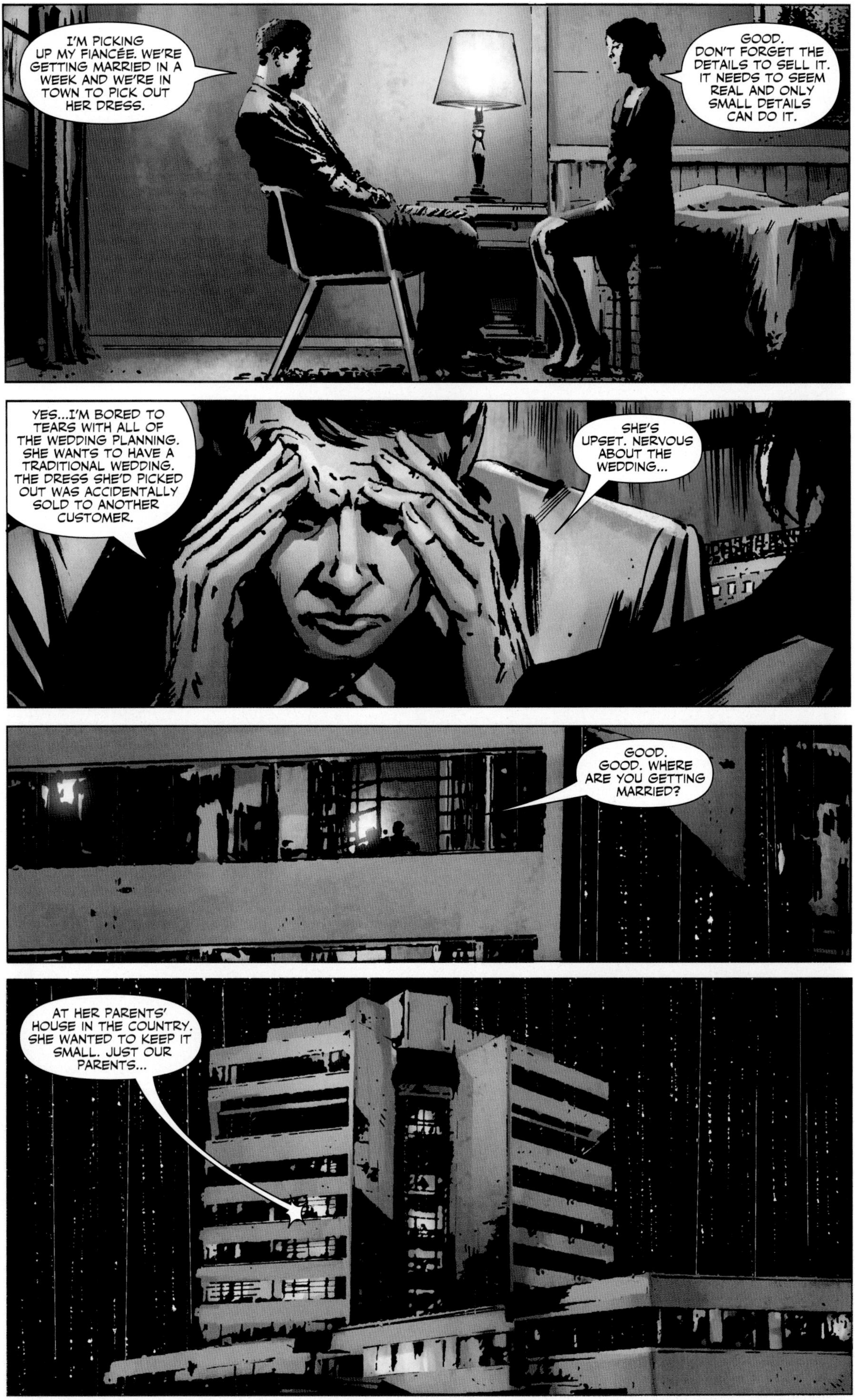
I'M PICKING UP MY FIANCÉE. WE'RE GETTING MARRIED IN A WEEK AND WE'RE IN TOWN TO PICK OUT HER DRESS.
GOOD. DON'T FORGET THE DETAILS TO SELL IT. IT NEEDS TO SEEM REAL AND ONLY SMALL DETAILS CAN DO IT.
YES...I'M BORED TO TEARS WITH ALL OF THE WEDDING PLANNING. SHE WANTS TO HAVE A TRADITIONAL WEDDING. THE DRESS SHE'D PICKED OUT WAS ACCIDENTALLY SOLD TO ANOTHER CUSTOMER.
SHE'S UPSET. NERVOUS ABOUT THE WEDDING...
GOOD. GOOD. WHERE ARE YOU GETTING MARRIED?
AT HER PARENTS' HOUSE IN THE COUNTRY. SHE WANTED TO KEEP IT SMALL. JUST OUR PARENTS...

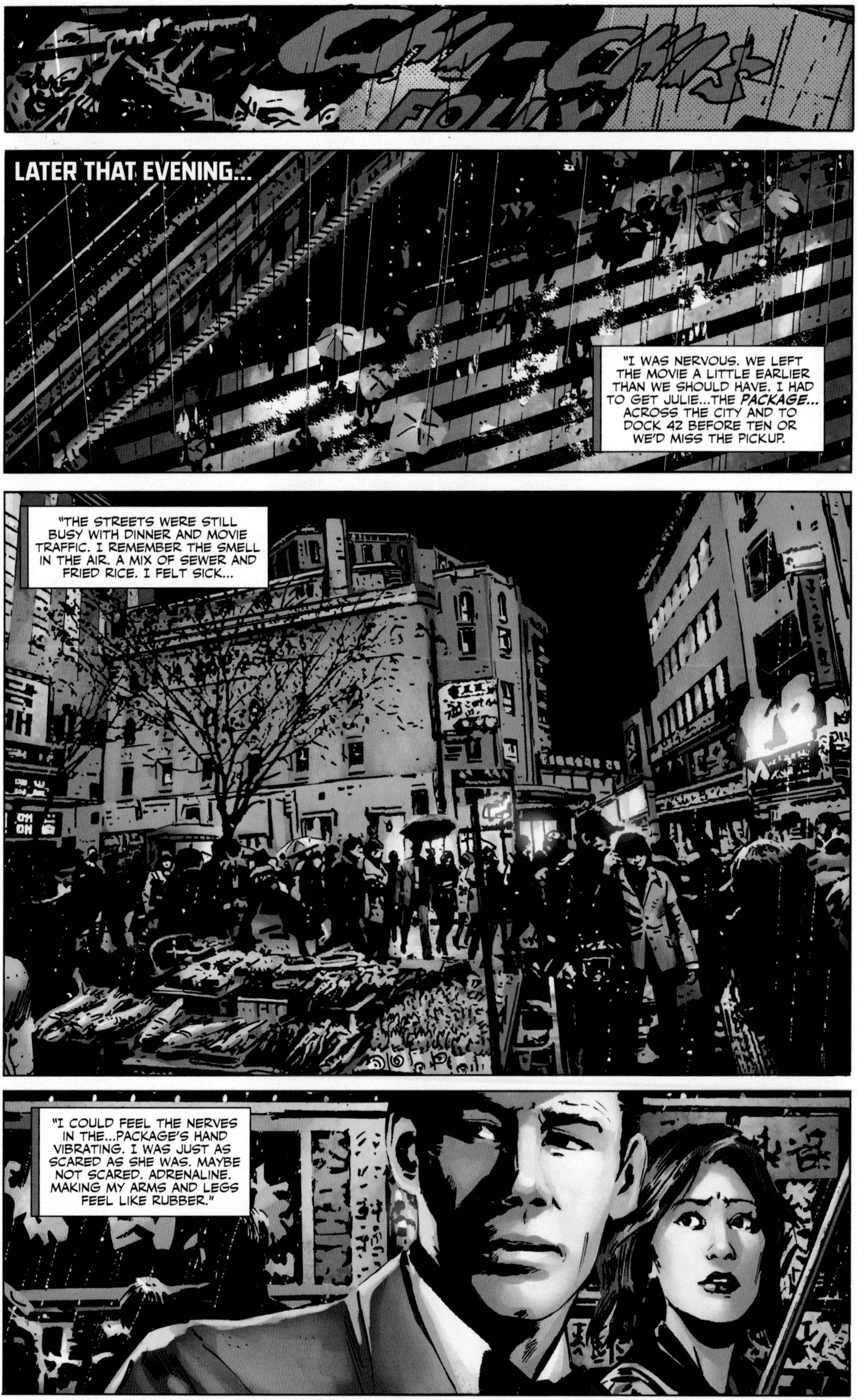

LATER THAT EVENING...
"I WAS NERVOUS. WE LEFT THE MOVIE A LITTLE EARLIER THAN WE SHOULD HAVE. I HAD TO GET JULIE...THE *PACKAGE...* ACROSS THE CITY AND TO DOCK 42 BEFORE TEN OR WE'D MISS THE PICKUP.
"THE STREETS WERE STILL BUSY WITH DINNER AND MOVIE TRAFFIC. I REMEMBER THE SMELL IN THE AIR. A MIX OF SEWER AND FRIED RICE. I FELT SICK...
"I COULD FEEL THE NERVES IN THE...PACKAGE'S HAND VIBRATING. I WAS JUST AS SCARED AS SHE WAS. MAYBE NOT SCARED. ADRENALINE. MAKING MY ARMS AND LEGS FEEL LIKE RUBBER."

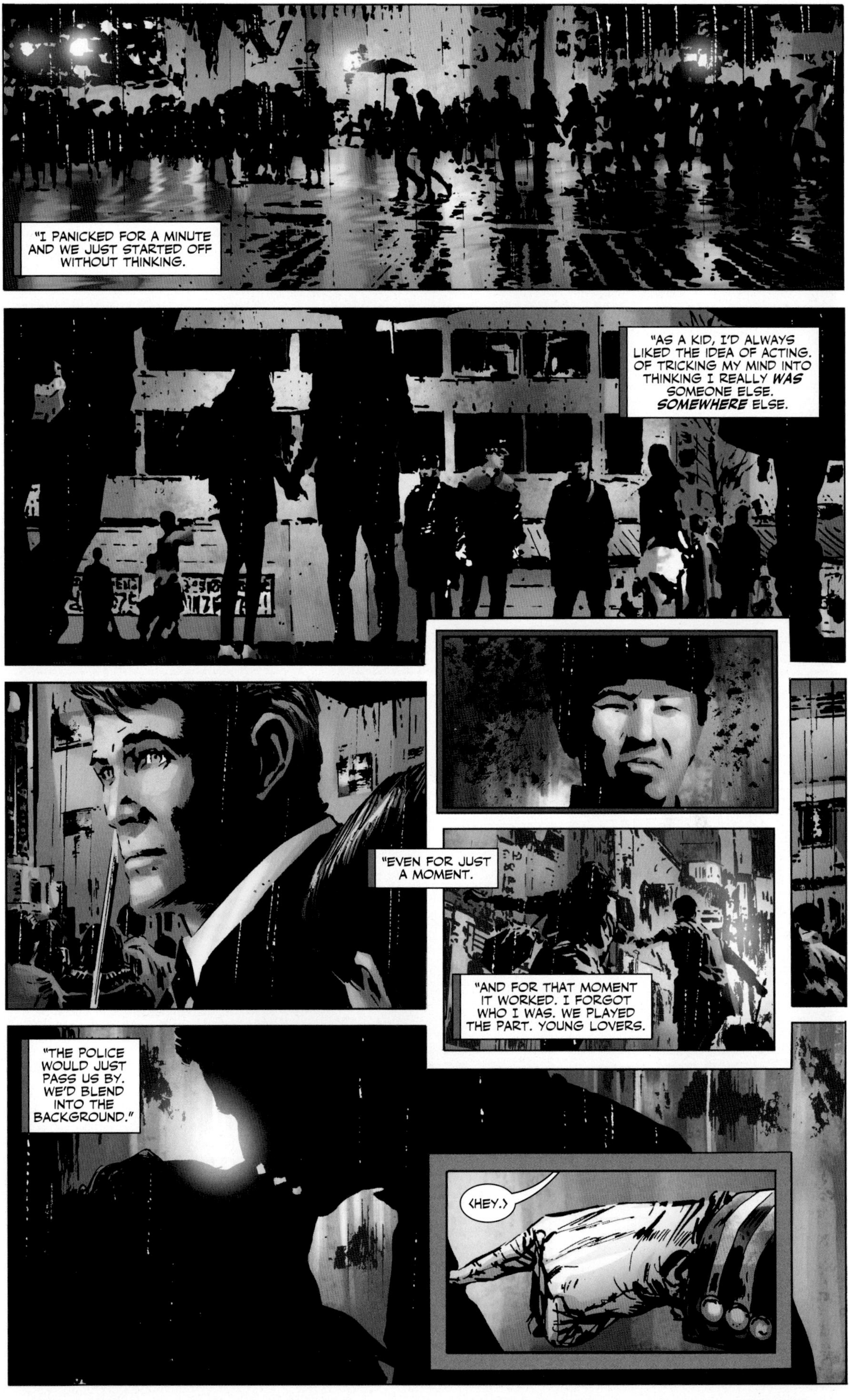
"I PANICKED FOR A MINUTE AND WE JUST STARTED OFF WITHOUT THINKING.
"AS A KID, I'D ALWAYS LIKED THE IDEA OF ACTING. OF TRICKING MY MIND INTO THINKING I REALLY *WAS* SOMEONE ELSE. *SOMEWHERE* ELSE.
"EVEN FOR JUST A MOMENT.
"AND FOR THAT MOMENT IT WORKED. I FORGOT WHO I WAS. WE PLAYED THE PART. YOUNG LOVERS.
"THE POLICE WOULD JUST PASS US BY. WE'D BLEND INTO THE BACKGROUND."
<HEY.>

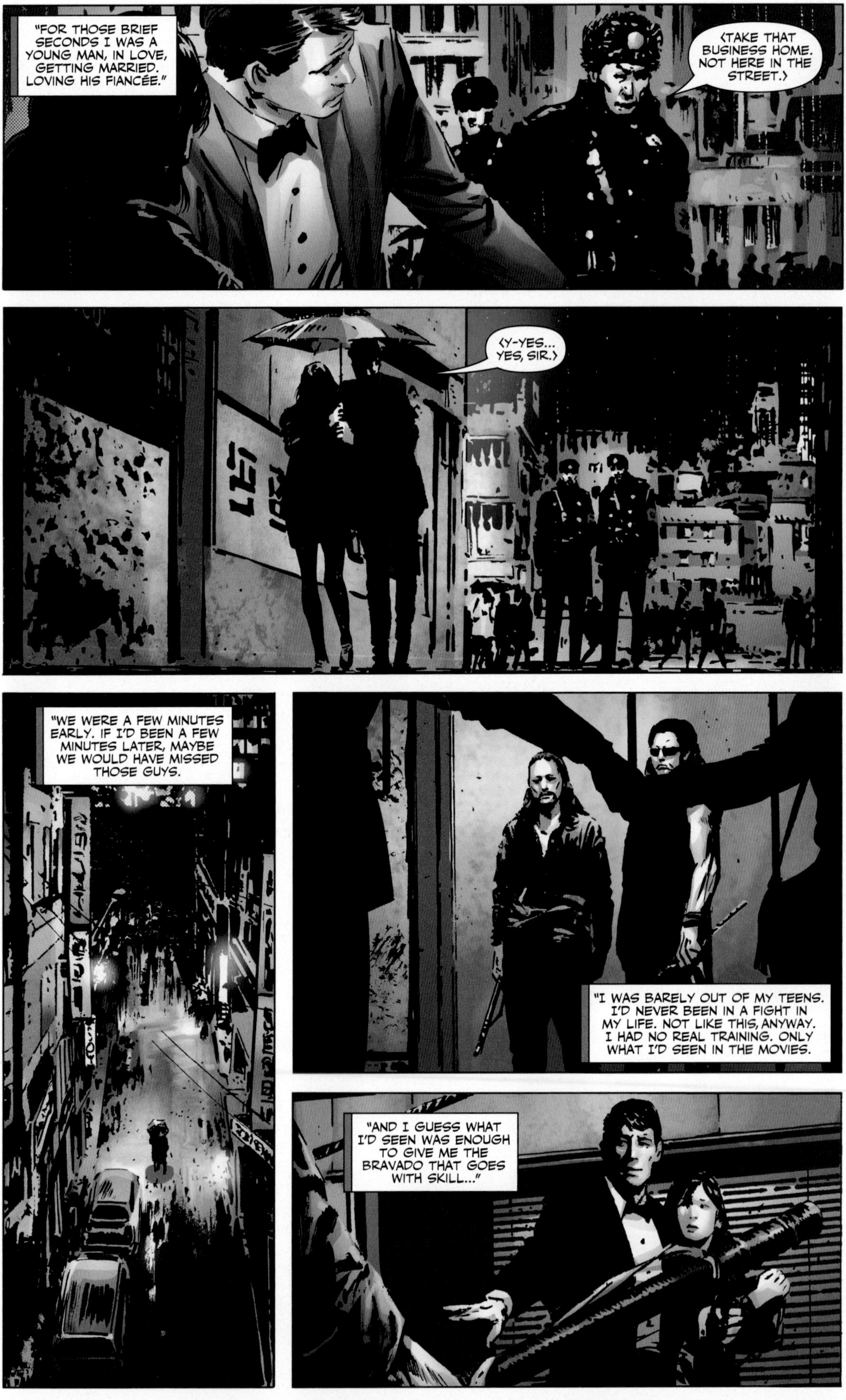
"FOR THOSE BRIEF SECONDS I WAS A YOUNG MAN, IN LOVE, GETTING MARRIED. LOVING HIS FIANCÉE."
‹TAKE THAT BUSINESS HOME. NOT HERE IN THE STREET.›
‹Y-YES... YES, SIR.›
"WE WERE A FEW MINUTES EARLY. IF I'D BEEN A FEW MINUTES LATER, MAYBE WE WOULD HAVE MISSED THOSE GUYS.
"I WAS BARELY OUT OF MY TEENS. I'D NEVER BEEN IN A FIGHT IN MY LIFE. NOT LIKE THIS, ANYWAY. I HAD NO REAL TRAINING. ONLY WHAT I'D SEEN IN THE MOVIES.
"AND I GUESS WHAT I'D SEEN WAS ENOUGH TO GIVE ME THE BRAVADO THAT GOES WITH SKILL..."

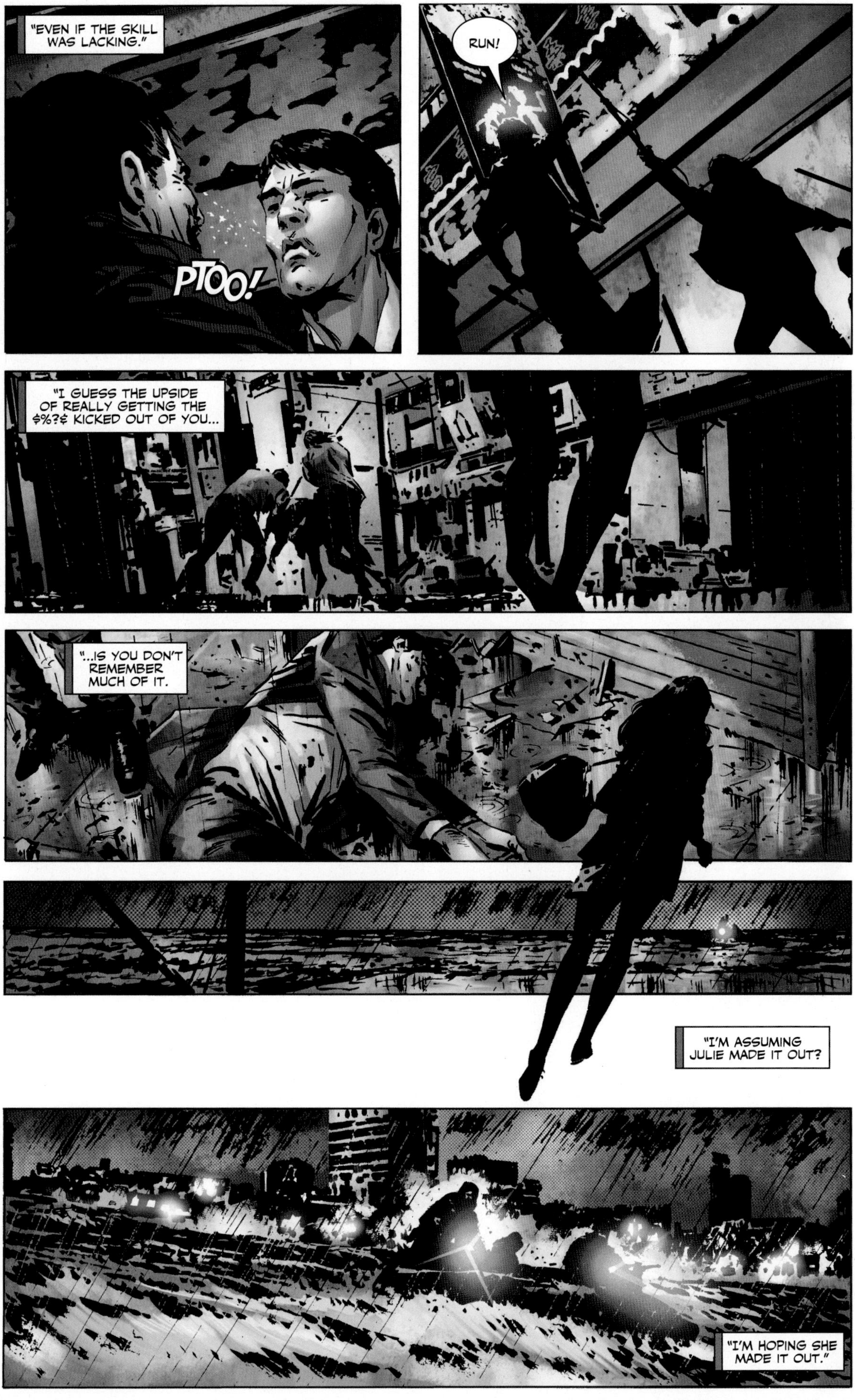
"EVEN IF THE SKILL WAS LACKING."
PTOO!
RUN!
"I GUESS THE UPSIDE OF REALLY GETTING THE $%?& KICKED OUT OF YOU...
"...IS YOU DON'T REMEMBER MUCH OF IT.
"I'M ASSUMING JULIE MADE IT OUT?
"I'M HOPING SHE MADE IT OUT."

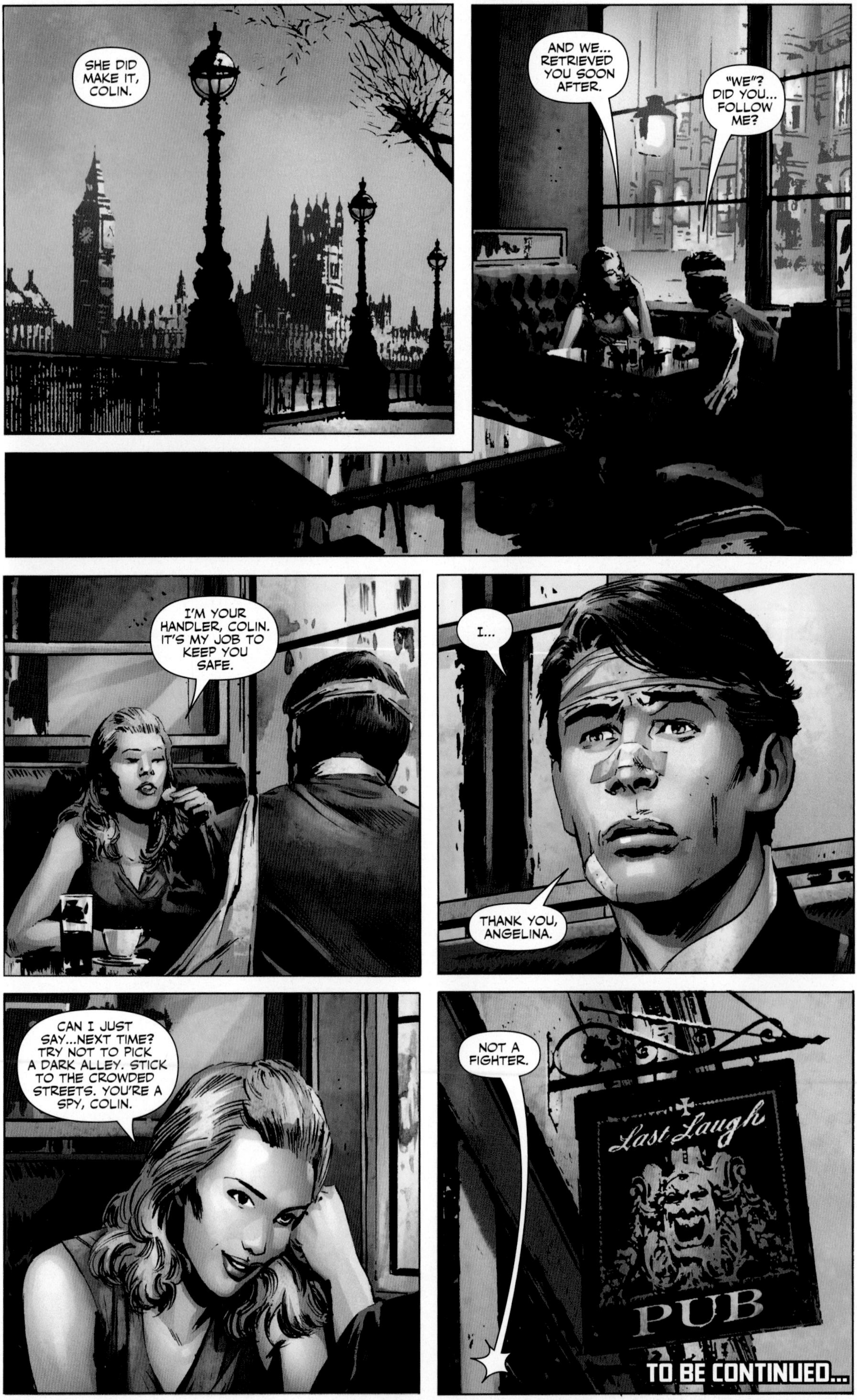
SHE DID MAKE IT, COLIN.
AND WE... RETRIEVED YOU SOON AFTER.
"WE"? DID YOU... FOLLOW ME?
I'M YOUR HANDLER, COLIN. IT'S MY JOB TO KEEP YOU SAFE.
I...
THANK YOU, ANGELINA.
CAN I JUST SAY...NEXT TIME? TRY NOT TO PICK A DARK ALLEY. STICK TO THE CROWDED STREETS. YOU'RE A SPY, COLIN.
NOT A FIGHTER.
Last Laugh
PUB
TO BE CONTINUED...

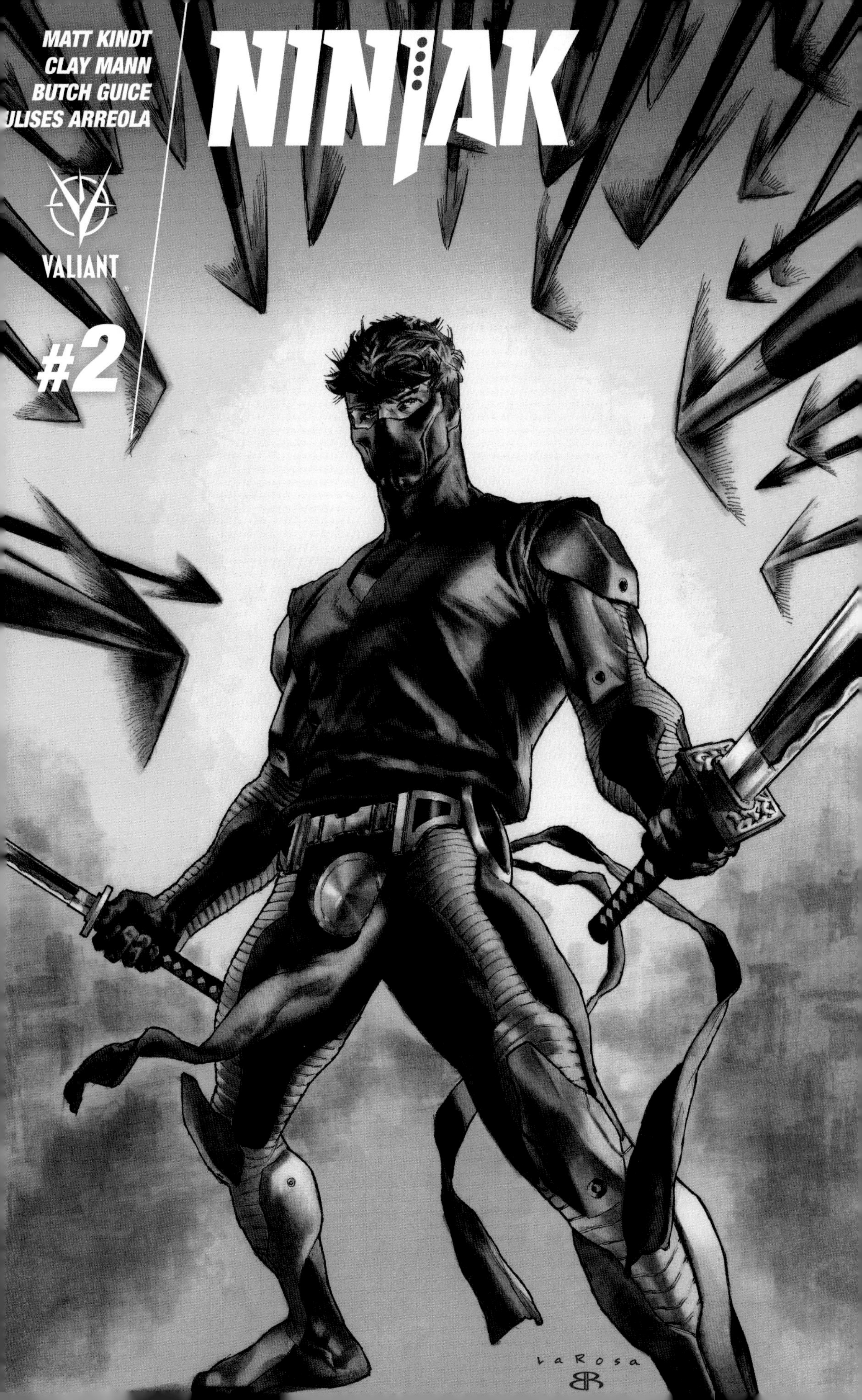
MATT KINDT
CLAY MANN
BUTCH GUICE
ULISES ARREOLA
NINJAK
VALIANT
#2
LaRosa

CLASSIFIED

NINJAK SPECIFICATIONS & INSIGHTS

Gauntlet with Chemical Loadout

STRONTIUM-90 RADIOACTIVE GRANULE. At all costs, he avoids close contact outside of the mission. In all probablity this is due to the traumatic loss of [redacted]

SODIUM AMYTAL (TRUTH SERUM). Subject is not susceptible to torture and interrogation techniques due to his inability or unwillingness to tell any simple truths.

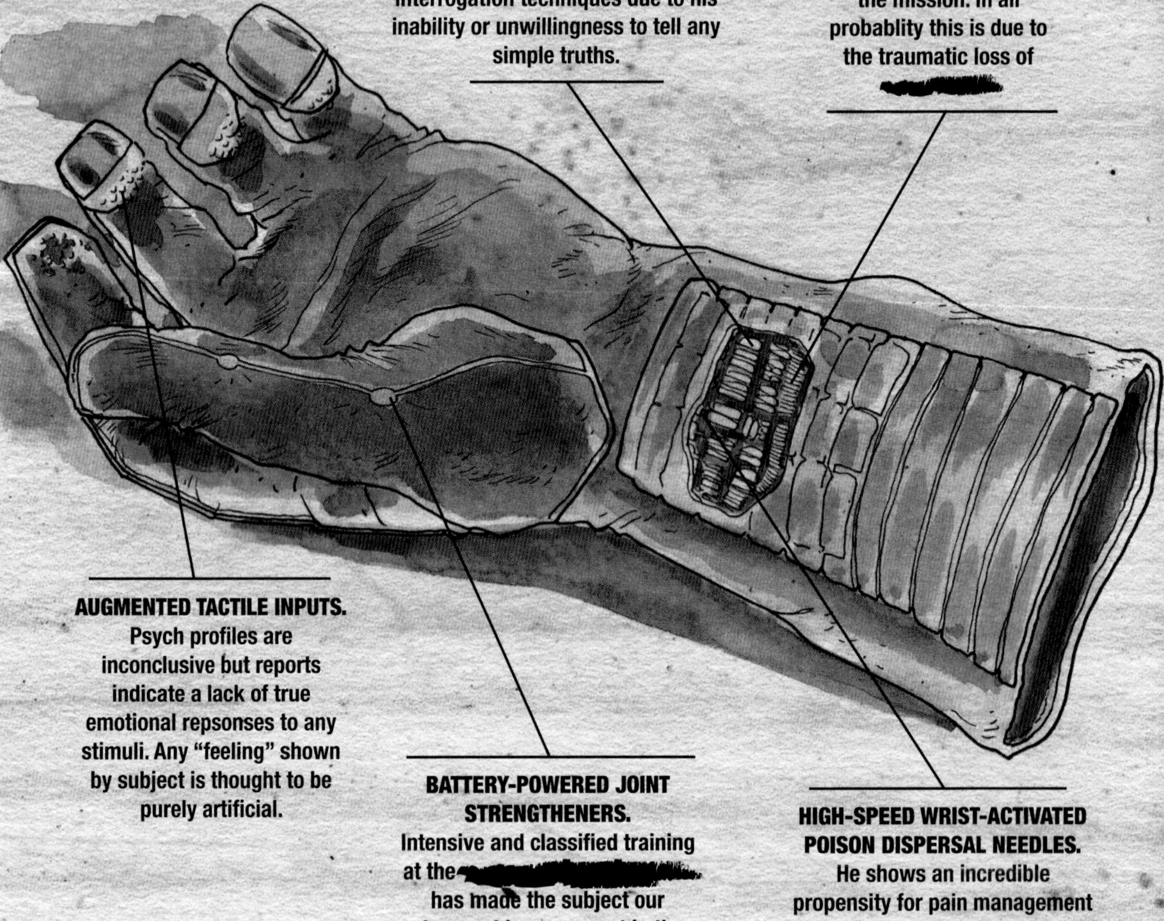

AUGMENTED TACTILE INPUTS. Psych profiles are inconclusive but reports indicate a lack of true emotional repsonses to any stimuli. Any "feeling" shown by subject is thought to be purely artificial.

BATTERY-POWERED JOINT STRENGTHENERS. Intensive and classified training at the [redacted] has made the subject our strongest human agent in the field. However it is feared that this strength makes him brittle and prone to a catastrohpic breakdown.

HIGH-SPEED WRIST-ACTIVATED POISON DISPERSAL NEEDLES. He shows an incredible propensity for pain management and is unflichingly—some say too eager—able to deal pain (both physical and emotional) to his targets.

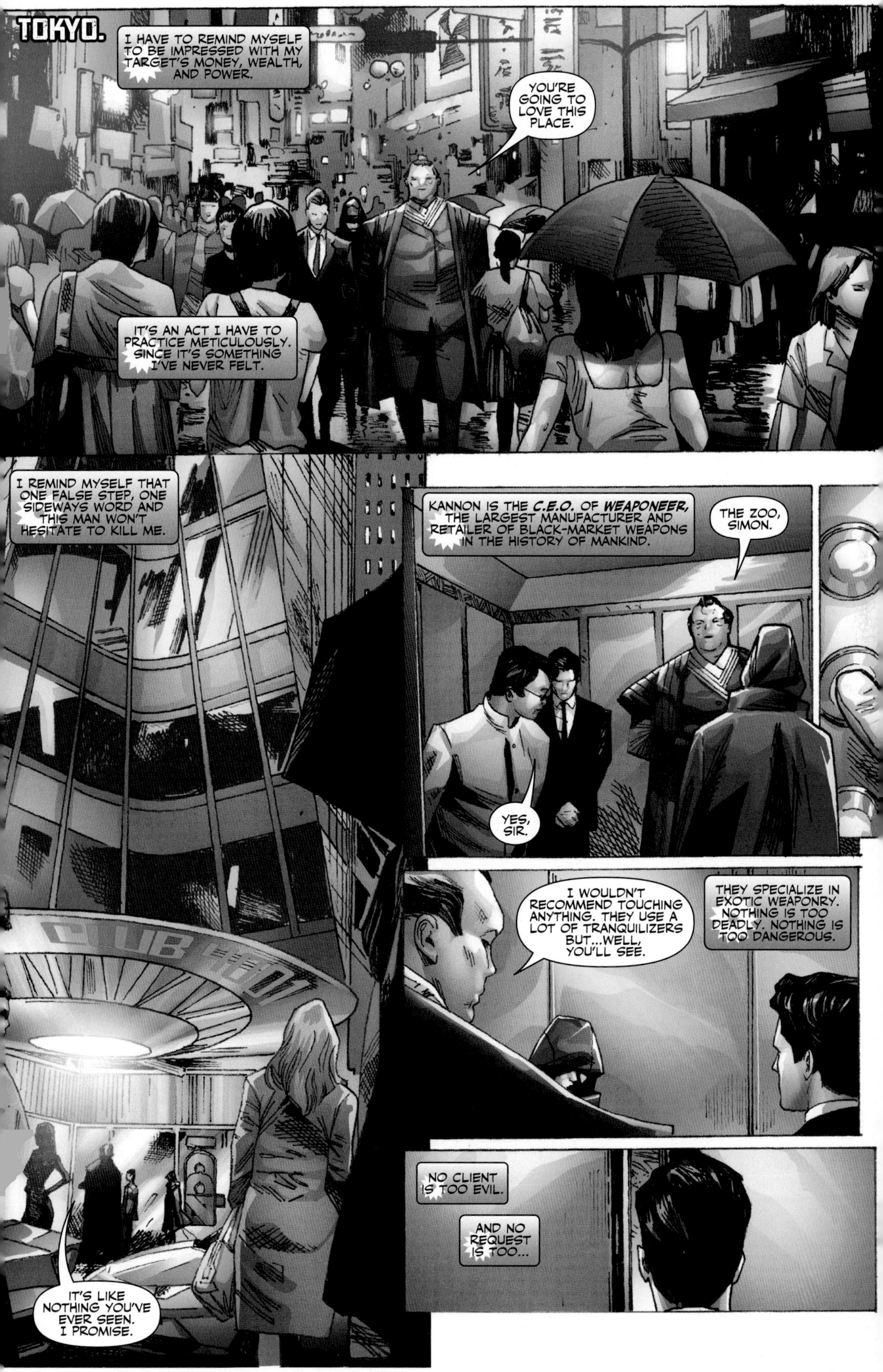
TOKYO.
I HAVE TO REMIND MYSELF TO BE IMPRESSED WITH MY TARGET'S MONEY, WEALTH, AND POWER.
YOU'RE GOING TO LOVE THIS PLACE.
IT'S AN ACT I HAVE TO PRACTICE METICULOUSLY. SINCE IT'S SOMETHING I'VE NEVER FELT.
I REMIND MYSELF THAT ONE FALSE STEP, ONE SIDEWAYS WORD AND THIS MAN WON'T HESITATE TO KILL ME.
CLUB 1001
IT'S LIKE NOTHING YOU'VE EVER SEEN. I PROMISE.
KANNON IS THE C.E.O. OF WEAPONEER, THE LARGEST MANUFACTURER AND RETAILER OF BLACK-MARKET WEAPONS IN THE HISTORY OF MANKIND.
THE ZOO, SIMON.
YES, SIR.
I WOULDN'T RECOMMEND TOUCHING ANYTHING. THEY USE A LOT OF TRANQUILIZERS BUT...WELL, YOU'LL SEE.
THEY SPECIALIZE IN EXOTIC WEAPONRY. NOTHING IS TOO DEADLY. NOTHING IS TOO DANGEROUS.
NO CLIENT IS TOO EVIL.
AND NO REQUEST IS TOO...

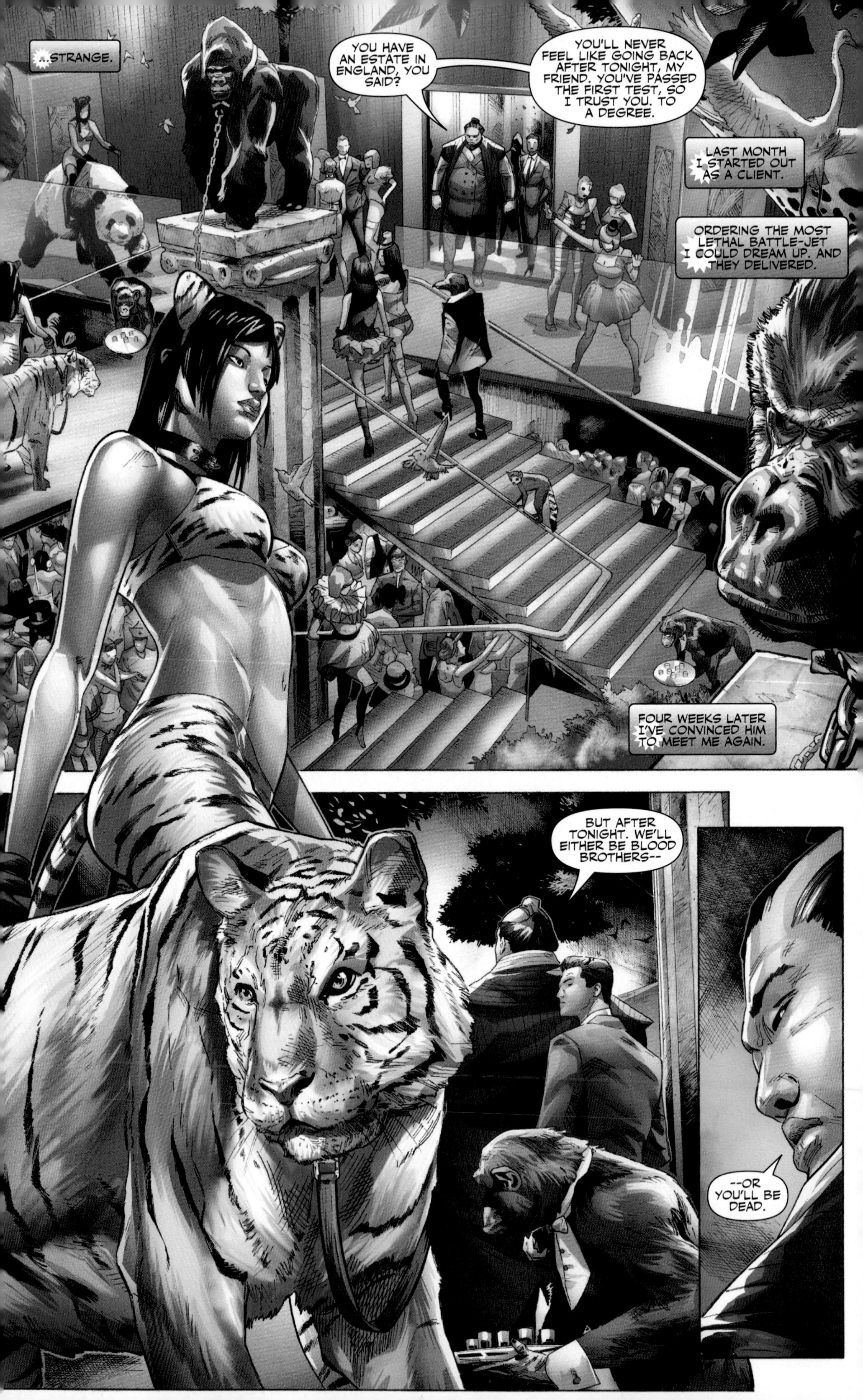
...STRANGE.
YOU HAVE AN ESTATE IN ENGLAND, YOU SAID?
YOU'LL NEVER FEEL LIKE GOING BACK AFTER TONIGHT, MY FRIEND. YOU'VE PASSED THE FIRST TEST, SO I TRUST YOU. TO A DEGREE.
LAST MONTH I STARTED OUT AS A CLIENT.
ORDERING THE MOST LETHAL BATTLE-JET I COULD DREAM UP. AND THEY DELIVERED.
FOUR WEEKS LATER I'VE CONVINCED HIM TO MEET ME AGAIN.
BUT AFTER TONIGHT. WE'LL EITHER BE BLOOD BROTHERS--
--OR YOU'LL BE DEAD.

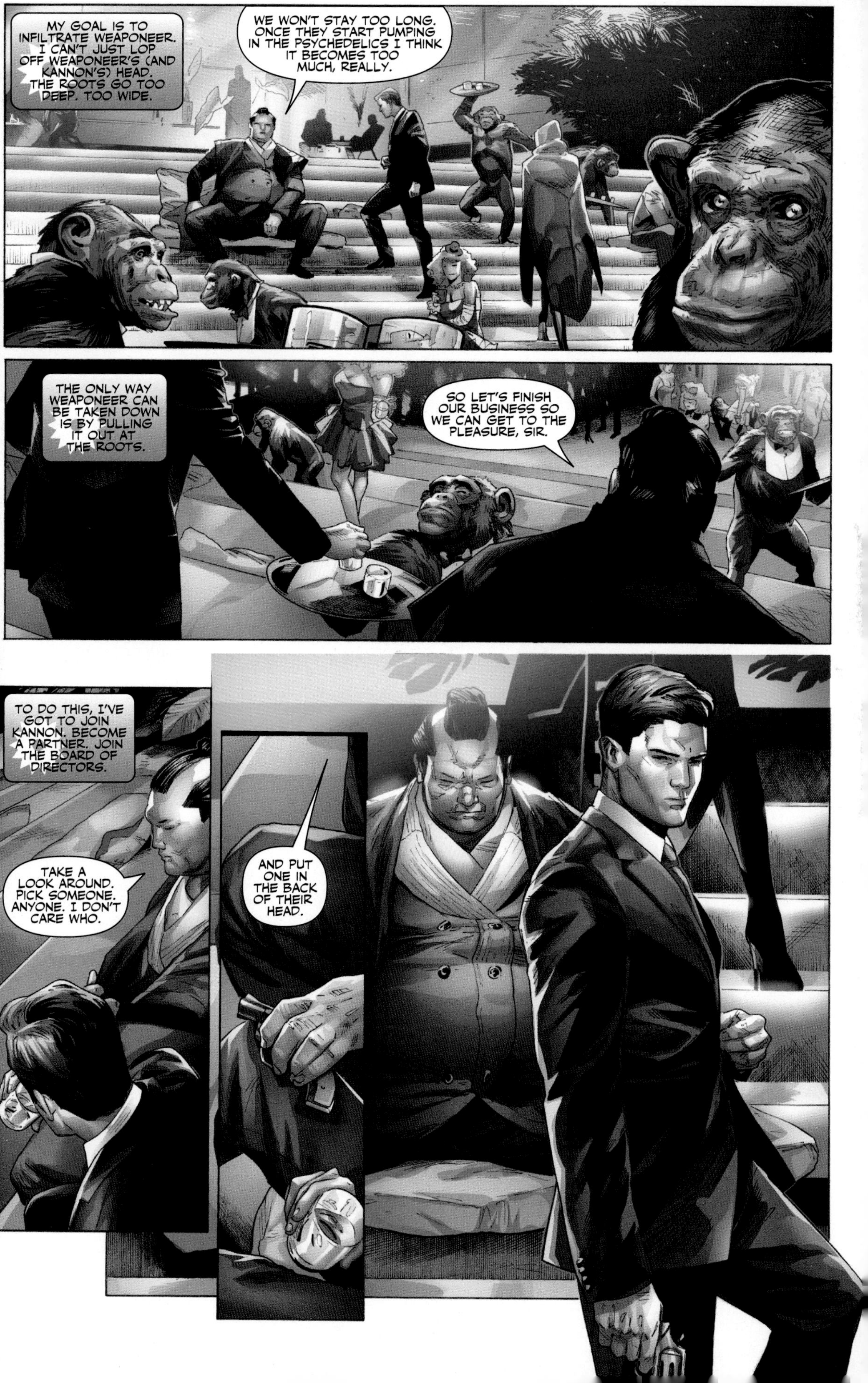
MY GOAL IS TO INFILTRATE WEAPONEER. I CAN'T JUST LOP OFF WEAPONEER'S (AND KANNON'S) HEAD. THE ROOTS GO TOO DEEP. TOO WIDE.
WE WON'T STAY TOO LONG. ONCE THEY START PUMPING IN THE PSYCHEDELICS I THINK IT BECOMES TOO MUCH, REALLY.
THE ONLY WAY WEAPONEER CAN BE TAKEN DOWN IS BY PULLING IT OUT AT THE ROOTS.
SO LET'S FINISH OUR BUSINESS SO WE CAN GET TO THE PLEASURE, SIR.
TO DO THIS, I'VE GOT TO JOIN KANNON. BECOME A PARTNER. JOIN THE BOARD OF DIRECTORS.
TAKE A LOOK AROUND. PICK SOMEONE. ANYONE. I DON'T CARE WHO.
AND PUT ONE IN THE BACK OF THEIR HEAD.

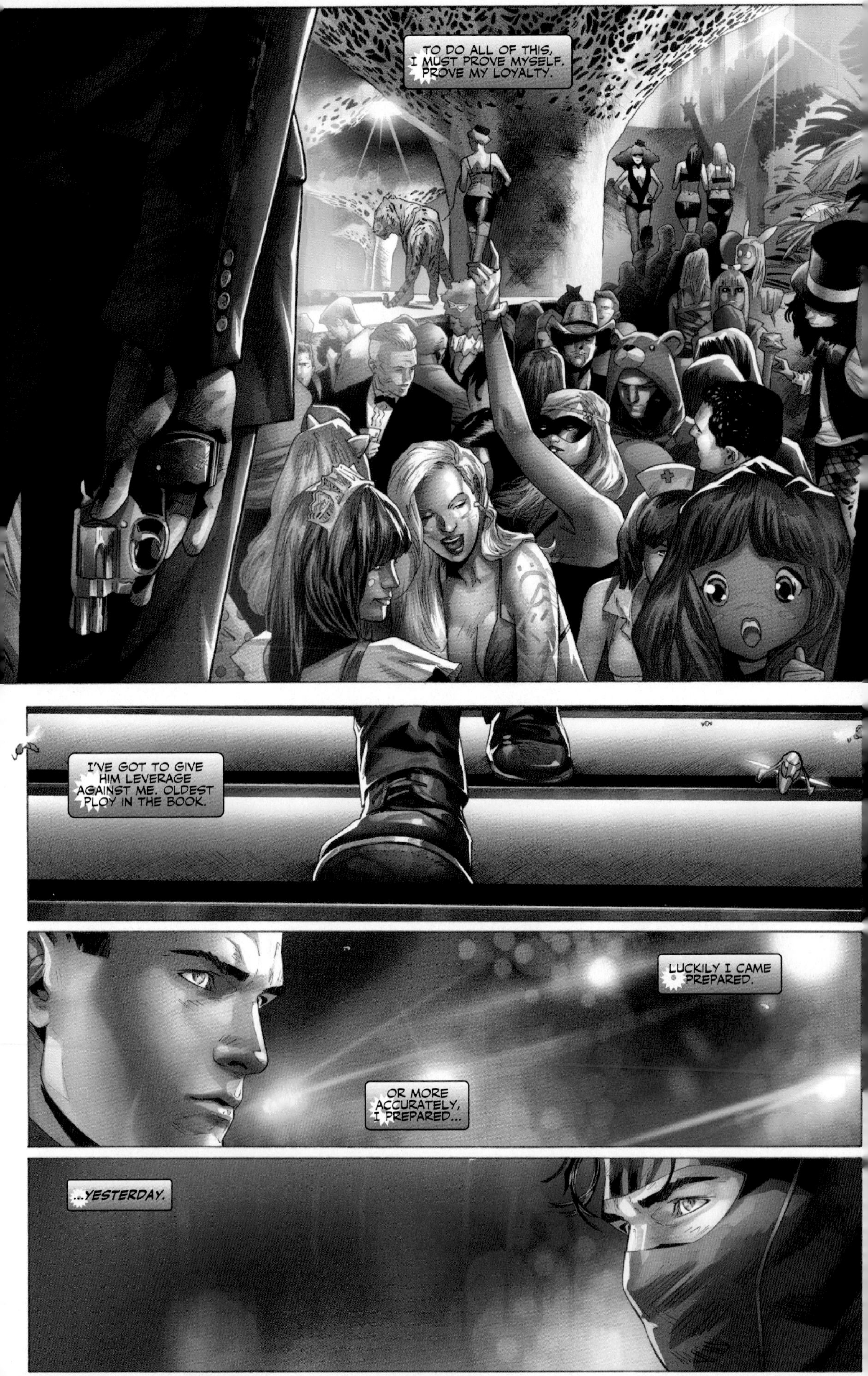

TO DO ALL OF THIS, I MUST PROVE MYSELF. PROVE MY LOYALTY.
I'VE GOT TO GIVE HIM LEVERAGE AGAINST ME. OLDEST PLOY IN THE BOOK.
LUCKILY I CAME PREPARED.
OR MORE ACCURATELY, I PREPARED...
...YESTERDAY.

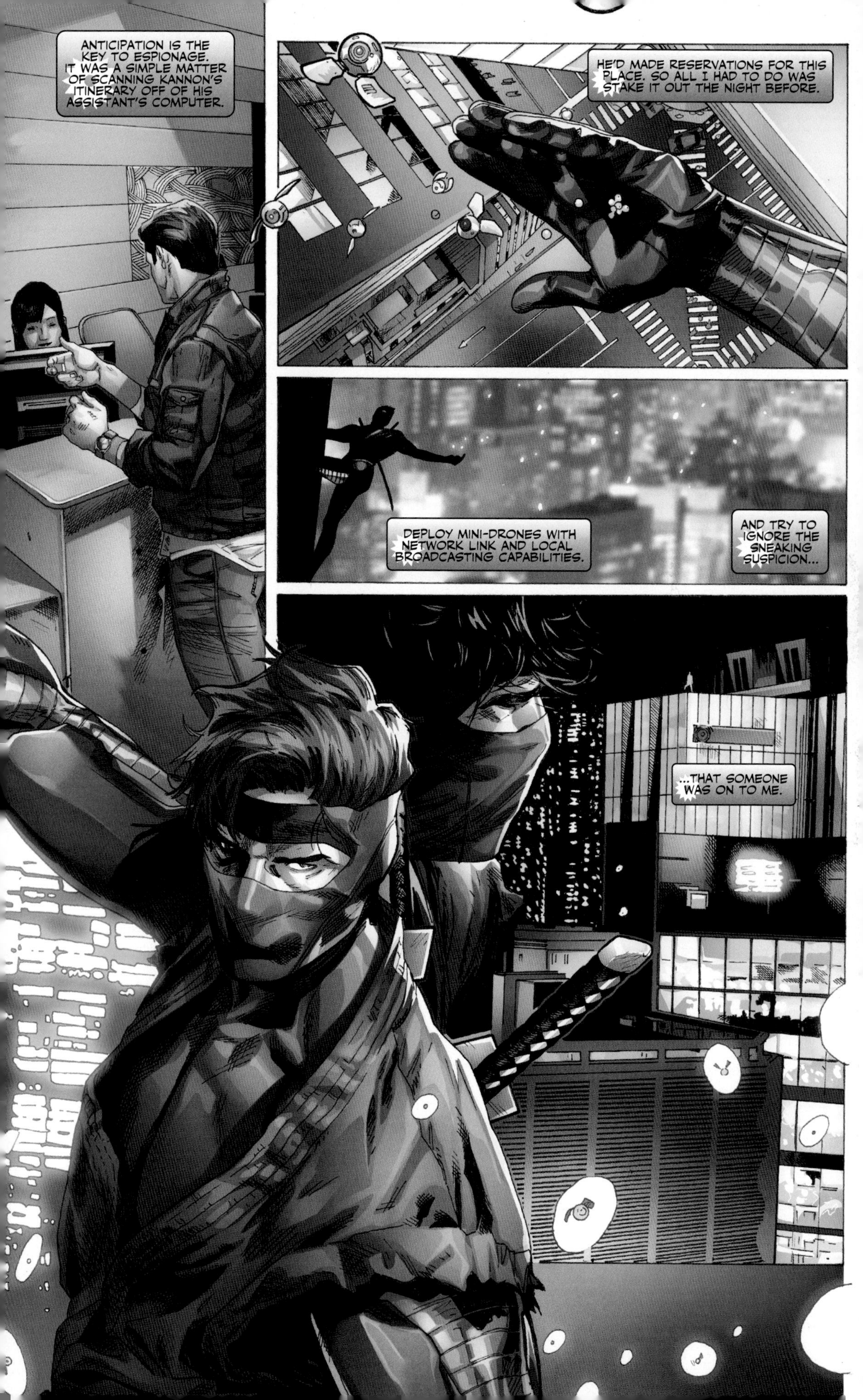
ANTICIPATION IS THE KEY TO ESPIONAGE. IT WAS A SIMPLE MATTER OF SCANNING KANNON'S ITINERARY OFF OF HIS ASSISTANT'S COMPUTER.
HE'D MADE RESERVATIONS FOR THIS PLACE. SO ALL I HAD TO DO WAS STAKE IT OUT THE NIGHT BEFORE.
DEPLOY MINI-DRONES WITH NETWORK LINK AND LOCAL BROADCASTING CAPABILITIES.
AND TRY TO IGNORE THE SNEAKING SUSPICION...
...THAT SOMEONE WAS ON TO ME.

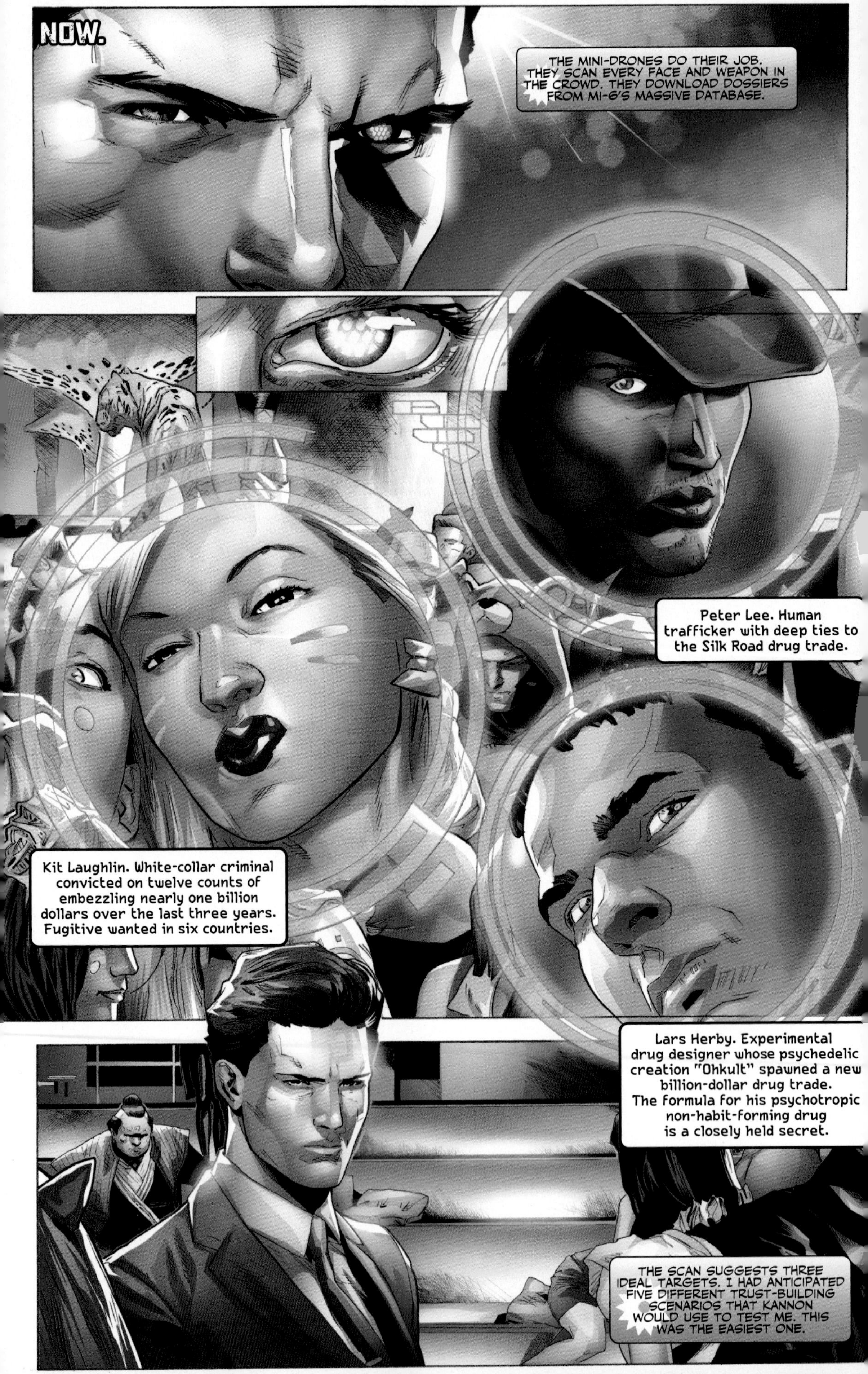
NOW.
THE MINI-DRONES DO THEIR JOB. THEY SCAN EVERY FACE AND WEAPON IN THE CROWD. THEY DOWNLOAD DOSSIERS FROM MI-6'S MASSIVE DATABASE.
Peter Lee. Human trafficker with deep ties to the Silk Road drug trade.
Kit Laughlin. White-collar criminal convicted on twelve counts of embezzling nearly one billion dollars over the last three years. Fugitive wanted in six countries.
Lars Herby. Experimental drug designer whose psychedelic creation "Ohkult" spawned a new billion-dollar drug trade. The formula for his psychotropic non-habit-forming drug is a closely held secret.
THE SCAN SUGGESTS THREE IDEAL TARGETS. I HAD ANTICIPATED FIVE DIFFERENT TRUST-BUILDING SCENARIOS THAT KANNON WOULD USE TO TEST ME. THIS WAS THE EASIEST ONE.

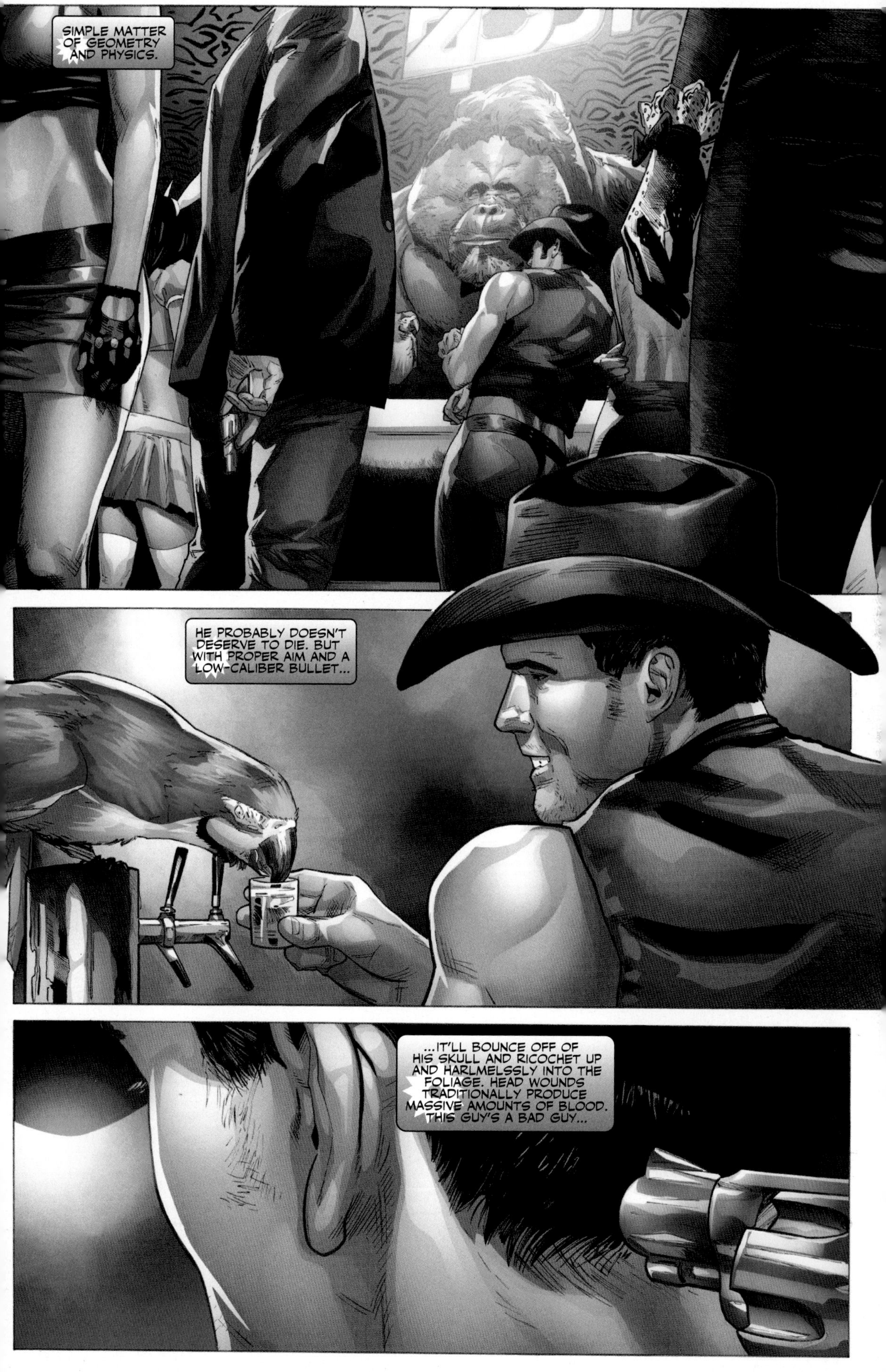
SIMPLE MATTER OF GEOMETRY AND PHYSICS.
HE PROBABLY DOESN'T DESERVE TO DIE. BUT WITH PROPER AIM AND A LOW-CALIBER BULLET...
...IT'LL BOUNCE OFF OF HIS SKULL AND RICOCHET UP AND HARLMELSSLY INTO THE FOLIAGE. HEAD WOUNDS TRADITIONALLY PRODUCE MASSIVE AMOUNTS OF BLOOD. THIS GUY'S A BAD GUY...

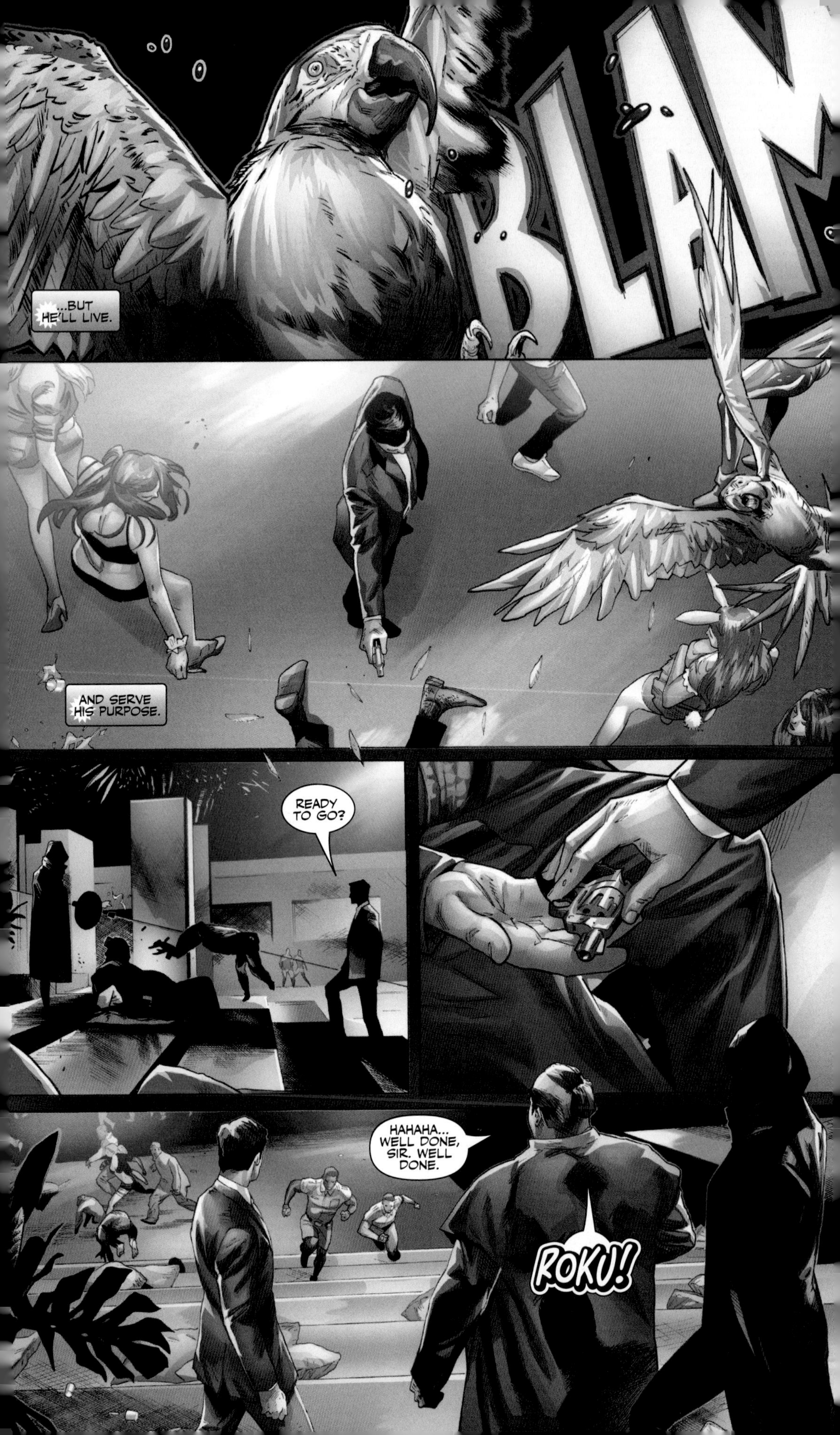
BLAM
...BUT HE'LL LIVE.
AND SERVE HIS PURPOSE.
READY TO GO?
HAHAHA... WELL DONE, SIR. WELL DONE.
ROKU!

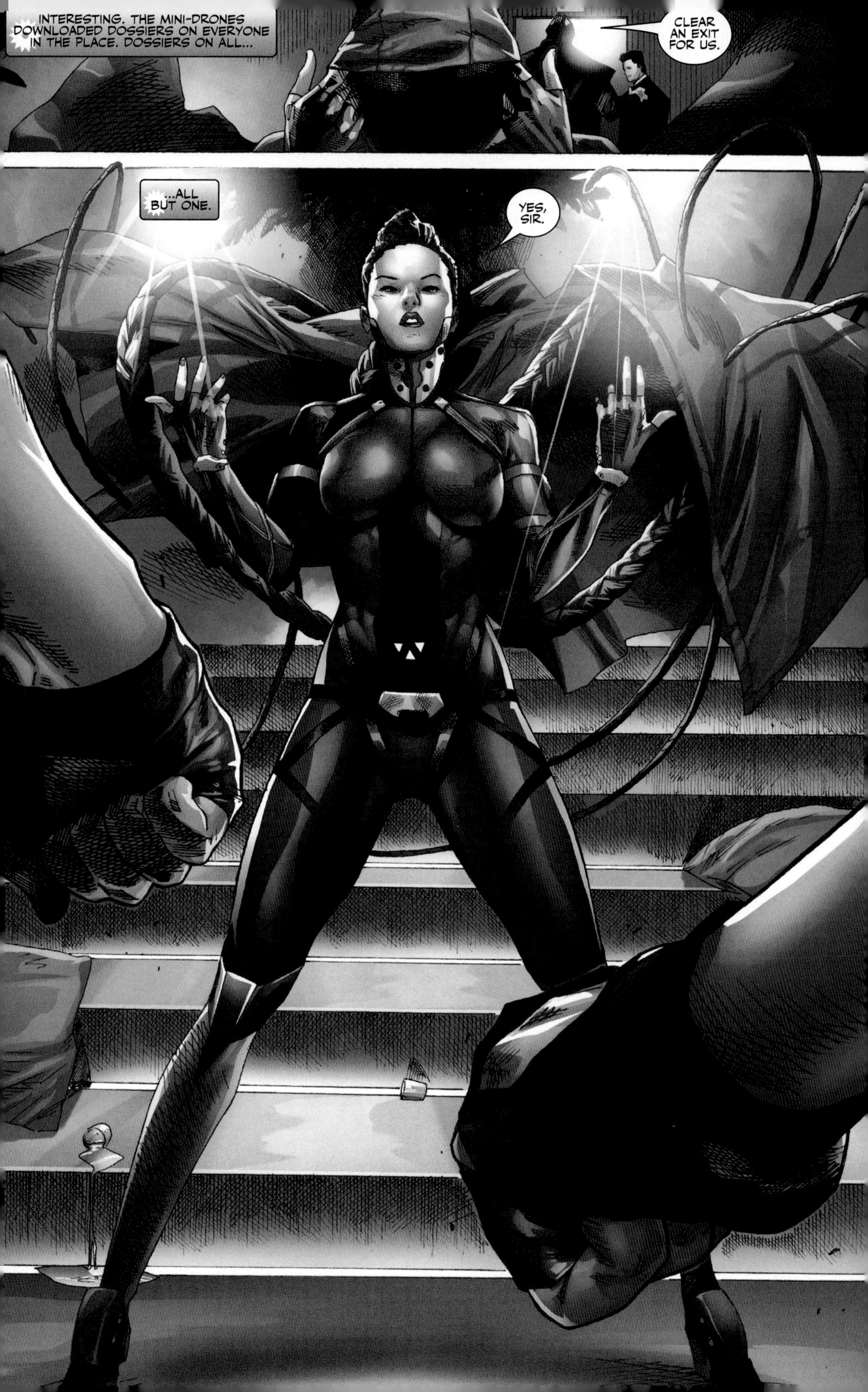
INTERESTING. THE MINI-DRONES DOWNLOADED DOSSIERS ON EVERYONE IN THE PLACE. DOSSIERS ON ALL...
CLEAR AN EXIT FOR US.
...ALL BUT ONE.
YES, SIR.

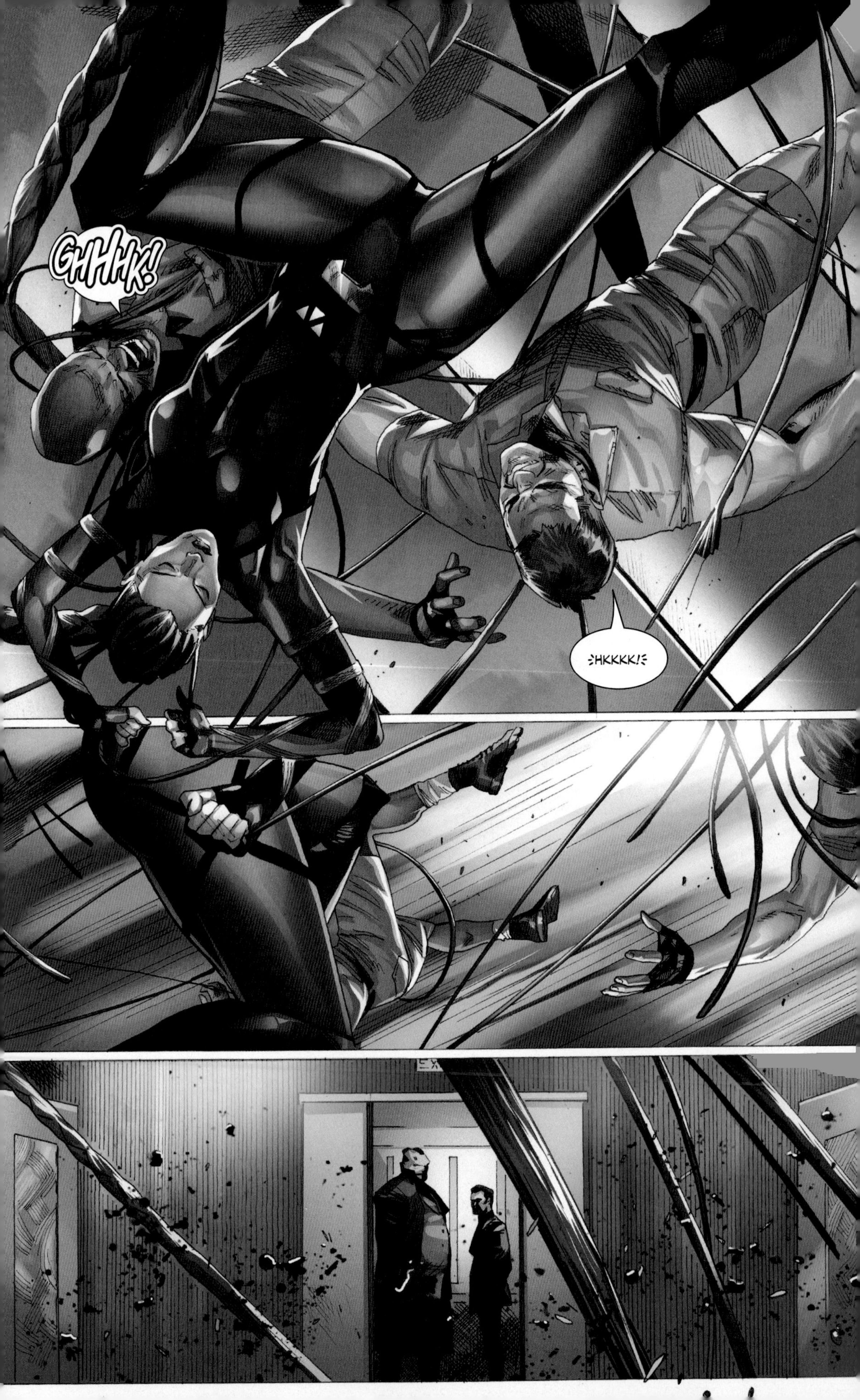
GHHHK!
HKKKK!

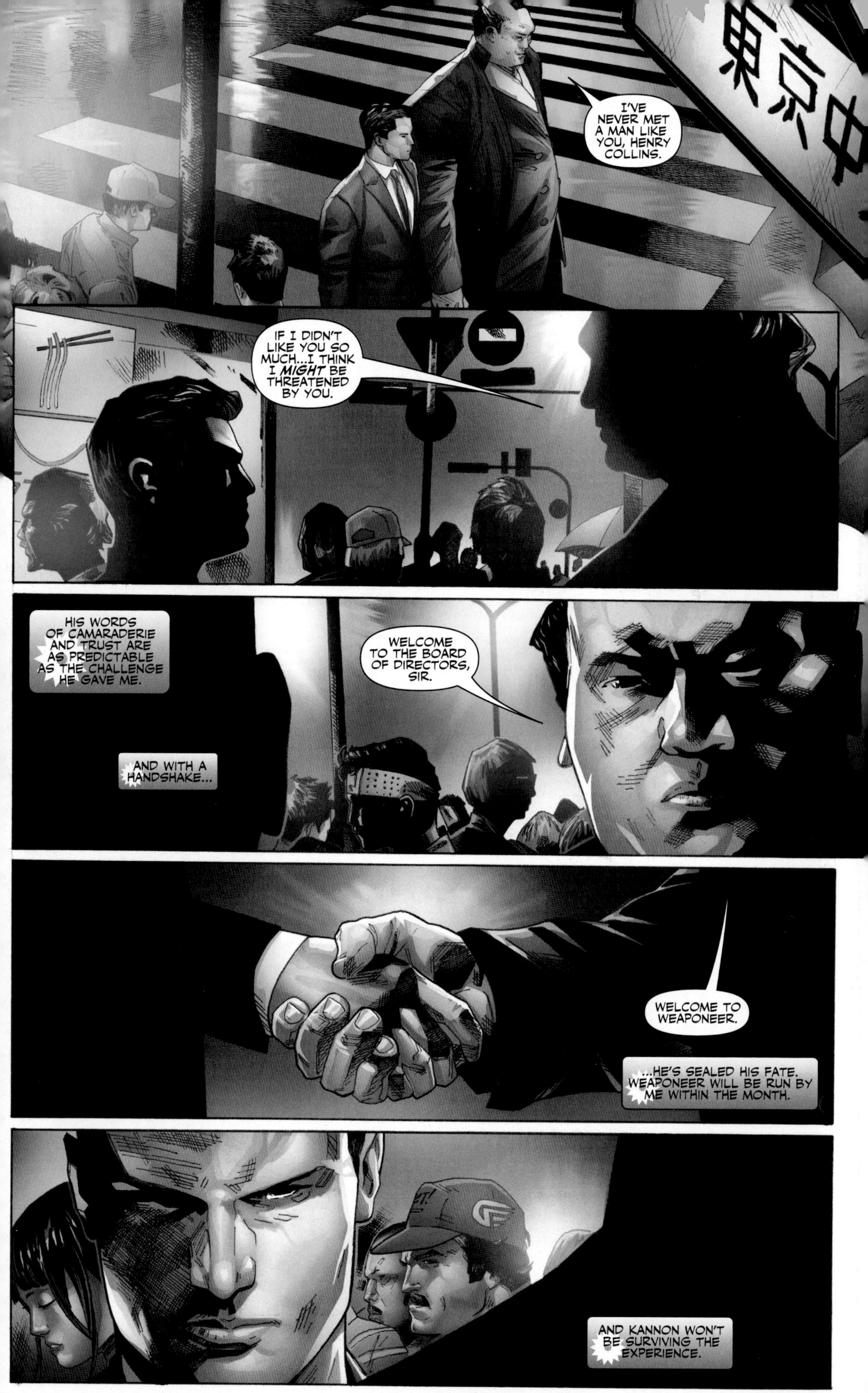
東京中
I'VE NEVER MET A MAN LIKE YOU, HENRY COLLINS.
IF I DIDN'T LIKE YOU SO MUCH...I THINK I *MIGHT* BE THREATENED BY YOU.
HIS WORDS OF CAMARADERIE AND TRUST ARE AS PREDICTABLE AS THE CHALLENGE HE GAVE ME.
WELCOME TO THE BOARD OF DIRECTORS, SIR.
AND WITH A HANDSHAKE...
WELCOME TO WEAPONEER.
...HE'S SEALED HIS FATE. WEAPONEER WILL BE RUN BY ME WITHIN THE MONTH.
AND KANNON WON'T BE SURVIVING THE EXPERIENCE.

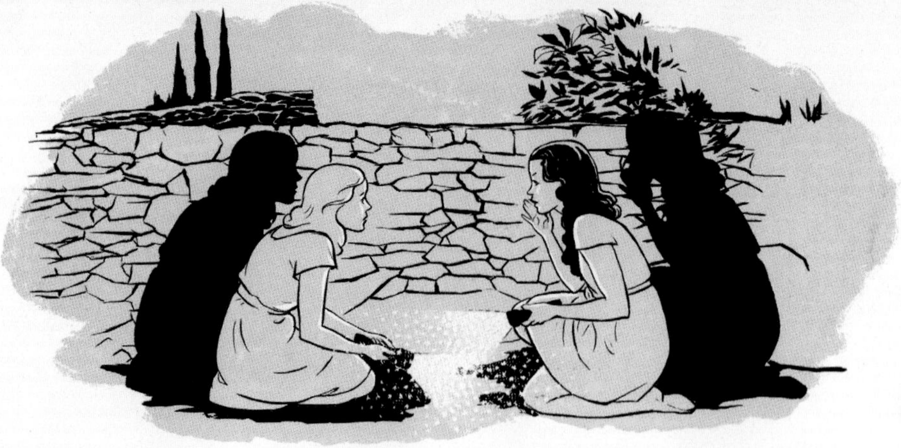

The suspicious girls whispered quietly as they traded information and evidence.

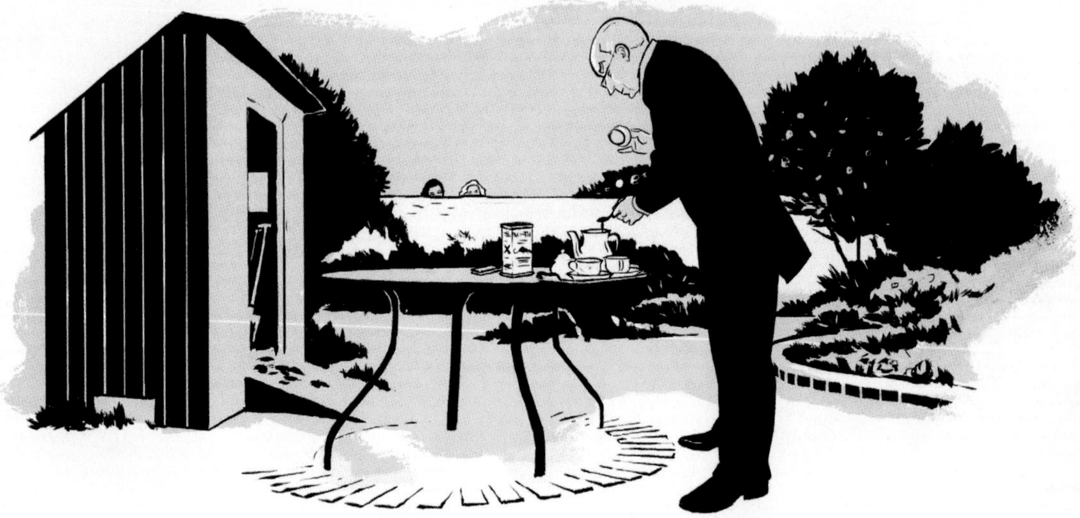

The housekeeper was definitely up to something.

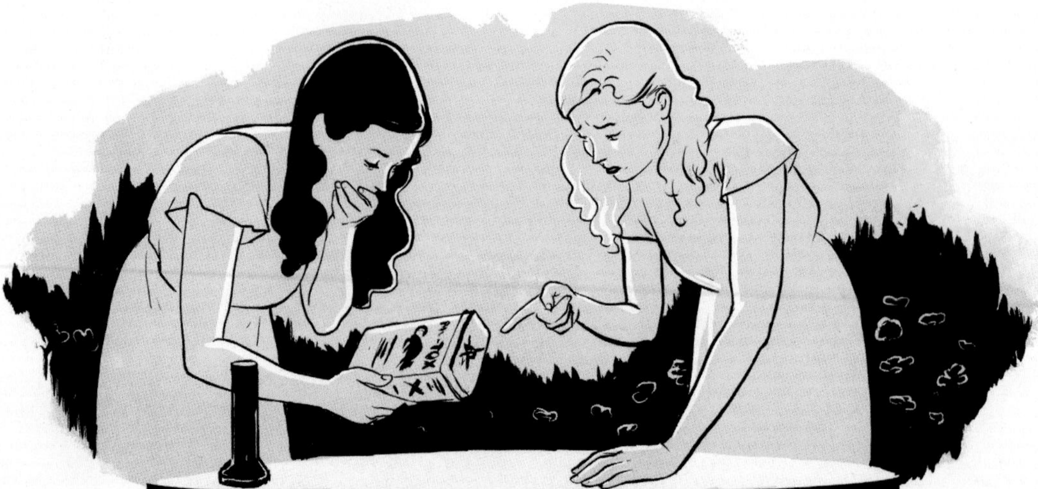

He'd been dosing the tea for weeks. Small doses that would have a cumulatively lethal effect over time.

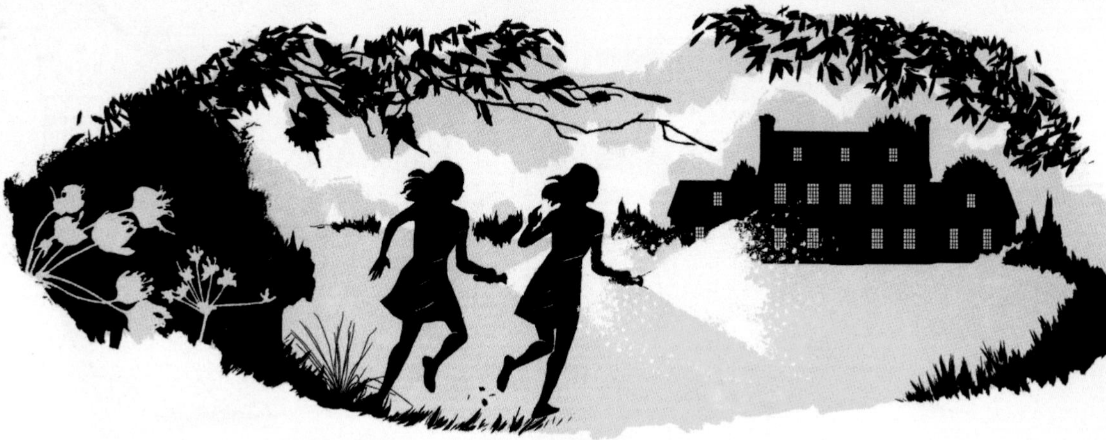

"How long had he been doing this?" they wondered.

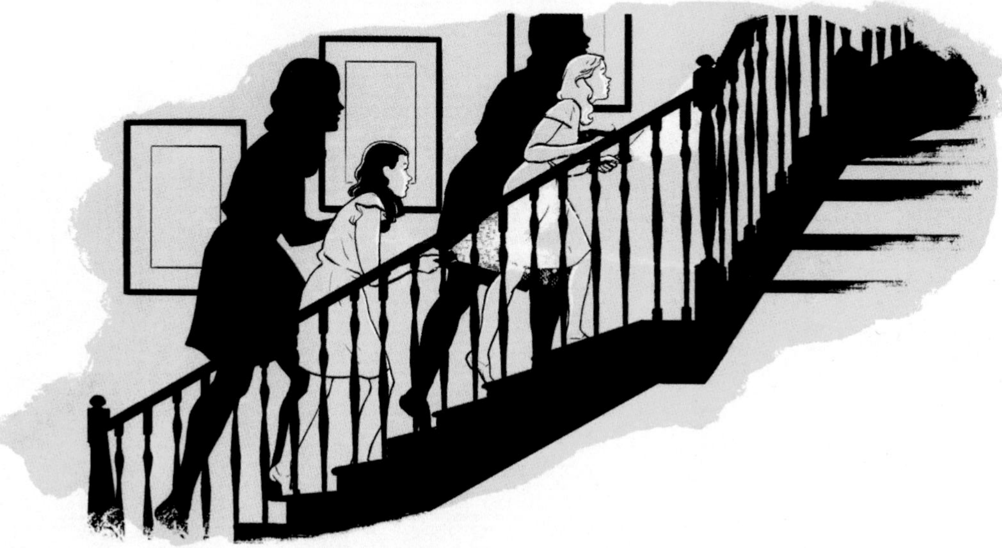

Would they be in time or was it already too late?

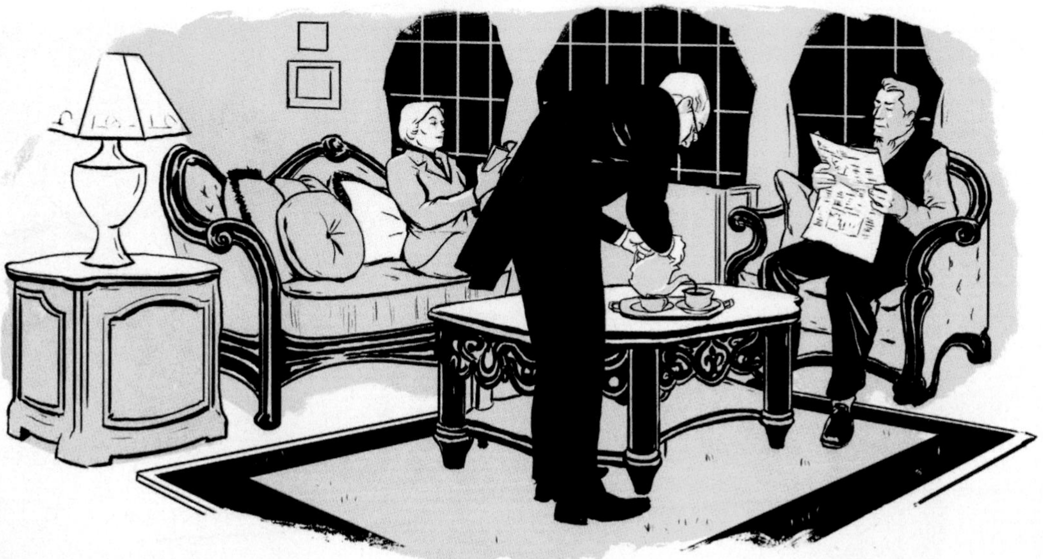

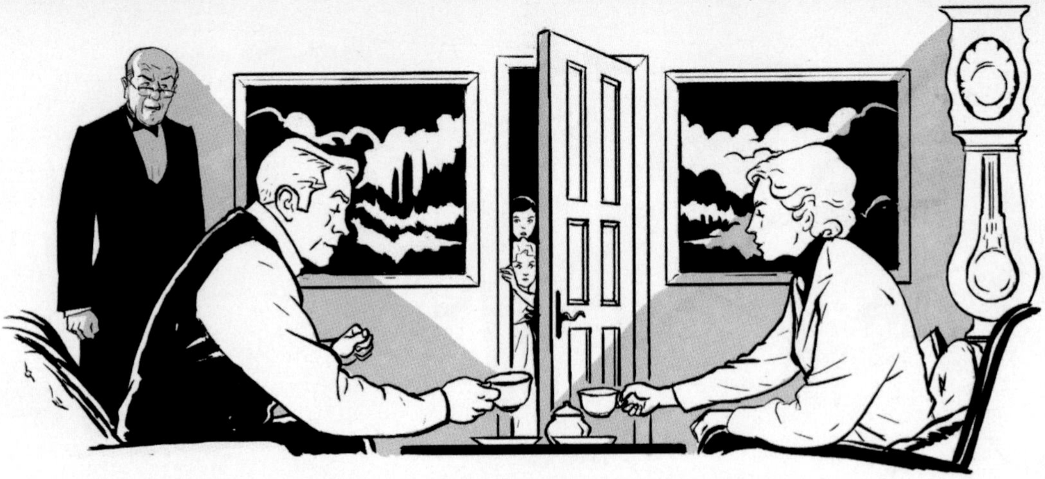

Only then would they feel confident enough to take action.
Otherwise, who would believe two teenage amateur sleuths?

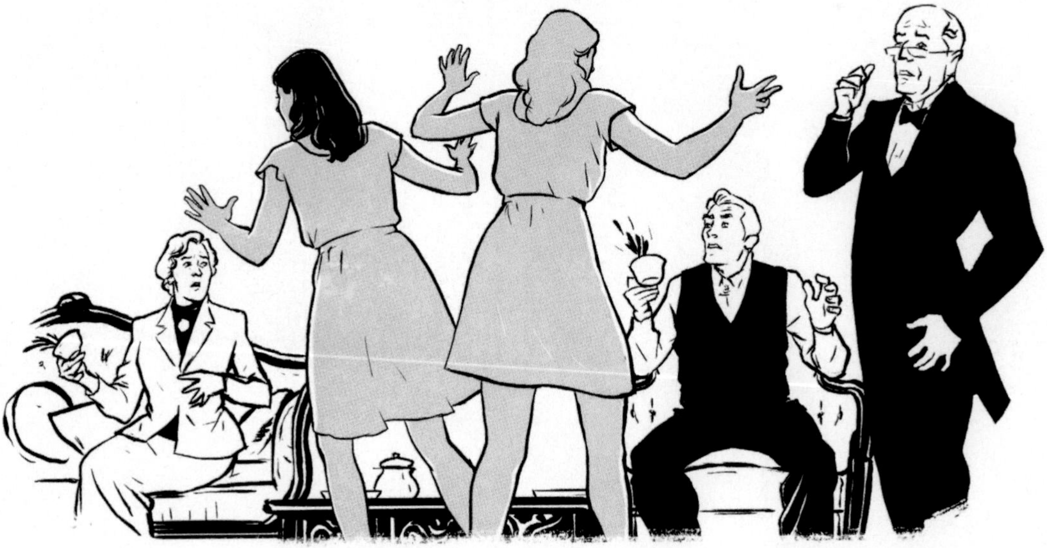

At last they take action! Saving the parents
from a certain and untimely death!

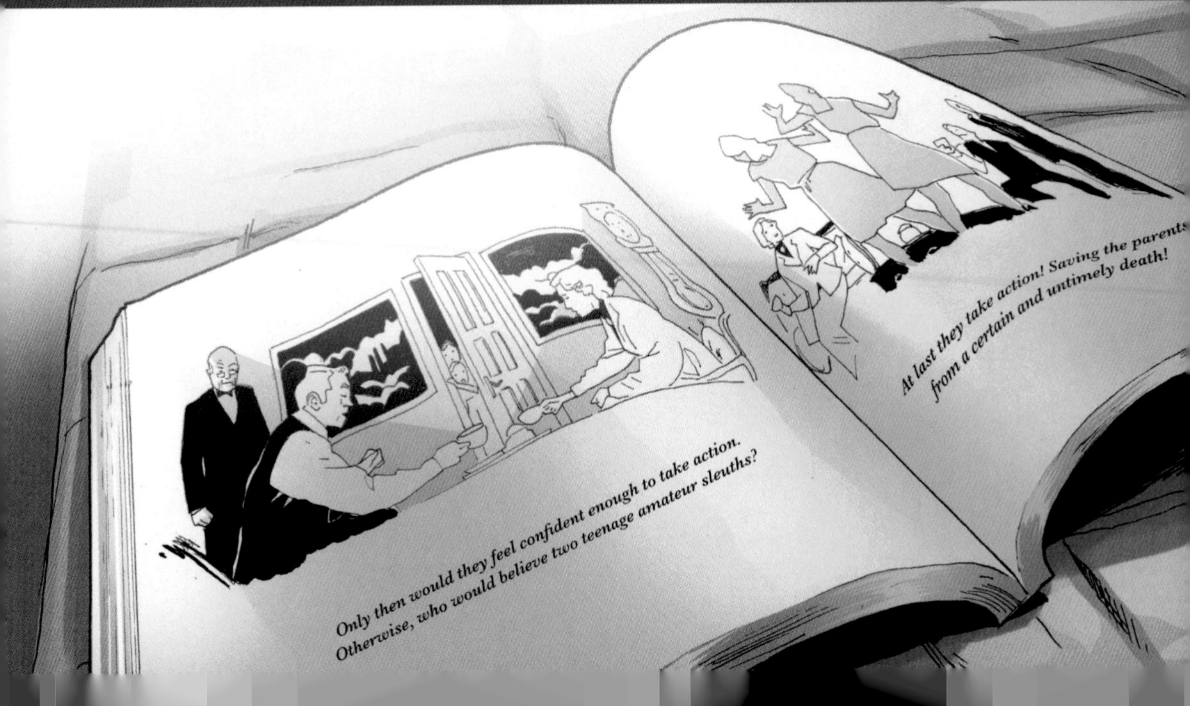
Only then would they feel confident enough to take action.
Otherwise, who would believe two teenage amateur sleuths?
At last they take action! Saving the parents
from a certain and untimely death!

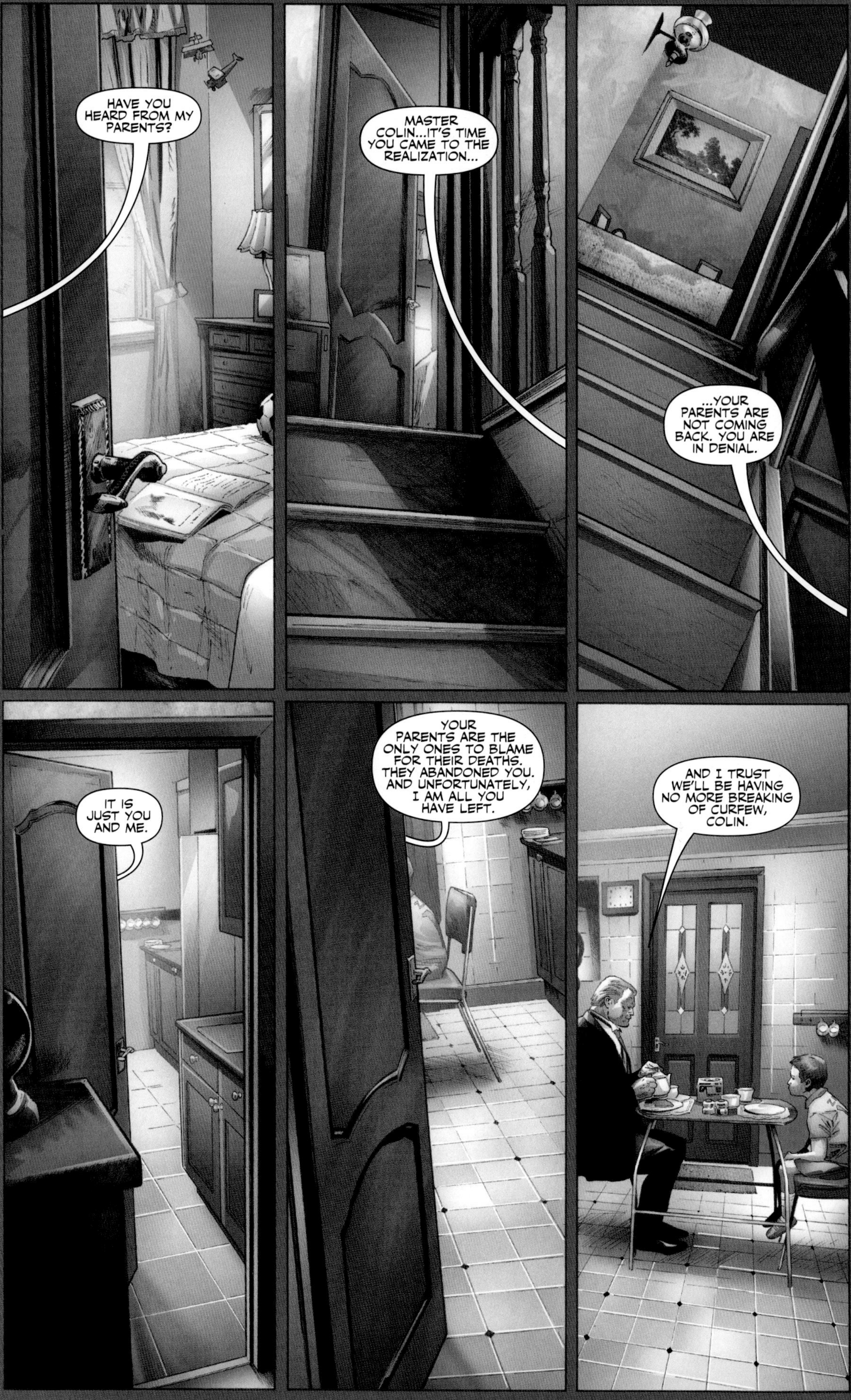
HAVE YOU HEARD FROM MY PARENTS?
MASTER COLIN...IT'S TIME YOU CAME TO THE REALIZATION...
...YOUR PARENTS ARE NOT COMING BACK. YOU ARE IN DENIAL.
IT IS JUST YOU AND ME.
YOUR PARENTS ARE THE ONLY ONES TO BLAME FOR THEIR DEATHS. THEY ABANDONED YOU. AND UNFORTUNATELY, I AM ALL YOU HAVE LEFT.
AND I TRUST WE'LL BE HAVING NO MORE BREAKING OF CURFEW, COLIN.

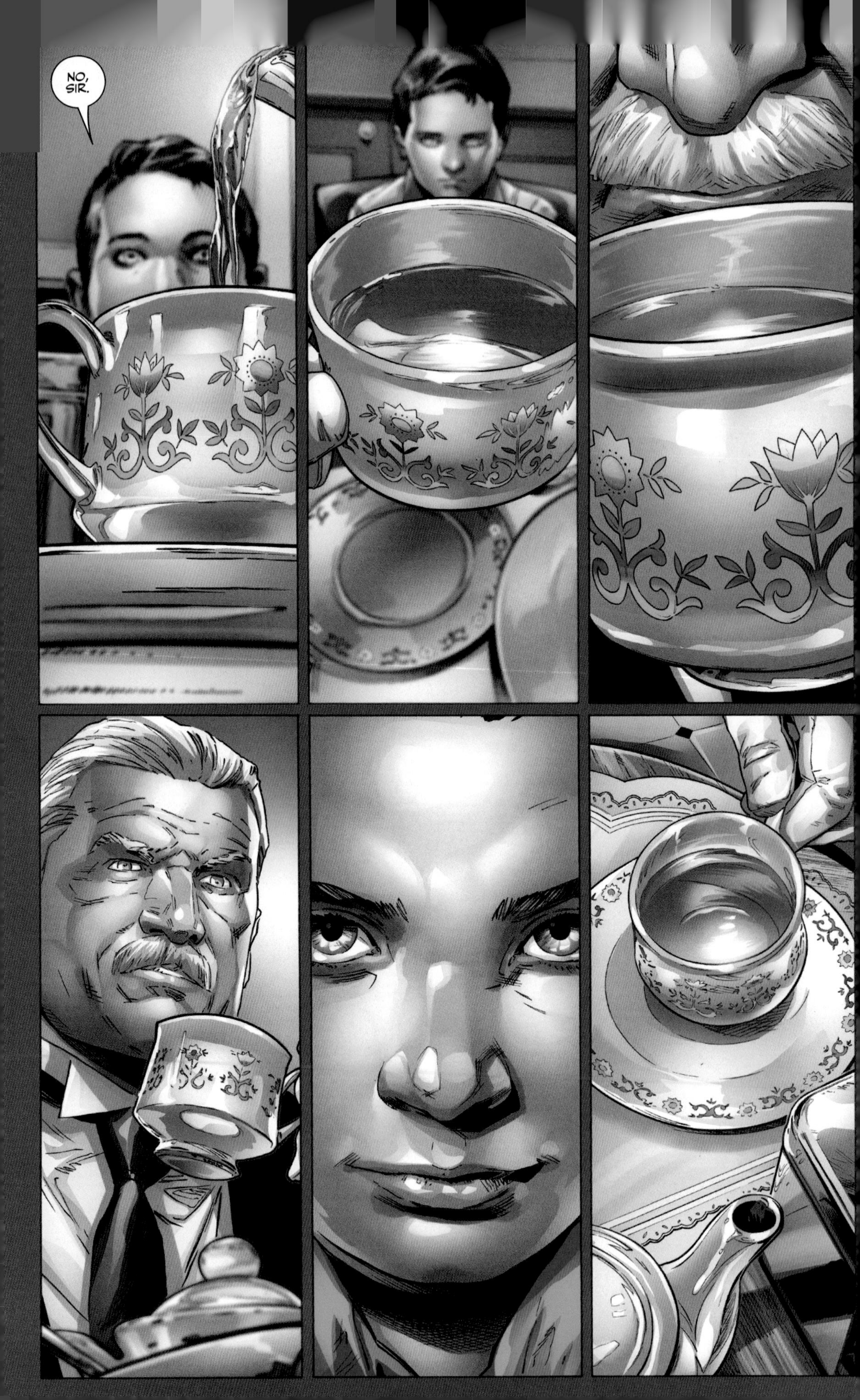
NO, SIR.

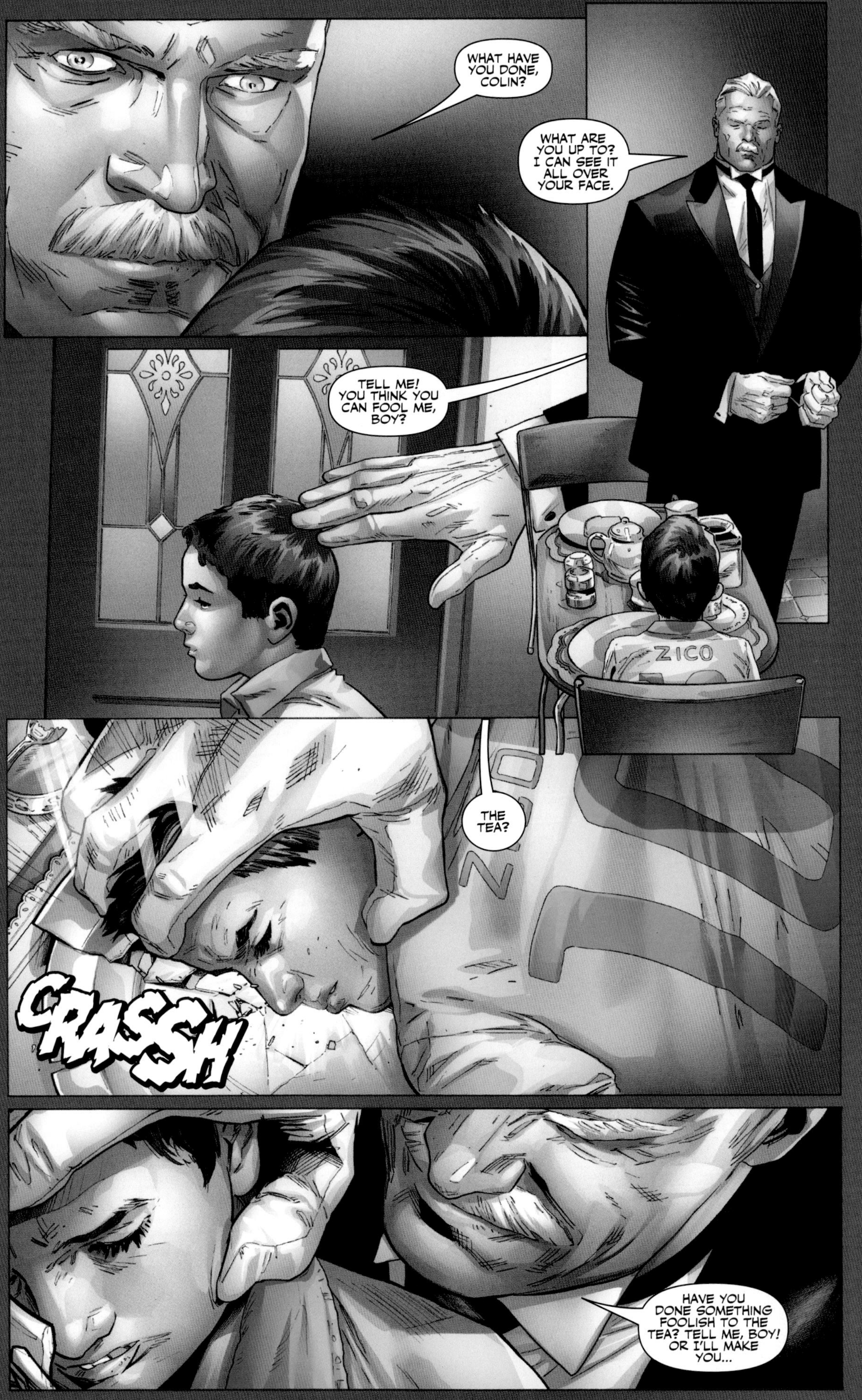
WHAT HAVE YOU DONE, COLIN?
WHAT ARE YOU UP TO? I CAN SEE IT ALL OVER YOUR FACE.
TELL ME! YOU THINK YOU CAN FOOL ME, BOY?
ZICO
THE TEA?
CRASSH
HAVE YOU DONE SOMETHING FOOLISH TO THE TEA? TELL ME, BOY! OR I'LL MAKE YOU...

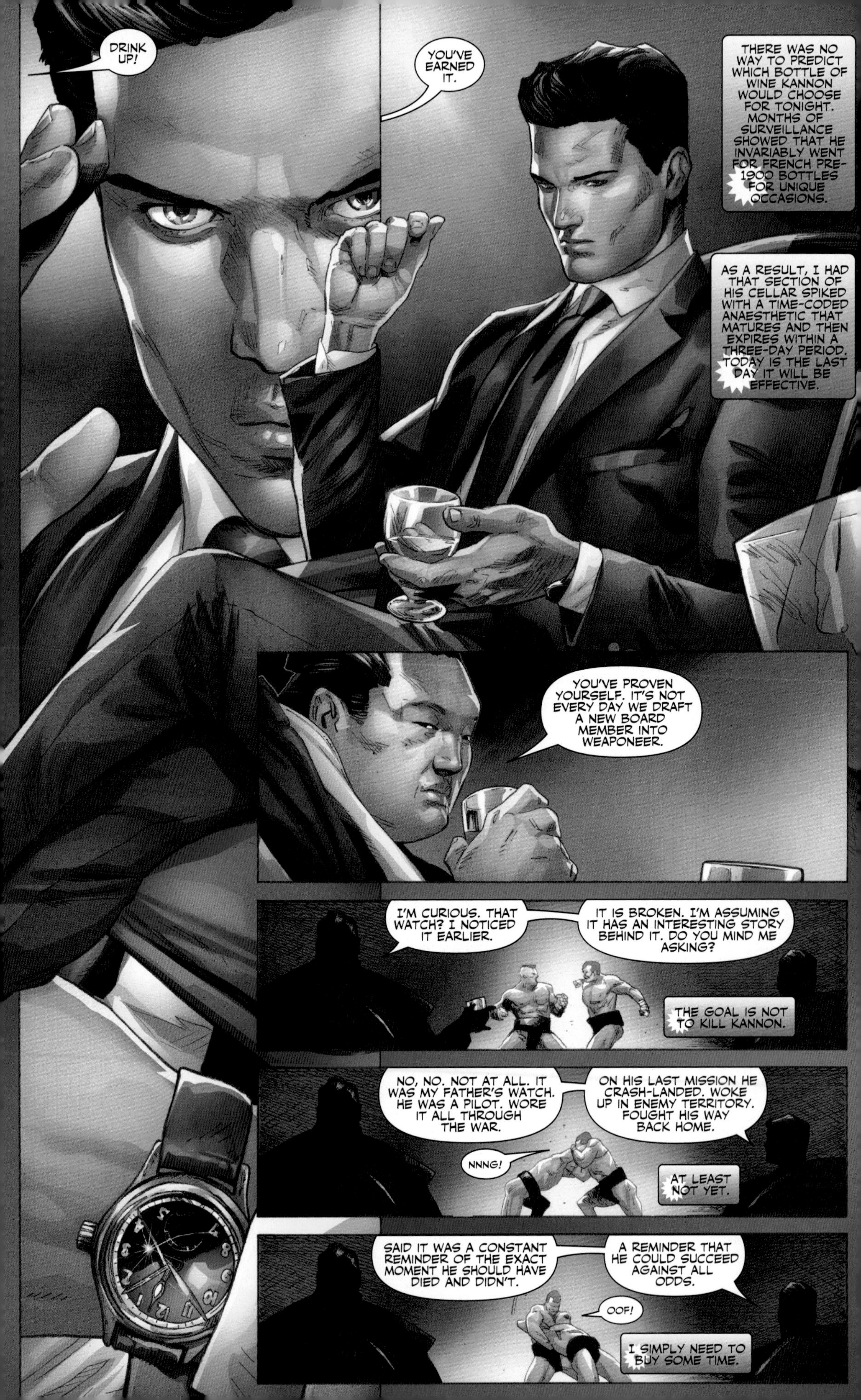
DRINK UP!
YOU'VE EARNED IT.
THERE WAS NO WAY TO PREDICT WHICH BOTTLE OF WINE KANNON WOULD CHOOSE FOR TONIGHT. MONTHS OF SURVEILLANCE SHOWED THAT HE INVARIABLY WENT FOR FRENCH PRE-1900 BOTTLES FOR UNIQUE OCCASIONS.
AS A RESULT, I HAD THAT SECTION OF HIS CELLAR SPIKED WITH A TIME-CODED ANAESTHETIC THAT MATURES AND THEN EXPIRES WITHIN A THREE-DAY PERIOD. TODAY IS THE LAST DAY IT WILL BE EFFECTIVE.
YOU'VE PROVEN YOURSELF. IT'S NOT EVERY DAY WE DRAFT A NEW BOARD MEMBER INTO WEAPONEER.
I'M CURIOUS. THAT WATCH? I NOTICED IT EARLIER.
IT IS BROKEN. I'M ASSUMING IT HAS AN INTERESTING STORY BEHIND IT. DO YOU MIND ME ASKING?
THE GOAL IS NOT TO KILL KANNON.
NO, NO. NOT AT ALL. IT WAS MY FATHER'S WATCH. HE WAS A PILOT. WORE IT ALL THROUGH THE WAR.
ON HIS LAST MISSION HE CRASH-LANDED. WOKE UP IN ENEMY TERRITORY. FOUGHT HIS WAY BACK HOME.
NNNG!
AT LEAST NOT YET.
SAID IT WAS A CONSTANT REMINDER OF THE EXACT MOMENT HE SHOULD HAVE DIED AND DIDN'T.
A REMINDER THAT HE COULD SUCCEED AGAINST ALL ODDS.
OOF!
I SIMPLY NEED TO BUY SOME TIME.

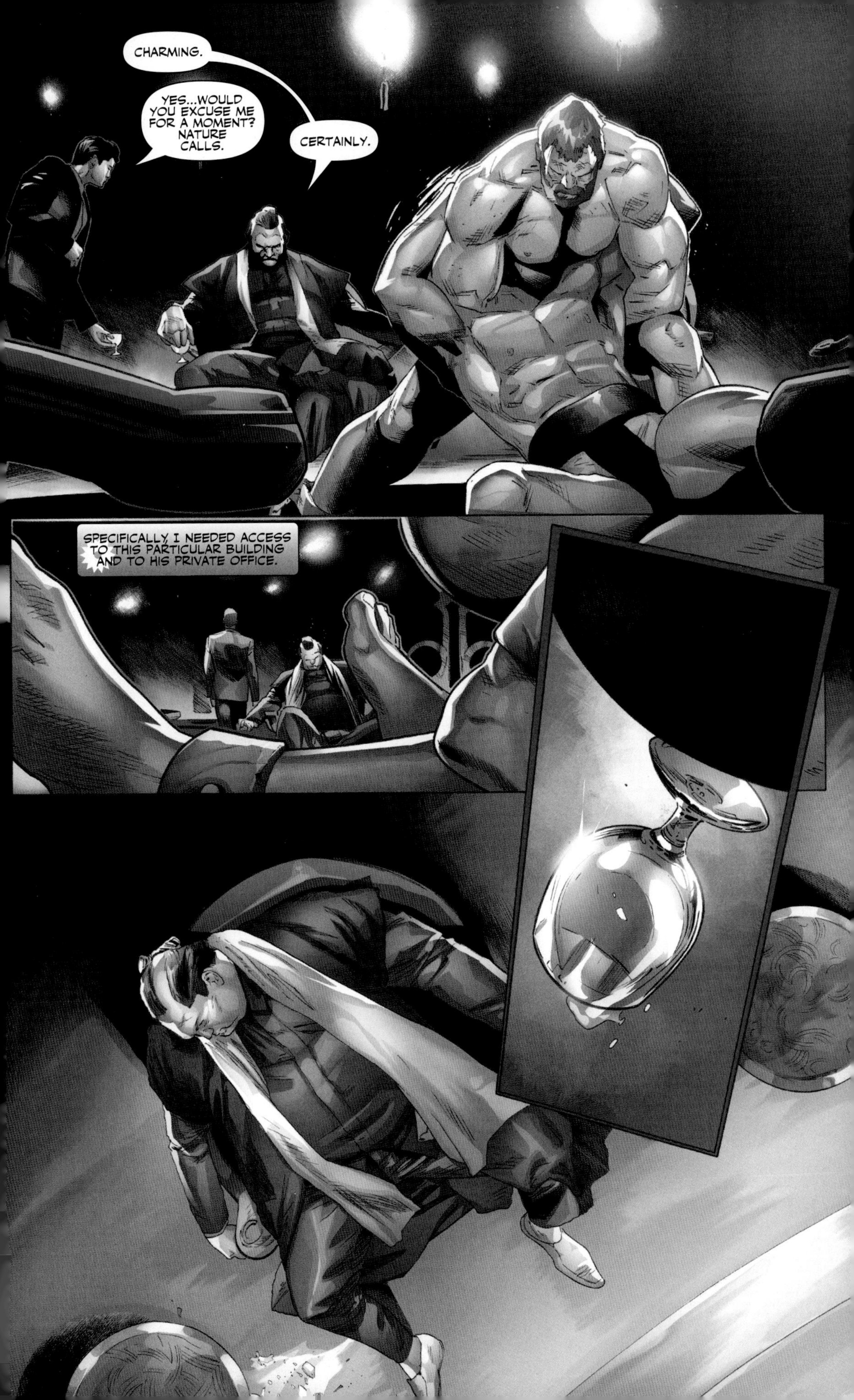
CHARMING.
YES...WOULD YOU EXCUSE ME FOR A MOMENT? NATURE CALLS.
CERTAINLY.
SPECIFICALLY, I NEEDED ACCESS TO THIS PARTICULAR BUILDING AND TO HIS PRIVATE OFFICE.

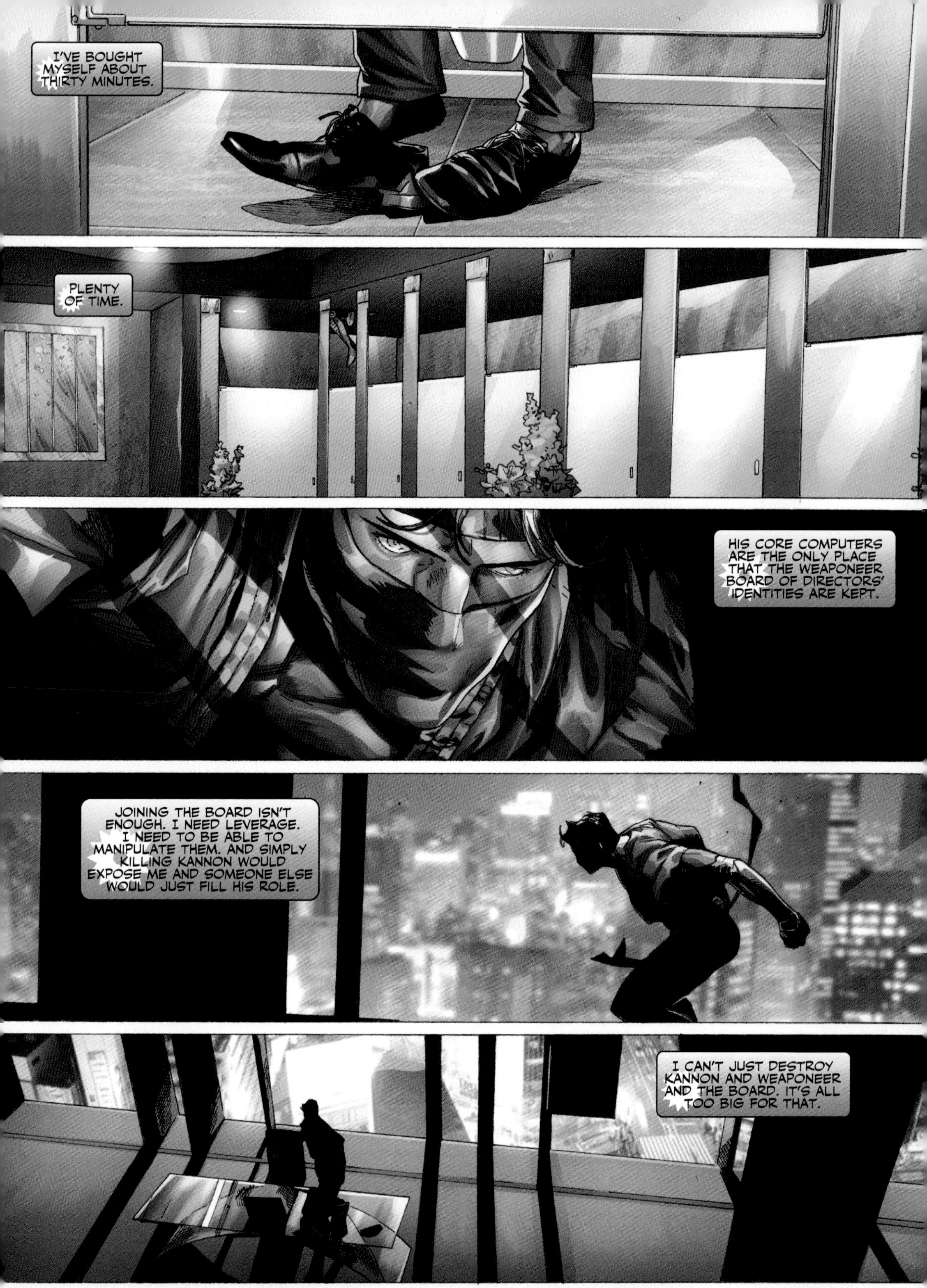
I'VE BOUGHT MYSELF ABOUT THIRTY MINUTES.
PLENTY OF TIME.
HIS CORE COMPUTERS ARE THE ONLY PLACE THAT THE WEAPONEER BOARD OF DIRECTORS' IDENTITIES ARE KEPT.
JOINING THE BOARD ISN'T ENOUGH. I NEED LEVERAGE. I NEED TO BE ABLE TO MANIPULATE THEM. AND SIMPLY KILLING KANNON WOULD EXPOSE ME AND SOMEONE ELSE WOULD JUST FILL HIS ROLE.
I CAN'T JUST DESTROY KANNON AND WEAPONEER AND THE BOARD. IT'S ALL TOO BIG FOR THAT.

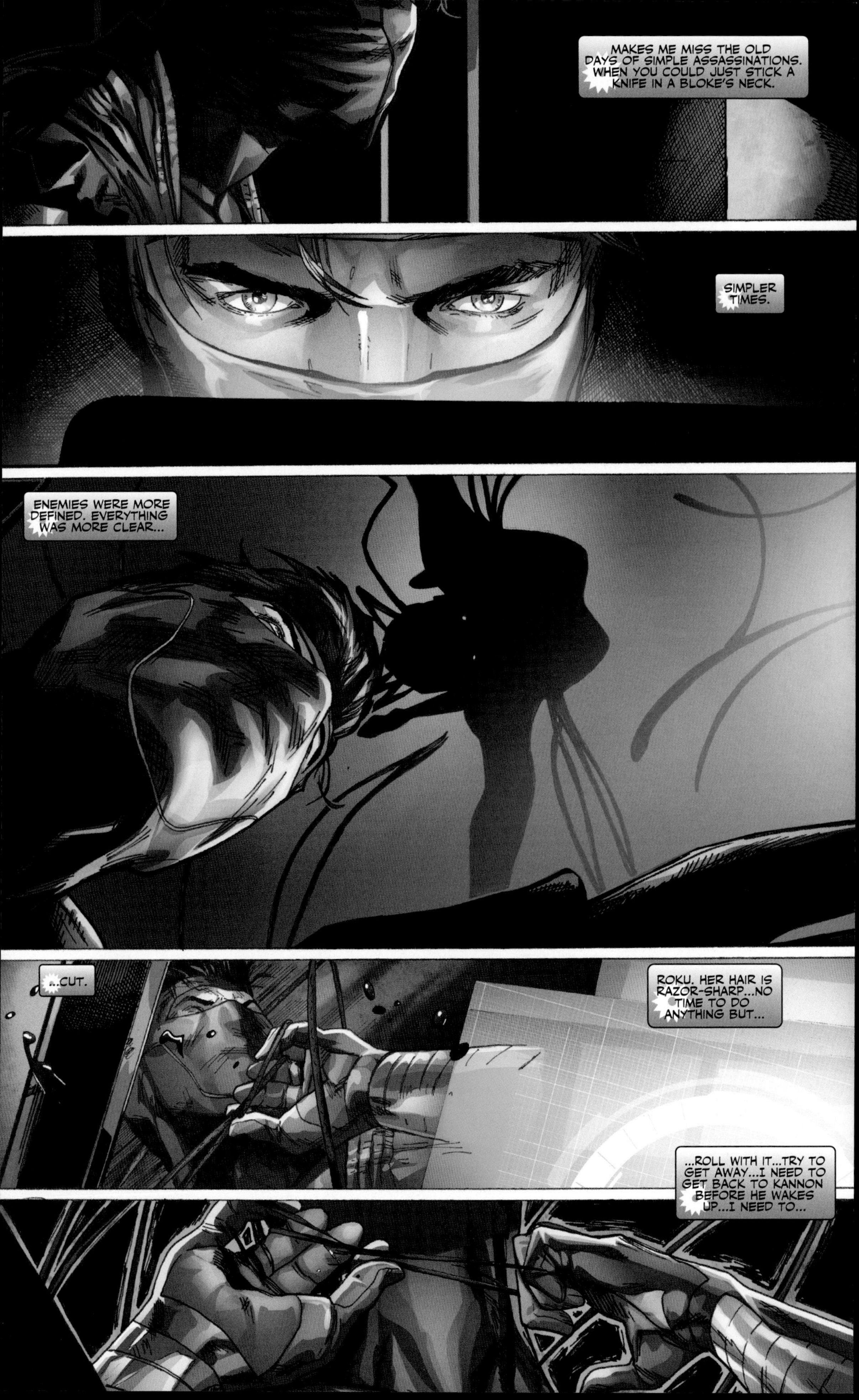
MAKES ME MISS THE OLD DAYS OF SIMPLE ASSASSINATIONS. WHEN YOU COULD JUST STICK A KNIFE IN A BLOKE'S NECK.
SIMPLER TIMES.
ENEMIES WERE MORE DEFINED. EVERYTHING WAS MORE CLEAR...
ROKU. HER HAIR IS RAZOR-SHARP...NO TIME TO DO ANYTHING BUT...
...CUT.
...ROLL WITH IT...TRY TO GET AWAY...I NEED TO GET BACK TO KANNON BEFORE HE WAKES UP...I NEED TO...

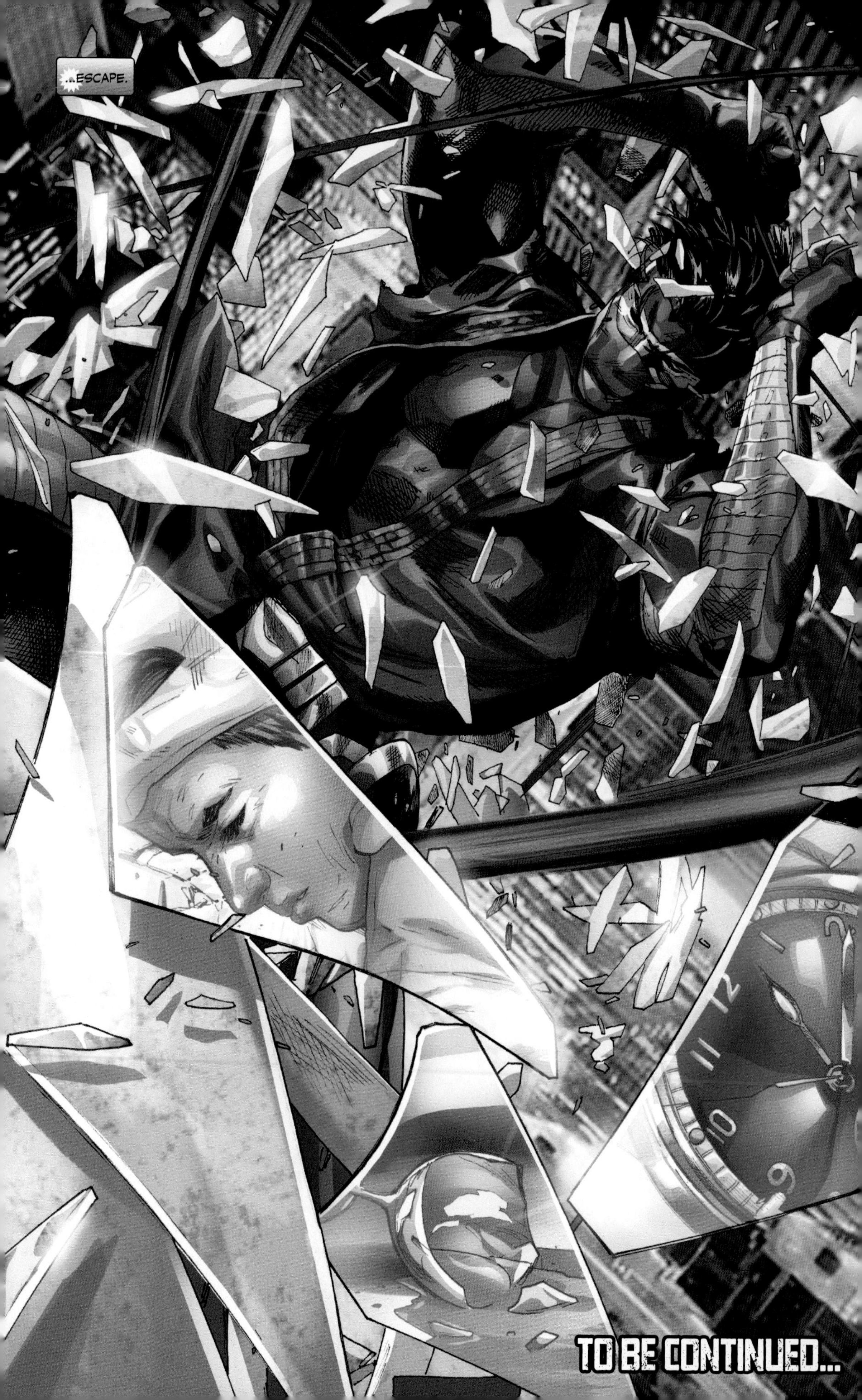
...ESCAPE.
TO BE CONTINUED...

THE LOST FILES

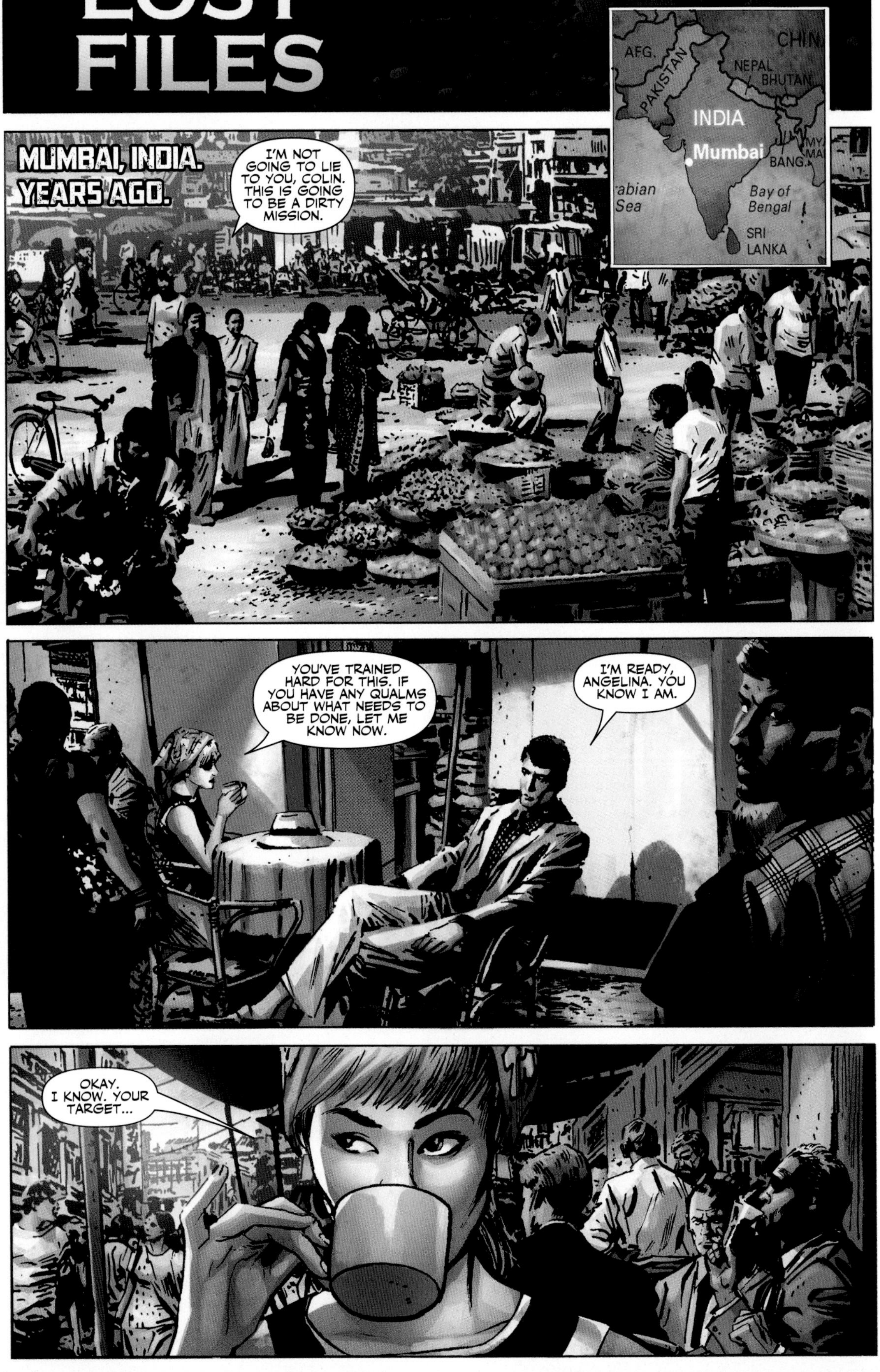
AFG.
PAKISTAN
NEPAL
BHUTAN
INDIA
Mumbai
BANG.
Bay of Bengal
SRI LANKA
MUMBAI, INDIA. YEARS AGO.
I'M NOT GOING TO LIE TO YOU, COLIN. THIS IS GOING TO BE A DIRTY MISSION.
YOU'VE TRAINED HARD FOR THIS. IF YOU HAVE ANY QUALMS ABOUT WHAT NEEDS TO BE DONE, LET ME KNOW NOW.
I'M READY, ANGELINA. YOU KNOW I AM.
OKAY. I KNOW. YOUR TARGET...

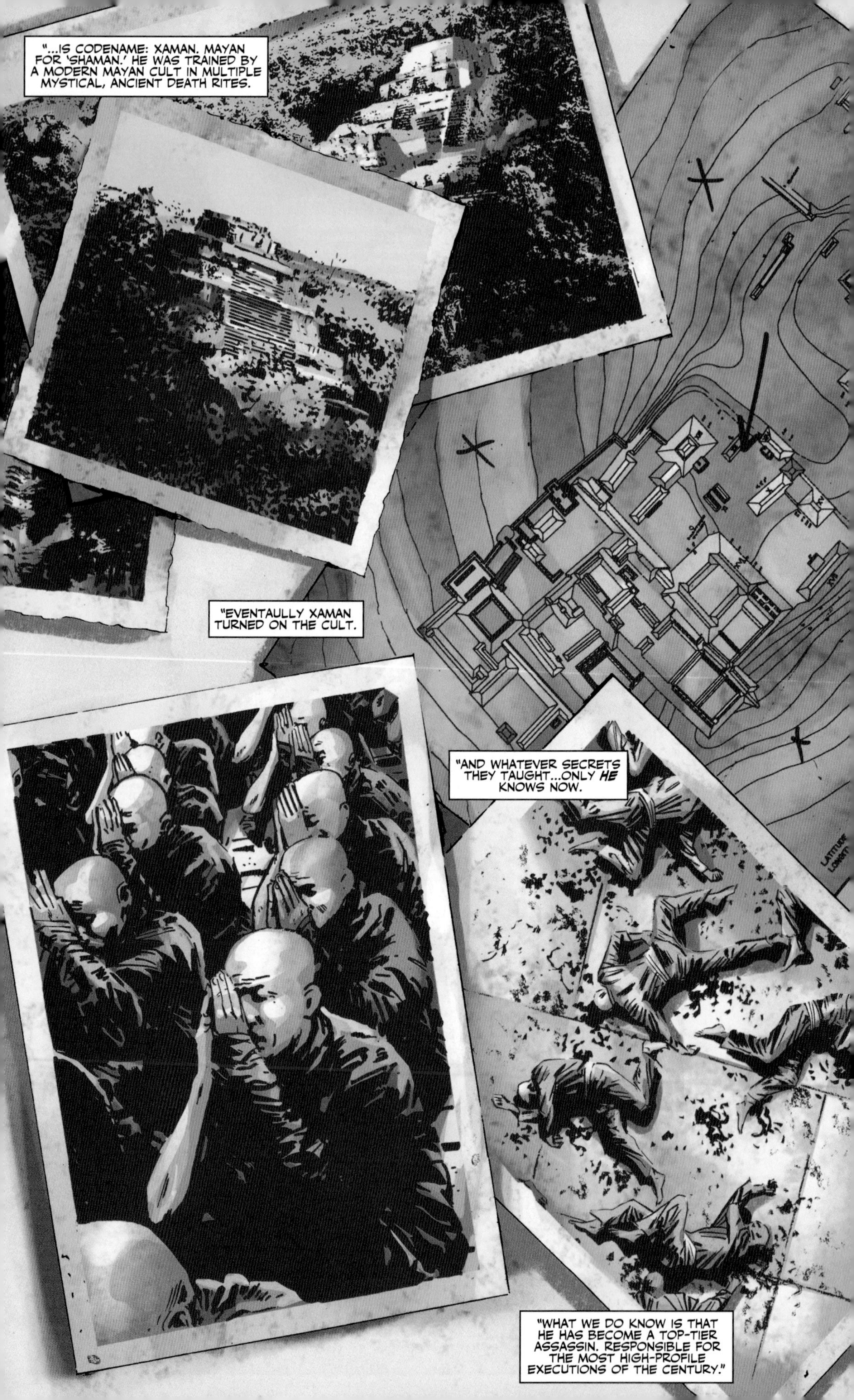
"...IS CODENAME: XAMAN. MAYAN FOR 'SHAMAN.' HE WAS TRAINED BY A MODERN MAYAN CULT IN MULTIPLE MYSTICAL, ANCIENT DEATH RITES.
"EVENTAULLY XAMAN TURNED ON THE CULT.
"AND WHATEVER SECRETS THEY TAUGHT...ONLY *HE* KNOWS NOW.
"WHAT WE DO KNOW IS THAT HE HAS BECOME A TOP-TIER ASSASSIN. RESPONSIBLE FOR THE MOST HIGH-PROFILE EXECUTIONS OF THE CENTURY."

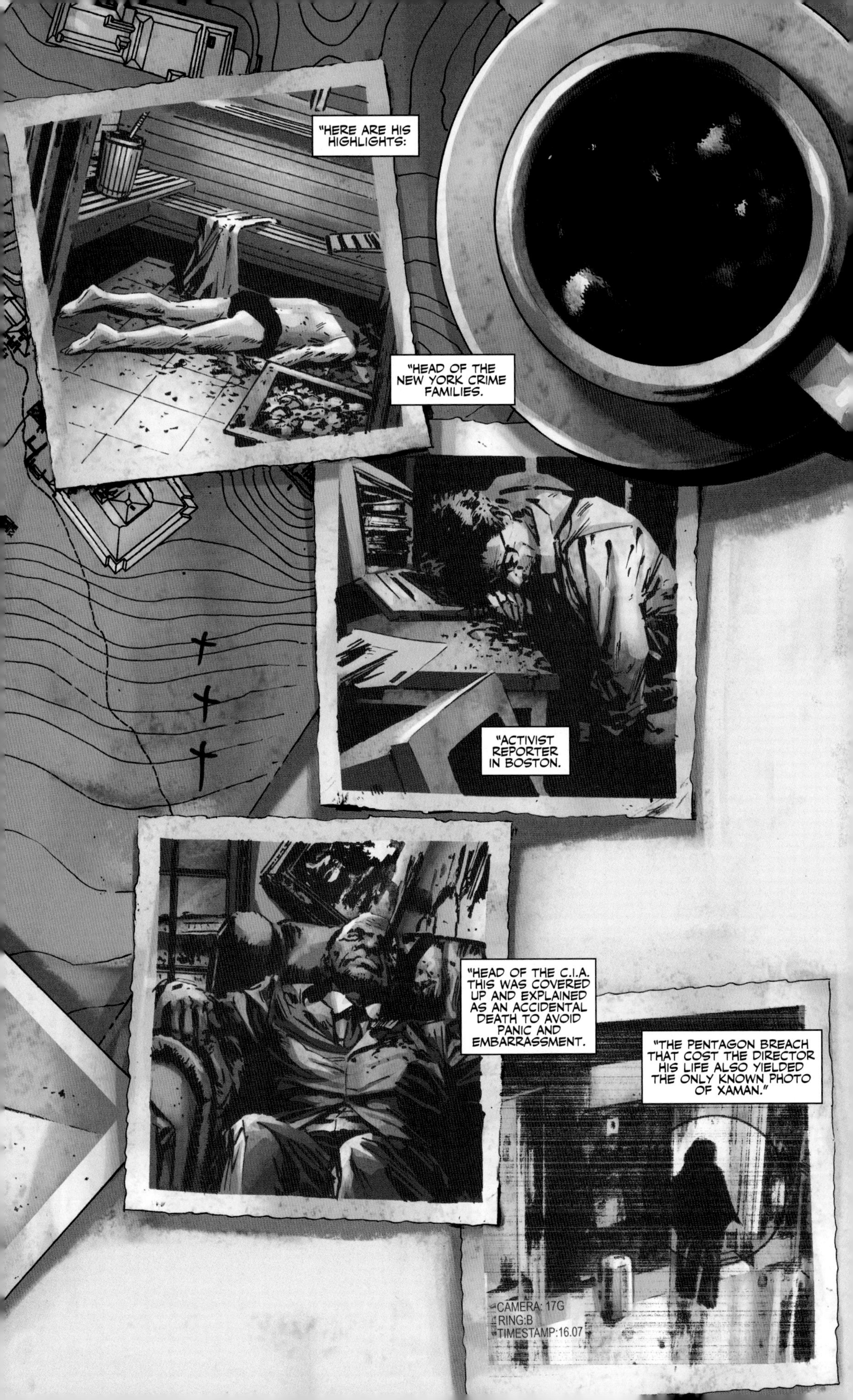
"HERE ARE HIS HIGHLIGHTS:
"HEAD OF THE NEW YORK CRIME FAMILIES.
"ACTIVIST REPORTER IN BOSTON.
"HEAD OF THE C.I.A. THIS WAS COVERED UP AND EXPLAINED AS AN ACCIDENTAL DEATH TO AVOID PANIC AND EMBARRASSMENT.
"THE PENTAGON BREACH THAT COST THE DIRECTOR HIS LIFE ALSO YIELDED THE ONLY KNOWN PHOTO OF XAMAN."
CAMERA: 17G
RING:B
TIMESTAMP:16.07

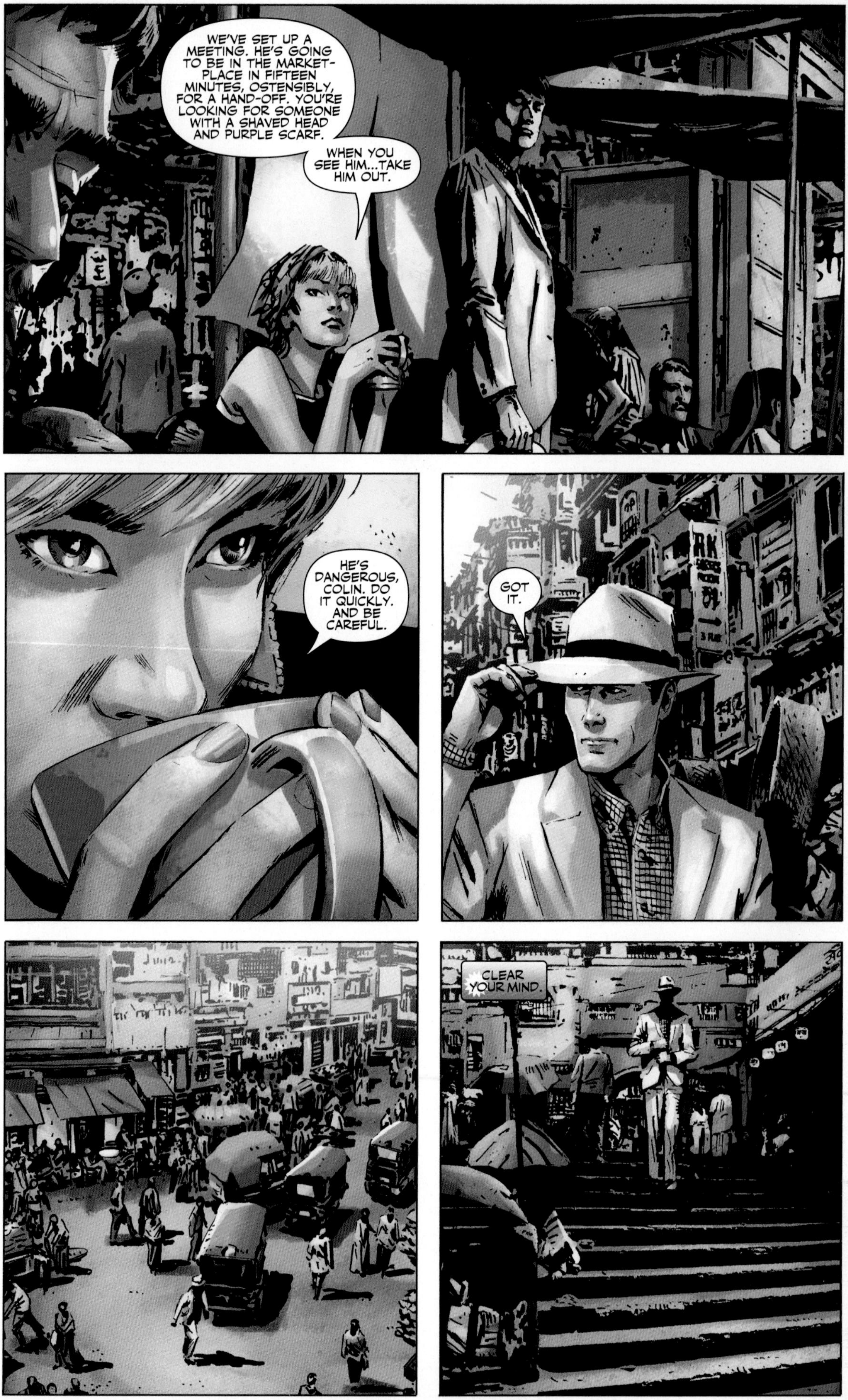
WE'VE SET UP A MEETING. HE'S GOING TO BE IN THE MARKET-PLACE IN FIFTEEN MINUTES, OSTENSIBLY, FOR A HAND-OFF. YOU'RE LOOKING FOR SOMEONE WITH A SHAVED HEAD AND PURPLE SCARF.
WHEN YOU SEE HIM...TAKE HIM OUT.
HE'S DANGEROUS, COLIN. DO IT QUICKLY. AND BE CAREFUL.
GOT IT.
CLEAR YOUR MIND.

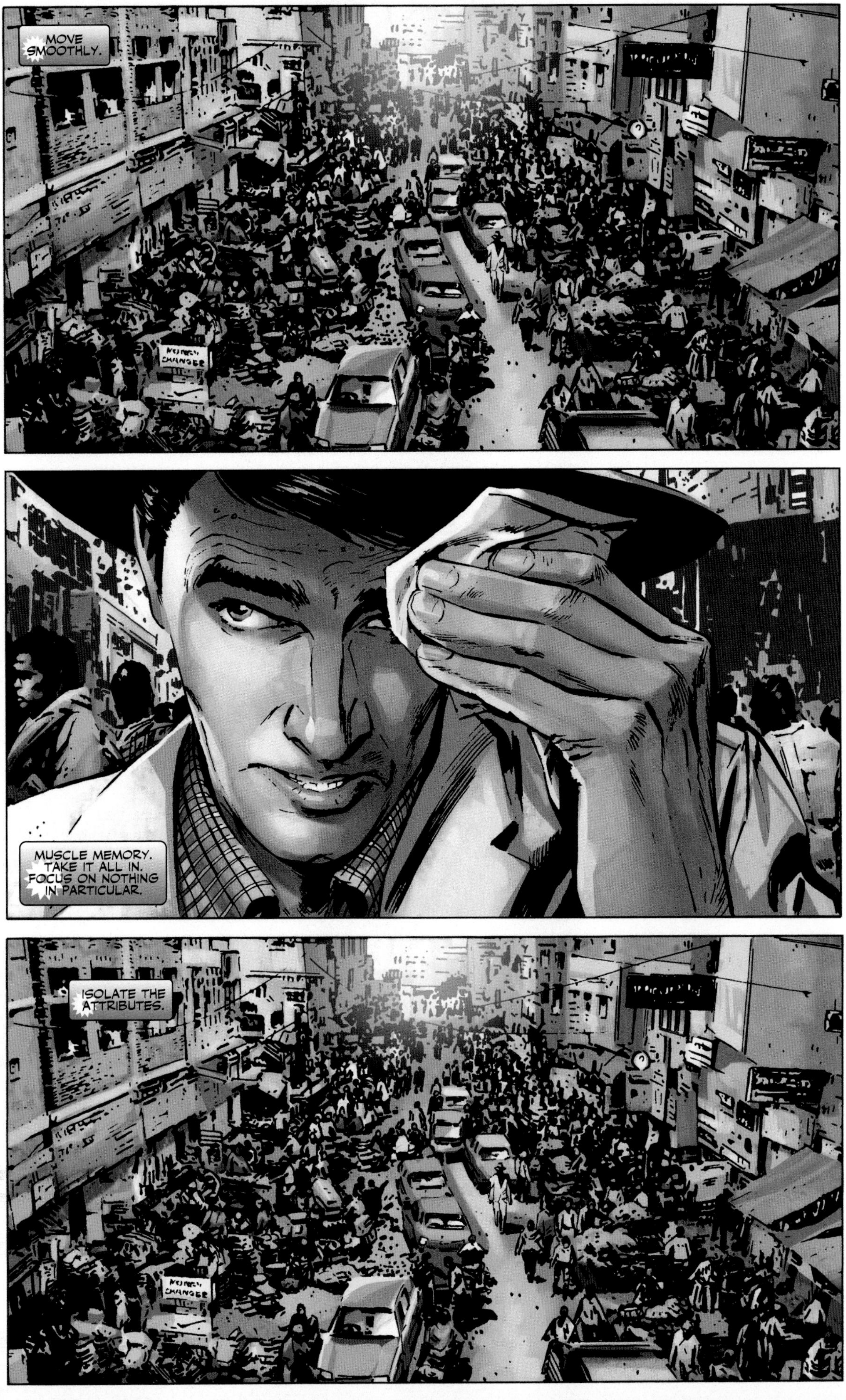
MOVE SMOOTHLY.
MUSCLE MEMORY. TAKE IT ALL IN. FOCUS ON NOTHING IN PARTICULAR.
ISOLATE THE ATTRIBUTES.

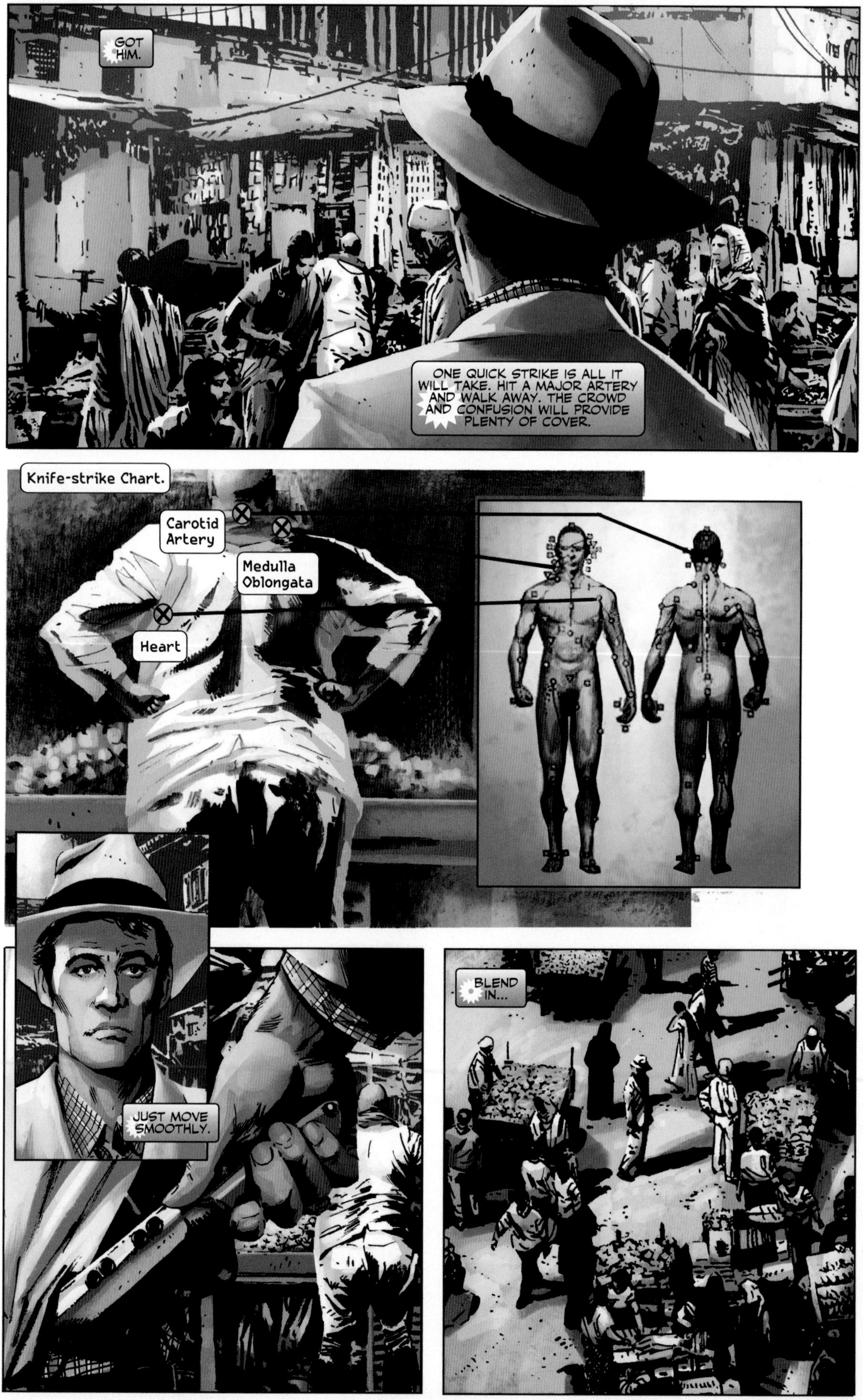
GOT HIM.
ONE QUICK STRIKE IS ALL IT WILL TAKE. HIT A MAJOR ARTERY AND WALK AWAY. THE CROWD AND CONFUSION WILL PROVIDE PLENTY OF COVER.
Knife-strike Chart.
Carotid Artery
Medulla Oblongata
Heart
JUST MOVE SMOOTHLY.
BLEND IN...

STRIKE QUICKLY--

WHAT--?!

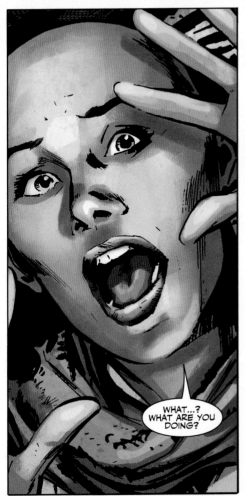

WHAT...? WHAT ARE YOU DOING?

PLEASE... LET ME GO...!

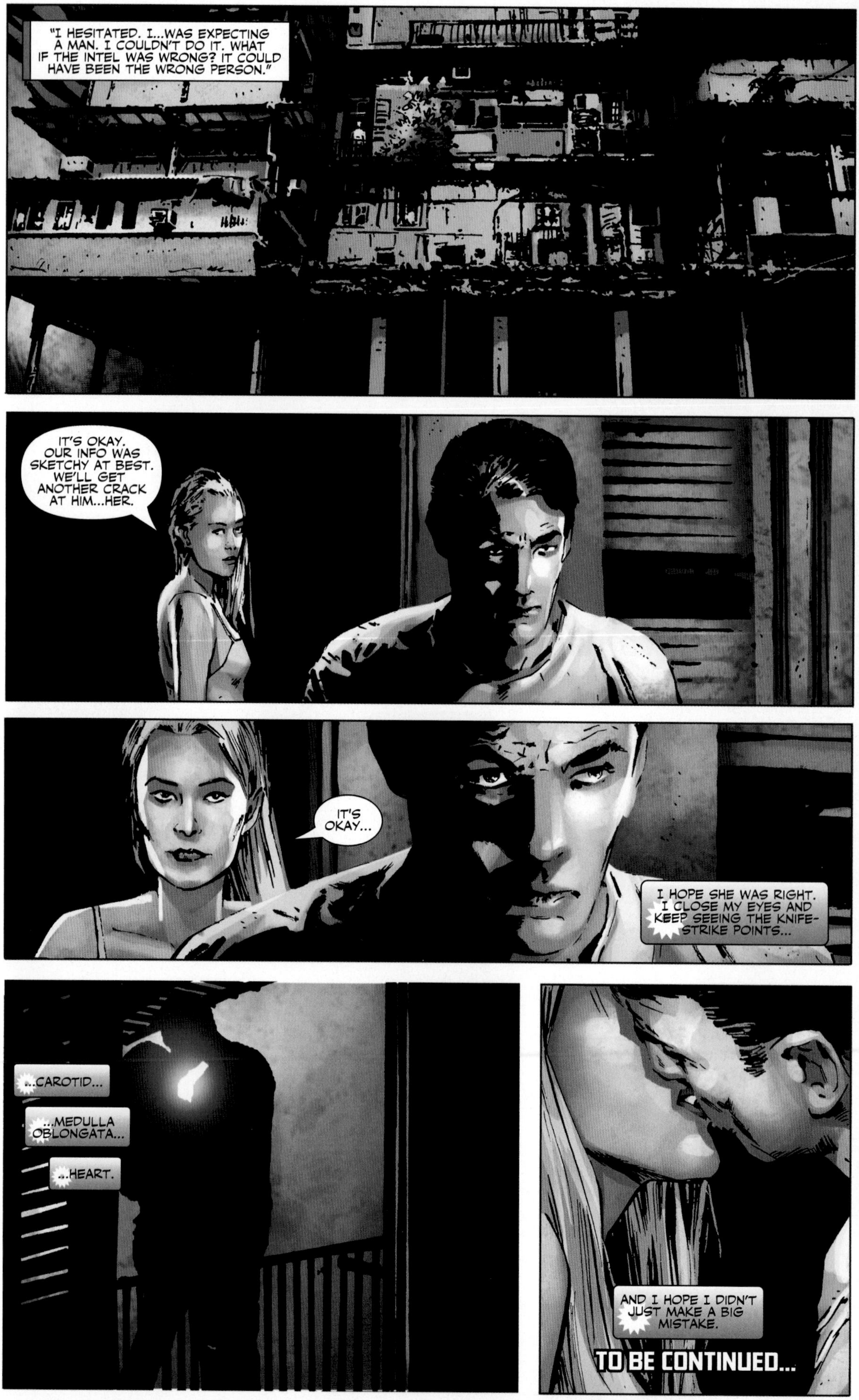
"I HESITATED. I...WAS EXPECTING A MAN. I COULDN'T DO IT. WHAT IF THE INTEL WAS WRONG? IT COULD HAVE BEEN THE WRONG PERSON."
IT'S OKAY. OUR INFO WAS SKETCHY AT BEST. WE'LL GET ANOTHER CRACK AT HIM...HER.
IT'S OKAY...
I HOPE SHE WAS RIGHT. I CLOSE MY EYES AND KEEP SEEING THE KNIFE-STRIKE POINTS...
...CAROTID...
...MEDULLA OBLONGATA...
...HEART.
AND I HOPE I DIDN'T JUST MAKE A BIG MISTAKE.
TO BE CONTINUED...

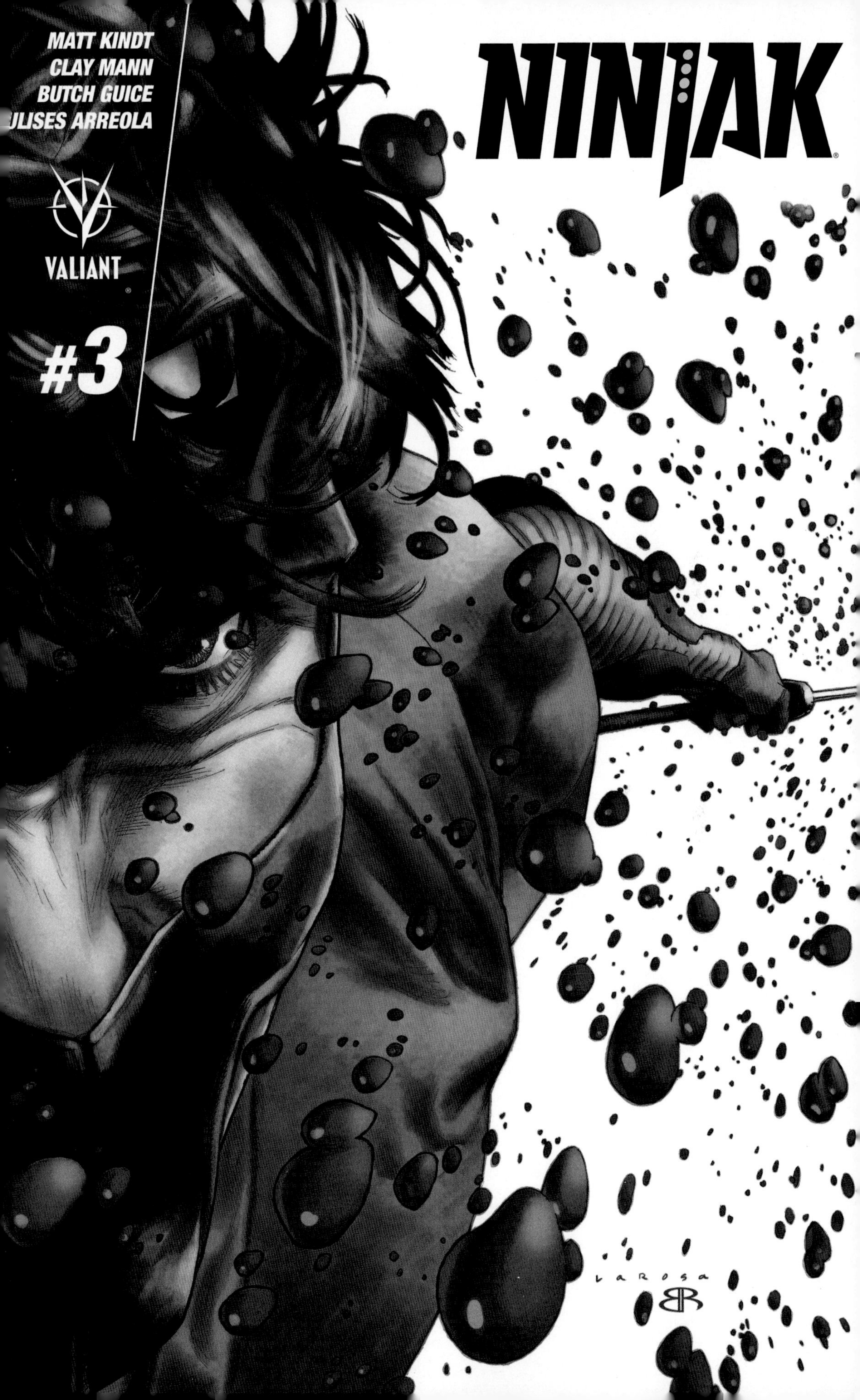
MATT KINDT
CLAY MANN
BUTCH GUICE
ULISES ARREOLA
VALIANT
#3
NINJAK

CLASSIFIED

NINJAK SPECIFICATIONS & INSIGHTS

Battle Boots

EXOTIC POISONS RELEASED ON IMPACT
Conspicuous lack of parental influence and control is a contributing factor to subject's disdain for honest relationships, making him an ideal candidate for advanced training.

ADJUSTABLE FORE-KICK BLADES
Sexuality is an enigma. While there have been several confirmed personal encounters, subject's aloof attitudes make him the most malleable of all eligible agents.

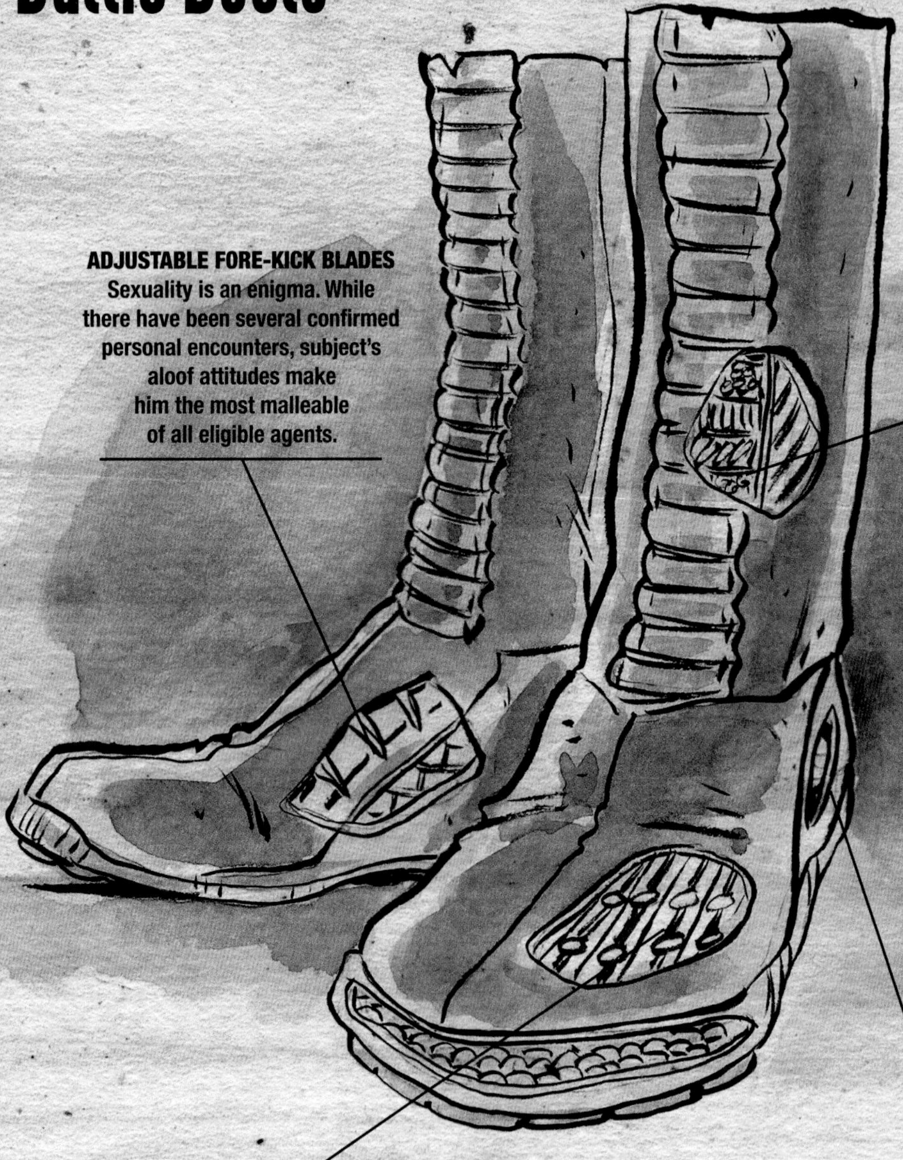

HOMING BEACON SPOOF
Agent has unique and deep ties to England that stretch back hundreds of years, further bolstering his loyalty attributes.

BIONIC SUPER-CHARGED EXO-SKELETON
Subject's tolerance for physical pain is nearly as limitless as his tolerance for emotional suffering. Hundreds of healed

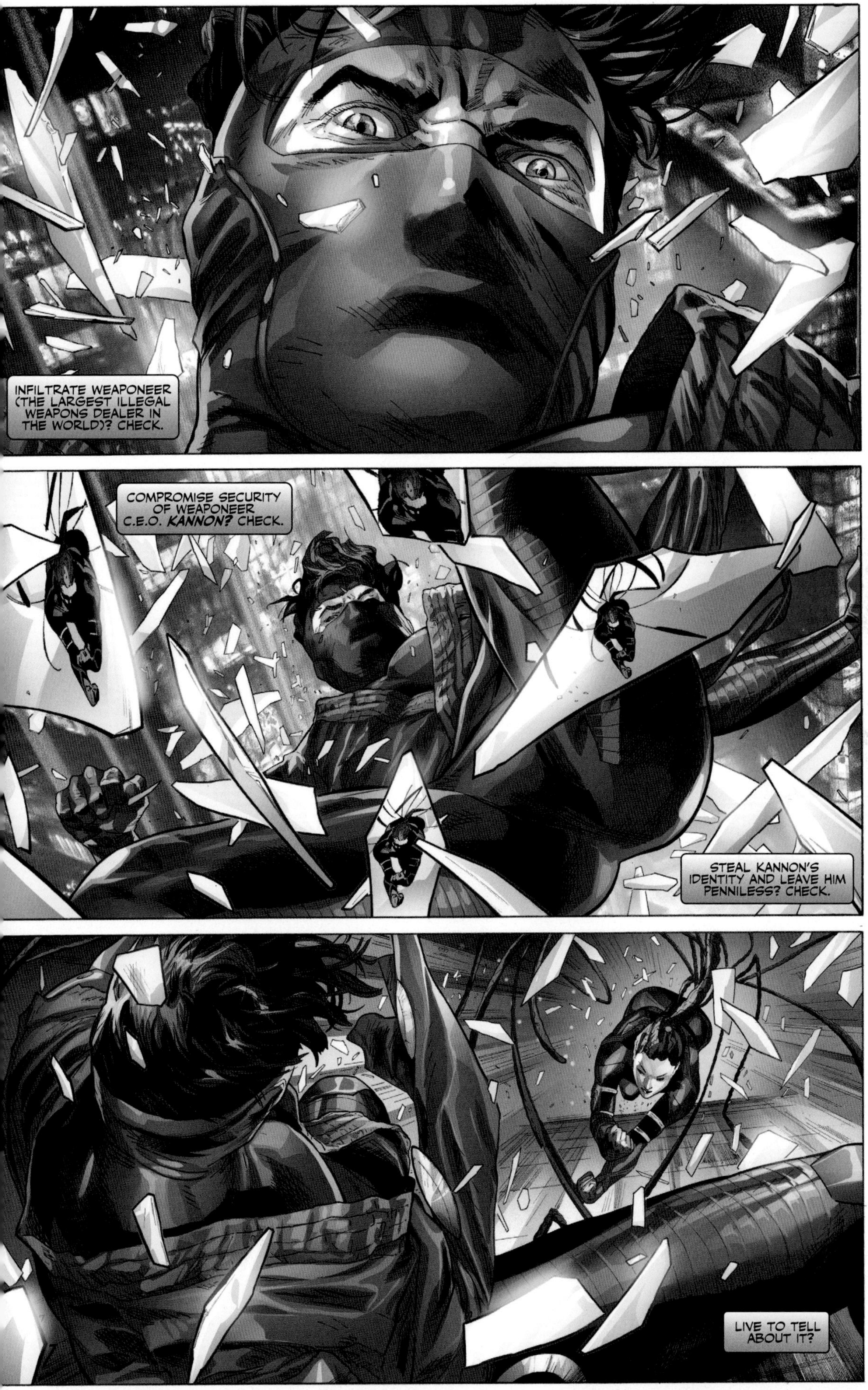
INFILTRATE WEAPONEER (THE LARGEST ILLEGAL WEAPONS DEALER IN THE WORLD)? CHECK.
COMPROMISE SECURITY OF WEAPONEER C.E.O. KANNON? CHECK.
STEAL KANNON'S IDENTITY AND LEAVE HIM PENNILESS? CHECK.
LIVE TO TELL ABOUT IT?

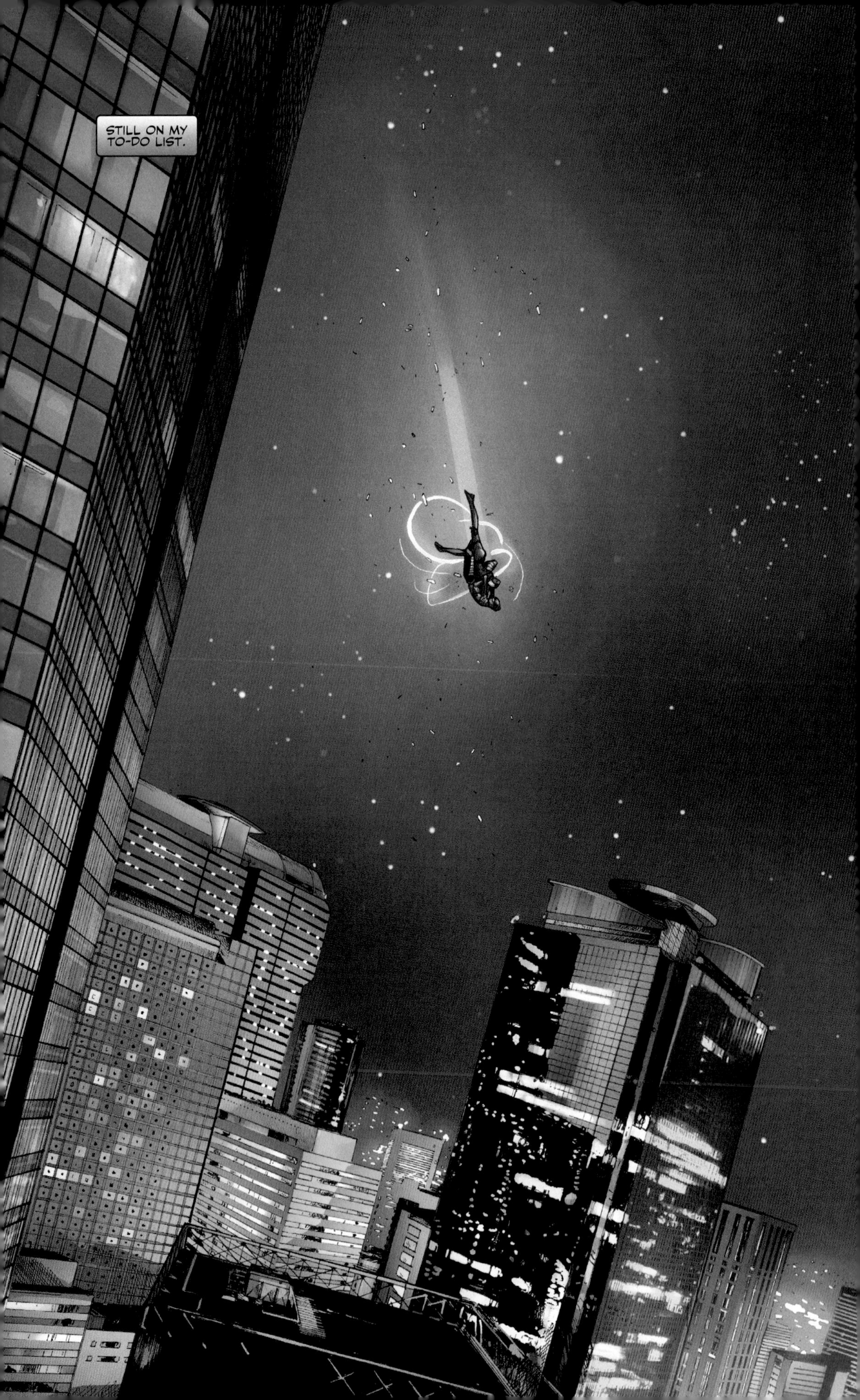
STILL ON MY TO-DO LIST.

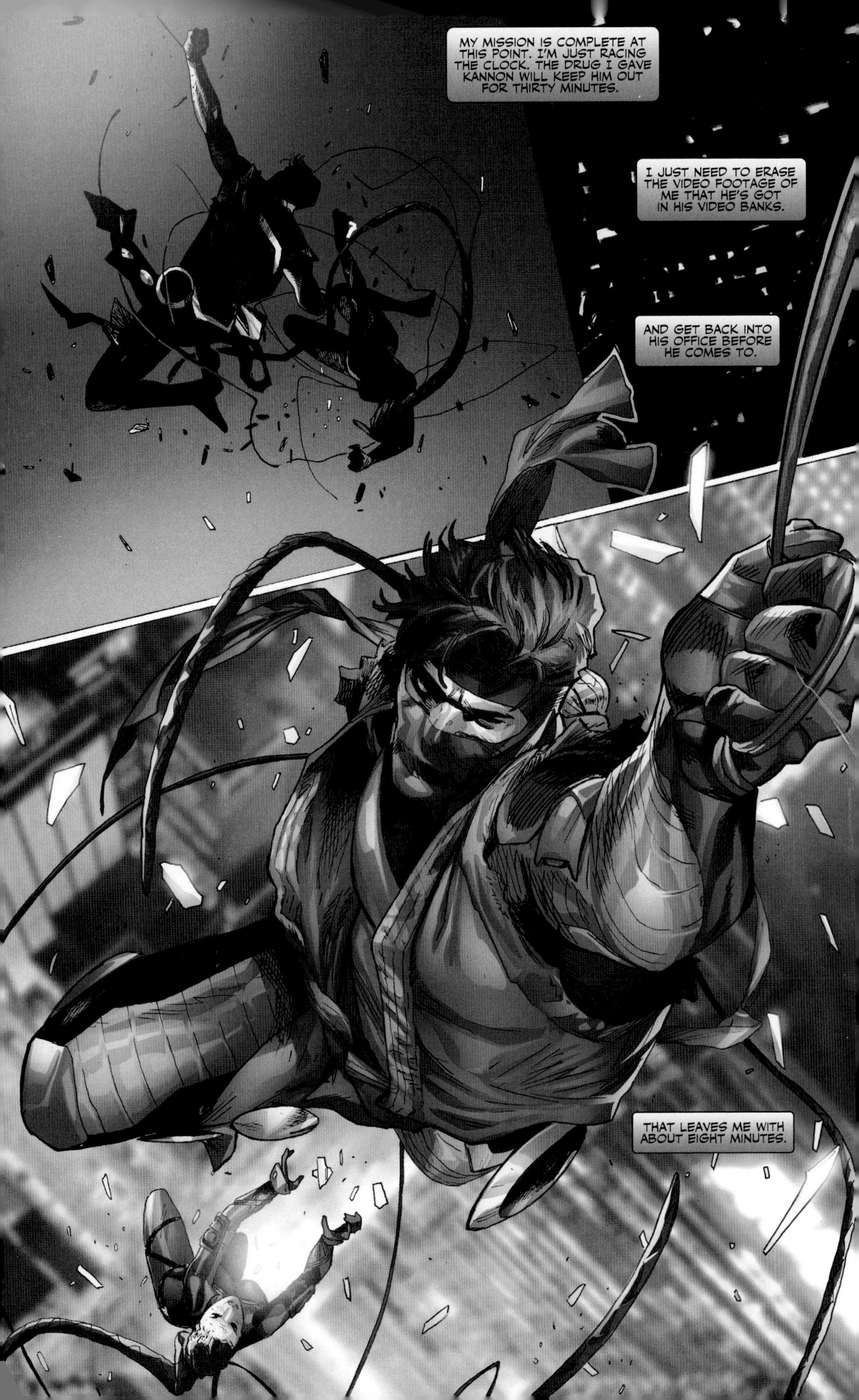
MY MISSION IS COMPLETE AT THIS POINT. I'M JUST RACING THE CLOCK. THE DRUG I GAVE KANNON WILL KEEP HIM OUT FOR THIRTY MINUTES.
I JUST NEED TO ERASE THE VIDEO FOOTAGE OF ME THAT HE'S GOT IN HIS VIDEO BANKS.
AND GET BACK INTO HIS OFFICE BEFORE HE COMES TO.
THAT LEAVES ME WITH ABOUT EIGHT MINUTES.

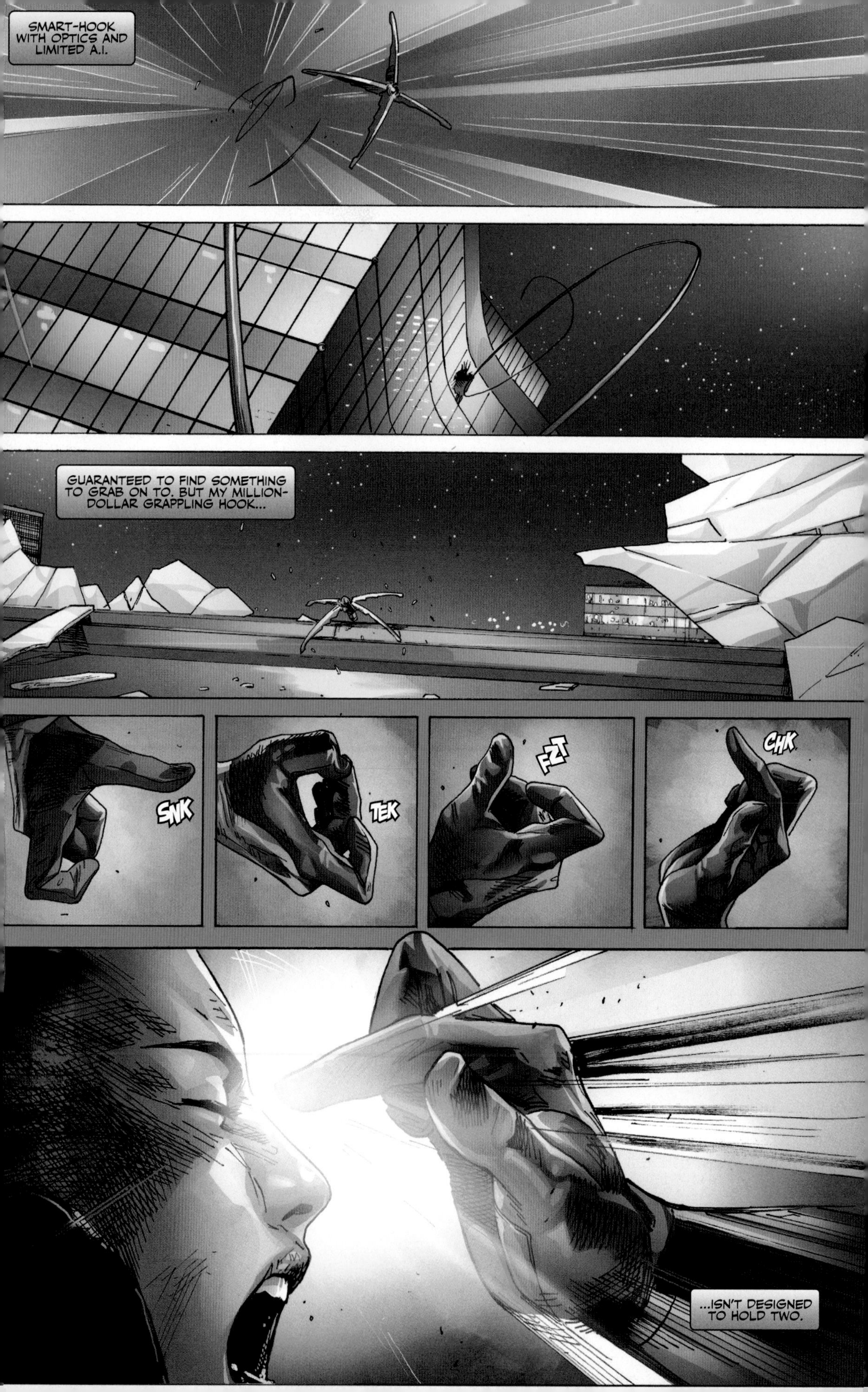
SMART-HOOK WITH OPTICS AND LIMITED A.I.
GUARANTEED TO FIND SOMETHING TO GRAB ON TO. BUT MY MILLION-DOLLAR GRAPPLING HOOK...
SNK
TEK
FZT
CHK
...ISN'T DESIGNED TO HOLD TWO.

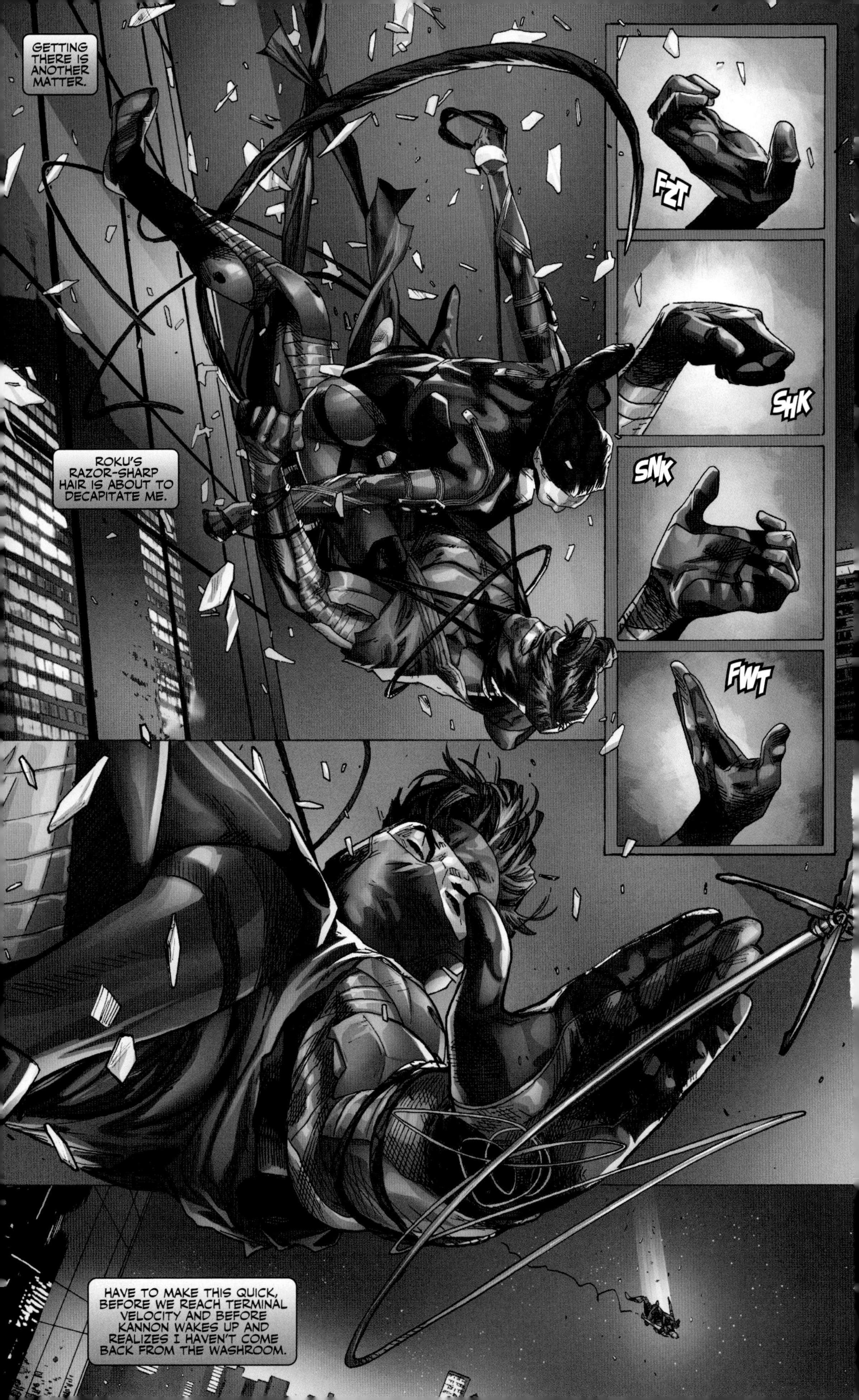
GETTING THERE IS ANOTHER MATTER.
FZT
SHK
SNK
FWT
ROKU'S RAZOR-SHARP HAIR IS ABOUT TO DECAPITATE ME.
HAVE TO MAKE THIS QUICK, BEFORE WE REACH TERMINAL VELOCITY AND BEFORE KANNON WAKES UP AND REALIZES I HAVEN'T COME BACK FROM THE WASHROOM.

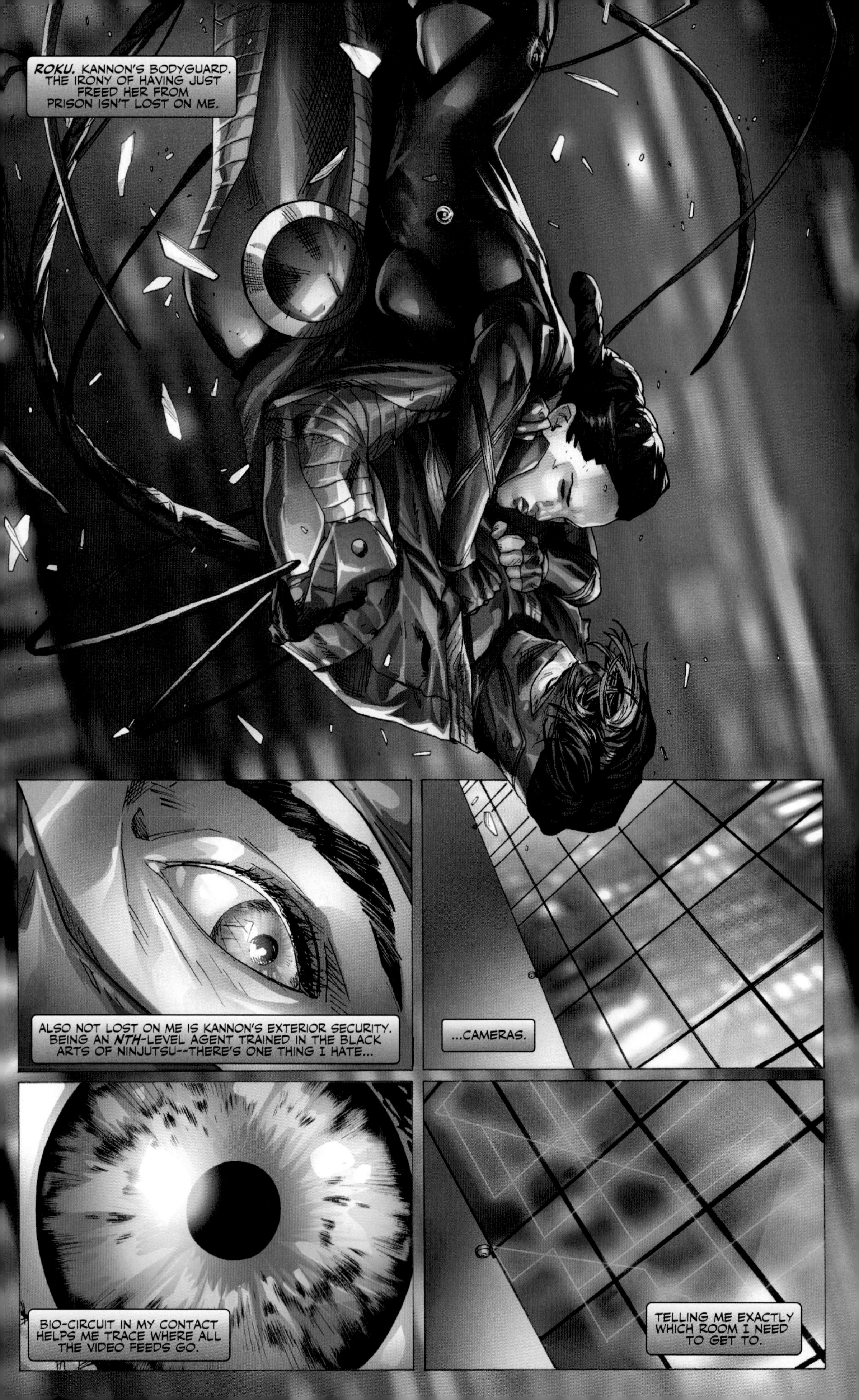
ROKU. KANNON'S BODYGUARD. THE IRONY OF HAVING JUST FREED HER FROM PRISON ISN'T LOST ON ME.
ALSO NOT LOST ON ME IS KANNON'S EXTERIOR SECURITY. BEING AN NTH-LEVEL AGENT TRAINED IN THE BLACK ARTS OF NINJUTSU--THERE'S ONE THING I HATE...
...CAMERAS.
BIO-CIRCUIT IN MY CONTACT HELPS ME TRACE WHERE ALL THE VIDEO FEEDS GO.
TELLING ME EXACTLY WHICH ROOM I NEED TO GET TO.

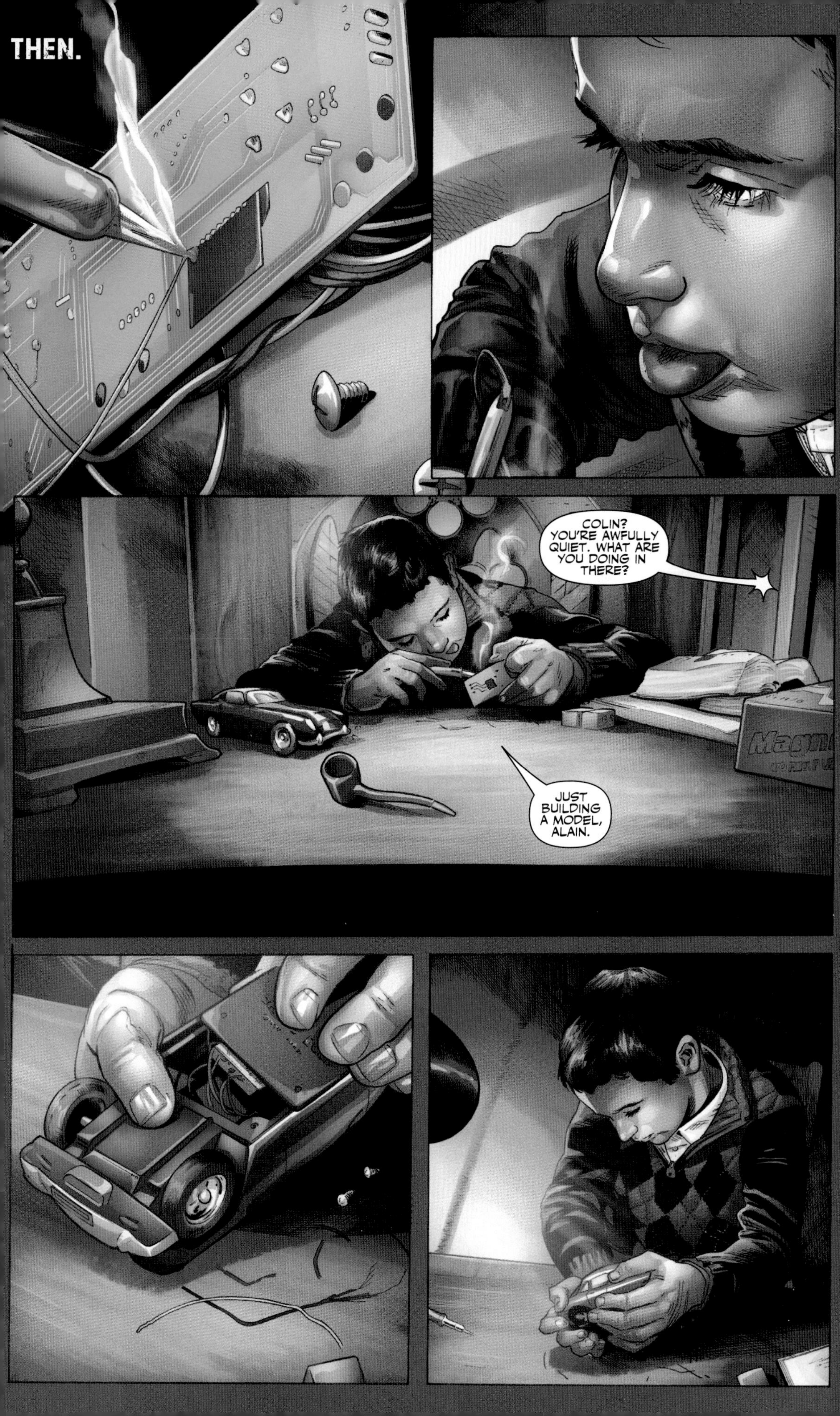
THEN.
COLIN? YOU'RE AWFULLY QUIET. WHAT ARE YOU DOING IN THERE?
JUST BUILDING A MODEL, ALAIN.

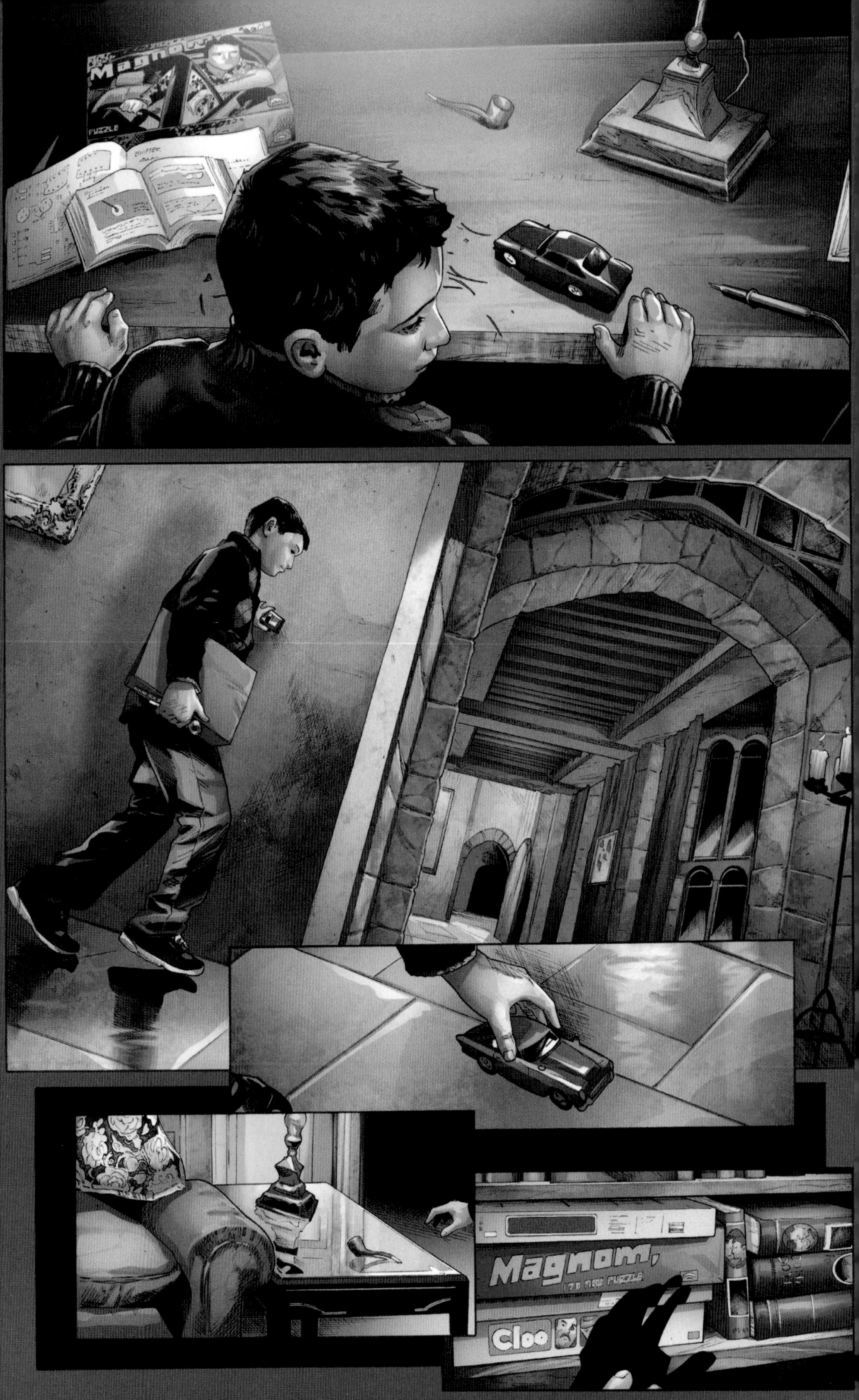
PUZZLE
Magnom,
Cloo

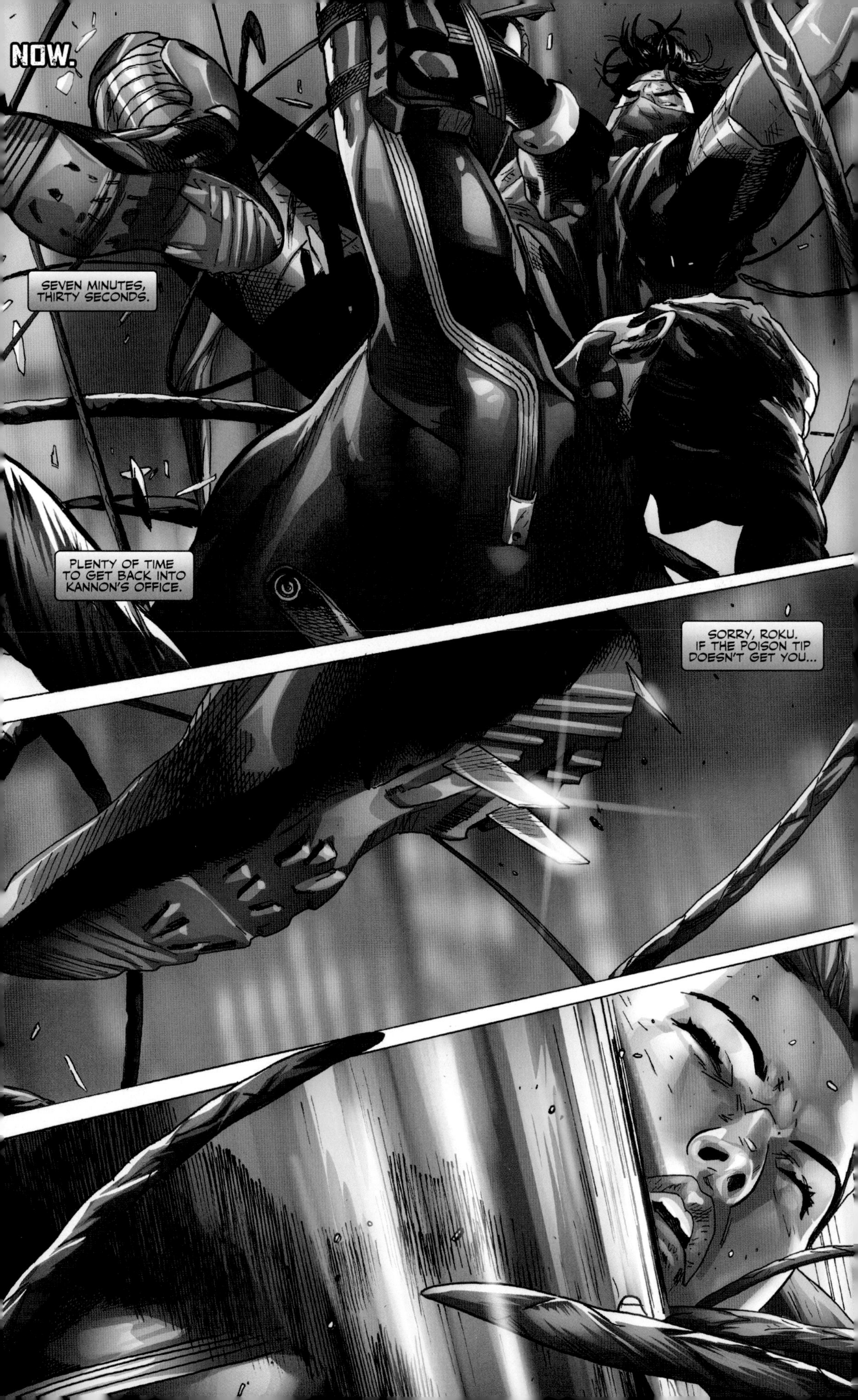
NOW.
SEVEN MINUTES, THIRTY SECONDS.
PLENTY OF TIME TO GET BACK INTO KANNON'S OFFICE.
SORRY, ROKU. IF THE POISON TIP DOESN'T GET YOU...

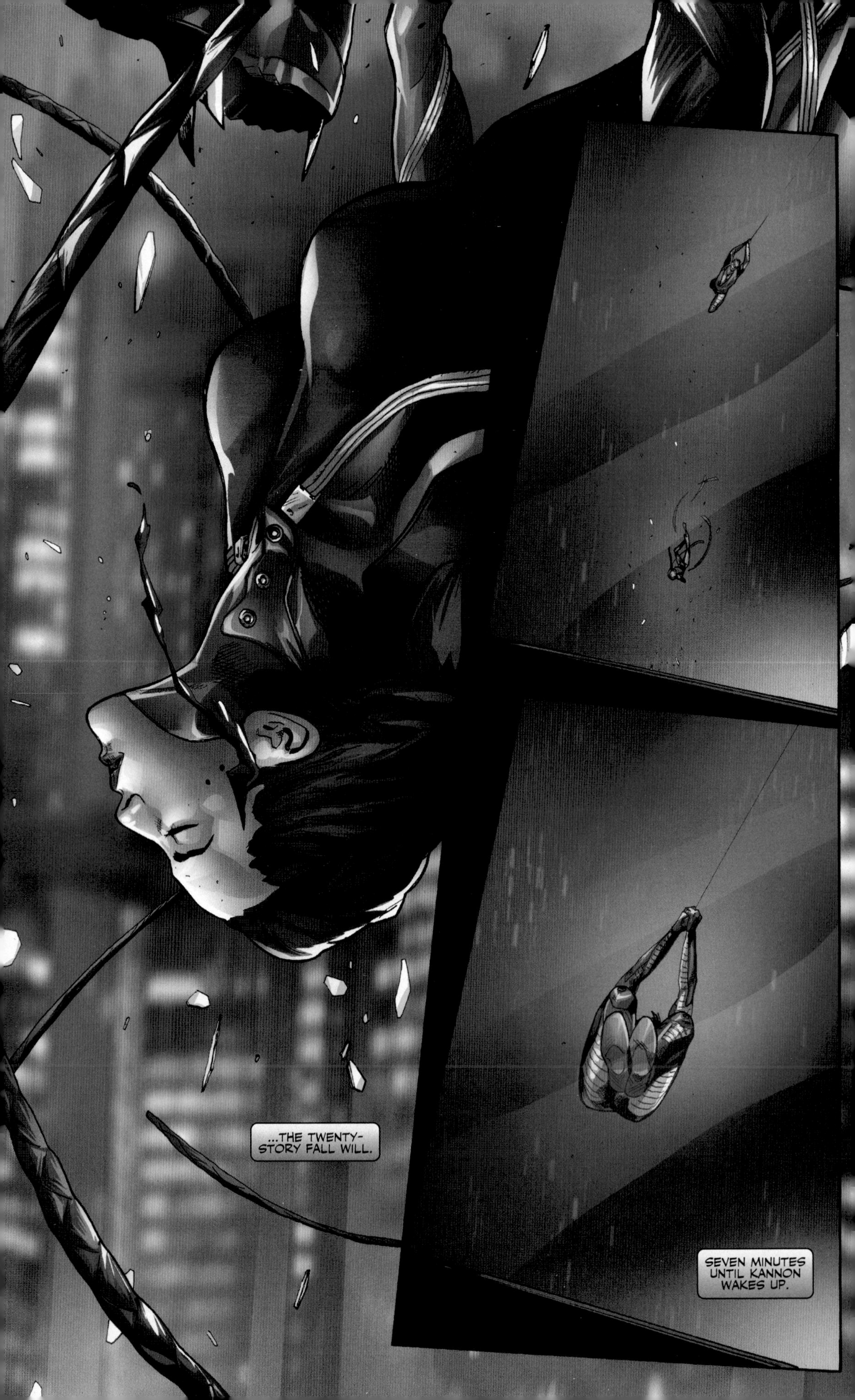
...THE TWENTY-STORY FALL WILL.
SEVEN MINUTES UNTIL KANNON WAKES UP.

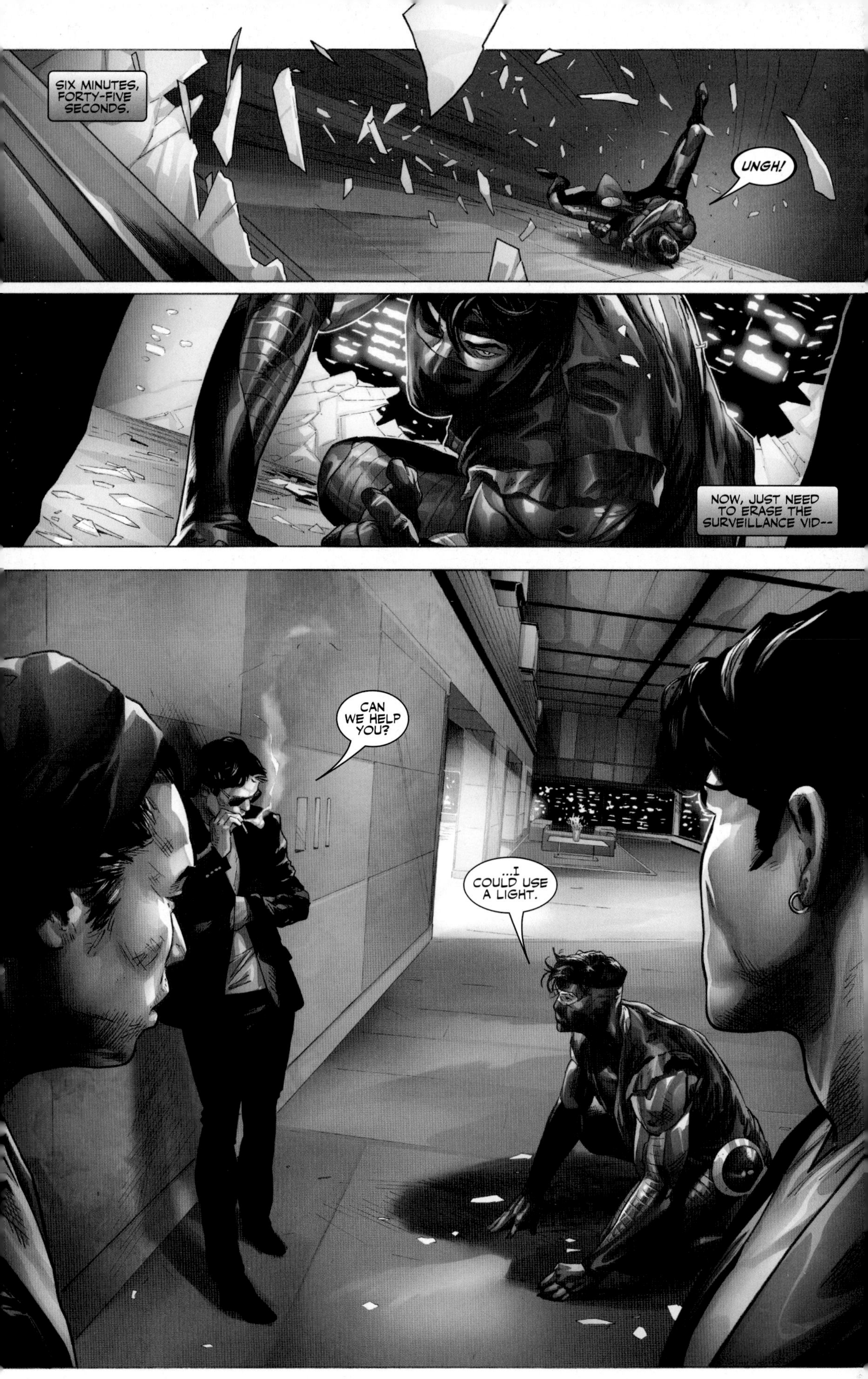
SIX MINUTES, FORTY-FIVE SECONDS.
UNGH!
NOW, JUST NEED TO ERASE THE SURVEILLANCE VID--
CAN WE HELP YOU?
...I COULD USE A LIGHT.

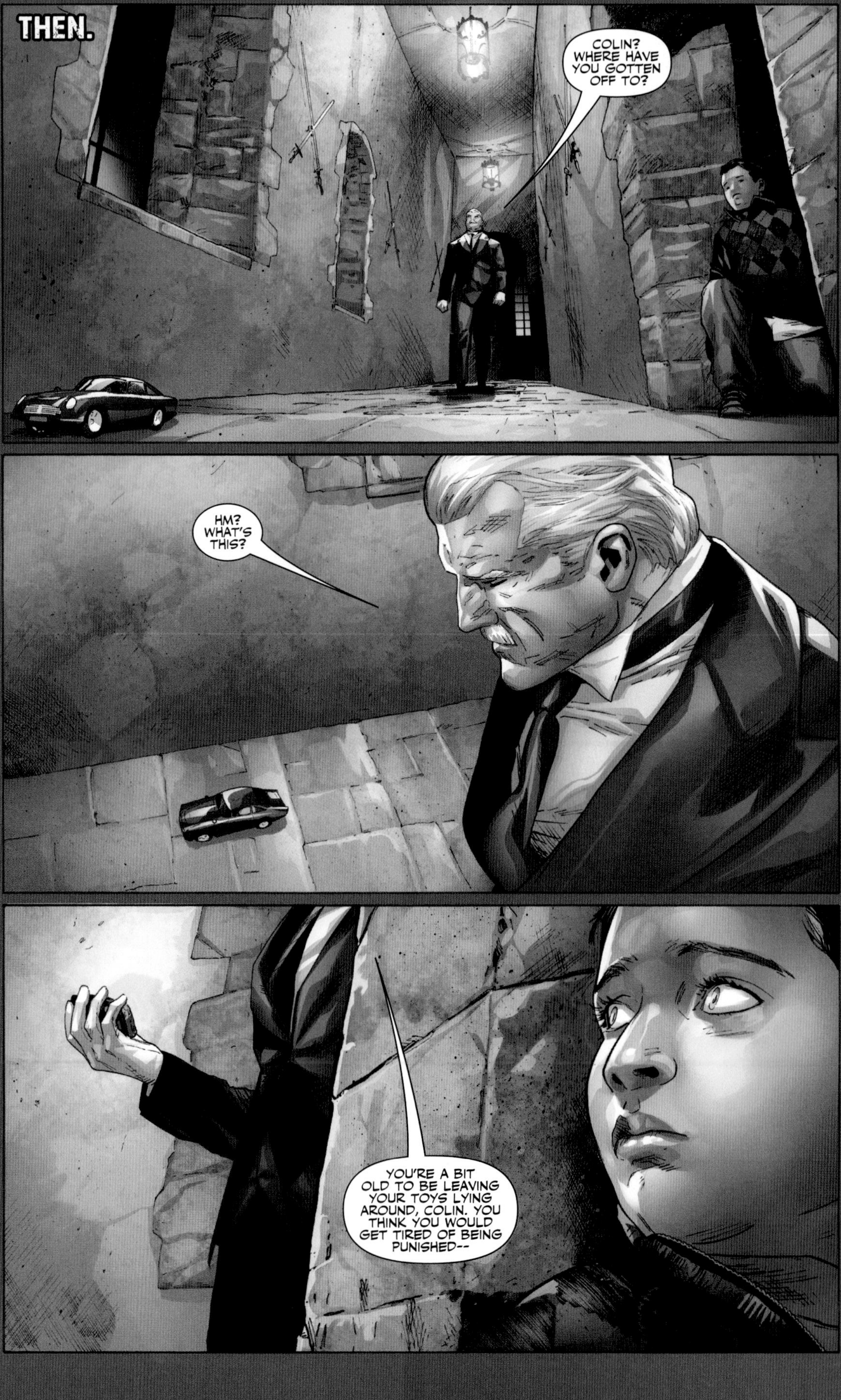
THEN.
COLIN? WHERE HAVE YOU GOTTEN OFF TO?
HM? WHAT'S THIS?
YOU'RE A BIT OLD TO BE LEAVING YOUR TOYS LYING AROUND, COLIN. YOU THINK YOU WOULD GET TIRED OF BEING PUNISHED--

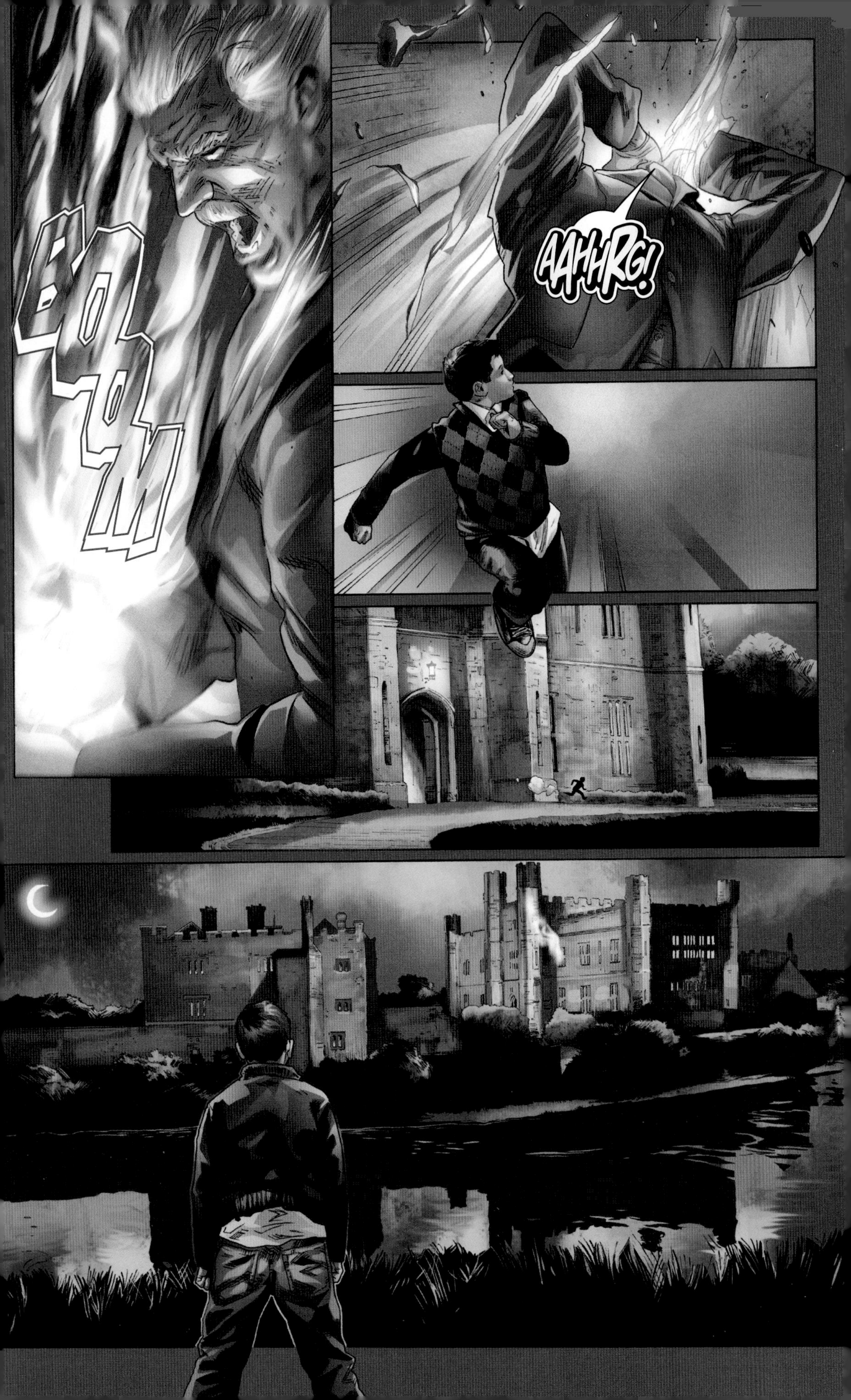
BOOOM
AAHHRG!

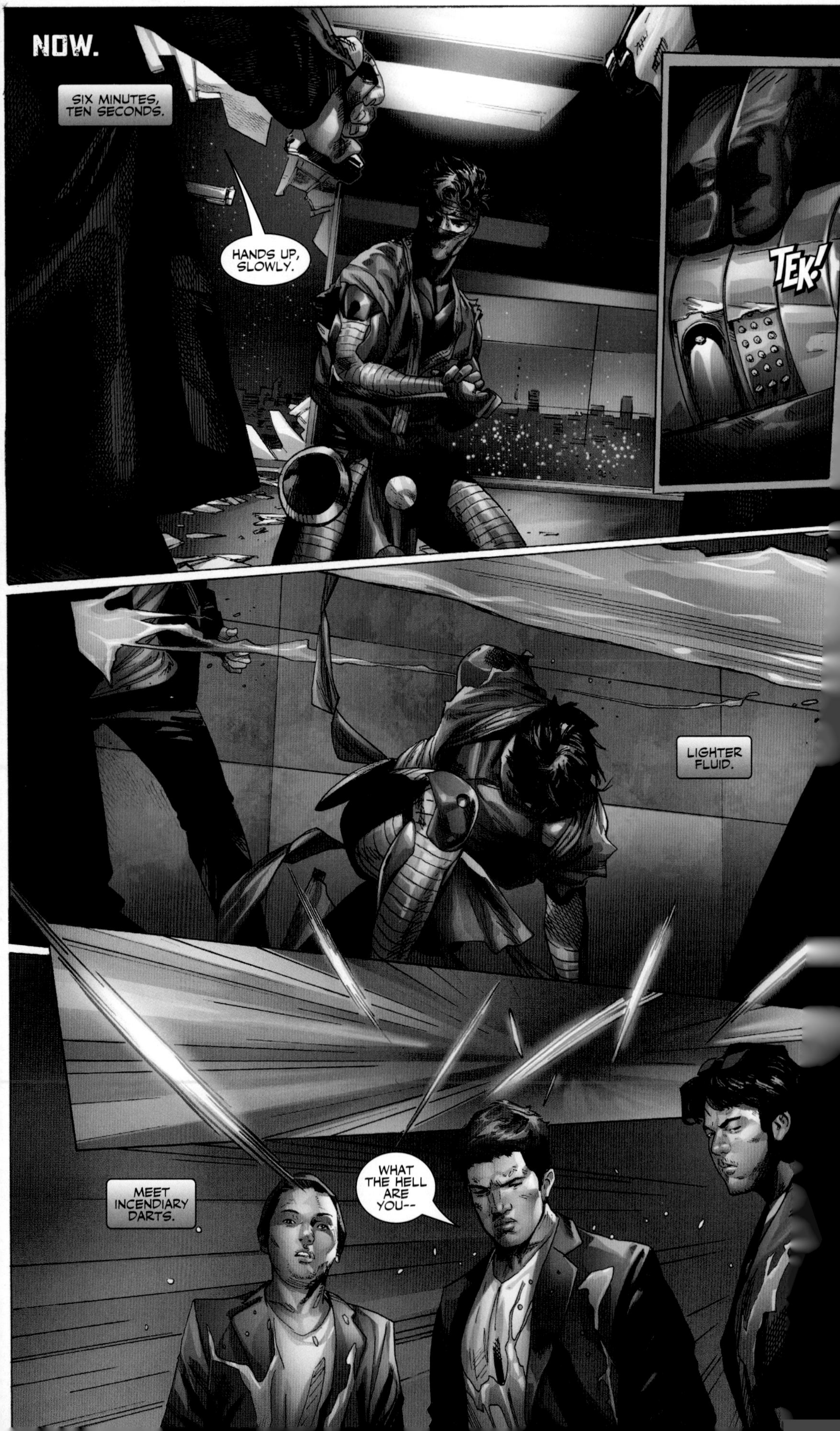
NOW.
SIX MINUTES, TEN SECONDS.
HANDS UP, SLOWLY.
TEK!
LIGHTER FLUID.
MEET INCENDIARY DARTS.
WHAT THE HELL ARE YOU--

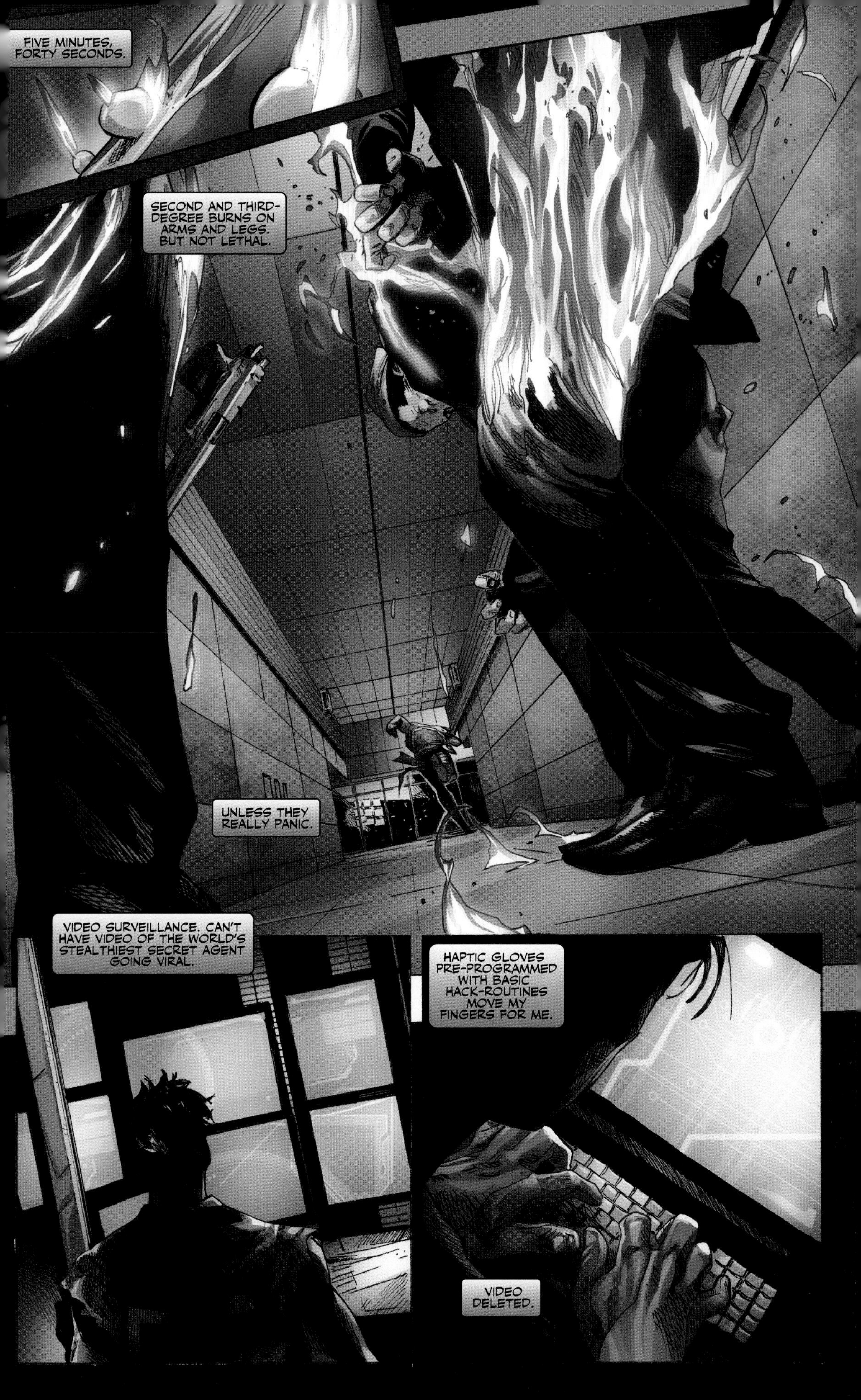
FIVE MINUTES, FORTY SECONDS.
SECOND AND THIRD-DEGREE BURNS ON ARMS AND LEGS. BUT NOT LETHAL.
UNLESS THEY REALLY PANIC.
VIDEO SURVEILLANCE. CAN'T HAVE VIDEO OF THE WORLD'S STEALTHIEST SECRET AGENT GOING VIRAL.
HAPTIC GLOVES PRE-PROGRAMMED WITH BASIC HACK-ROUTINES MOVE MY FINGERS FOR ME.
VIDEO DELETED.

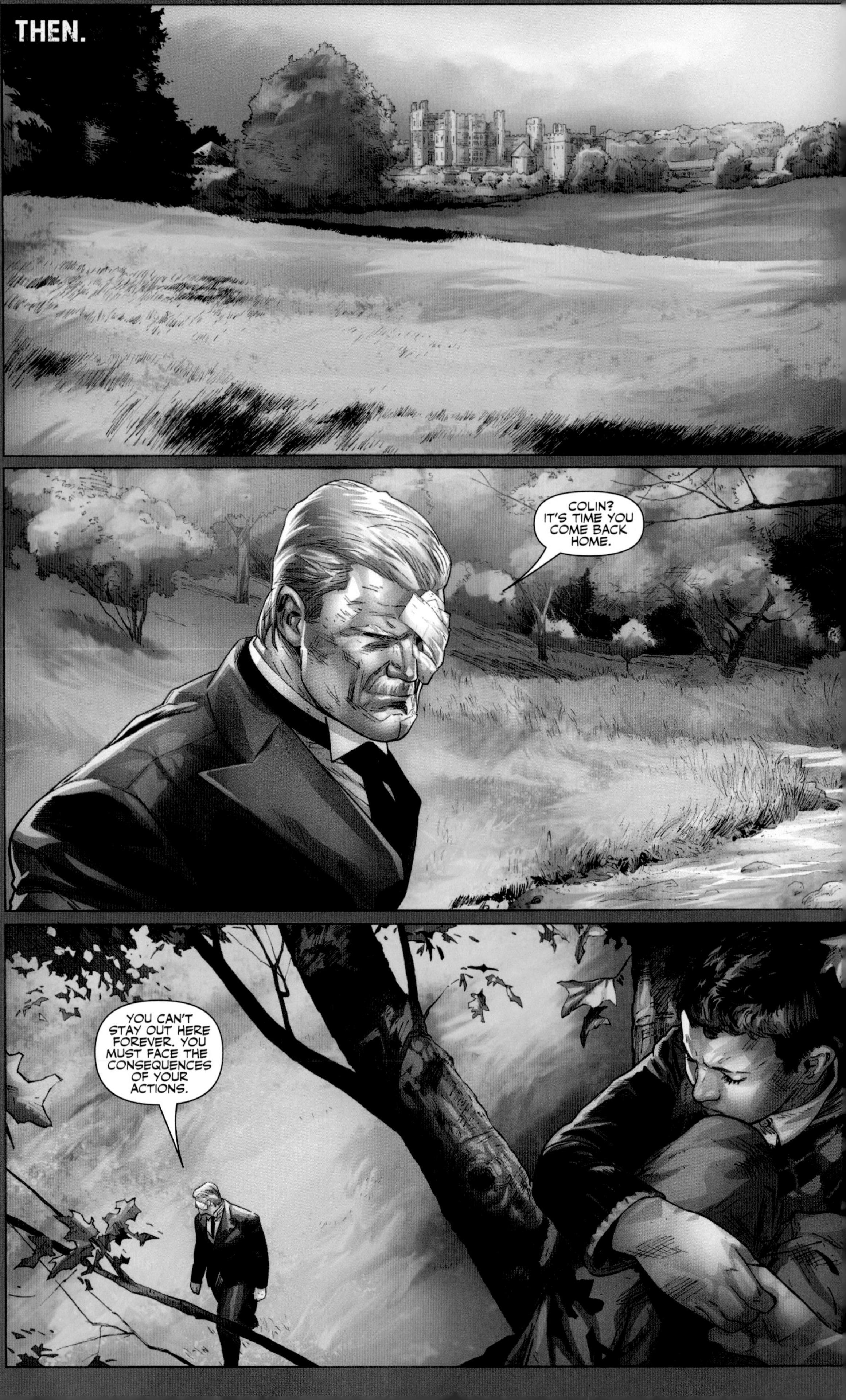
THEN.
COLIN? IT'S TIME YOU COME BACK HOME.
YOU CAN'T STAY OUT HERE FOREVER. YOU MUST FACE THE CONSEQUENCES OF YOUR ACTIONS.

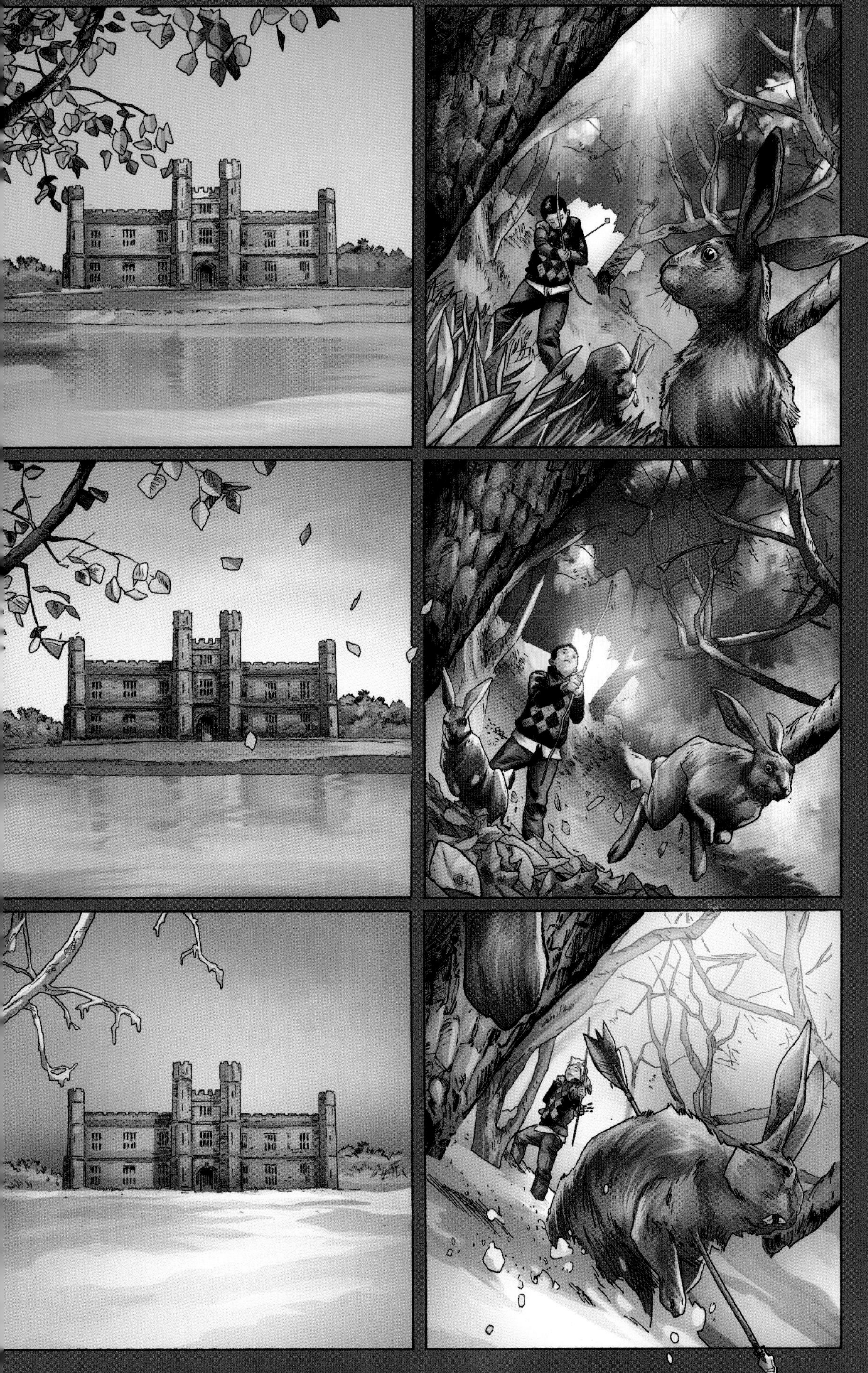

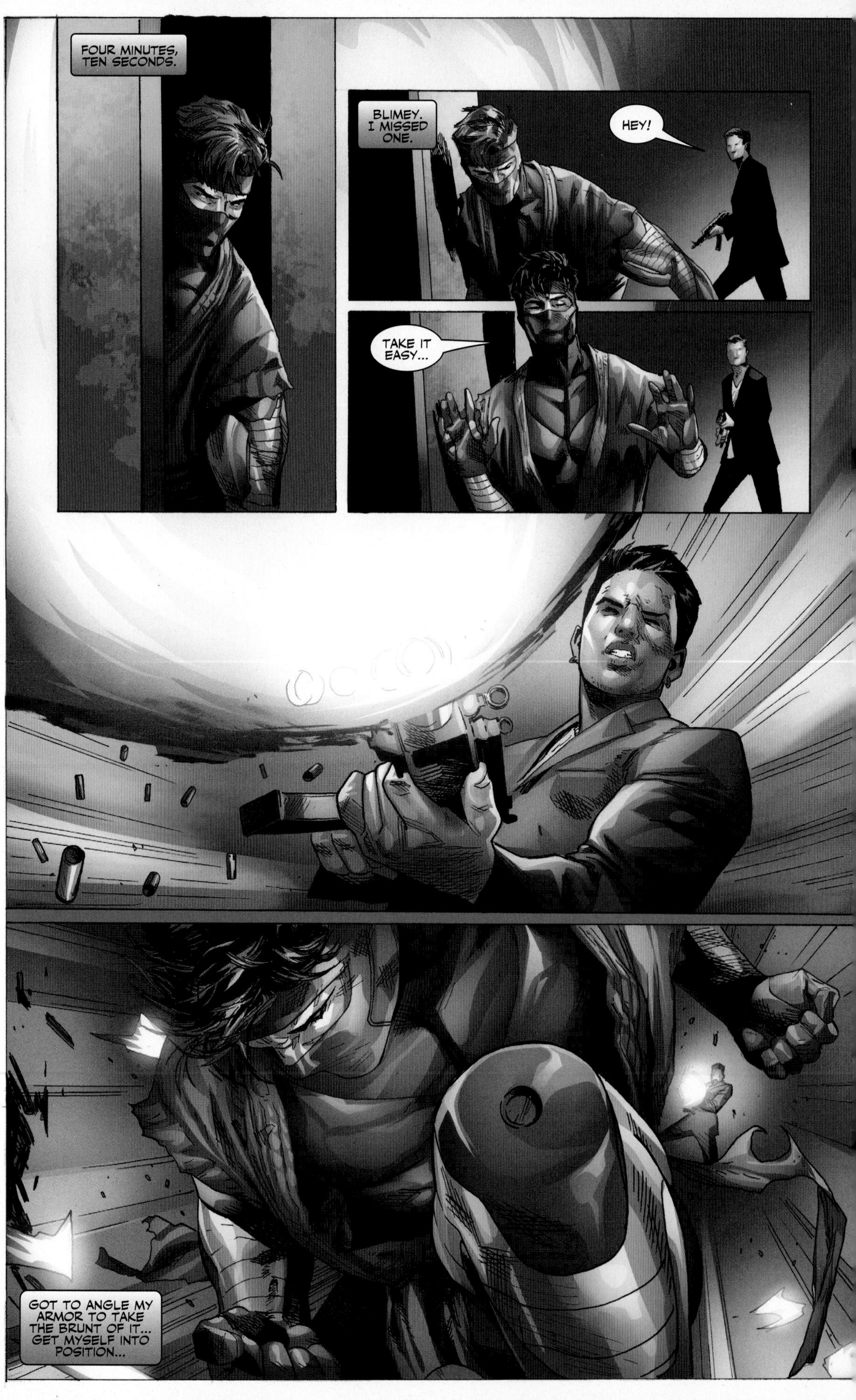
FOUR MINUTES, TEN SECONDS.
BLIMEY. I MISSED ONE.
HEY!
TAKE IT EASY...
GOT TO ANGLE MY ARMOR TO TAKE THE BRUNT OF IT... GET MYSELF INTO POSITION...

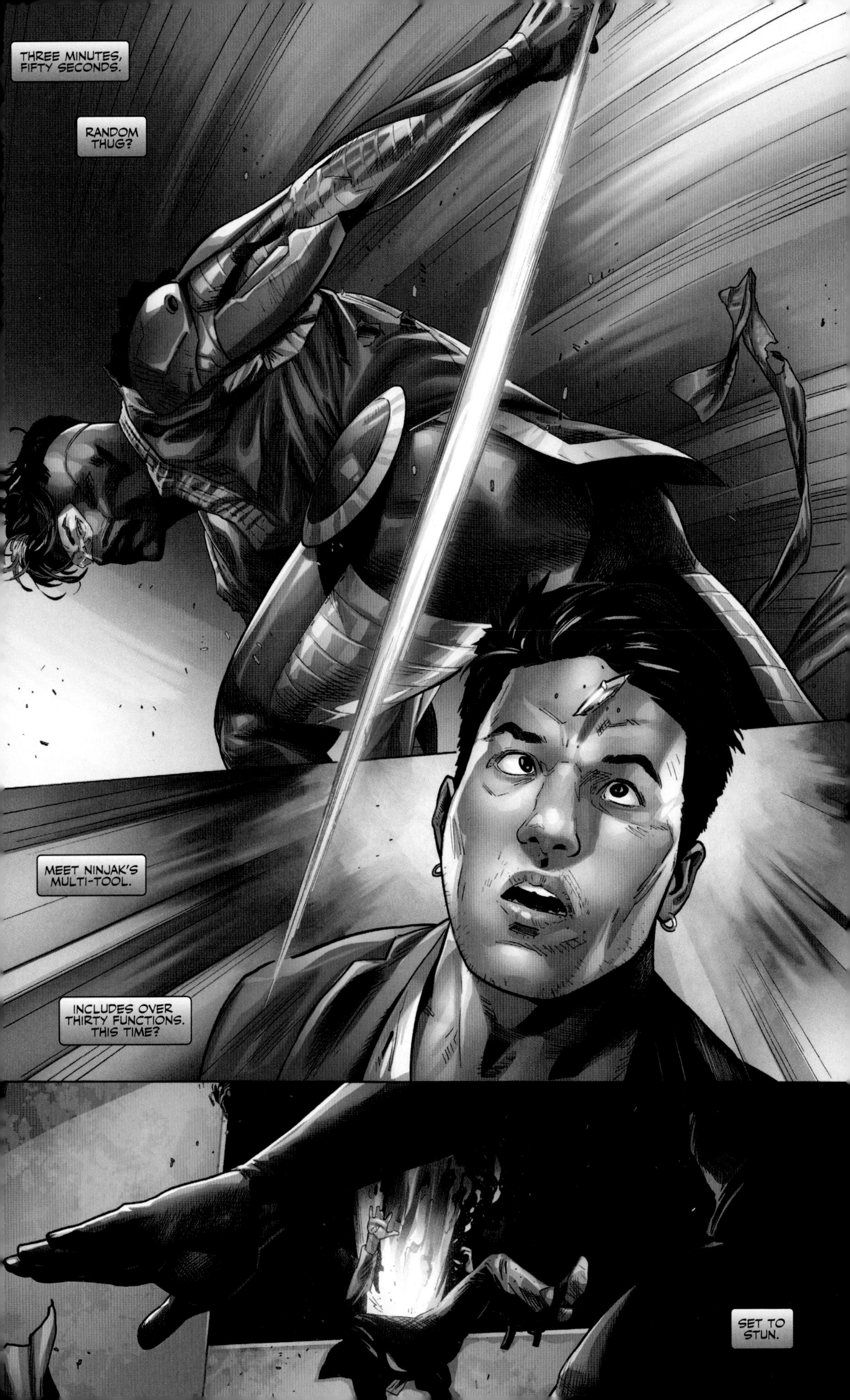
THREE MINUTES, FIFTY SECONDS.
RANDOM THUG?
MEET NINJAK'S MULTI-TOOL.
INCLUDES OVER THIRTY FUNCTIONS. THIS TIME?
SET TO STUN.

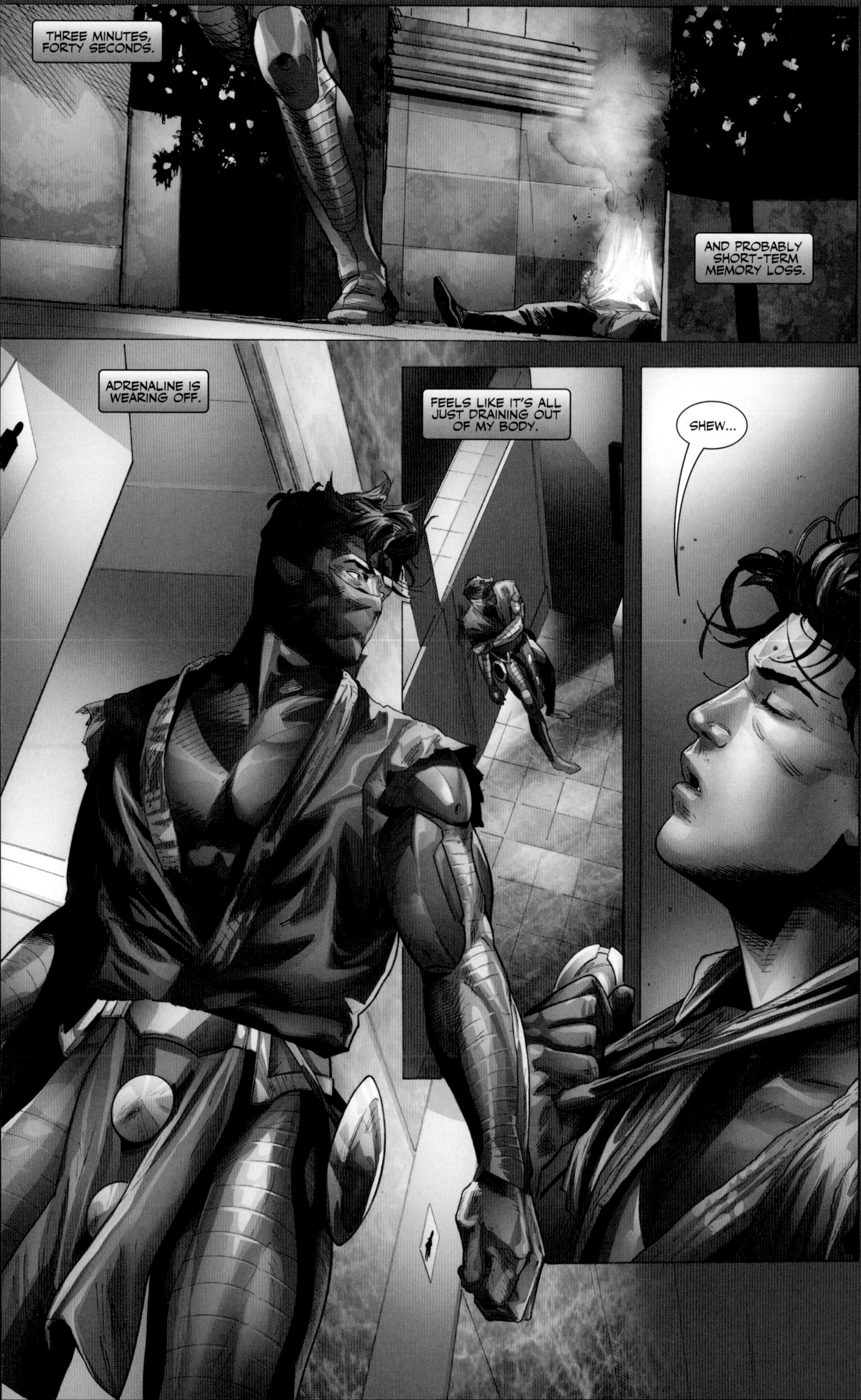
THREE MINUTES, FORTY SECONDS.
AND PROBABLY SHORT-TERM MEMORY LOSS.
ADRENALINE IS WEARING OFF.
FEELS LIKE IT'S ALL JUST DRAINING OUT OF MY BODY.
SHEW...

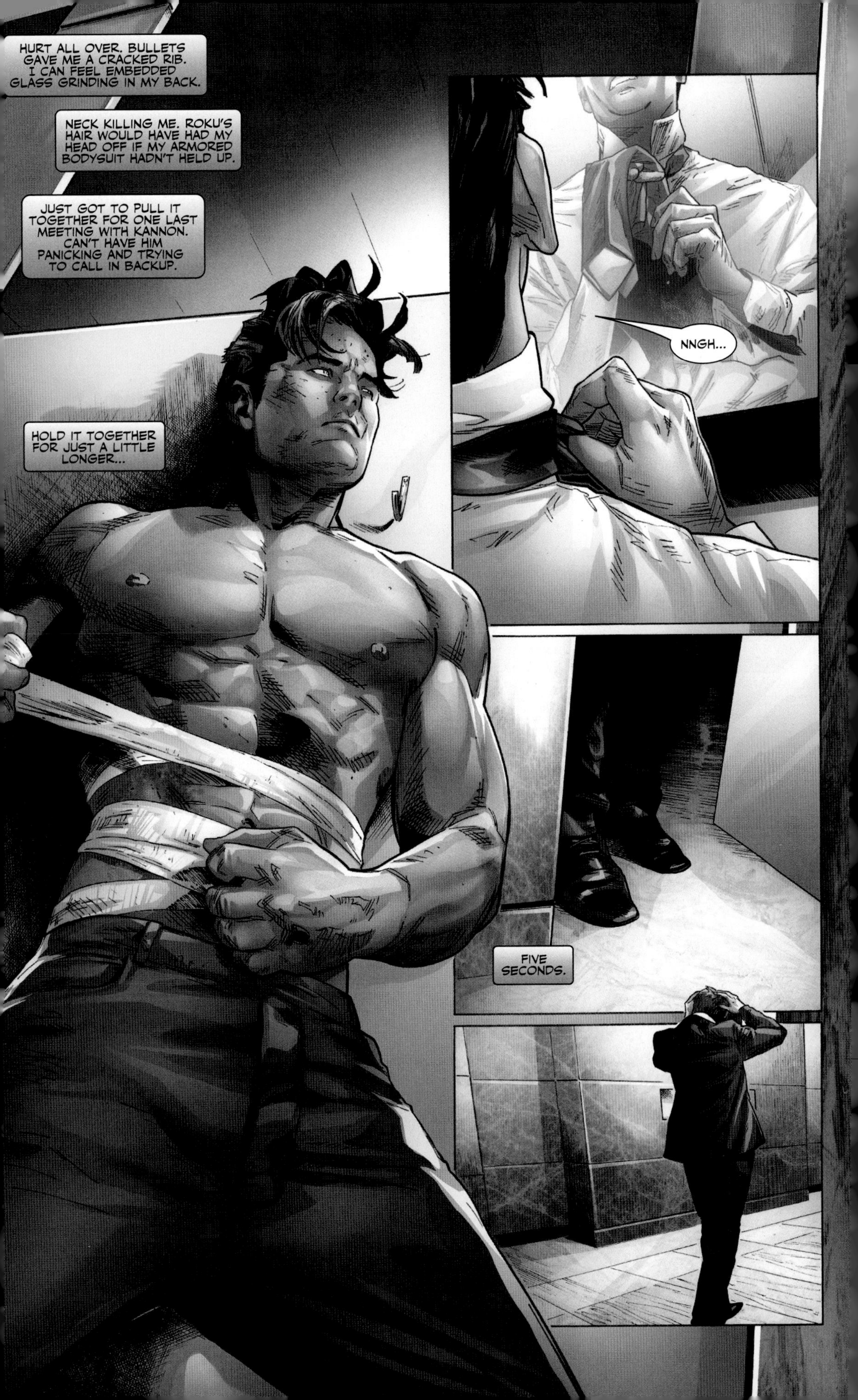
HURT ALL OVER. BULLETS GAVE ME A CRACKED RIB. I CAN FEEL EMBEDDED GLASS GRINDING IN MY BACK.
NECK KILLING ME. ROKU'S HAIR WOULD HAVE HAD MY HEAD OFF IF MY ARMORED BODYSUIT HADN'T HELD UP.
JUST GOT TO PULL IT TOGETHER FOR ONE LAST MEETING WITH KANNON. CAN'T HAVE HIM PANICKING AND TRYING TO CALL IN BACKUP.
HOLD IT TOGETHER FOR JUST A LITTLE LONGER...
NNGH...
FIVE SECONDS.

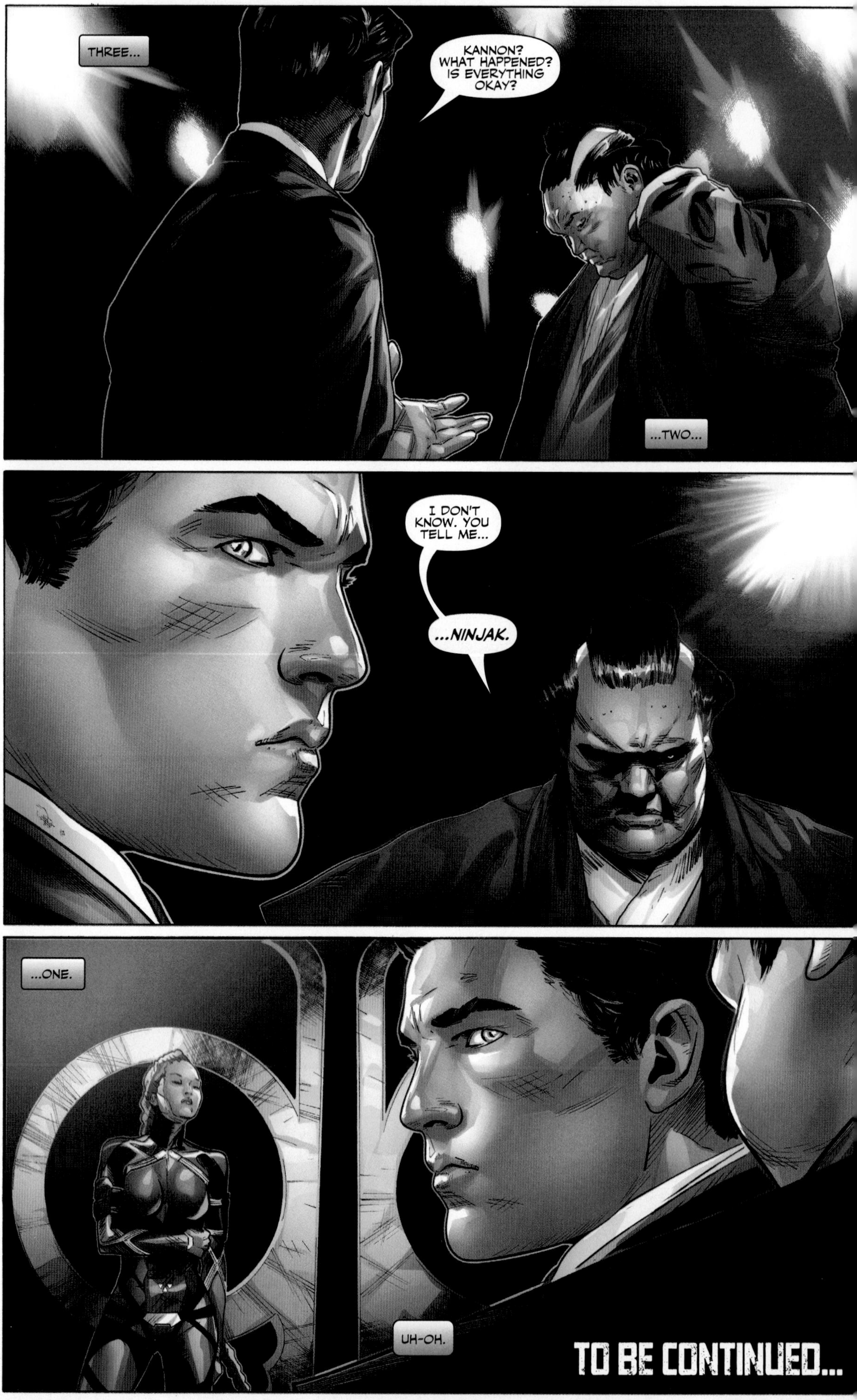
THREE...
KANNON? WHAT HAPPENED? IS EVERYTHING OKAY?
...TWO...
I DON'T KNOW. YOU TELL ME...
...NINJAK.
...ONE.
UH-OH.
TO BE CONTINUED...

THE LOST FILES

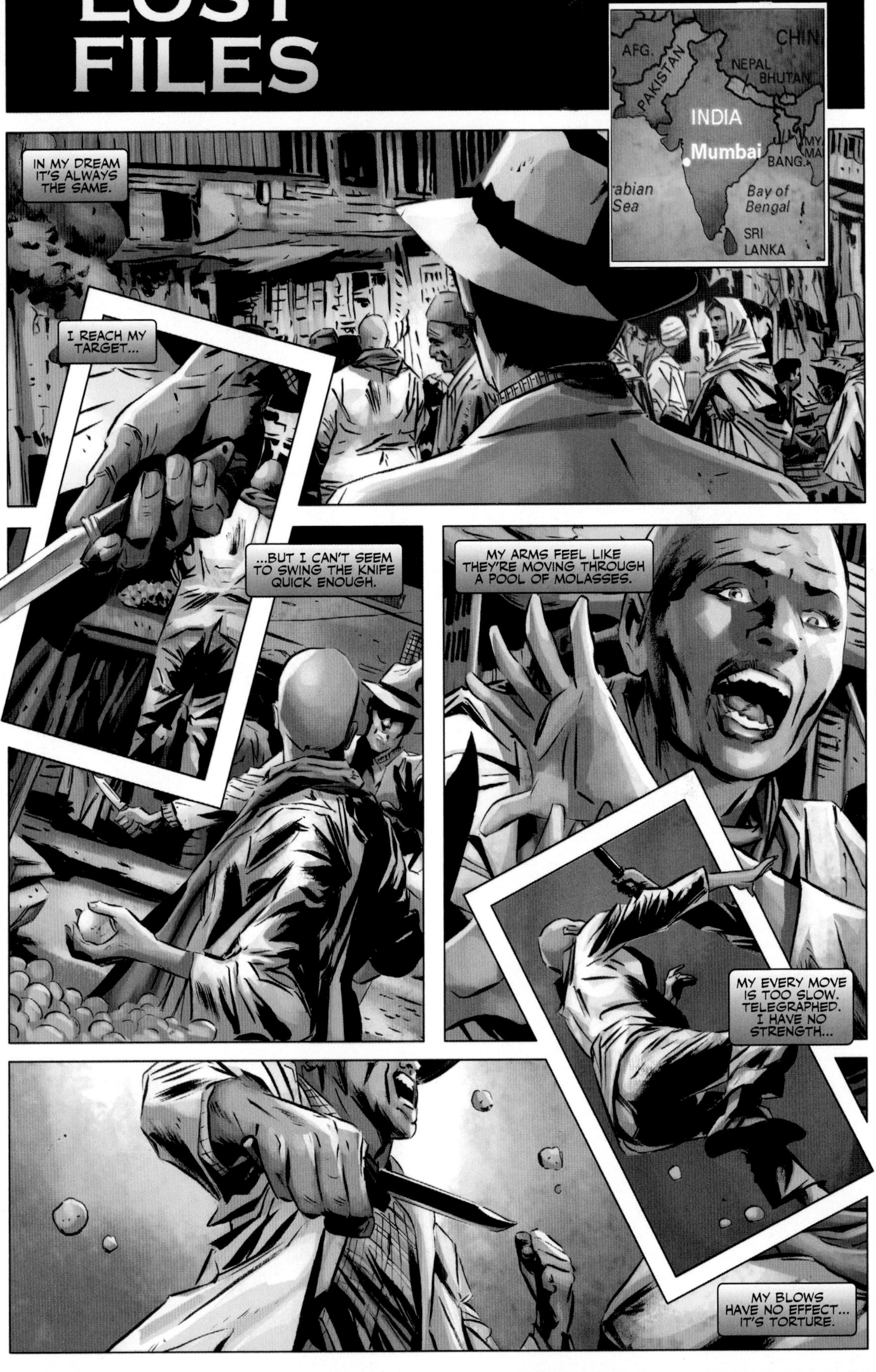
AFG.
PAKISTAN
NEPAL
BHUTAN
INDIA
Mumbai
BANG.
Bay of Bengal
SRI LANKA
IN MY DREAM IT'S ALWAYS THE SAME.
I REACH MY TARGET...
...BUT I CAN'T SEEM TO SWING THE KNIFE QUICK ENOUGH.
MY ARMS FEEL LIKE THEY'RE MOVING THROUGH A POOL OF MOLASSES.
MY EVERY MOVE IS TOO SLOW. TELEGRAPHED. I HAVE NO STRENGTH...
MY BLOWS HAVE NO EFFECT... IT'S TORTURE.

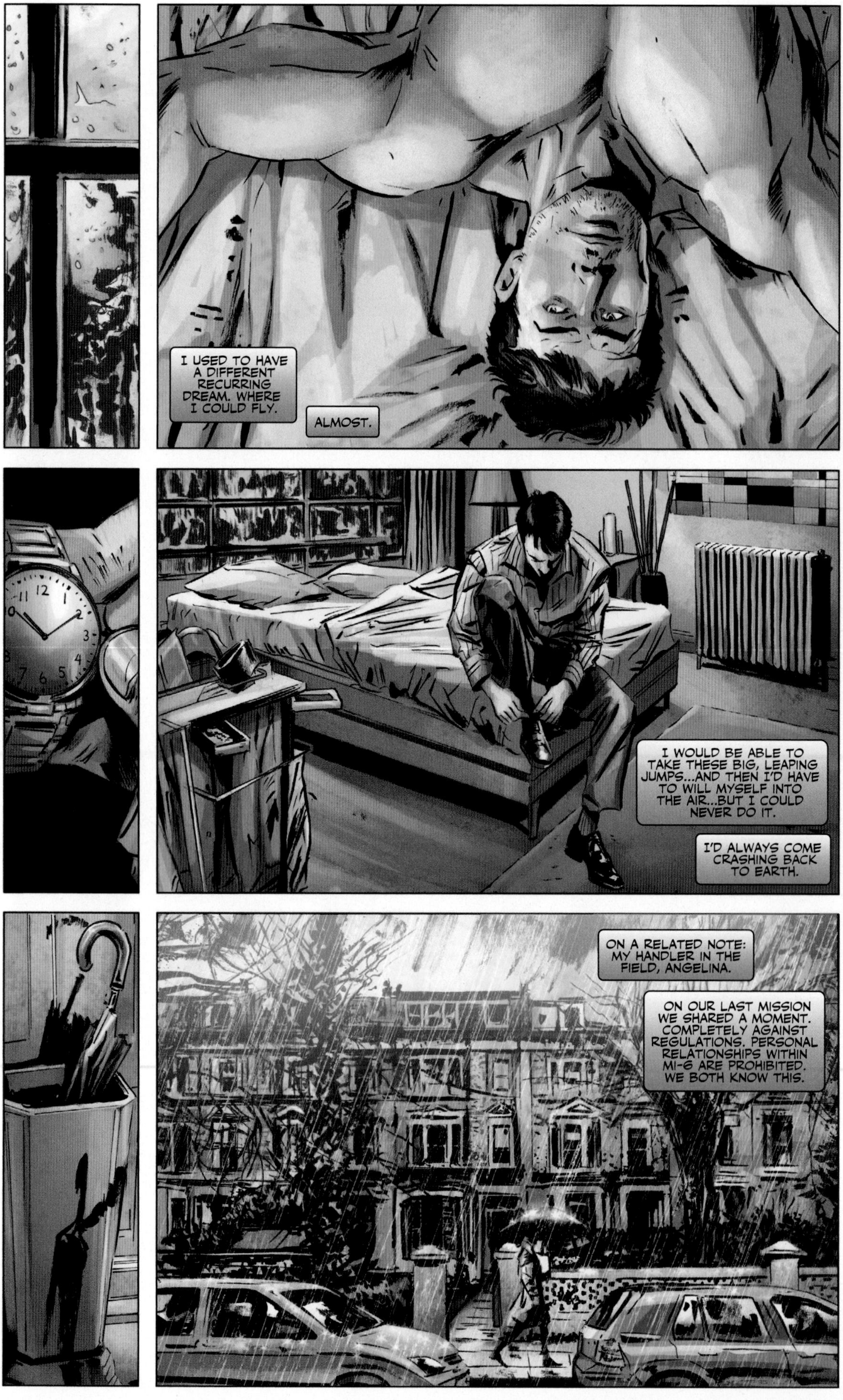
I USED TO HAVE A DIFFERENT RECURRING DREAM. WHERE I COULD FLY.
ALMOST.
I WOULD BE ABLE TO TAKE THESE BIG, LEAPING JUMPS...AND THEN I'D HAVE TO WILL MYSELF INTO THE AIR...BUT I COULD NEVER DO IT.
I'D ALWAYS COME CRASHING BACK TO EARTH.
ON A RELATED NOTE: MY HANDLER IN THE FIELD, ANGELINA.
ON OUR LAST MISSION WE SHARED A MOMENT. COMPLETELY AGAINST REGULATIONS. PERSONAL RELATIONSHIPS WITHIN MI-6 ARE PROHIBITED. WE BOTH KNOW THIS.

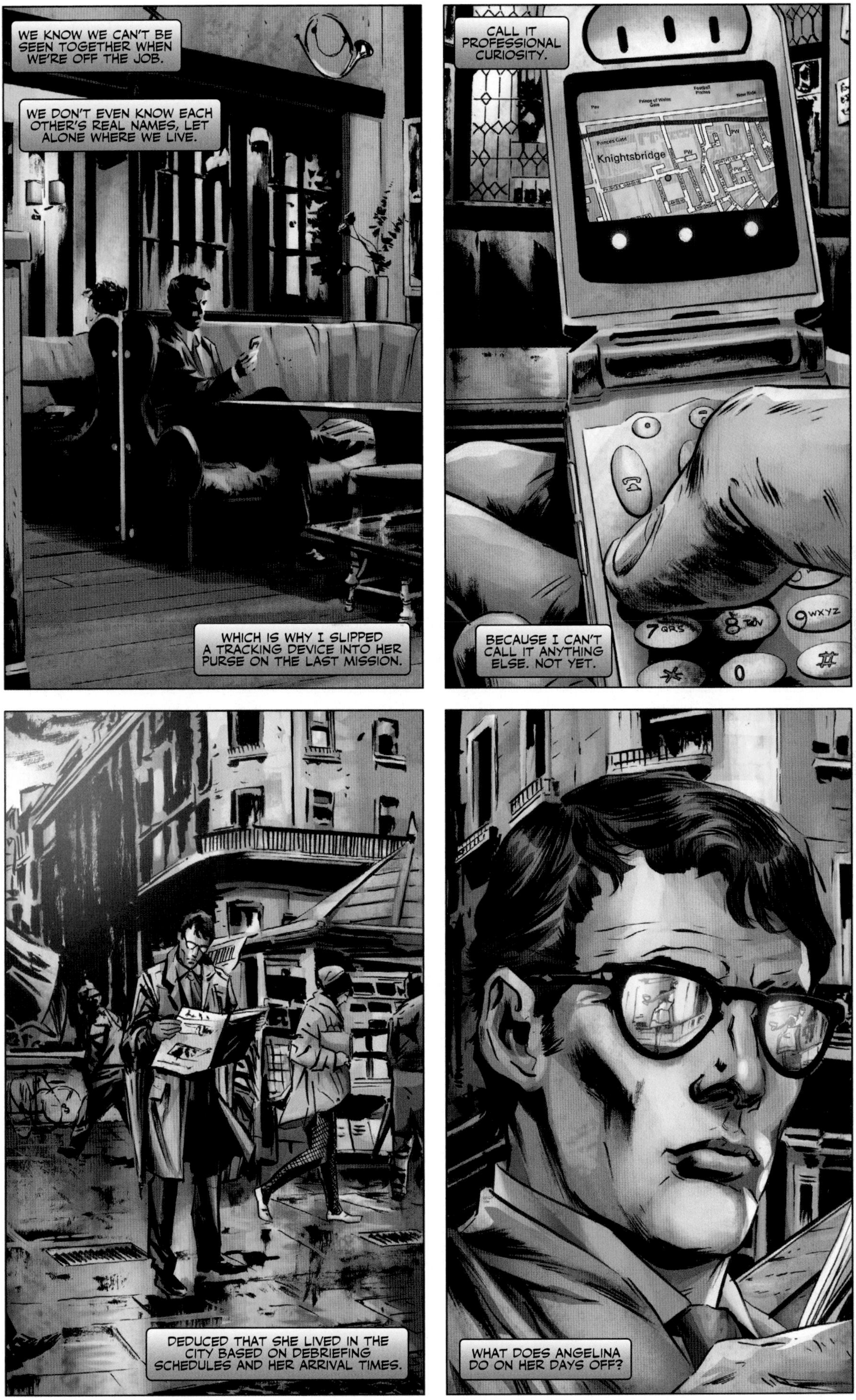

WE KNOW WE CAN'T BE SEEN TOGETHER WHEN WE'RE OFF THE JOB.
WE DON'T EVEN KNOW EACH OTHER'S REAL NAMES, LET ALONE WHERE WE LIVE.
WHICH IS WHY I SLIPPED A TRACKING DEVICE INTO HER PURSE ON THE LAST MISSION.
CALL IT PROFESSIONAL CURIOSITY.
Princes Gate
Knightsbridge
BECAUSE I CAN'T CALL IT ANYTHING ELSE. NOT YET.
DEDUCED THAT SHE LIVED IN THE CITY BASED ON DEBRIEFING SCHEDULES AND HER ARRIVAL TIMES.
WHAT DOES ANGELINA DO ON HER DAYS OFF?

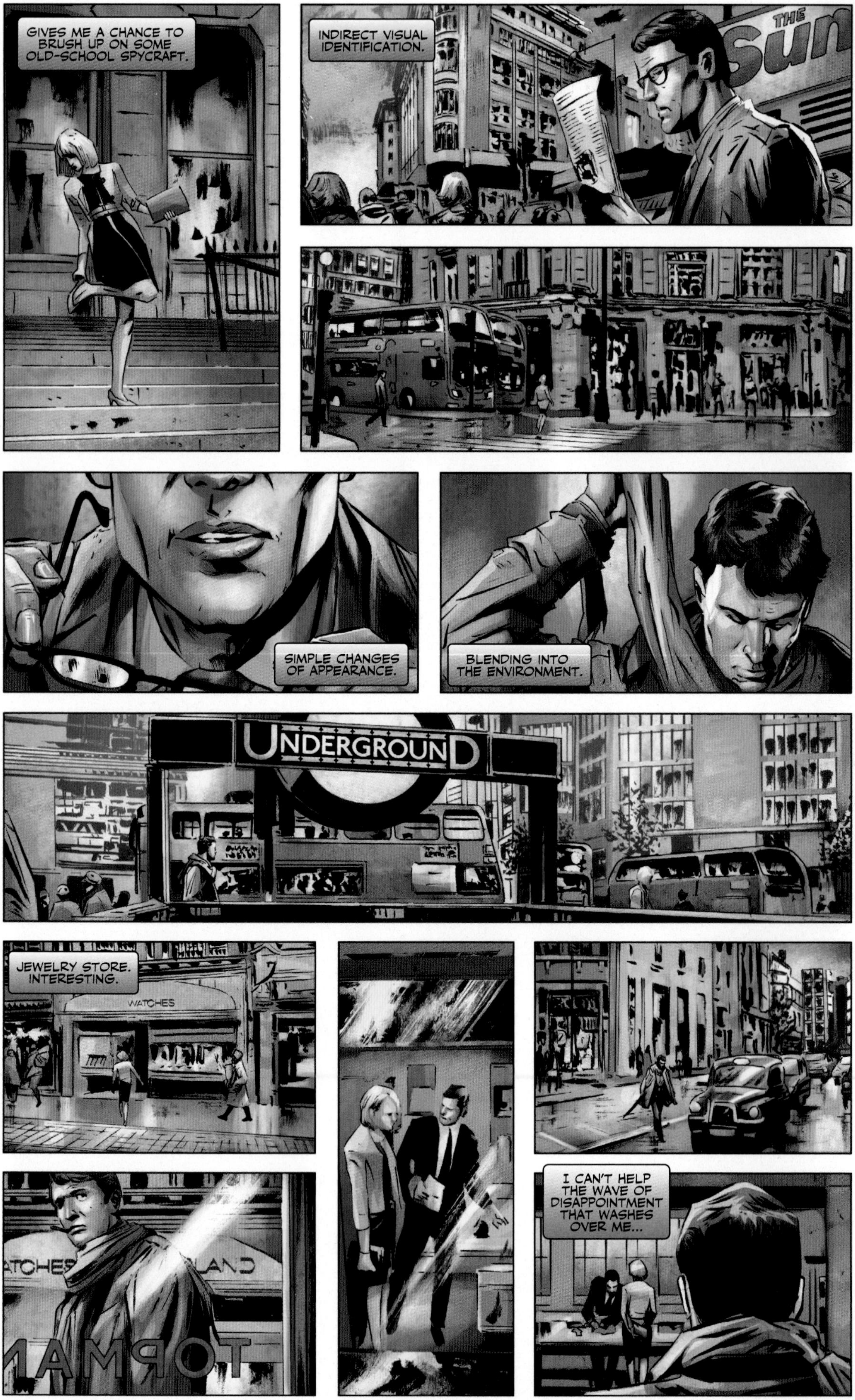
GIVES ME A CHANCE TO BRUSH UP ON SOME OLD-SCHOOL SPYCRAFT.
INDIRECT VISUAL IDENTIFICATION.
THE Sun
SIMPLE CHANGES OF APPEARANCE.
BLENDING INTO THE ENVIRONMENT.
UNDERGROUND
JEWELRY STORE. INTERESTING.
WATCHES
I CAN'T HELP THE WAVE OF DISAPPOINTMENT THAT WASHES OVER ME...

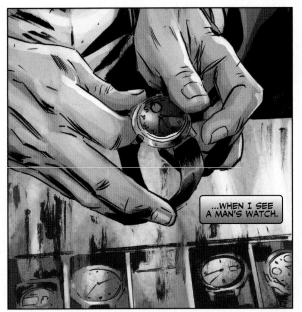

...WHEN I SEE A MAN'S WATCH.

OF COURSE SHE HAS A LIFE ON THE OUTSIDE. SOMEONE ELSE.

WE'RE CO-WORKERS.

STRICTLY PROFESSIONAL.

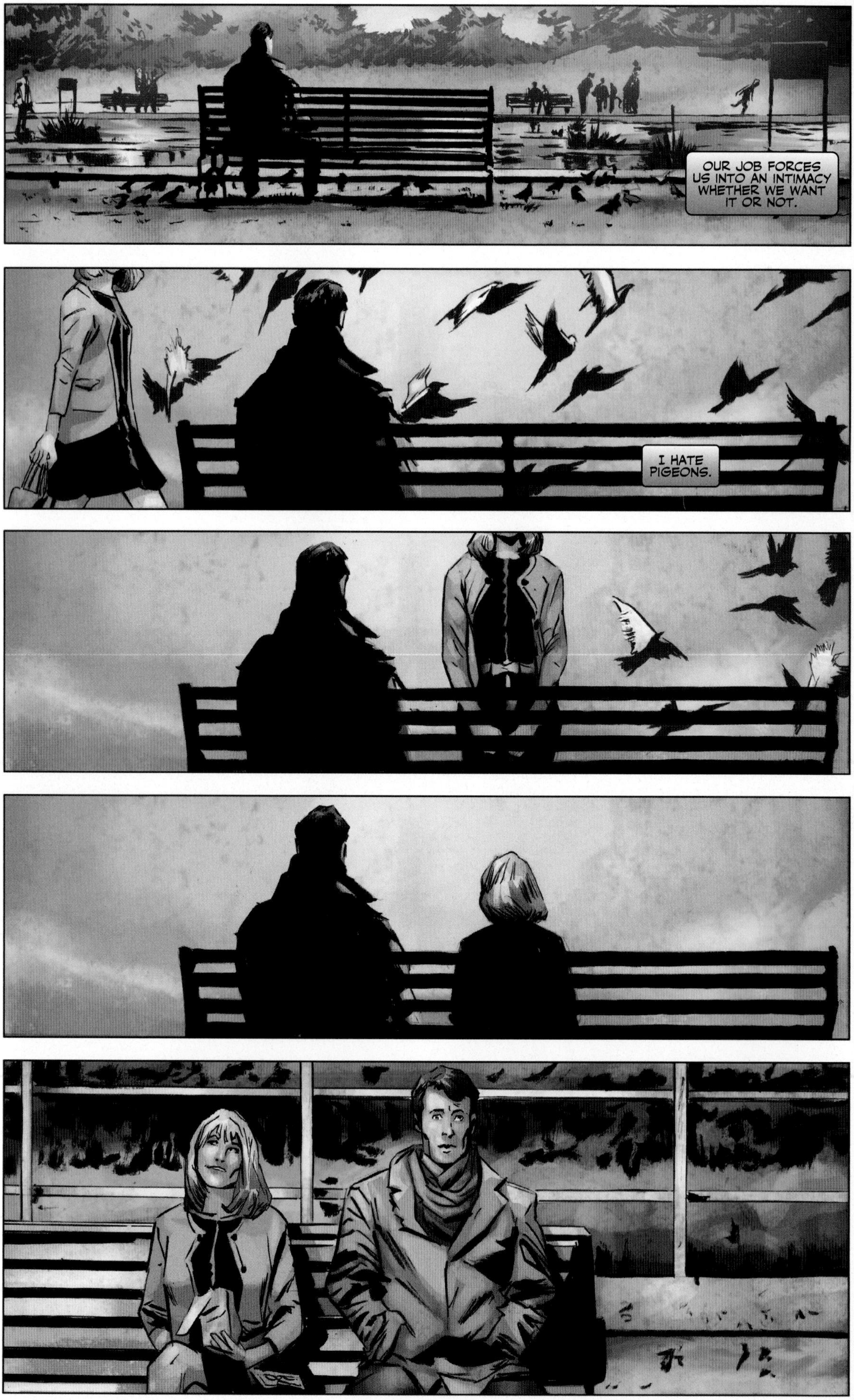
OUR JOB FORCES US INTO AN INTIMACY WHETHER WE WANT IT OR NOT.
I HATE PIGEONS.

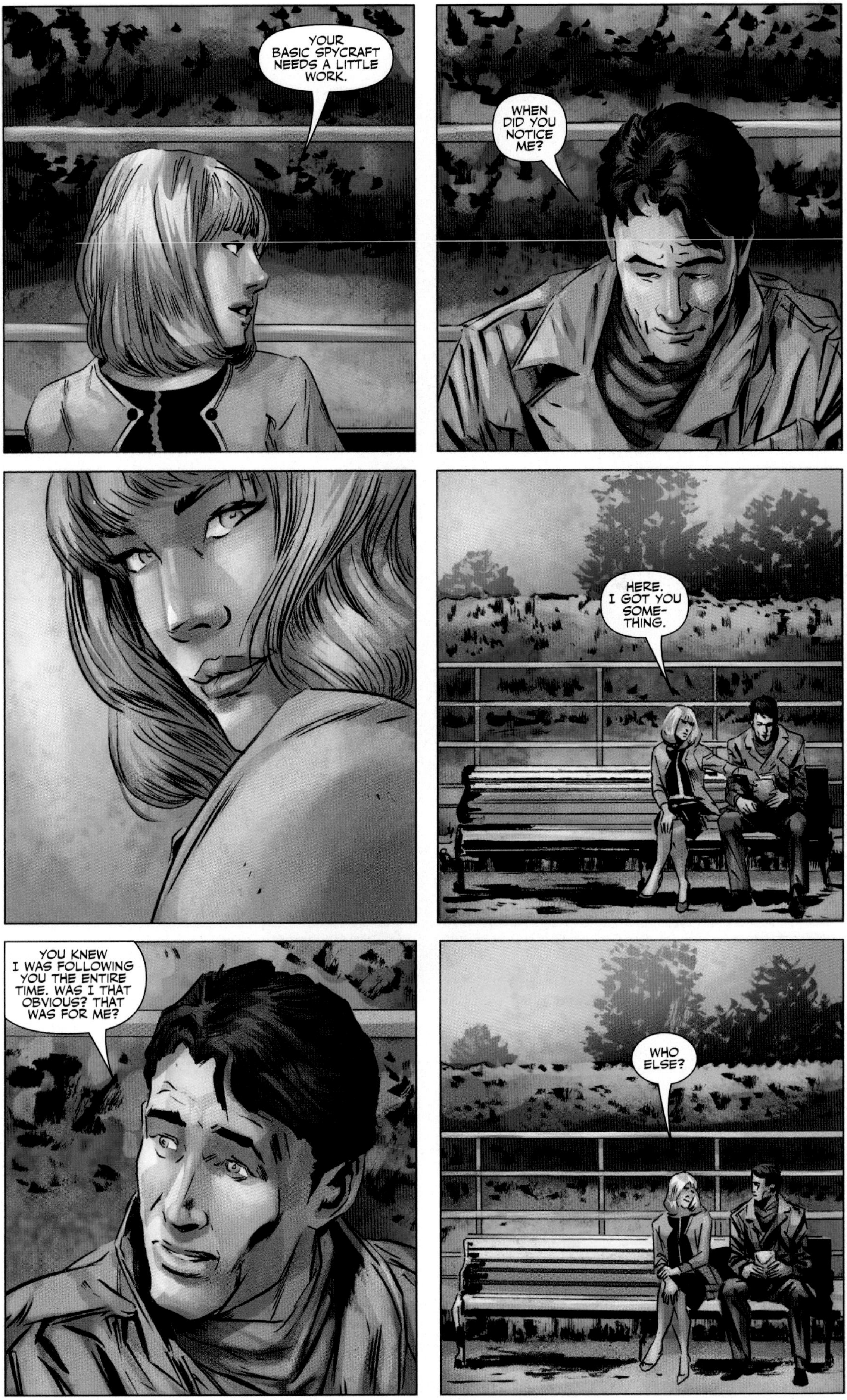
YOUR BASIC SPYCRAFT NEEDS A LITTLE WORK.
WHEN DID YOU NOTICE ME?
HERE. I GOT YOU SOME-THING.
YOU KNEW I WAS FOLLOWING YOU THE ENTIRE TIME. WAS I THAT OBVIOUS? THAT WAS FOR ME?
WHO ELSE?

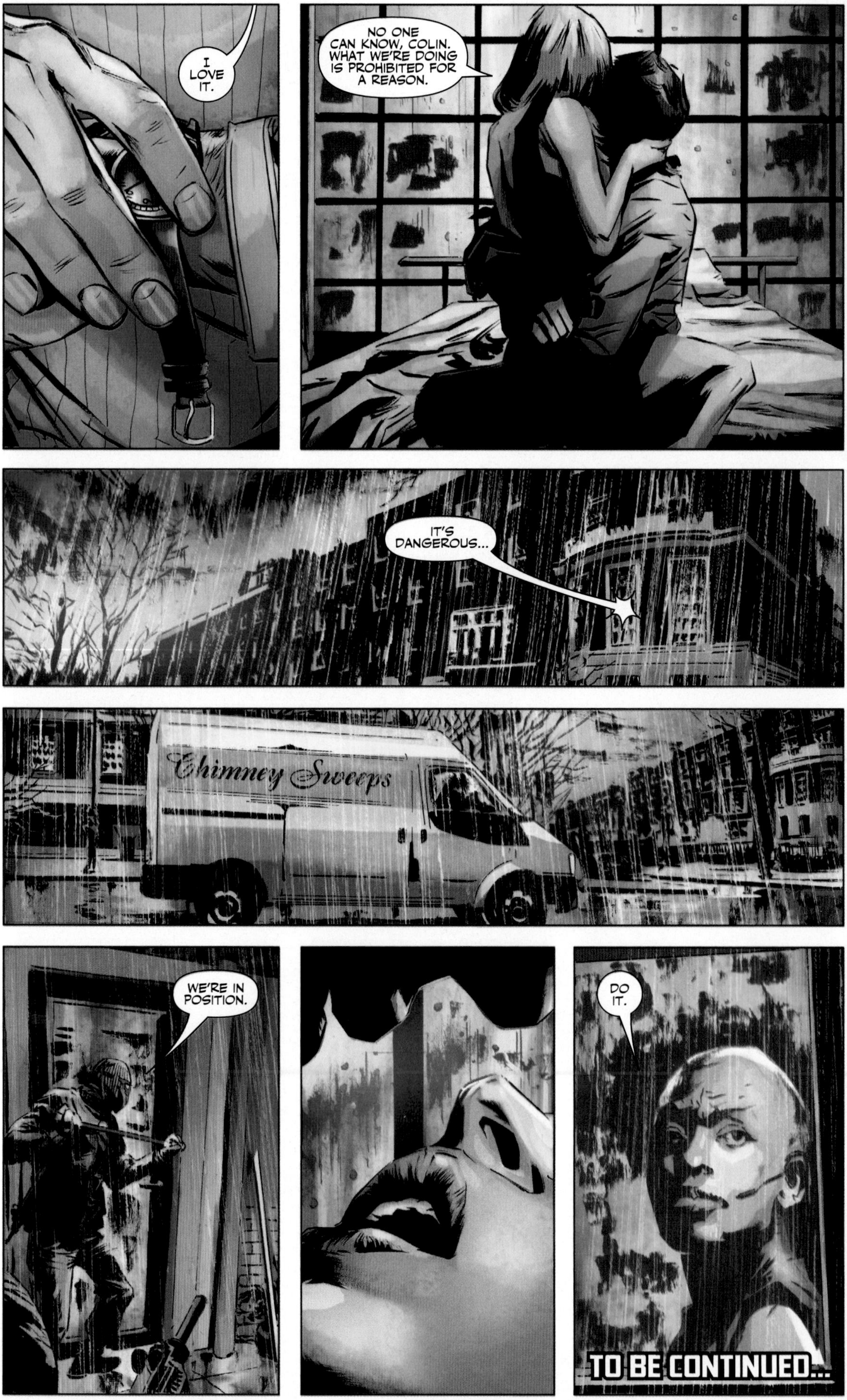
I LOVE IT.
NO ONE CAN KNOW, COLIN. WHAT WE'RE DOING IS PROHIBITED FOR A REASON.
IT'S DANGEROUS...
Chimney Sweeps
WE'RE IN POSITION.
DO IT.
TO BE CONTINUED...

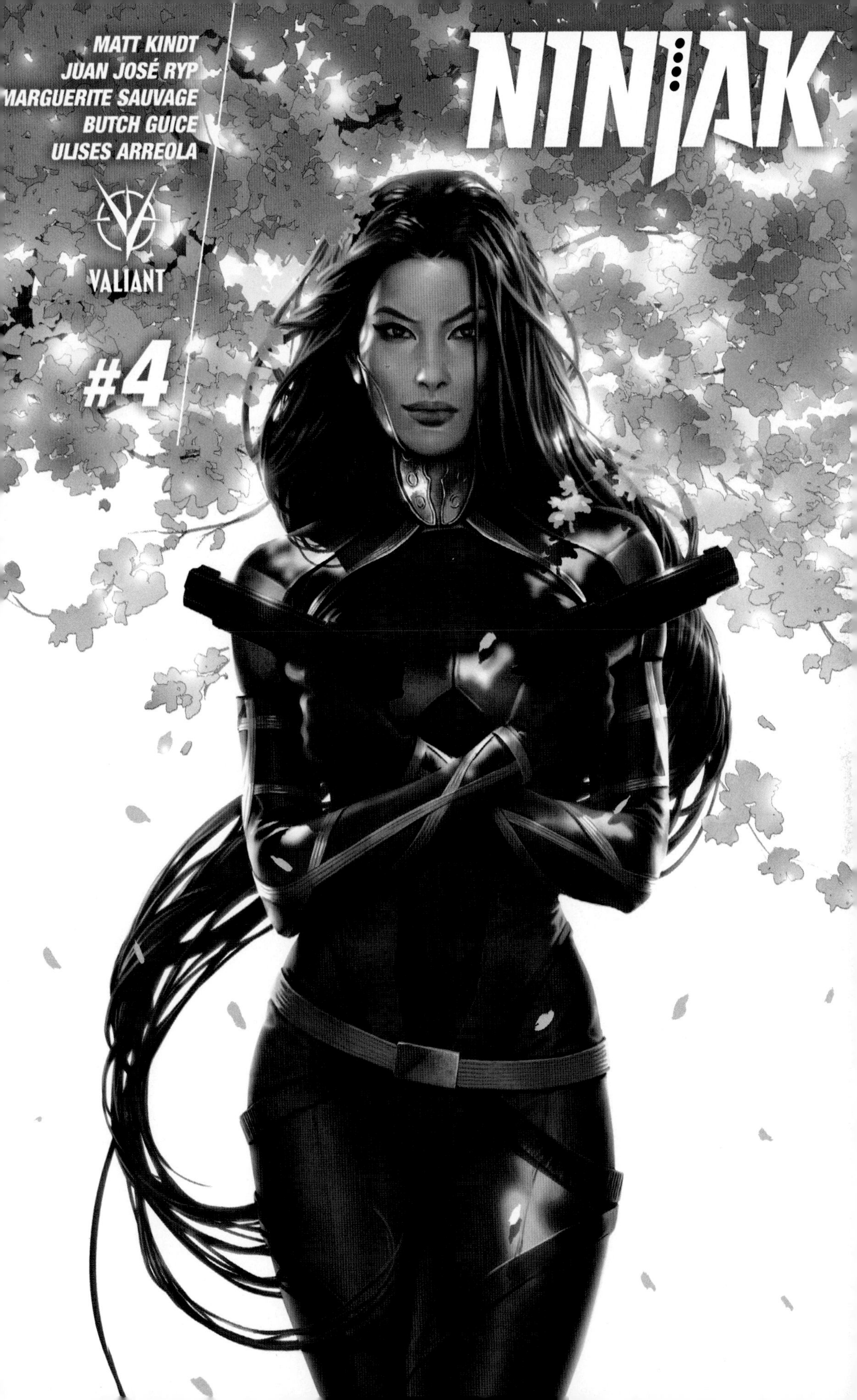
MATT KINDT
JUAN JOSÉ RYP
MARGUERITE SAUVAGE
BUTCH GUICE
ULISES ARREOLA
VALIANT
#4
NINJAK

CLASSIFIED

ROKU SPECIFICATIONS
& INSIGHTS

Psychokinetic Hair

FOLLICLE DETAIL
Only one strand of hair has been recovered to date but the lab is theorizing that the follicles have migrated through the skull and into the brain. This gives each section of hair different and unique capabilities.

DOCUMENTED CAPABILITY
Intense heat/fire generation.

DOCUMENTED CAPABILITY
Enhanced strength/durability.

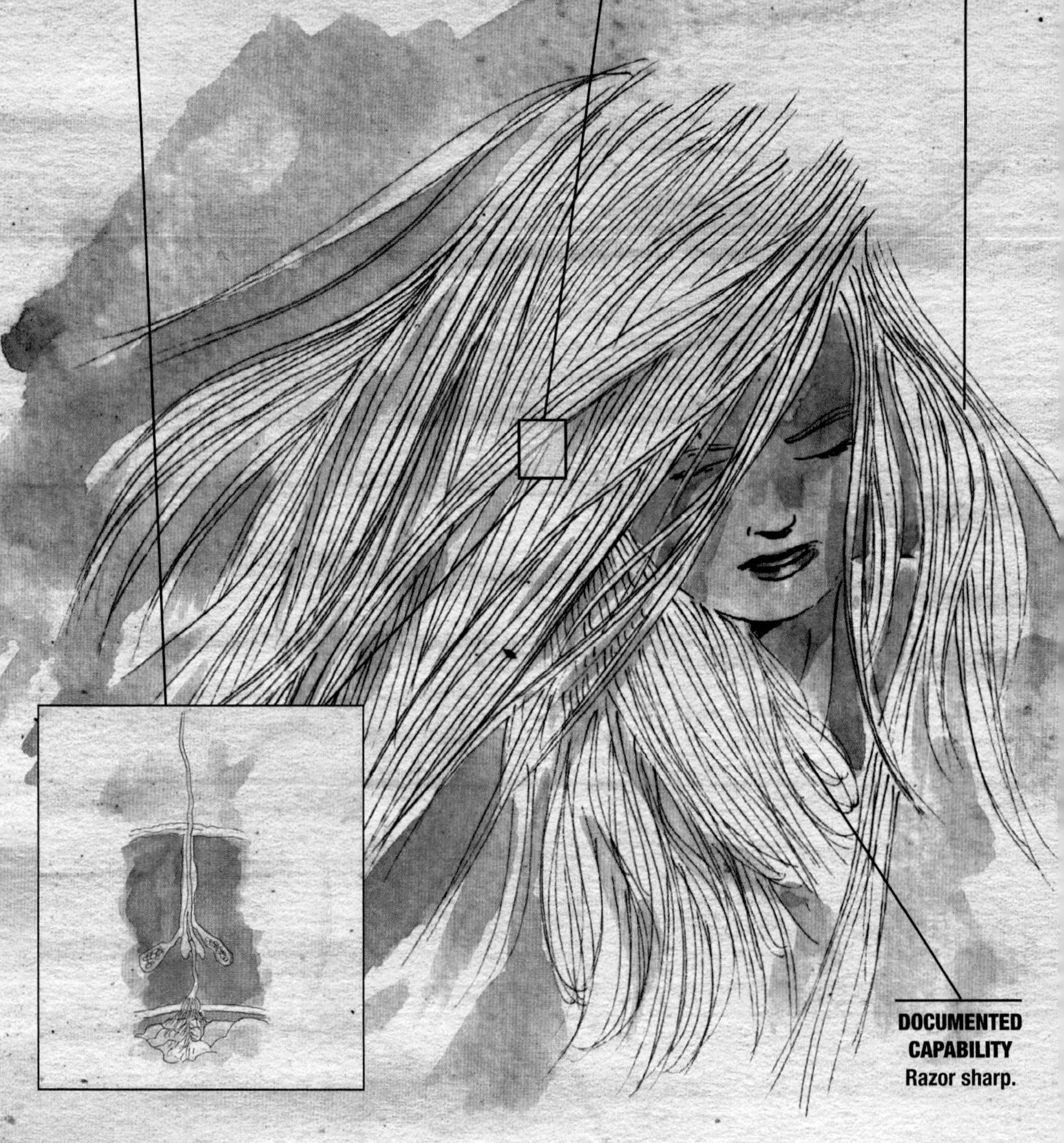

DOCUMENTED CAPABILITY
Razor sharp.

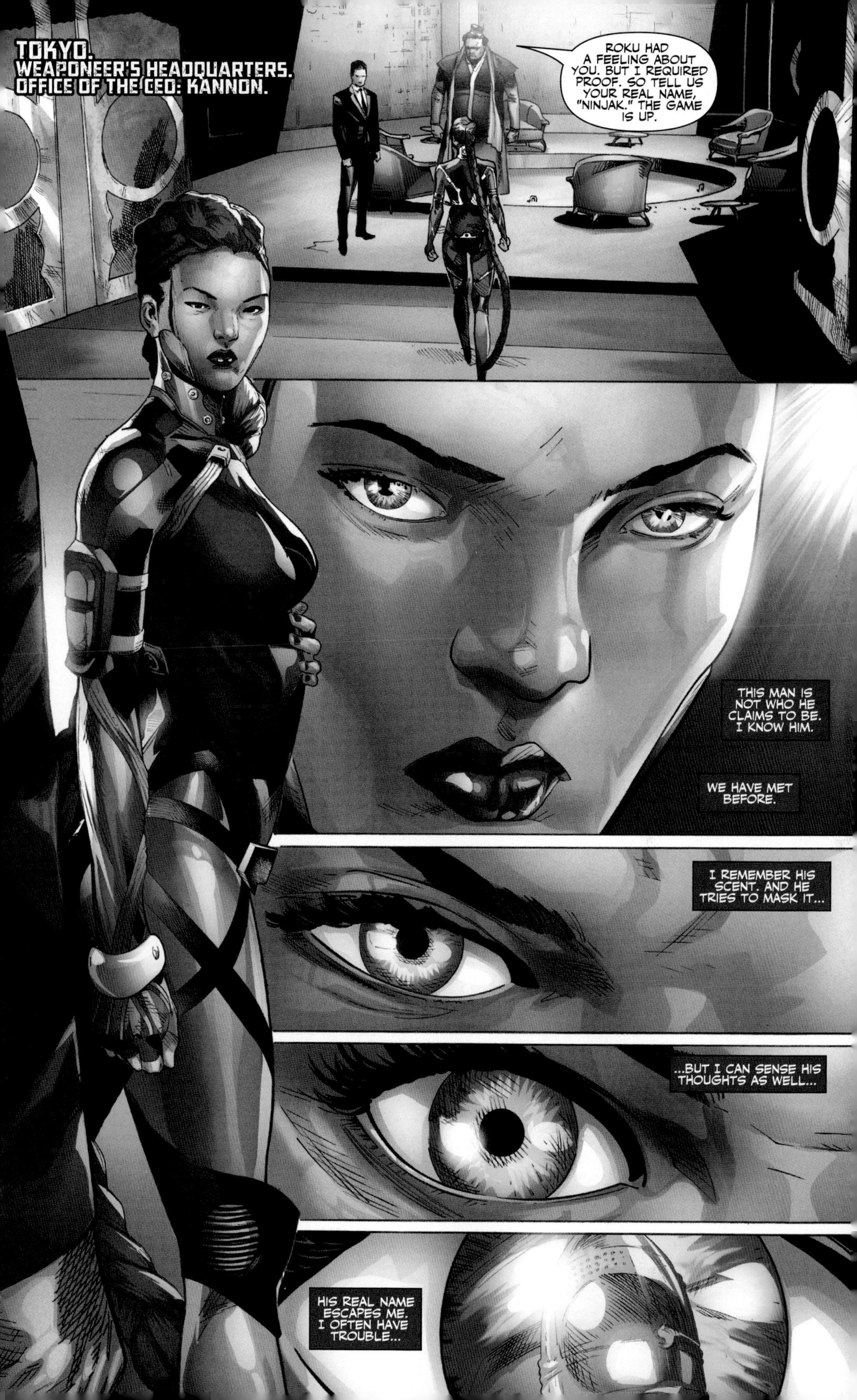
TOKYO.
WEAPONEER'S HEADQUARTERS.
OFFICE OF THE CEO: KANNON.
ROKU HAD A FEELING ABOUT YOU. BUT I REQUIRED PROOF. SO TELL US YOUR REAL NAME, "NINJAK." THE GAME IS UP.
THIS MAN IS NOT WHO HE CLAIMS TO BE. I KNOW HIM.
WE HAVE MET BEFORE.
I REMEMBER HIS SCENT. AND HE TRIES TO MASK IT...
...BUT I CAN SENSE HIS THOUGHTS AS WELL...
HIS REAL NAME ESCAPES ME. I OFTEN HAVE TROUBLE...

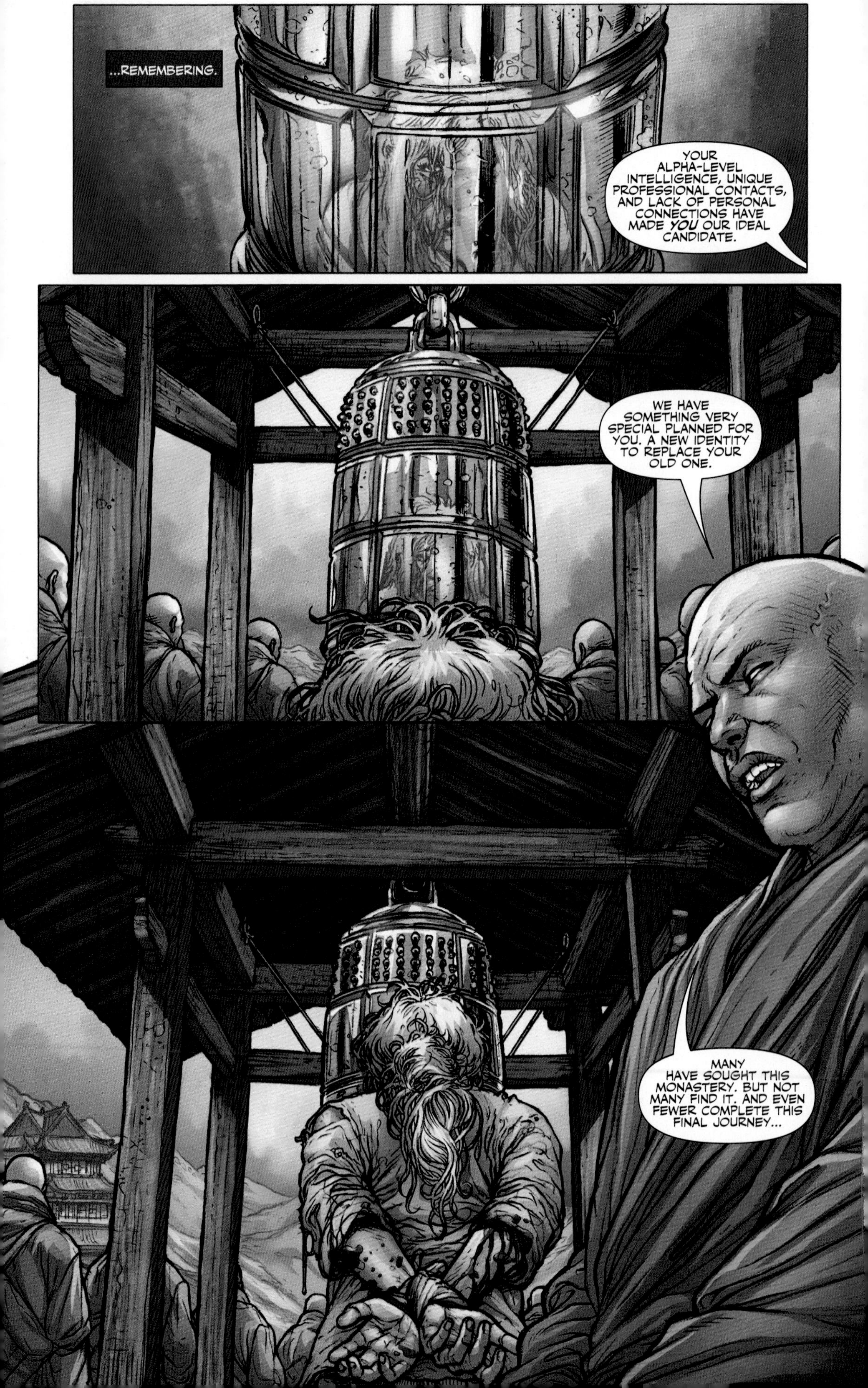
...REMEMBERING.
YOUR ALPHA-LEVEL INTELLIGENCE, UNIQUE PROFESSIONAL CONTACTS, AND LACK OF PERSONAL CONNECTIONS HAVE MADE YOU OUR IDEAL CANDIDATE.
WE HAVE SOMETHING VERY SPECIAL PLANNED FOR YOU. A NEW IDENTITY TO REPLACE YOUR OLD ONE.
MANY HAVE SOUGHT THIS MONASTERY. BUT NOT MANY FIND IT. AND EVEN FEWER COMPLETE THIS FINAL JOURNEY...

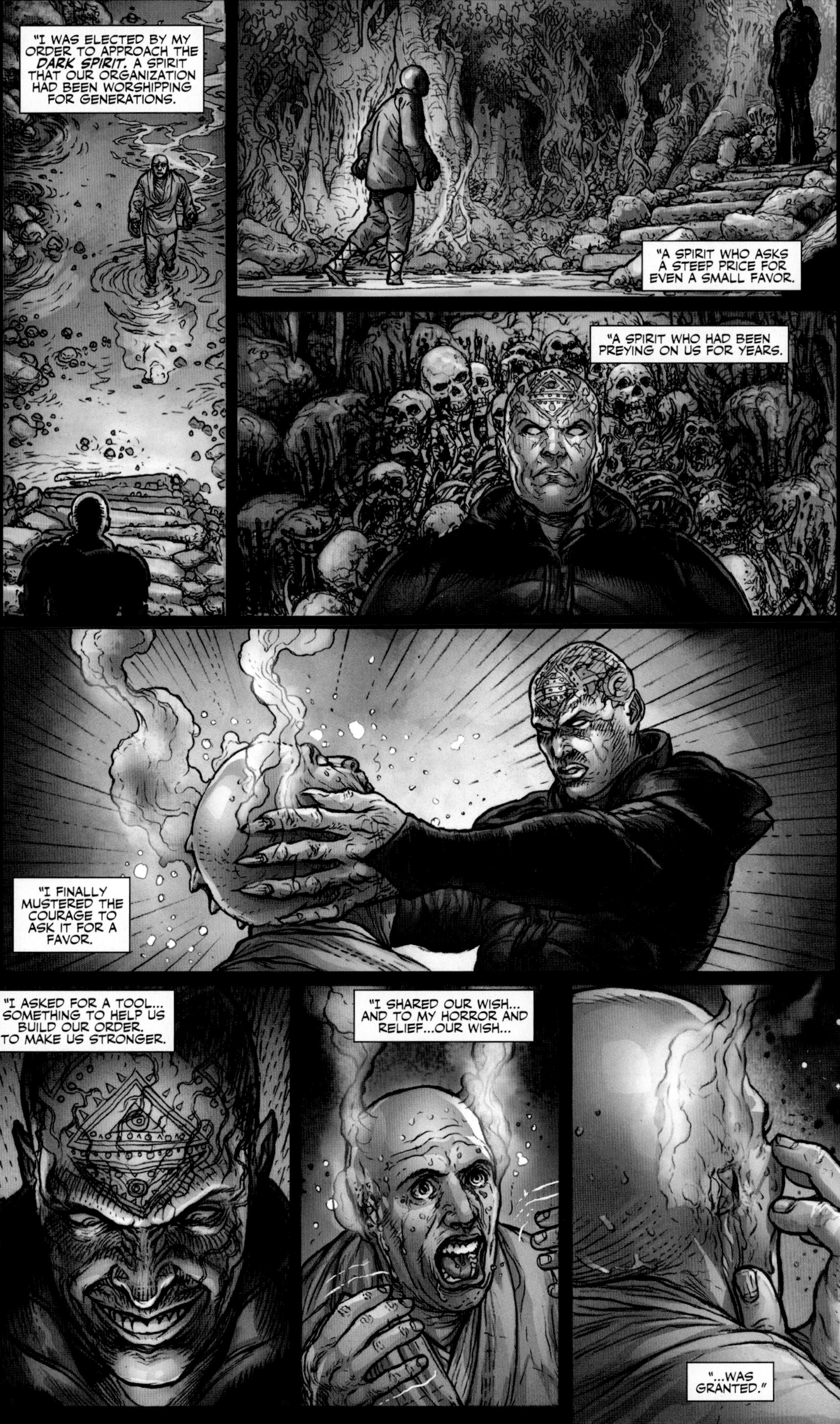
"I WAS ELECTED BY MY ORDER TO APPROACH THE *DARK SPIRIT.* A SPIRIT THAT OUR ORGANIZATION HAD BEEN WORSHIPPING FOR GENERATIONS.
"A SPIRIT WHO ASKS A STEEP PRICE FOR EVEN A SMALL FAVOR.
"A SPIRIT WHO HAD BEEN PREYING ON US FOR YEARS.
"I FINALLY MUSTERED THE COURAGE TO ASK IT FOR A FAVOR.
"I ASKED FOR A TOOL... SOMETHING TO HELP US BUILD OUR ORDER. TO MAKE US STRONGER.
"I SHARED OUR WISH... AND TO MY HORROR AND RELIEF...OUR WISH...
"...WAS GRANTED."

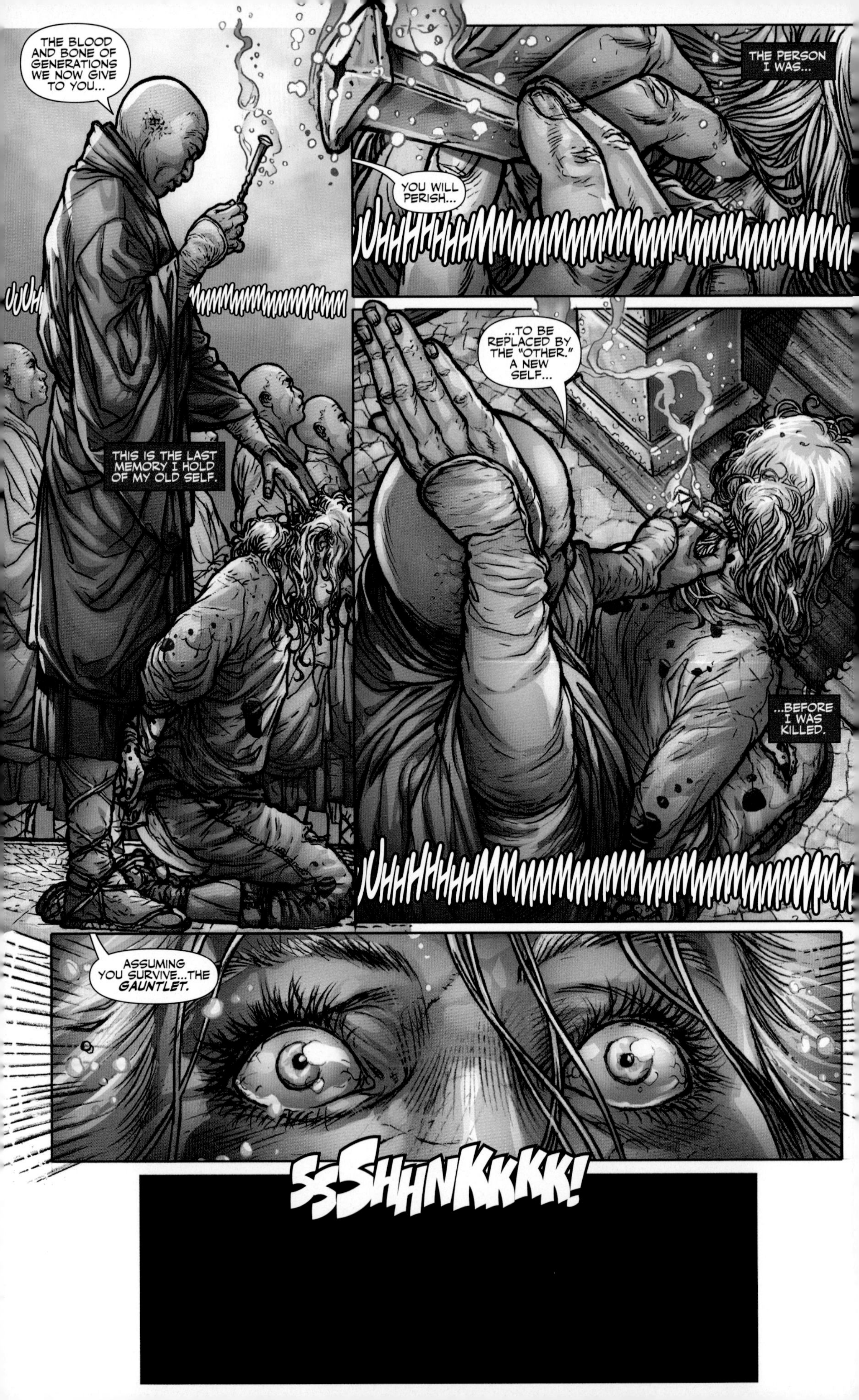
THE BLOOD AND BONE OF GENERATIONS WE NOW GIVE TO YOU...
THE PERSON I WAS...
YOU WILL PERISH...
UUHHHHHHHMMMMMMMMMMMMMMMMMMMMMMMMMMMMMMM
UUHMMMMMMMMMMMMMMMMMM
THIS IS THE LAST MEMORY I HOLD OF MY OLD SELF.
...TO BE REPLACED BY THE "OTHER." A NEW SELF...
...BEFORE I WAS KILLED.
UUHHHHHHHHMMMMMMMMMMMMMMMMMMMMMMMMMMMMMM
ASSUMING YOU SURVIVE...THE *GAUNTLET.*
SSSHHNKKKK!

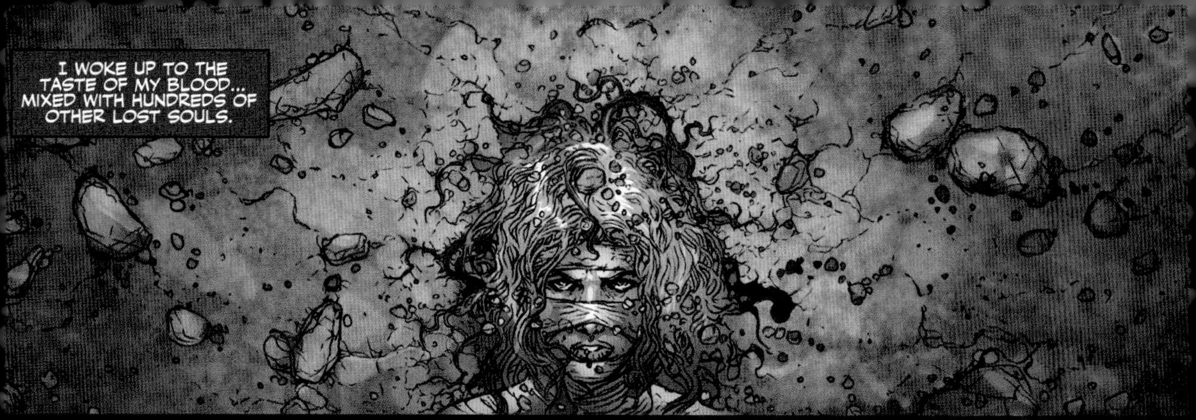
I WOKE UP TO THE TASTE OF MY BLOOD... MIXED WITH HUNDREDS OF OTHER LOST SOULS.

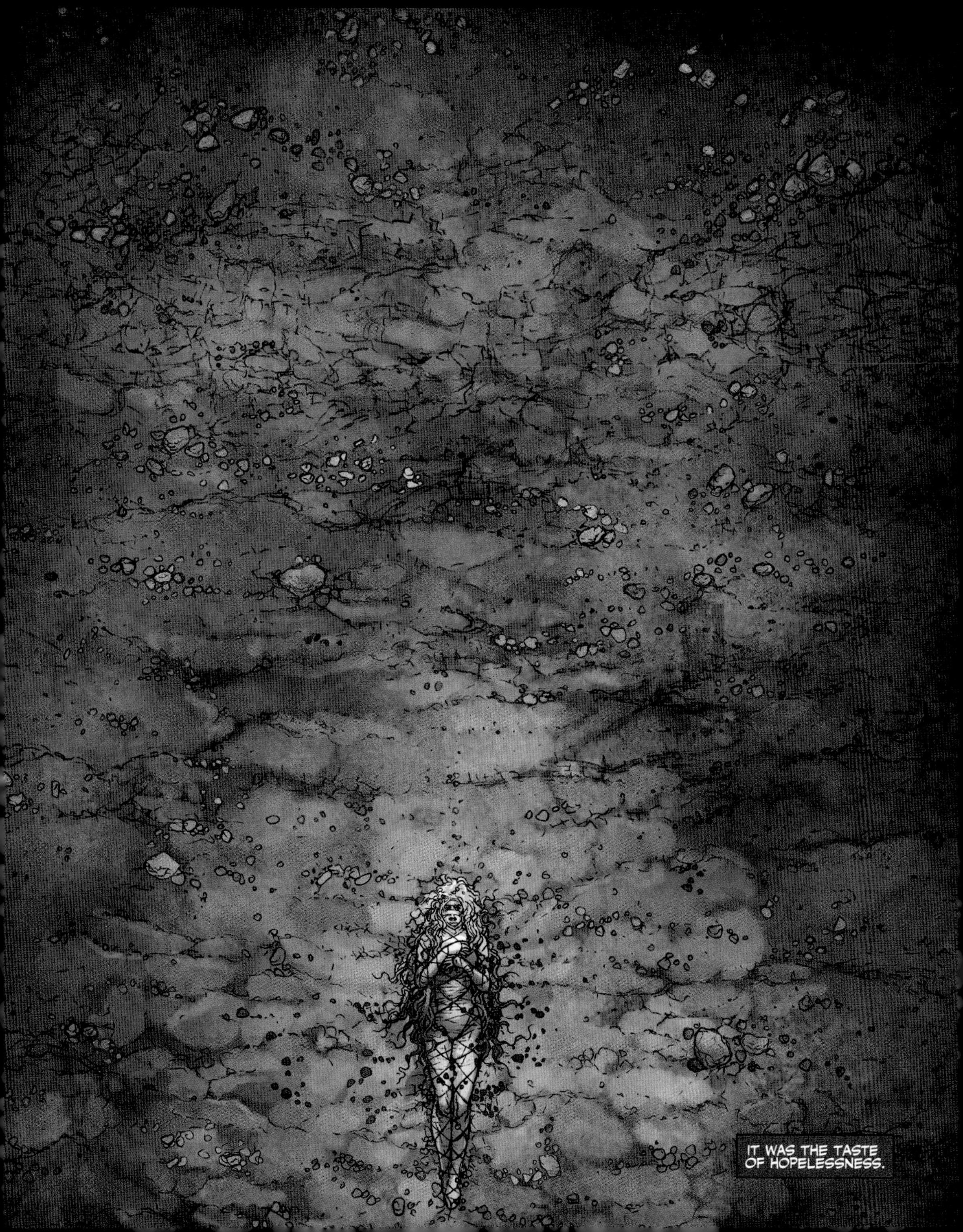
IT WAS THE TASTE OF HOPELESSNESS.

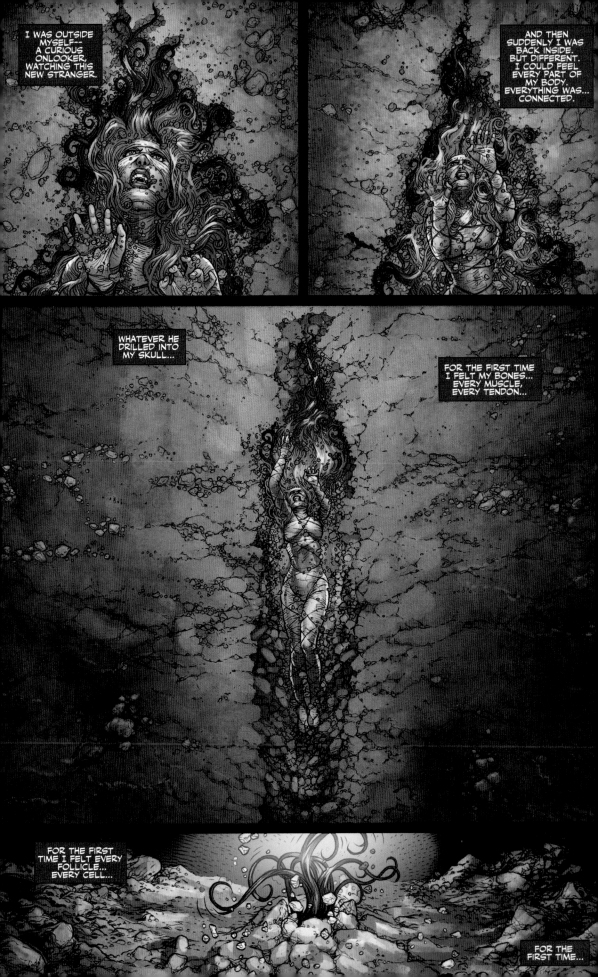

I WAS OUTSIDE MYSELF— A CURIOUS ONLOOKER, WATCHING THIS NEW STRANGER.

AND THEN SUDDENLY I WAS BACK INSIDE. BUT DIFFERENT. I COULD FEEL EVERY PART OF MY BODY. EVERYTHING WAS... CONNECTED.

WHATEVER HE DRILLED INTO MY SKULL...

FOR THE FIRST TIME I FELT MY BONES... EVERY MUSCLE. EVERY TENDON...

FOR THE FIRST TIME I FELT EVERY FOLLICLE... EVERY CELL...

FOR THE FIRST TIME...

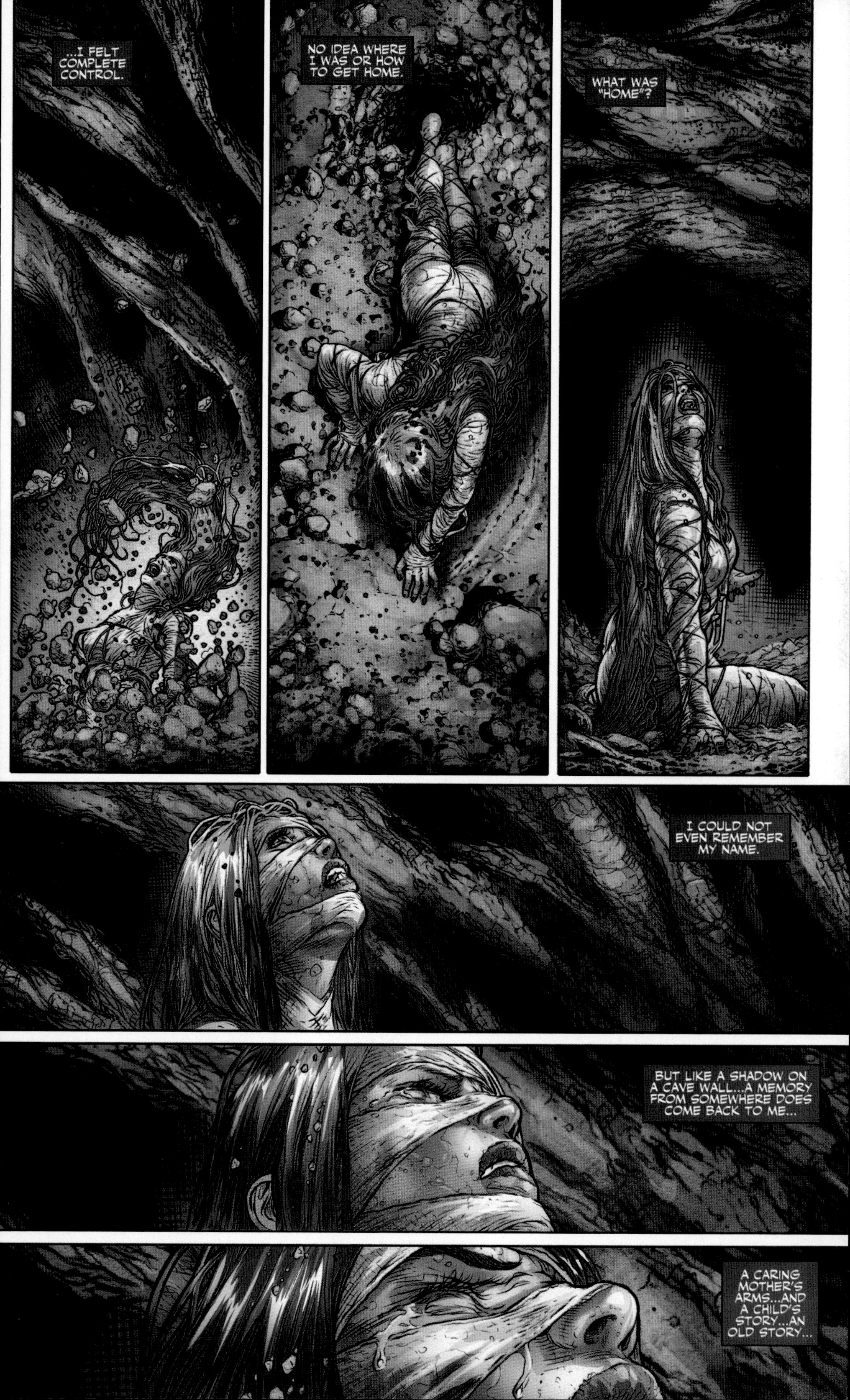
...I FELT COMPLETE CONTROL.
NO IDEA WHERE I WAS OR HOW TO GET HOME.
WHAT WAS "HOME"?
I COULD NOT EVEN REMEMBER MY NAME.
BUT LIKE A SHADOW ON A CAVE WALL...A MEMORY FROM SOMEWHERE DOES COME BACK TO ME...
A CARING MOTHER'S ARMS...AND A CHILD'S STORY...AN OLD STORY...

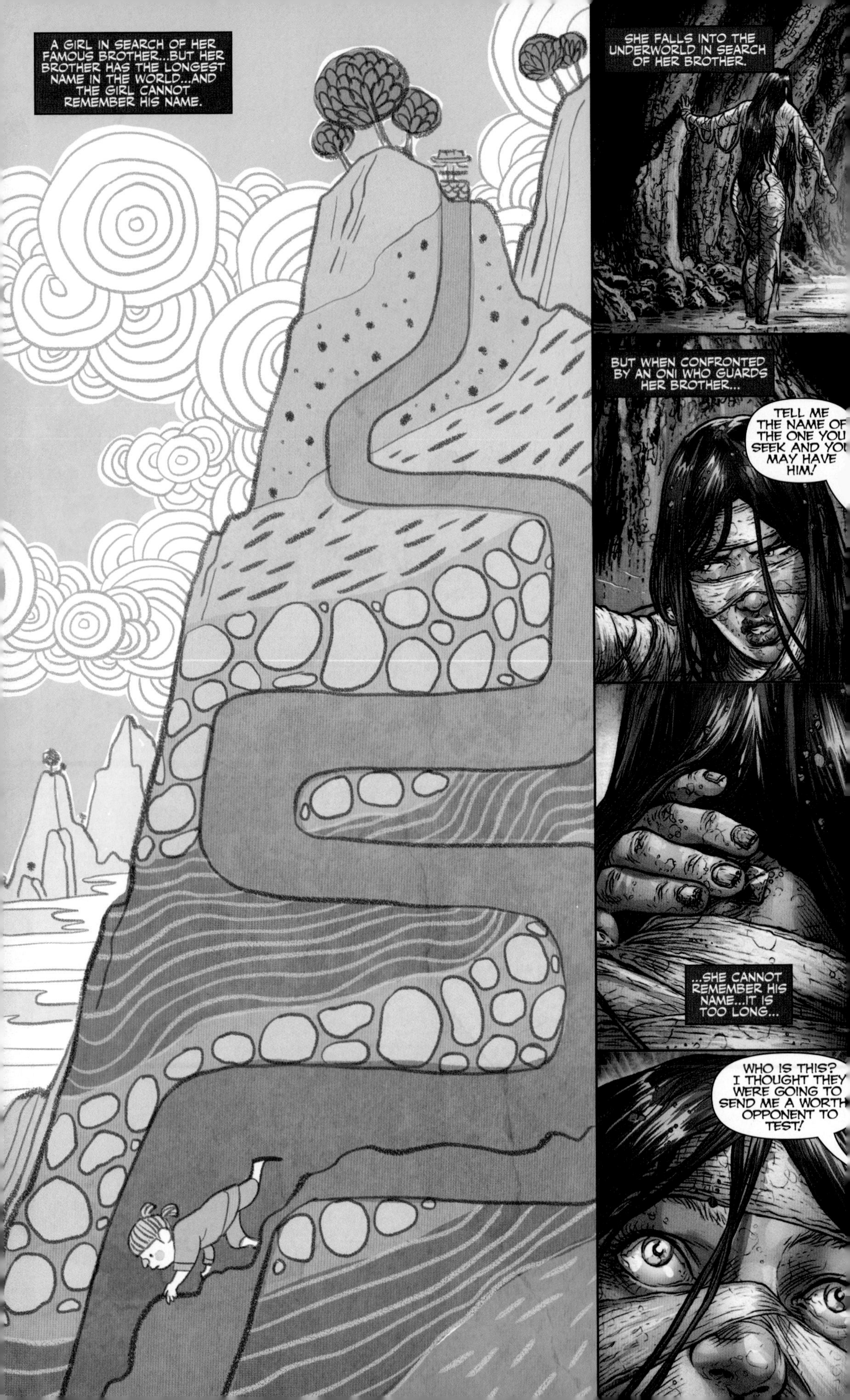
A GIRL IN SEARCH OF HER FAMOUS BROTHER...BUT HER BROTHER HAS THE LONGEST NAME IN THE WORLD...AND THE GIRL CANNOT REMEMBER HIS NAME.
SHE FALLS INTO THE UNDERWORLD IN SEARCH OF HER BROTHER.
BUT WHEN CONFRONTED BY AN ONI WHO GUARDS HER BROTHER...
TELL ME THE NAME OF THE ONE YOU SEEK AND YO MAY HAVE HIM!
...SHE CANNOT REMEMBER HIS NAME...IT IS TOO LONG...
WHO IS THIS? I THOUGHT THEY WERE GOING TO SEND ME A WORTH OPPONENT TO TEST!

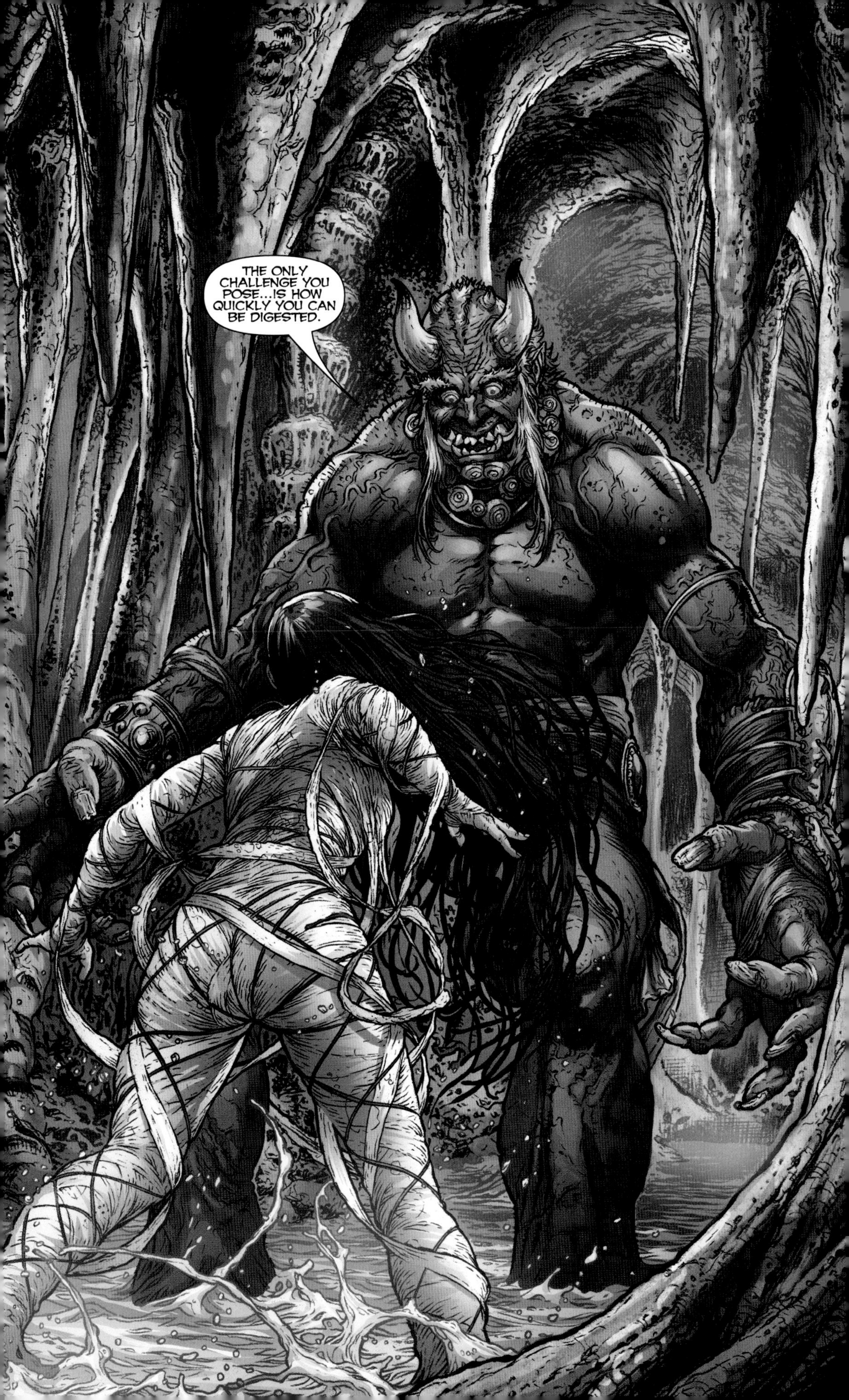
THE ONLY CHALLENGE YOU POSE...IS HOW QUICKLY YOU CAN BE DIGESTED.

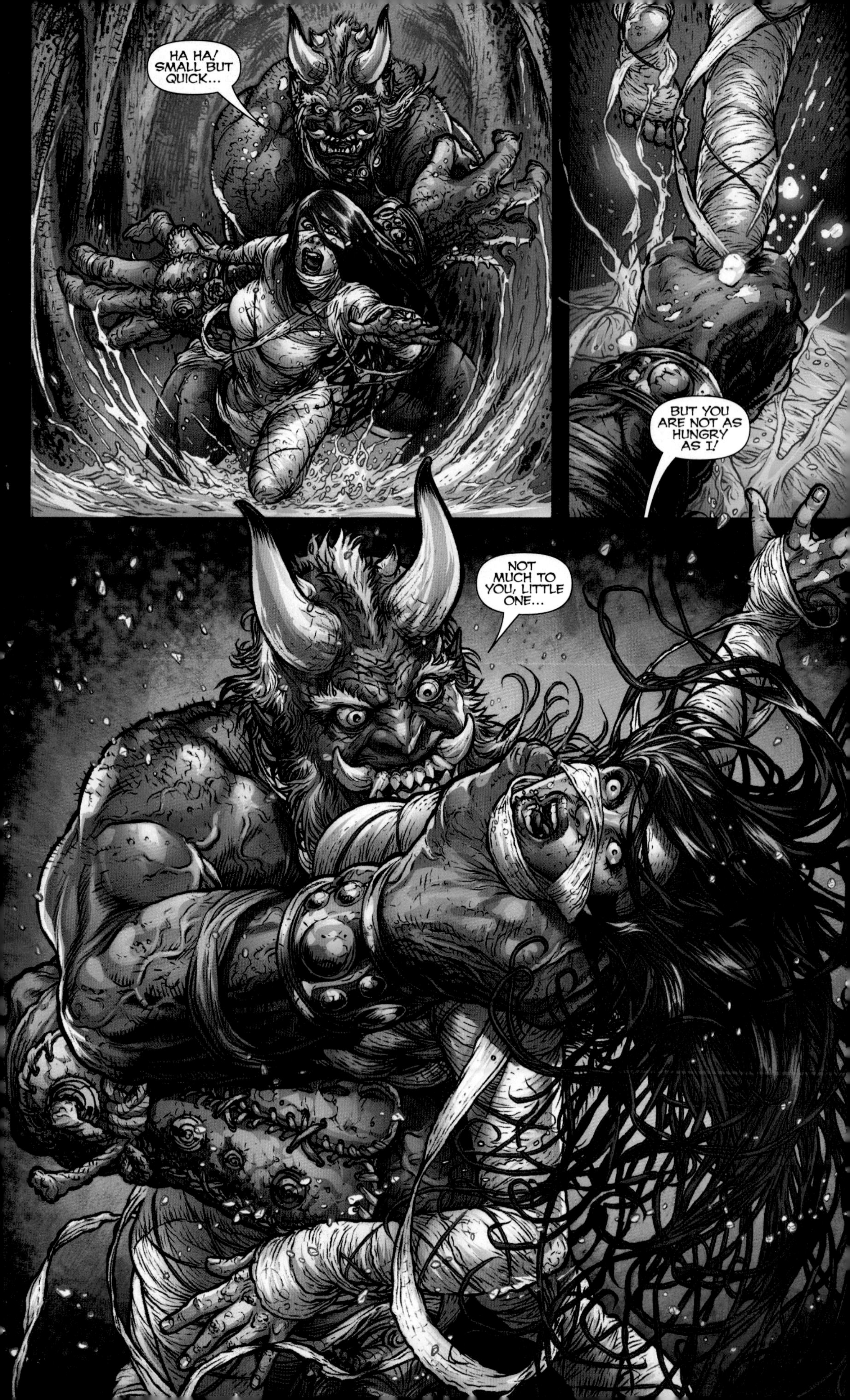
HA HA! SMALL BUT QUICK...
BUT YOU ARE NOT AS HUNGRY AS I!
NOT MUCH TO YOU, LITTLE ONE...

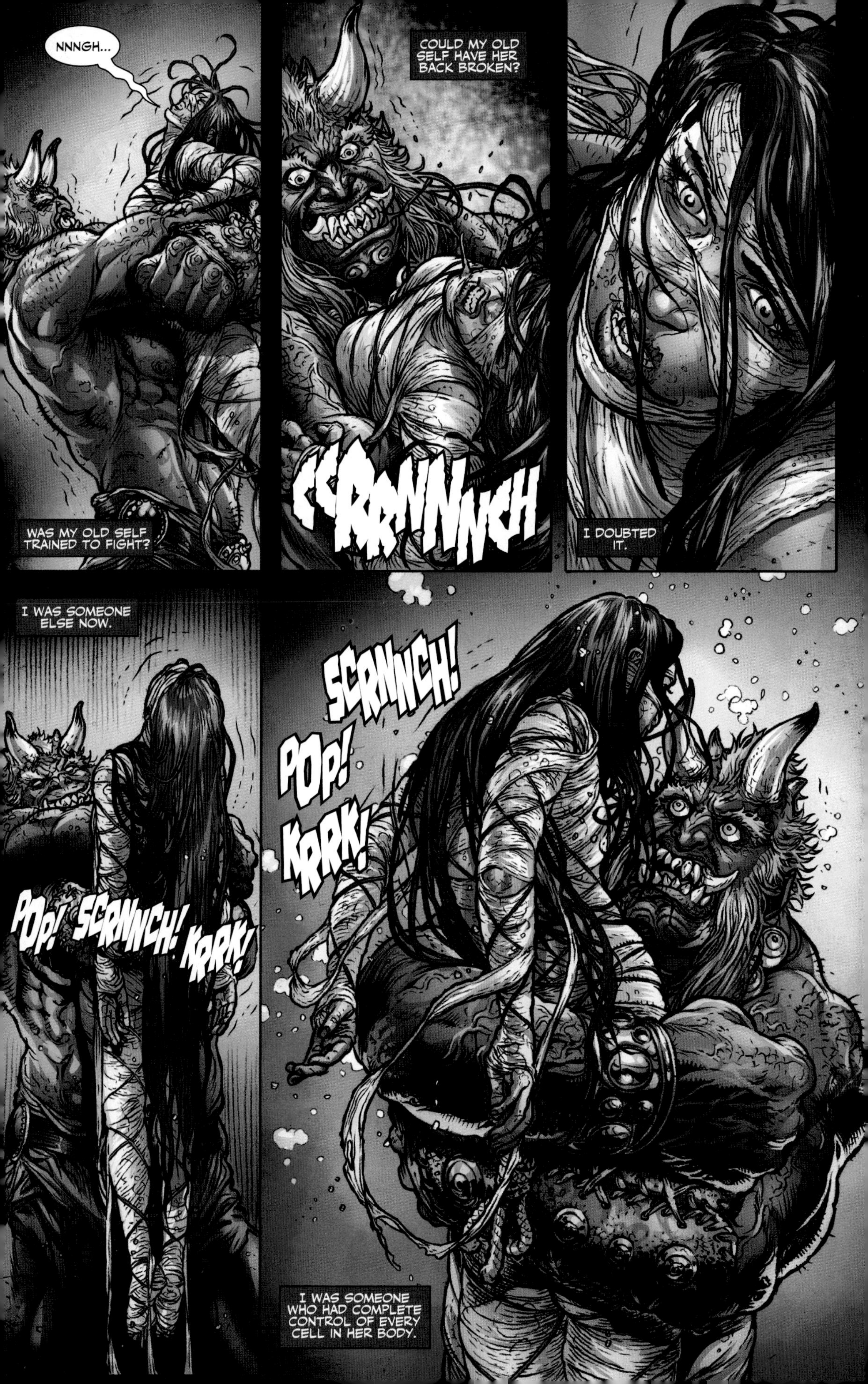
NNNGH...
WAS MY OLD SELF TRAINED TO FIGHT?
COULD MY OLD SELF HAVE HER BACK BROKEN?
SCRNNNCH
I DOUBTED IT.
I WAS SOMEONE ELSE NOW.
POP! SCRNNCH! KRRK!
SCRNNCH!
POP!
KRRK!
I WAS SOMEONE WHO HAD COMPLETE CONTROL OF EVERY CELL IN HER BODY.

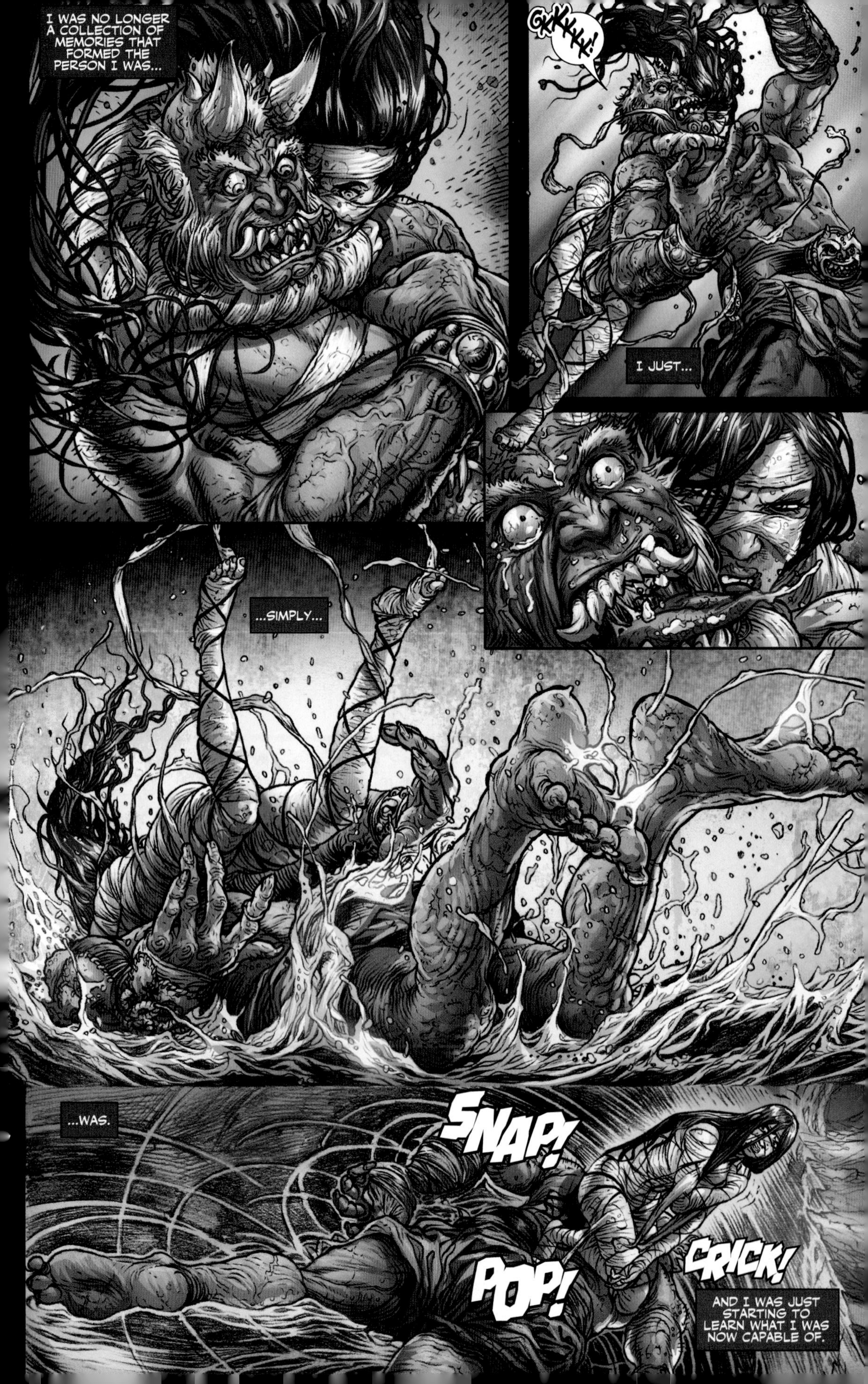
I WAS NO LONGER A COLLECTION OF MEMORIES THAT FORMED THE PERSON I WAS...
GKKKKK!
I JUST...
...SIMPLY...
...WAS.
SNAP!
POP!
CRICK!
AND I WAS JUST STARTING TO LEARN WHAT I WAS NOW CAPABLE OF.

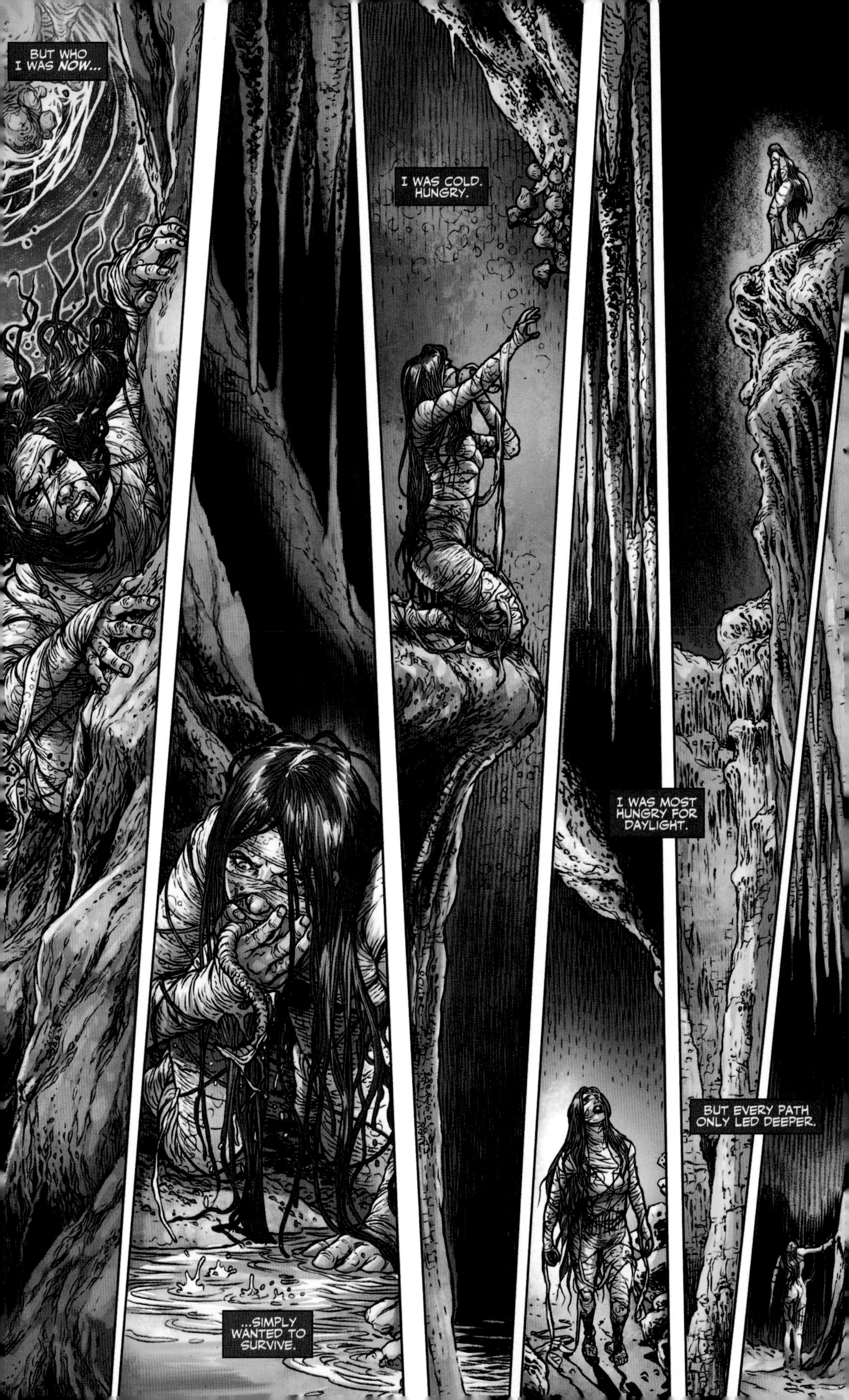
BUT WHO I WAS *NOW*...
...SIMPLY WANTED TO SURVIVE.
I WAS COLD. HUNGRY.
I WAS MOST HUNGRY FOR DAYLIGHT.
BUT EVERY PATH ONLY LED DEEPER.

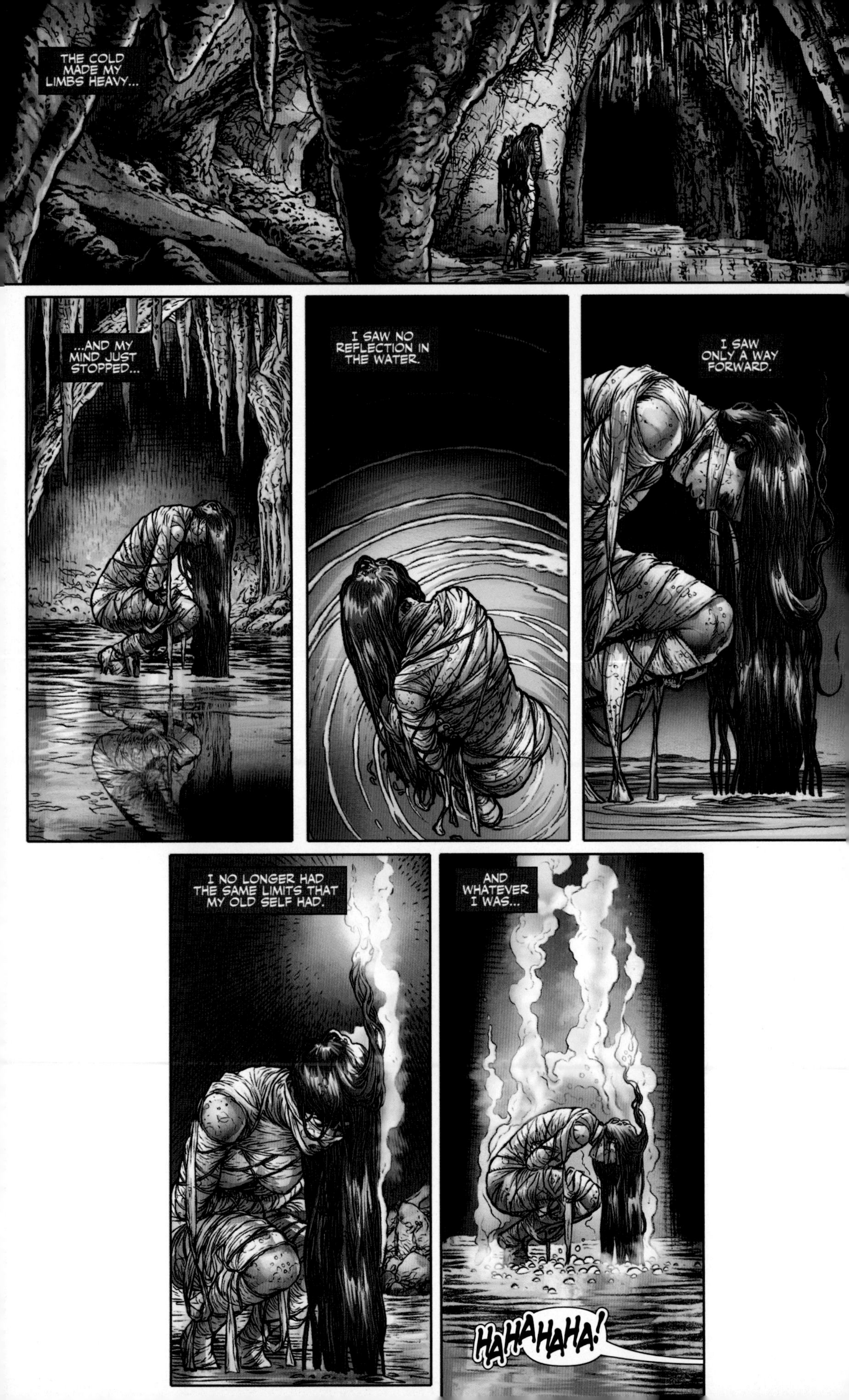
THE COLD MADE MY LIMBS HEAVY...
...AND MY MIND JUST STOPPED...
I SAW NO REFLECTION IN THE WATER.
I SAW ONLY A WAY FORWARD.
I NO LONGER HAD THE SAME LIMITS THAT MY OLD SELF HAD.
AND WHATEVER I WAS...
HAHAHAHA!

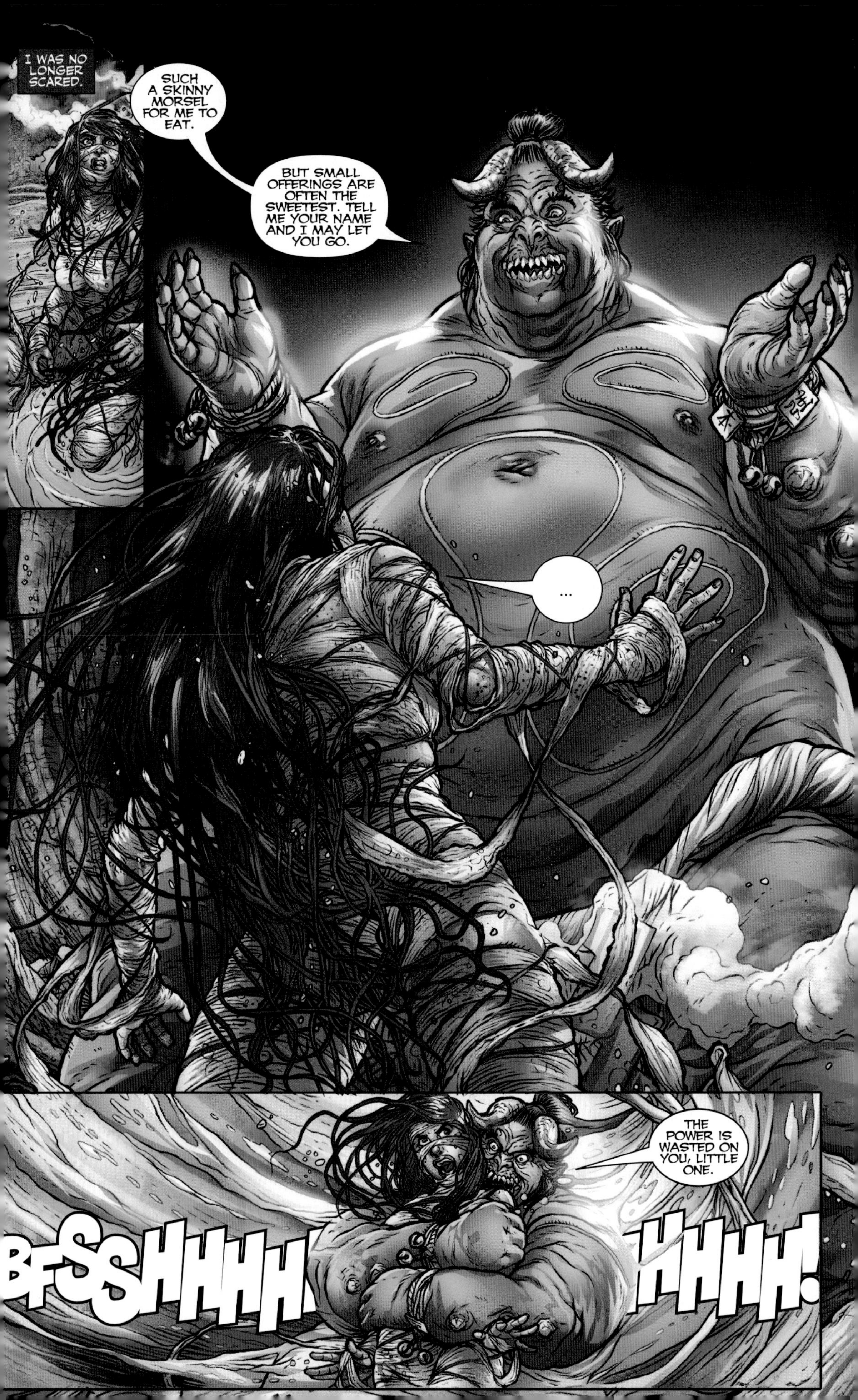
I WAS NO LONGER SCARED.
SUCH A SKINNY MORSEL FOR ME TO EAT.
BUT SMALL OFFERINGS ARE OFTEN THE SWEETEST. TELL ME YOUR NAME AND I MAY LET YOU GO.
...
THE POWER IS WASTED ON YOU, LITTLE ONE.
BFSSHHHHHHHHHHHHH!

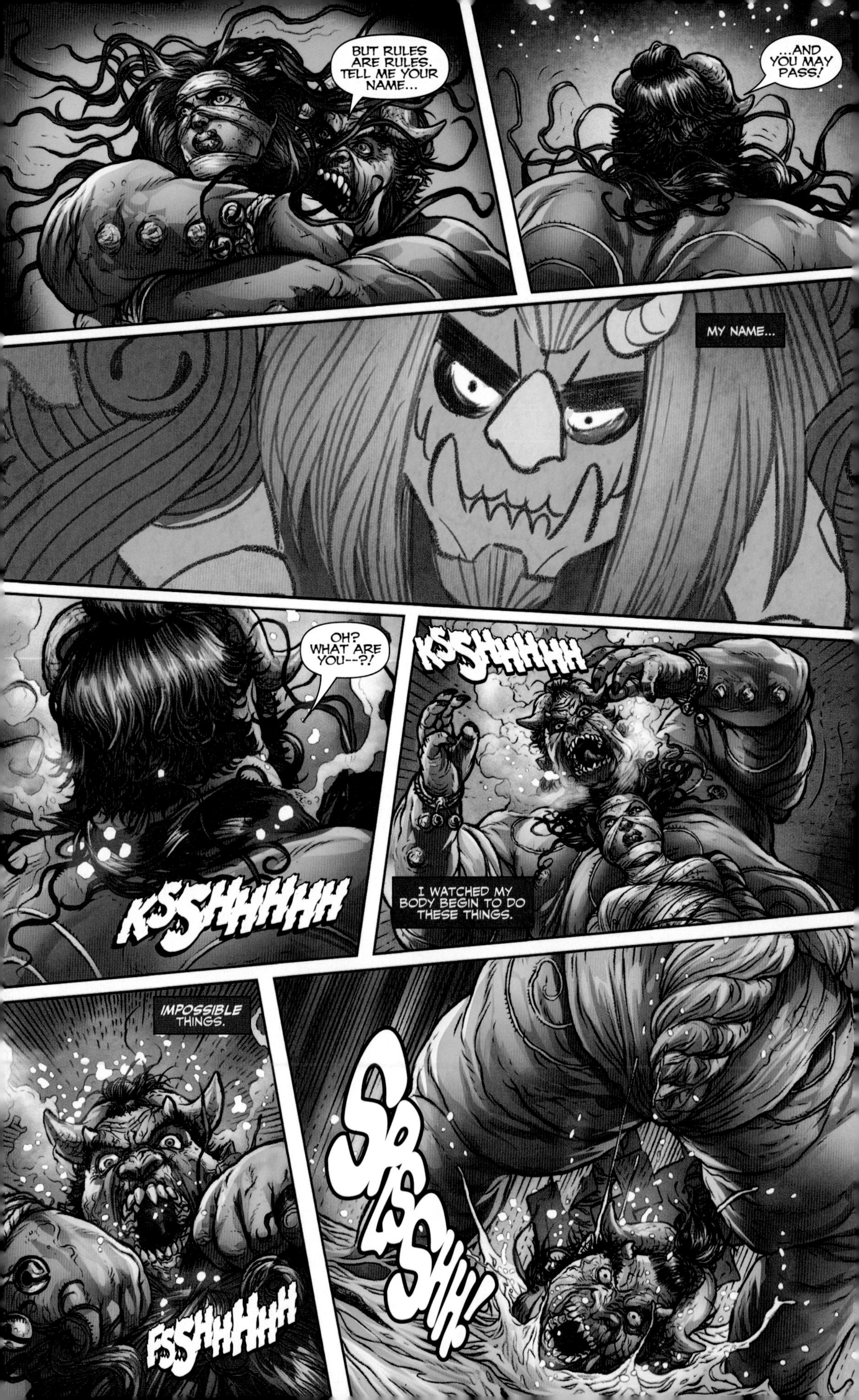

BUT RULES ARE RULES. TELL ME YOUR NAME...
...AND YOU MAY PASS!
MY NAME...
OH? WHAT ARE YOU--?!
KSSHHHHHH
KSSHHHHHH
I WATCHED MY BODY BEGIN TO DO THESE THINGS.
IMPOSSIBLE THINGS.
SPLOOSHHH!
FSSHHHHHH

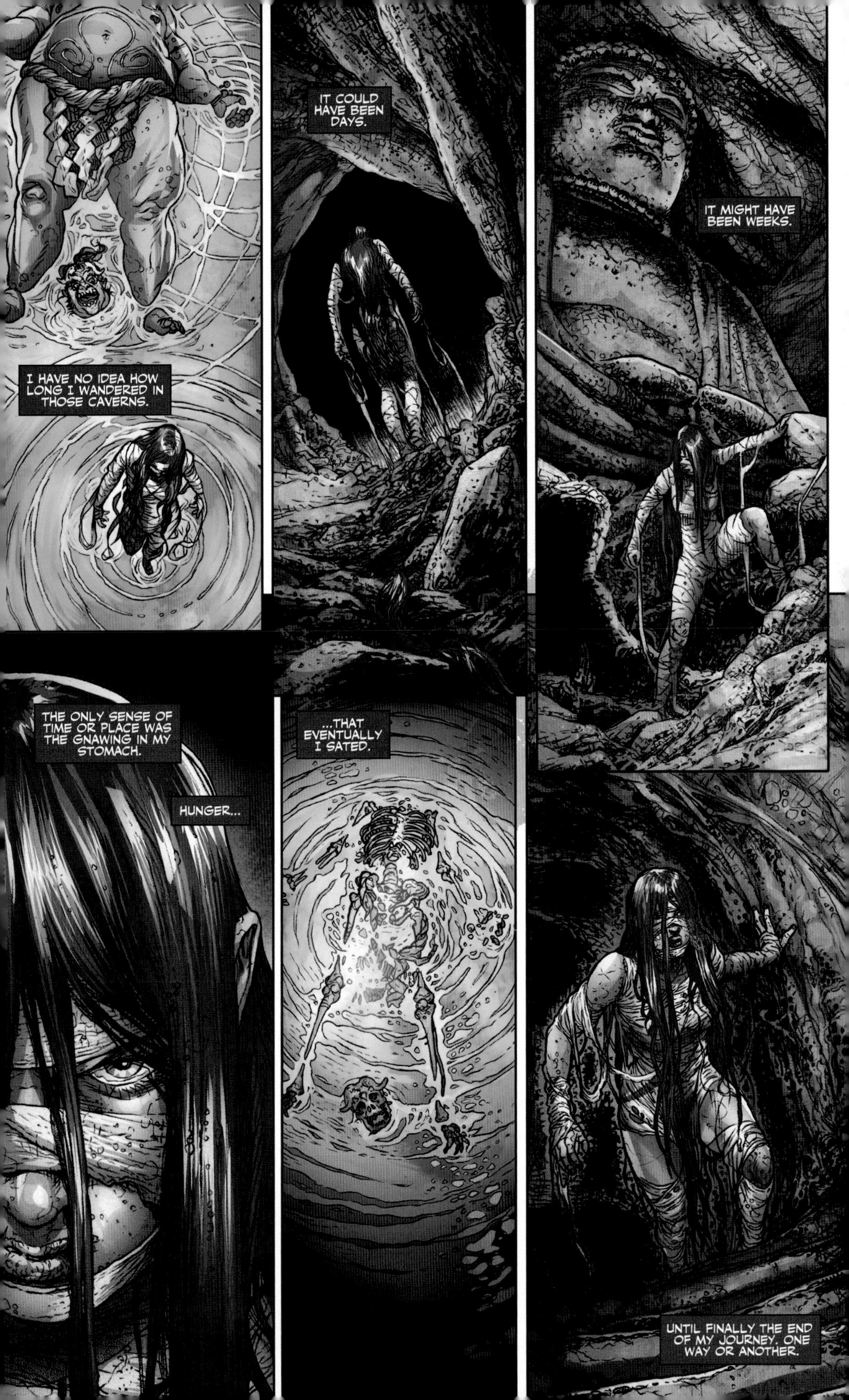
I HAVE NO IDEA HOW LONG I WANDERED IN THOSE CAVERNS.
IT COULD HAVE BEEN DAYS.
IT MIGHT HAVE BEEN WEEKS.
THE ONLY SENSE OF TIME OR PLACE WAS THE GNAWING IN MY STOMACH.
HUNGER...
...THAT EVENTUALLY I SATED.
UNTIL FINALLY THE END OF MY JOURNEY. ONE WAY OR ANOTHER.

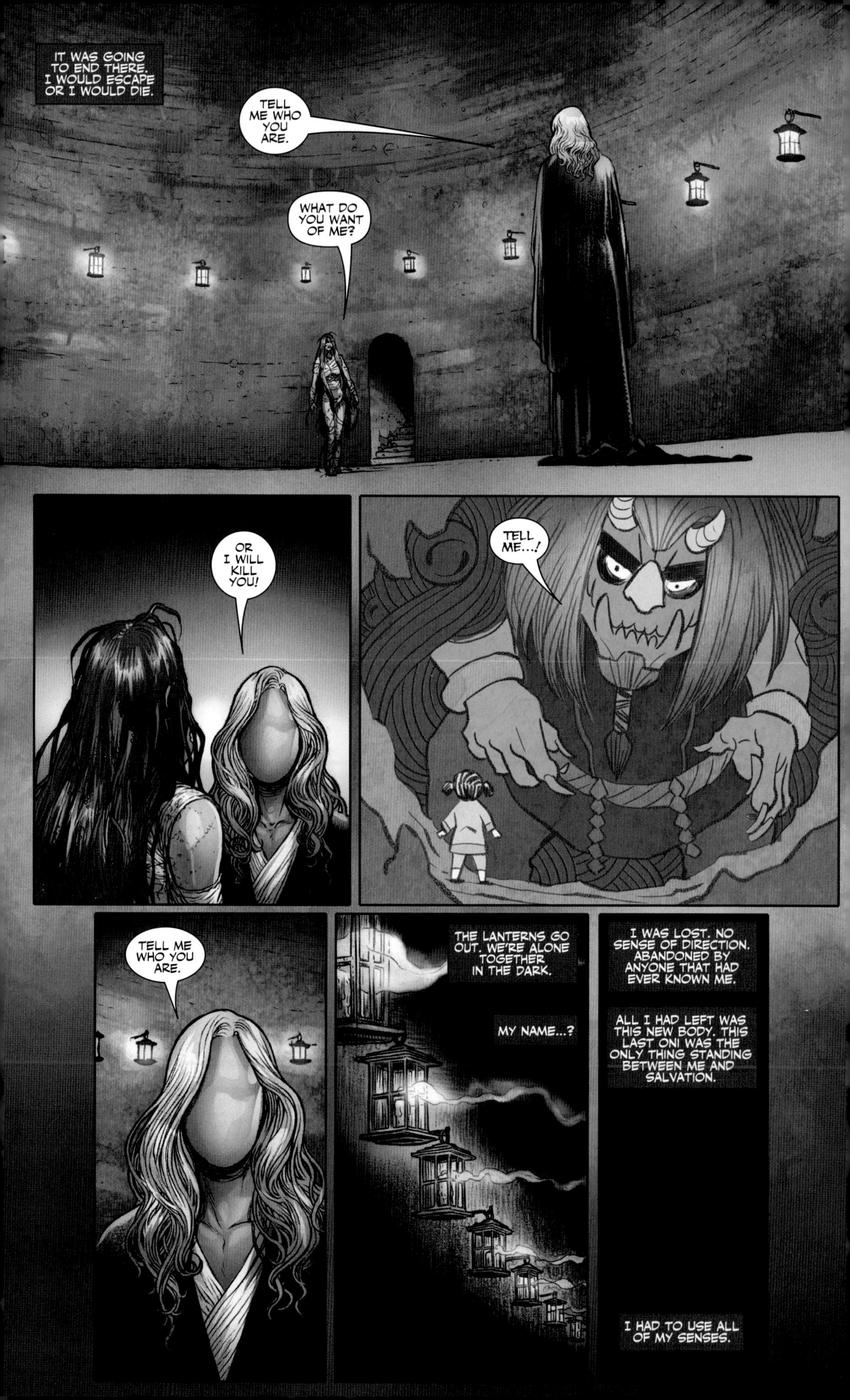
IT WAS GOING TO END THERE. I WOULD ESCAPE OR I WOULD DIE.
TELL ME WHO YOU ARE.
WHAT DO YOU WANT OF ME?
OR I WILL KILL YOU!
TELL ME...!
TELL ME WHO YOU ARE.
THE LANTERNS GO OUT. WE'RE ALONE TOGETHER IN THE DARK.
MY NAME...?
I WAS LOST. NO SENSE OF DIRECTION. ABANDONED BY ANYONE THAT HAD EVER KNOWN ME.
ALL I HAD LEFT WAS THIS NEW BODY. THIS LAST ONI WAS THE ONLY THING STANDING BETWEEN ME AND SALVATION.
I HAD TO USE ALL OF MY SENSES.

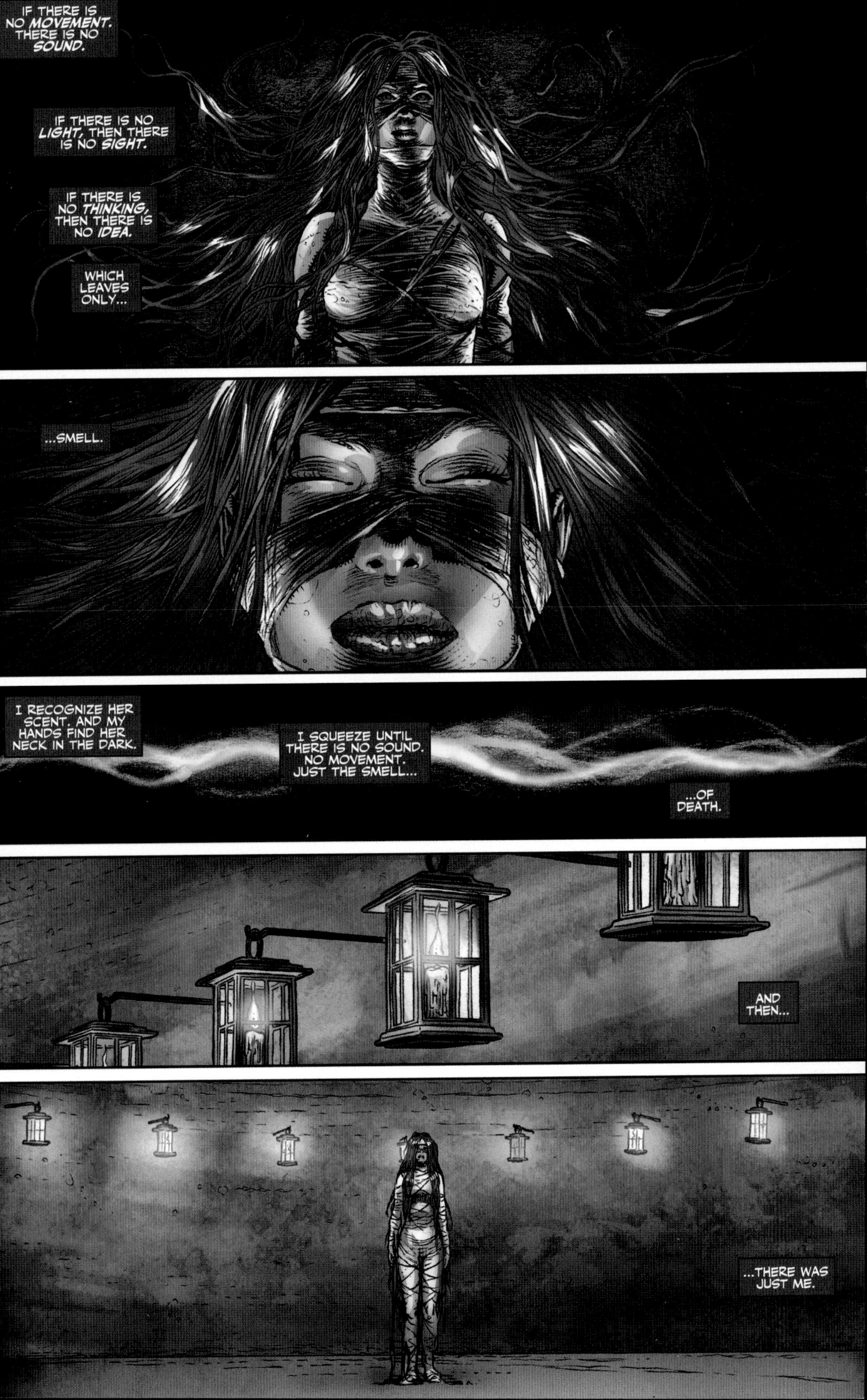
IF THERE IS NO *MOVEMENT*. THERE IS NO *SOUND*.
IF THERE IS NO *LIGHT*, THEN THERE IS NO *SIGHT*.
IF THERE IS NO *THINKING*, THEN THERE IS NO *IDEA*.
WHICH LEAVES ONLY...
...SMELL.
I RECOGNIZE HER SCENT. AND MY HANDS FIND HER NECK IN THE DARK.
I SQUEEZE UNTIL THERE IS NO SOUND. NO MOVEMENT. JUST THE SMELL...
...OF DEATH.
AND THEN...
...THERE WAS JUST ME.

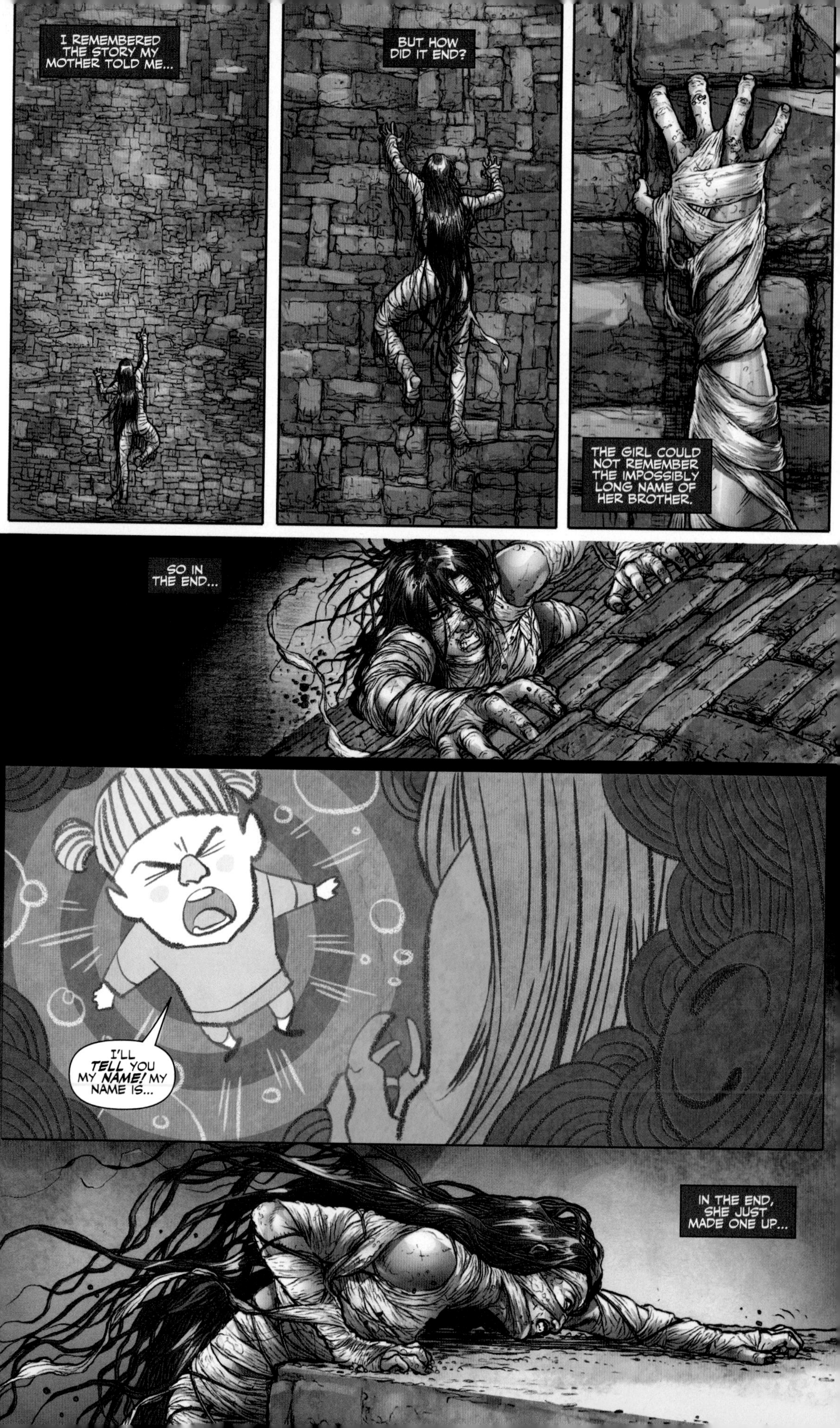

I REMEMBERED THE STORY MY MOTHER TOLD ME...
BUT HOW DID IT END?
THE GIRL COULD NOT REMEMBER THE IMPOSSIBLY LONG NAME OF HER BROTHER.
SO IN THE END...
I'LL TELL YOU MY NAME! MY NAME IS...
IN THE END, SHE JUST MADE ONE UP...

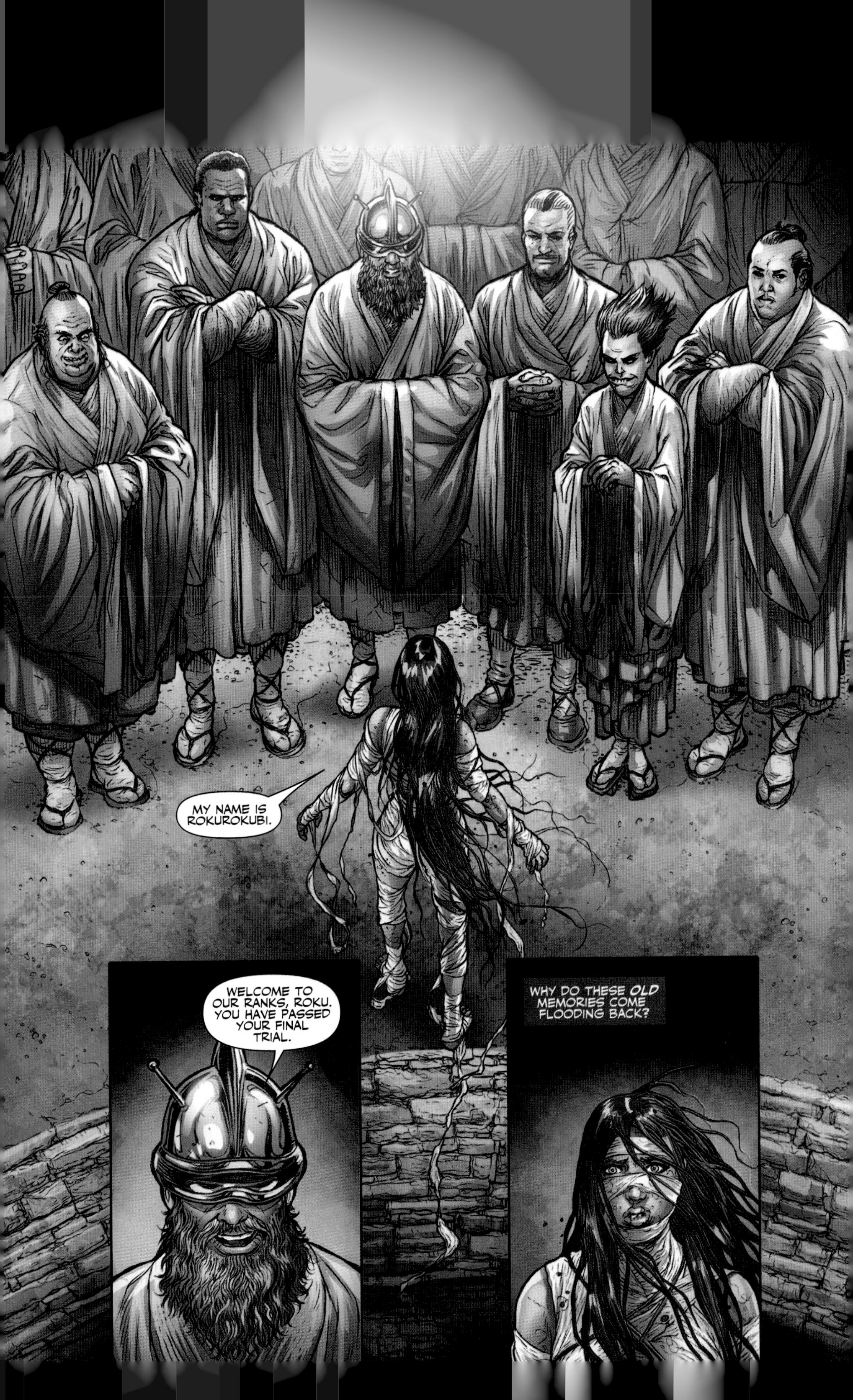
MY NAME IS ROKUROKUBI.
WELCOME TO OUR RANKS, ROKU. YOU HAVE PASSED YOUR FINAL TRIAL.
WHY DO THESE *OLD* MEMORIES COME FLOODING BACK?

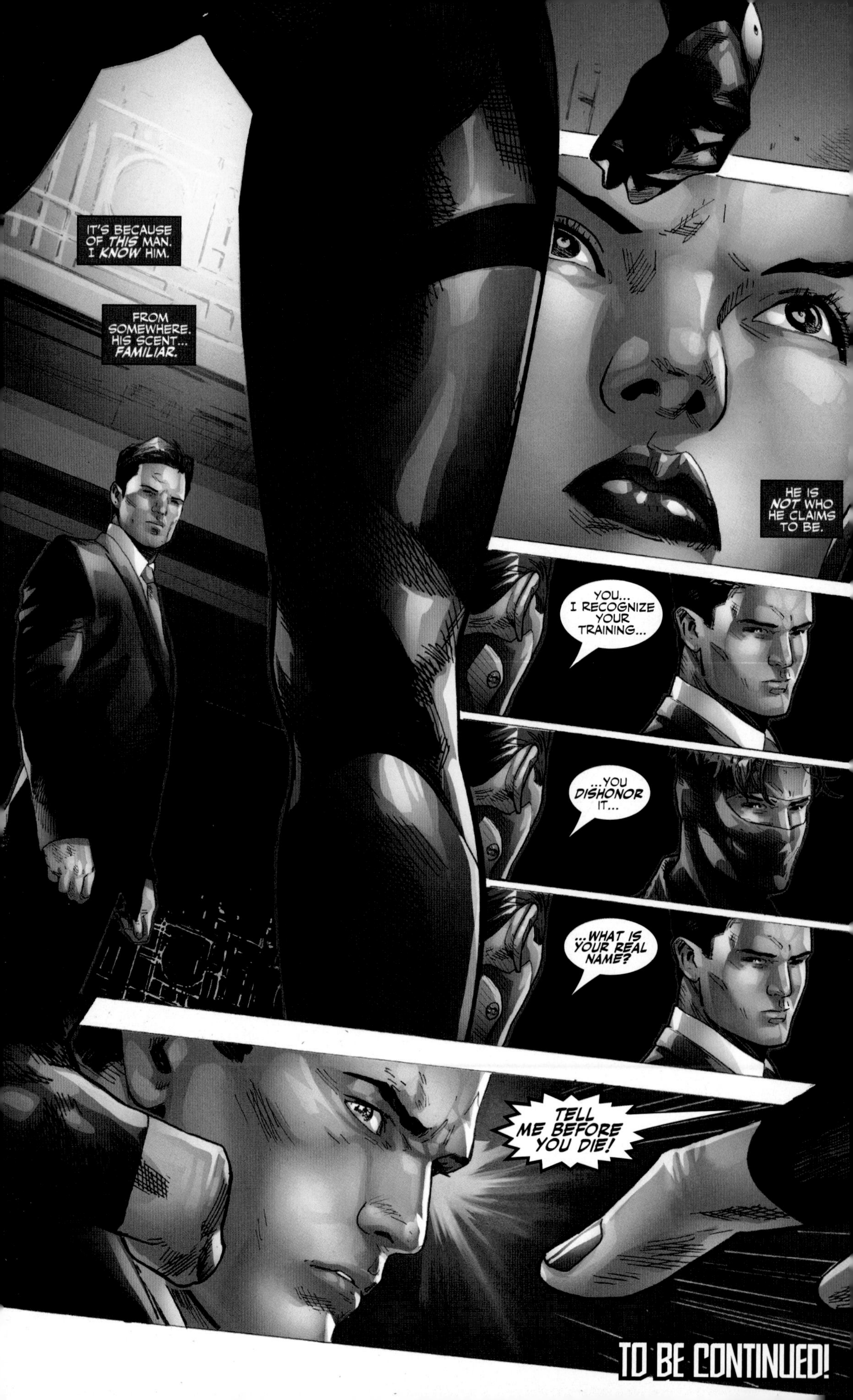
IT'S BECAUSE OF THIS MAN. I KNOW HIM.
FROM SOMEWHERE. HIS SCENT... FAMILIAR.
HE IS NOT WHO HE CLAIMS TO BE.
YOU... I RECOGNIZE YOUR TRAINING...
...YOU DISHONOR IT...
...WHAT IS YOUR REAL NAME?
TELL ME BEFORE YOU DIE!
TO BE CONTINUED!

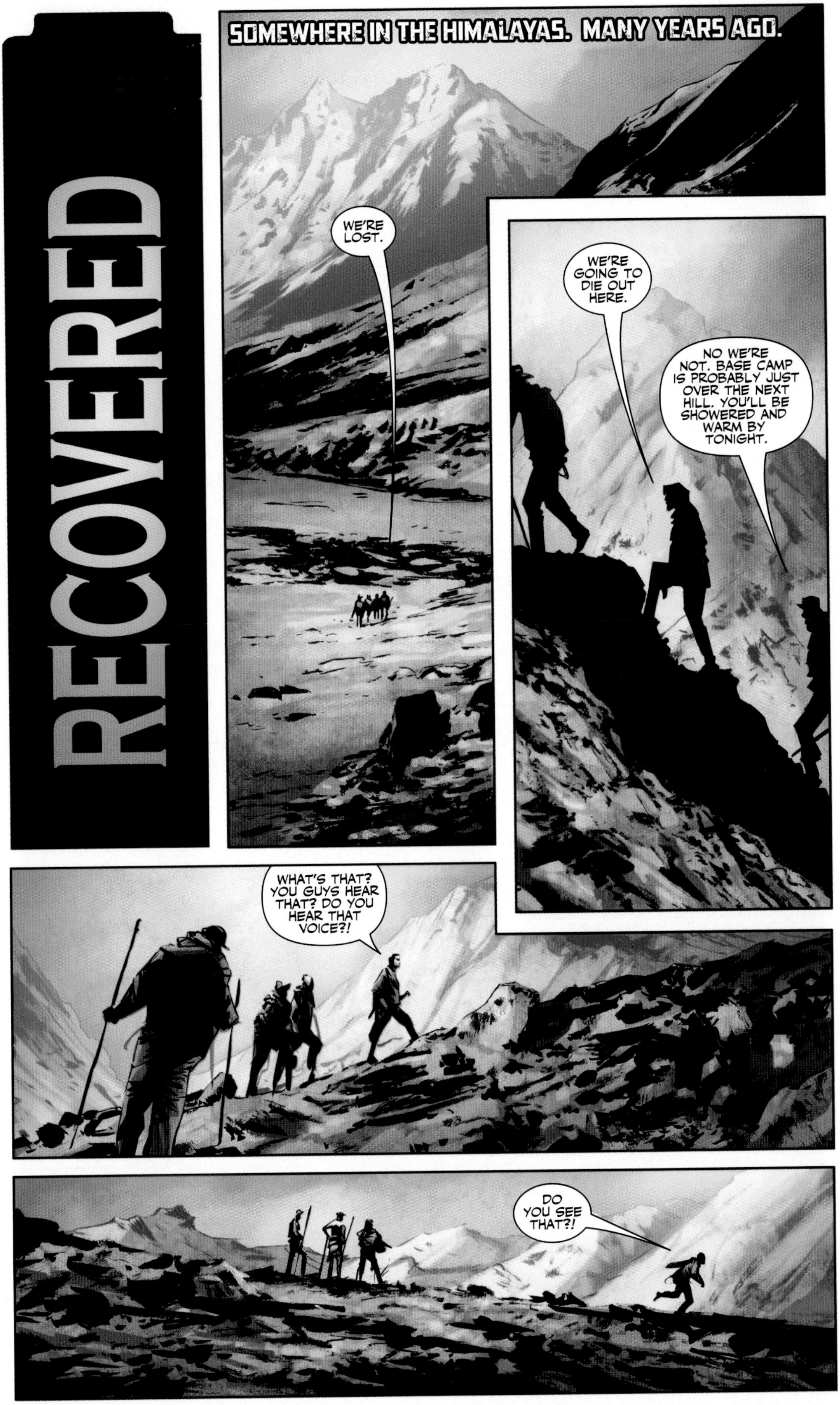
RECOVERED
SOMEWHERE IN THE HIMALAYAS. MANY YEARS AGO.
WE'RE LOST.
WE'RE GOING TO DIE OUT HERE.
NO WE'RE NOT. BASE CAMP IS PROBABLY JUST OVER THE NEXT HILL. YOU'LL BE SHOWERED AND WARM BY TONIGHT.
WHAT'S THAT? YOU GUYS HEAR THAT? DO YOU HEAR THAT VOICE?!
DO YOU SEE THAT?!

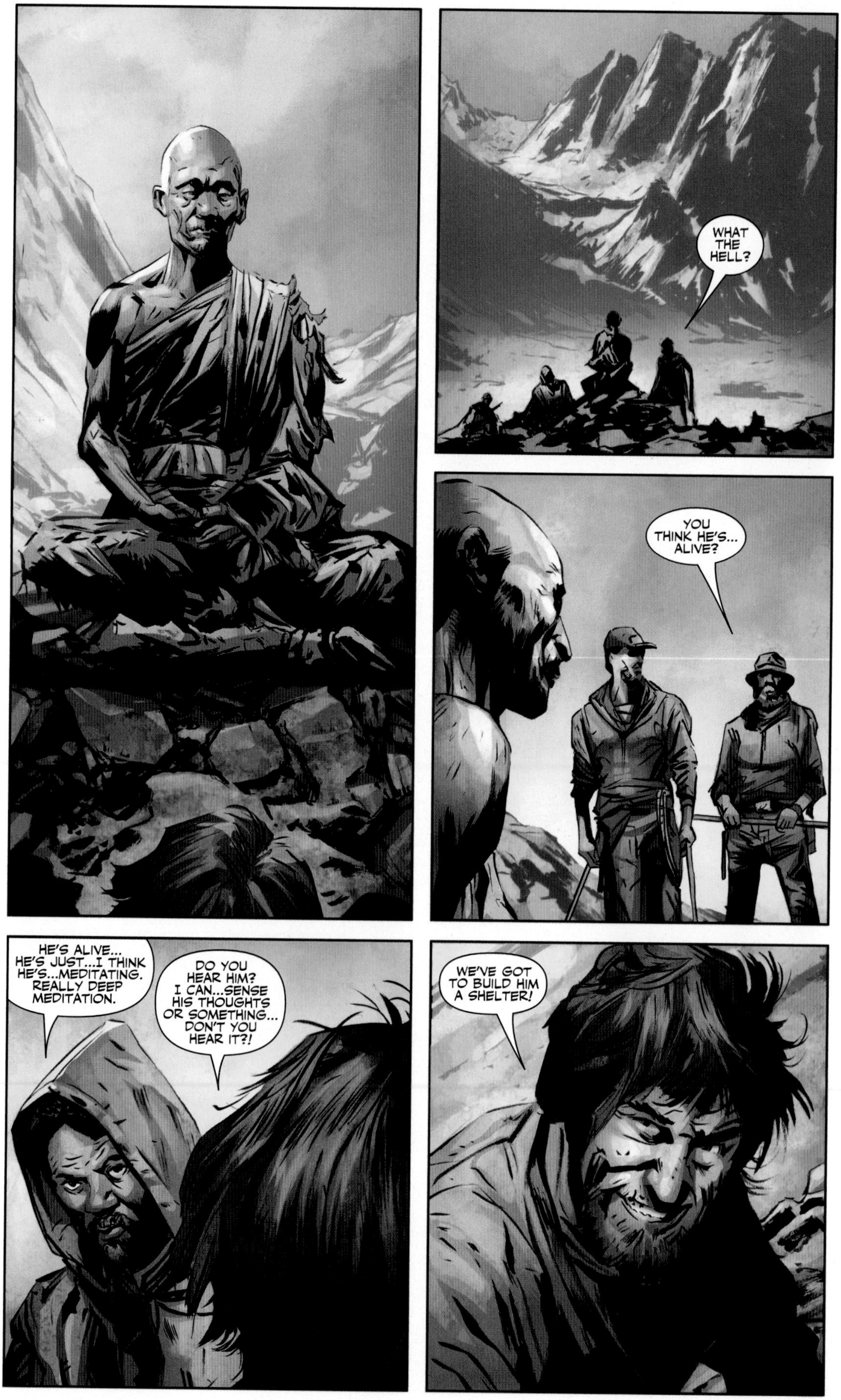
WHAT THE HELL?
YOU THINK HE'S... ALIVE?
HE'S ALIVE... HE'S JUST...I THINK HE'S...MEDITATING. REALLY DEEP MEDITATION.
DO YOU HEAR HIM? I CAN...SENSE HIS THOUGHTS OR SOMETHING... DON'T YOU HEAR IT?!
WE'VE GOT TO BUILD HIM A SHELTER!

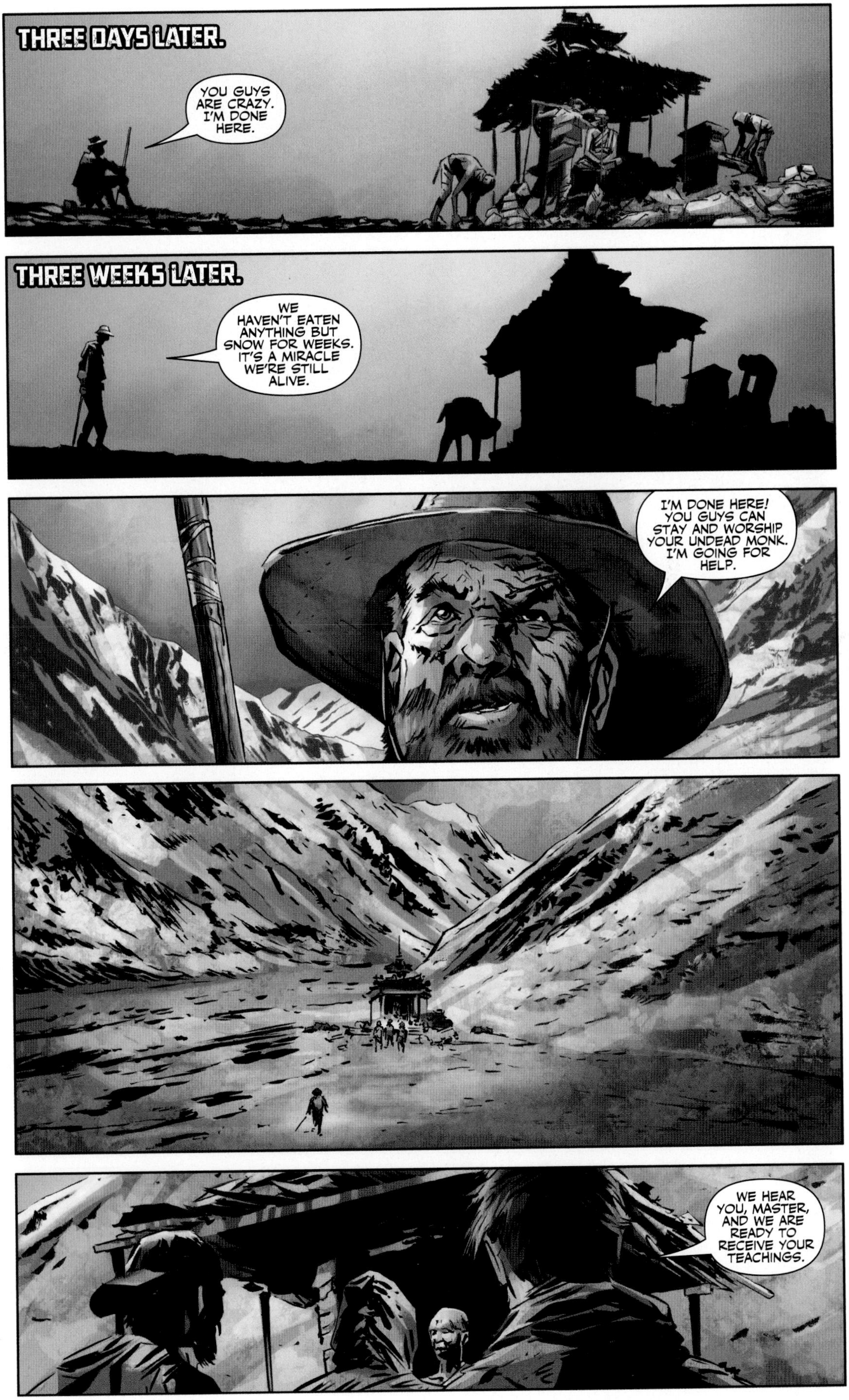
THREE DAYS LATER.
YOU GUYS ARE CRAZY. I'M DONE HERE.
THREE WEEKS LATER.
WE HAVEN'T EATEN ANYTHING BUT SNOW FOR WEEKS. IT'S A MIRACLE WE'RE STILL ALIVE.
I'M DONE HERE! YOU GUYS CAN STAY AND WORSHIP YOUR UNDEAD MONK. I'M GOING FOR HELP.
WE HEAR YOU, MASTER, AND WE ARE READY TO RECEIVE YOUR TEACHINGS.

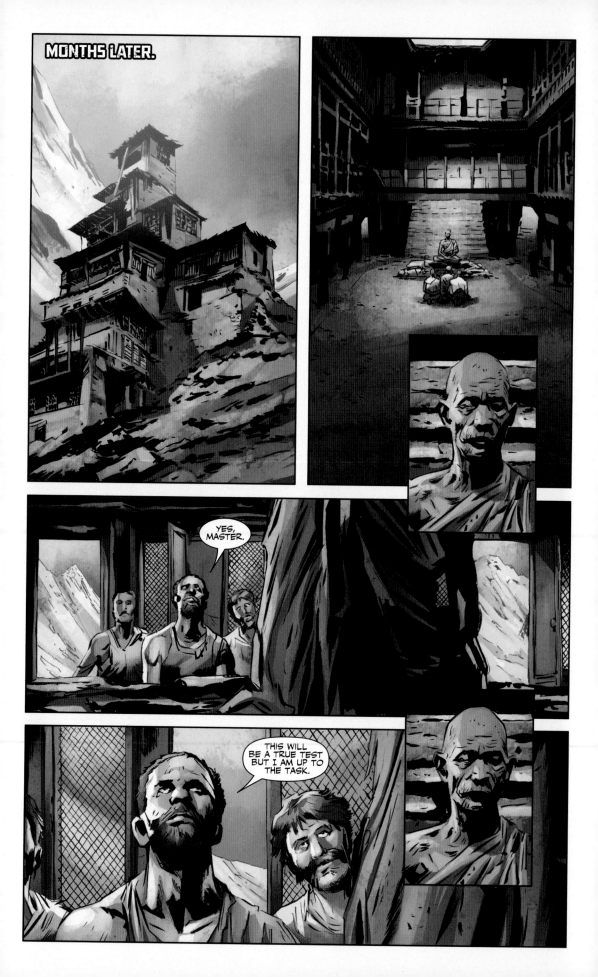

MONTHS LATER.

YES, MASTER.

THIS WILL BE A TRUE TEST BUT I AM UP TO THE TASK.

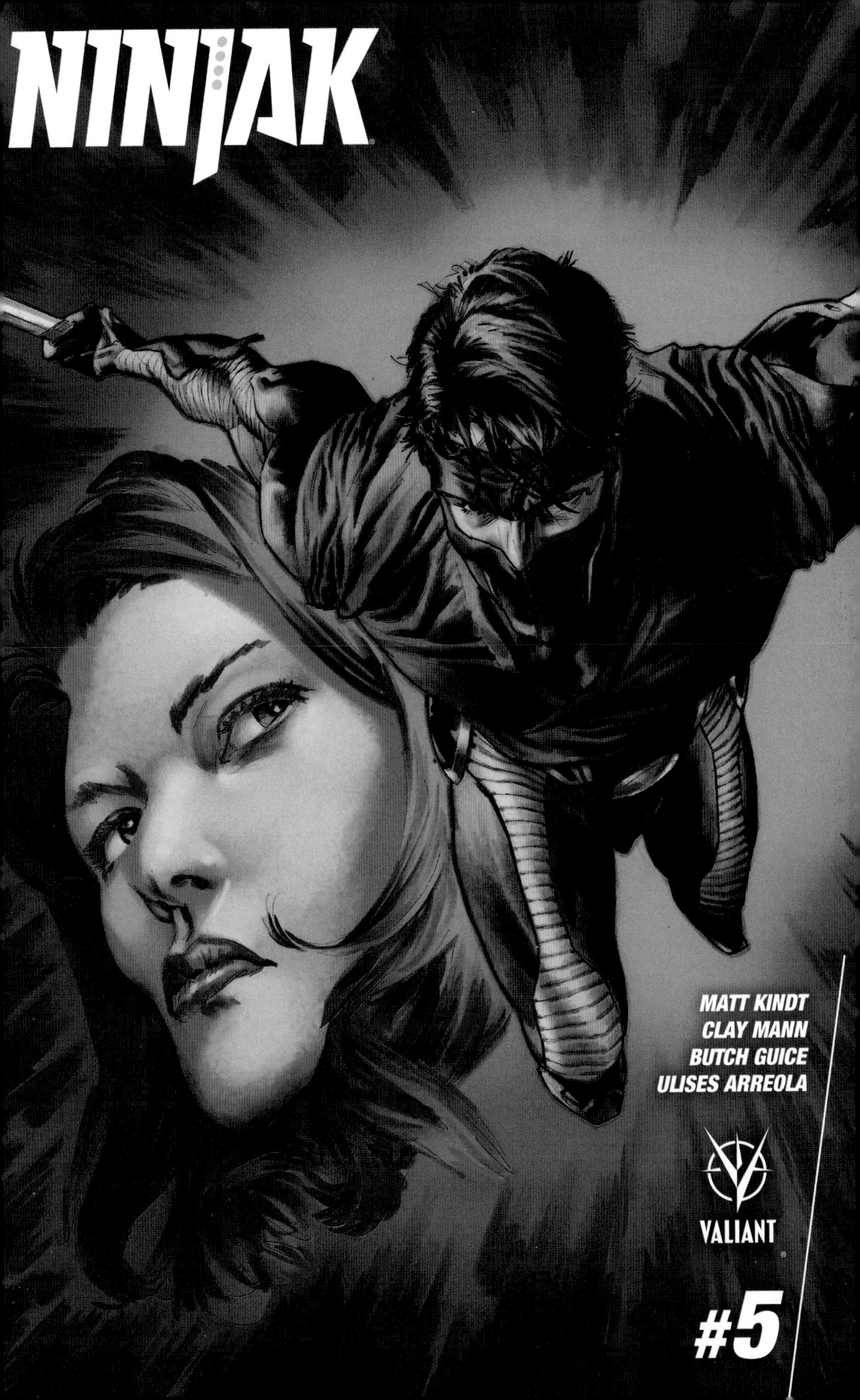
NINJAK
MATT KINDT
CLAY MANN
BUTCH GUICE
ULISES ARREOLA
VALIANT
#5

CLASSIFIED

NINJAK SPECIFICATIONS
& INSIGHTS

Battle Vest

TITANIUM IMPACT RESISTANT CAGE
He has established a wide range of contacts in order to shield himself from any unwanted outside relationships and/or personal contact.

HEART FIBRILLATION CONTROL
A strained relationship with parents is thought to be the reason that he has trouble [redacted]

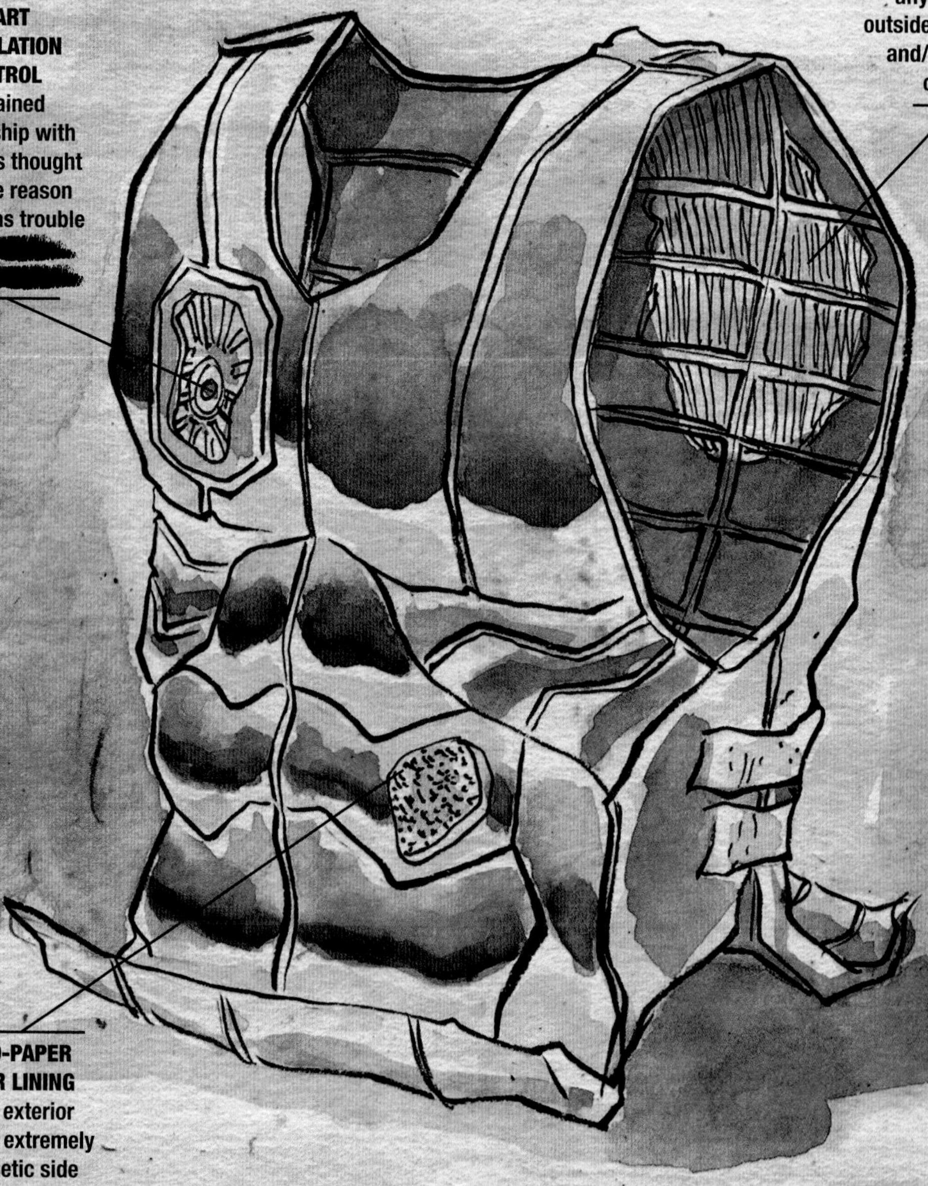

MICRO-PAPER ARMOR LINING
Colin's exterior belies an extremely empathetic side that is rarely exposed.

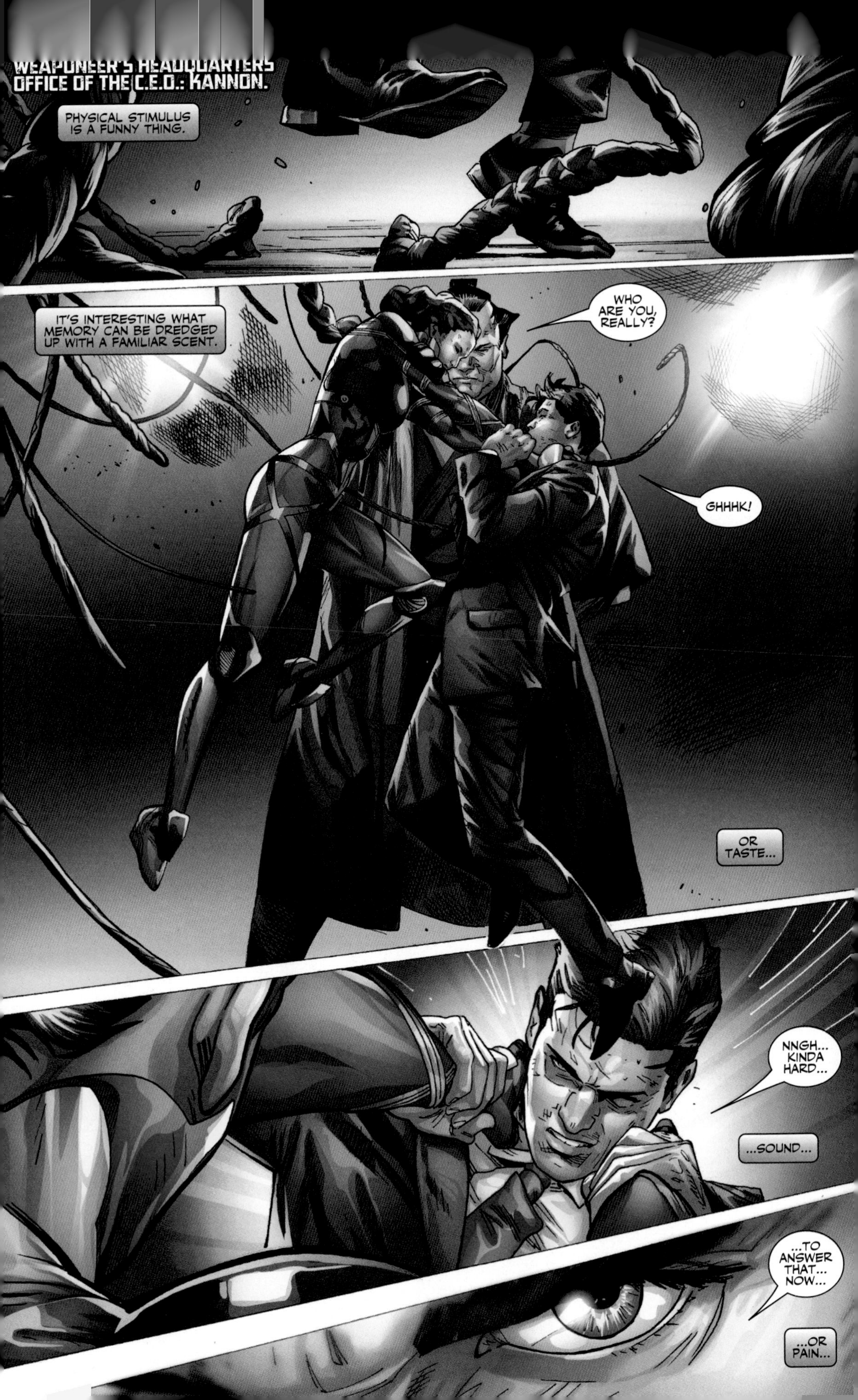
WEAPONEER'S HEADQUARTERS
OFFICE OF THE C.E.O.: KANNON.
PHYSICAL STIMULUS IS A FUNNY THING.
IT'S INTERESTING WHAT MEMORY CAN BE DREDGED UP WITH A FAMILIAR SCENT.
WHO ARE YOU, REALLY?
GHHHK!
OR TASTE...
NNGH... KINDA HARD...
...SOUND...
...TO ANSWER THAT... NOW...
...OR PAIN...

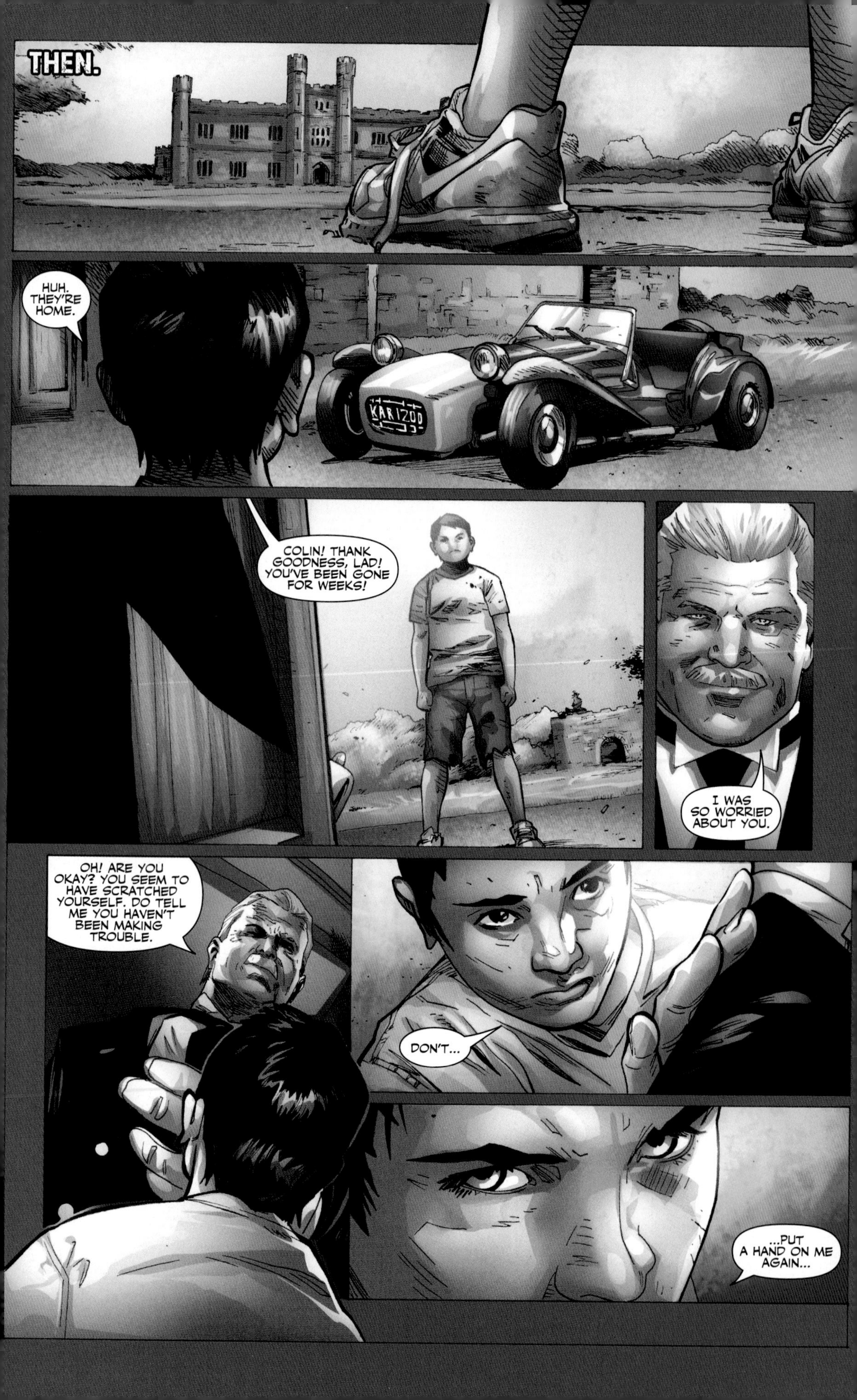
THEN.
HUH. THEY'RE HOME.
KARIZOD
COLIN! THANK GOODNESS, LAD! YOU'VE BEEN GONE FOR WEEKS!
I WAS SO WORRIED ABOUT YOU.
OH! ARE YOU OKAY? YOU SEEM TO HAVE SCRATCHED YOURSELF. DO TELL ME YOU HAVEN'T BEEN MAKING TROUBLE.
DON'T...
...PUT A HAND ON ME AGAIN...

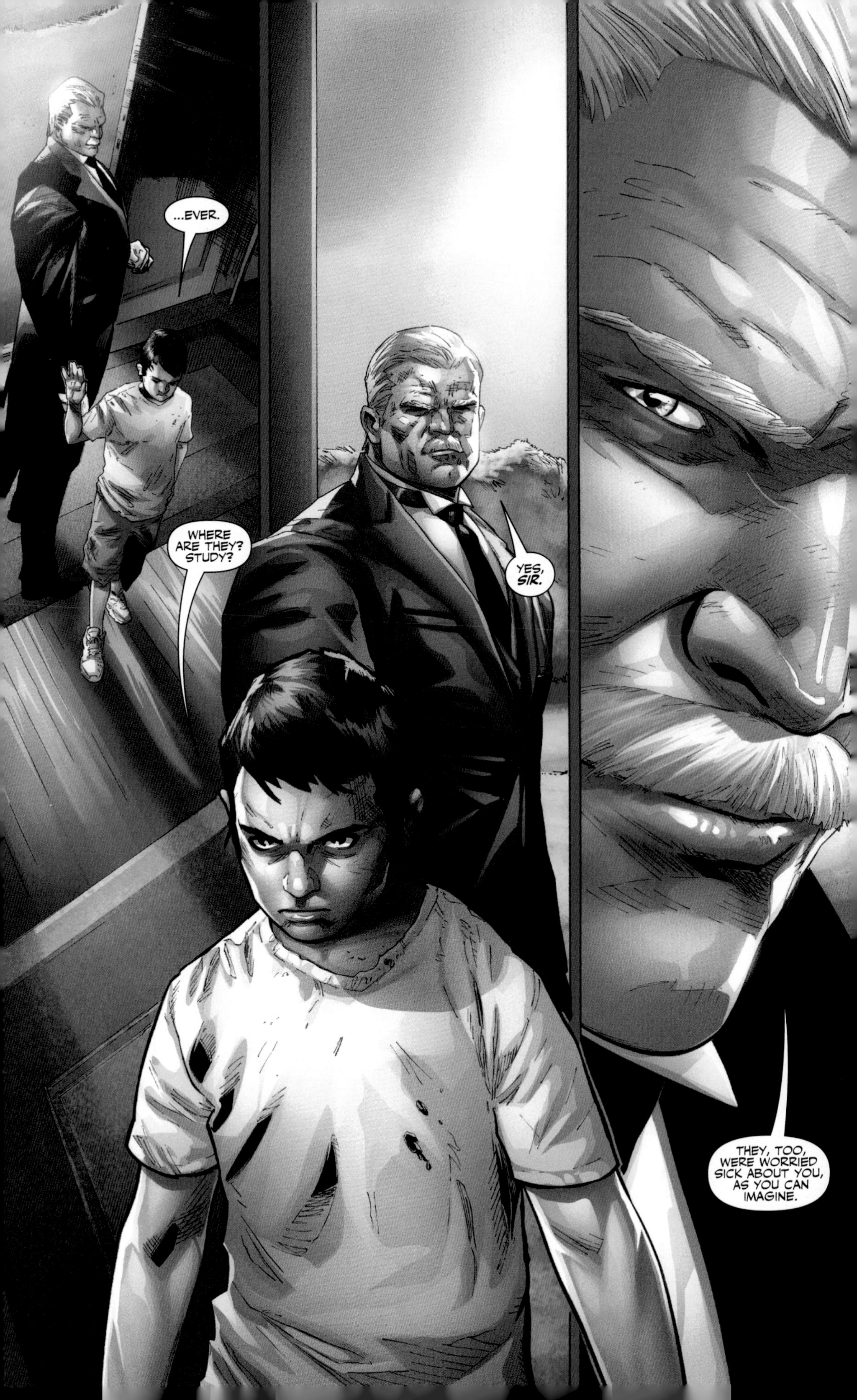
...EVER.
WHERE ARE THEY? STUDY?
YES, SIR.
THEY, TOO, WERE WORRIED SICK ABOUT YOU, AS YOU CAN IMAGINE.

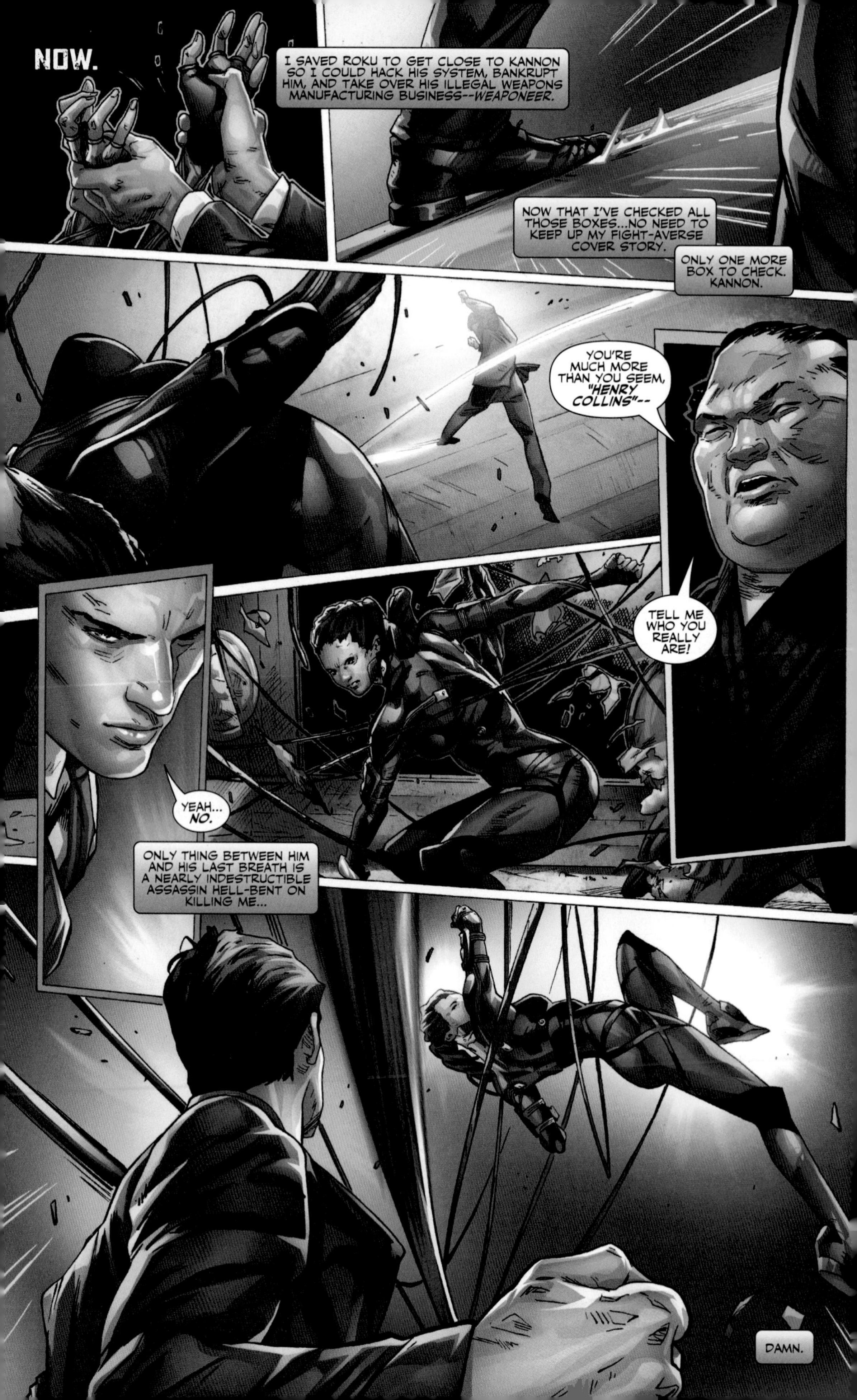
NOW.
I SAVED ROKU TO GET CLOSE TO KANNON SO I COULD HACK HIS SYSTEM, BANKRUPT HIM, AND TAKE OVER HIS ILLEGAL WEAPONS MANUFACTURING BUSINESS--WEAPONEER.
NOW THAT I'VE CHECKED ALL THOSE BOXES...NO NEED TO KEEP UP MY FIGHT-AVERSE COVER STORY.
ONLY ONE MORE BOX TO CHECK. KANNON.
YOU'RE MUCH MORE THAN YOU SEEM, "HENRY COLLINS"--
TELL ME WHO YOU REALLY ARE!
YEAH... NO.
ONLY THING BETWEEN HIM AND HIS LAST BREATH IS A NEARLY INDESTRUCTIBLE ASSASSIN HELL-BENT ON KILLING ME...
DAMN.

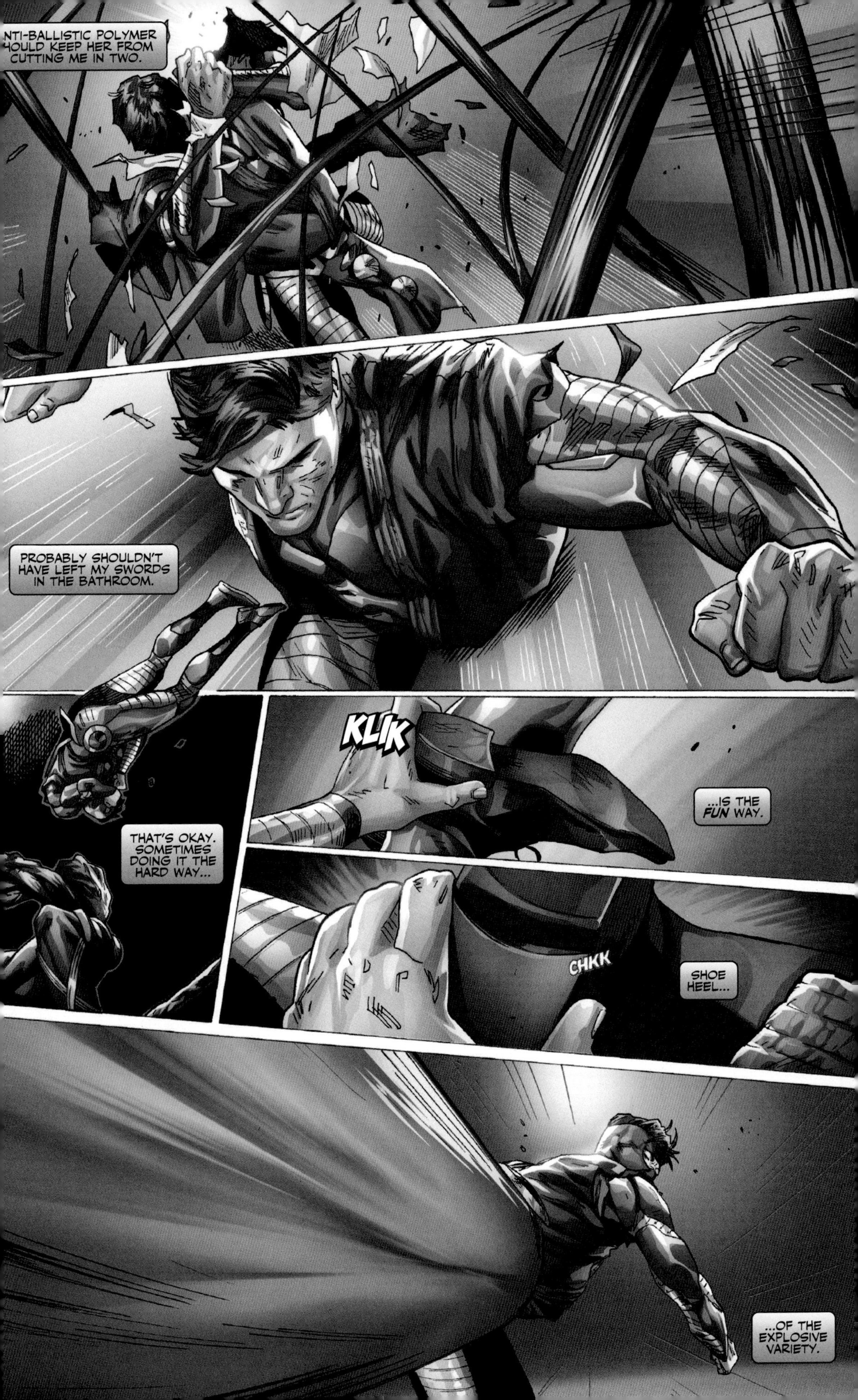

NTI-BALLISTIC POLYMER
HOULD KEEP HER FROM
CUTTING ME IN TWO.
PROBABLY SHOULDN'T HAVE LEFT MY SWORDS IN THE BATHROOM.
THAT'S OKAY. SOMETIMES DOING IT THE HARD WAY...
KLIK
...IS THE FUN WAY.
CHKK
SHOE HEEL...
...OF THE EXPLOSIVE VARIETY.

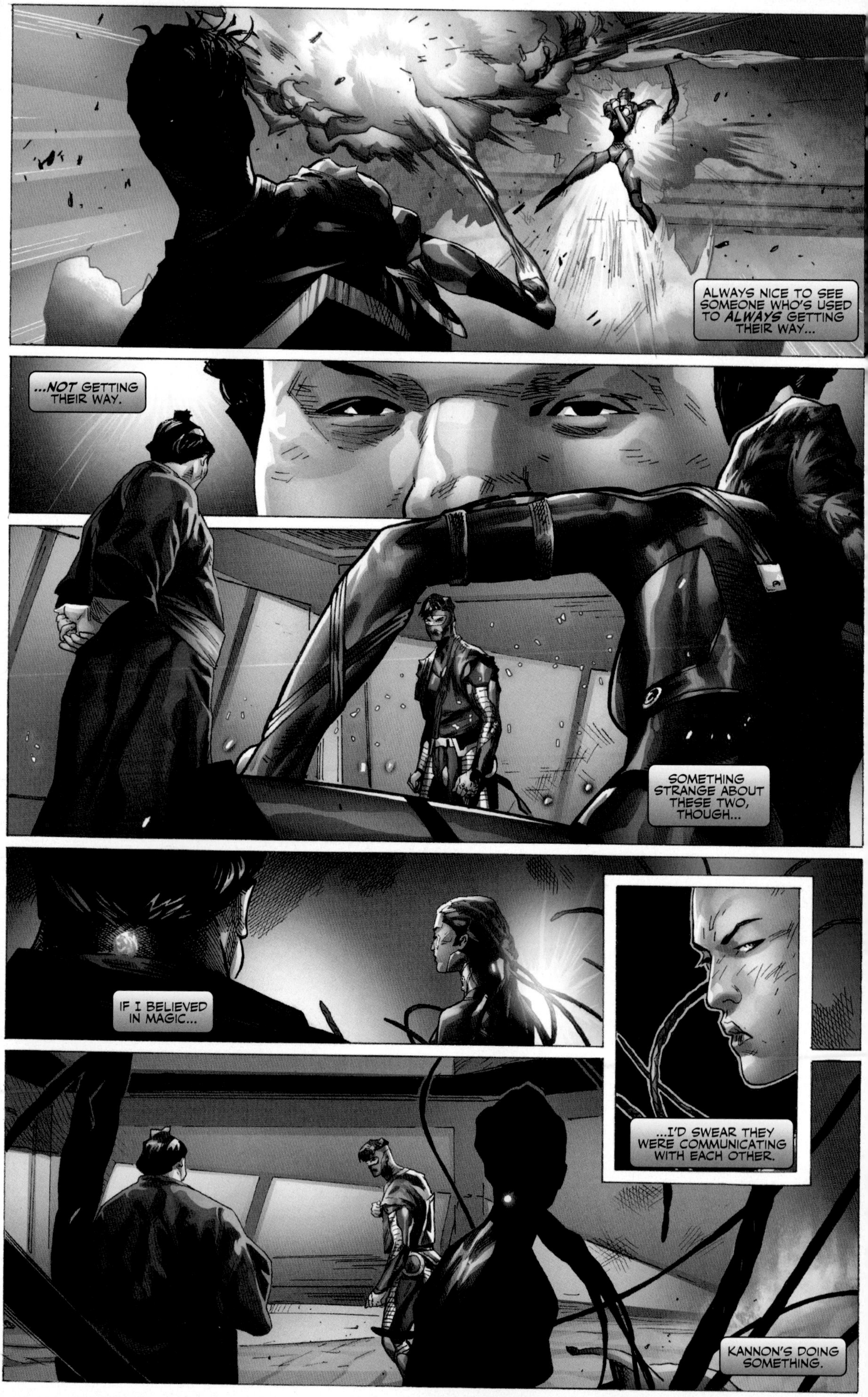
ALWAYS NICE TO SEE SOMEONE WHO'S USED TO *ALWAYS* GETTING THEIR WAY...
...*NOT* GETTING THEIR WAY.
SOMETHING STRANGE ABOUT THESE TWO, THOUGH...
IF I BELIEVED IN MAGIC...
...I'D SWEAR THEY WERE COMMUNICATING WITH EACH OTHER.
KANNON'S DOING SOMETHING.

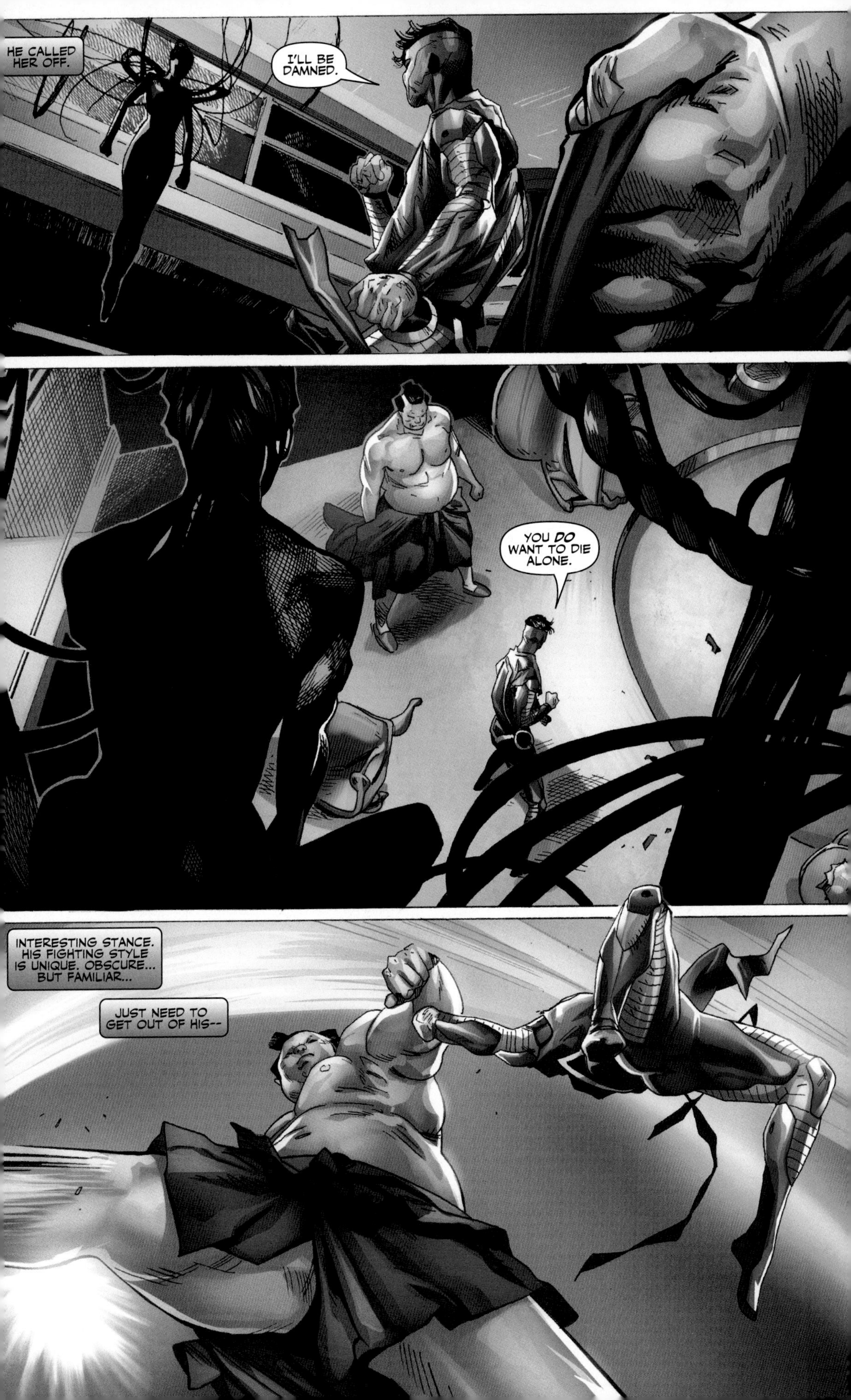

HE CALLED HER OFF.
I'LL BE DAMNED.
YOU DO WANT TO DIE ALONE.
INTERESTING STANCE. HIS FIGHTING STYLE IS UNIQUE. OBSCURE... BUT FAMILIAR...
JUST NEED TO GET OUT OF HIS--

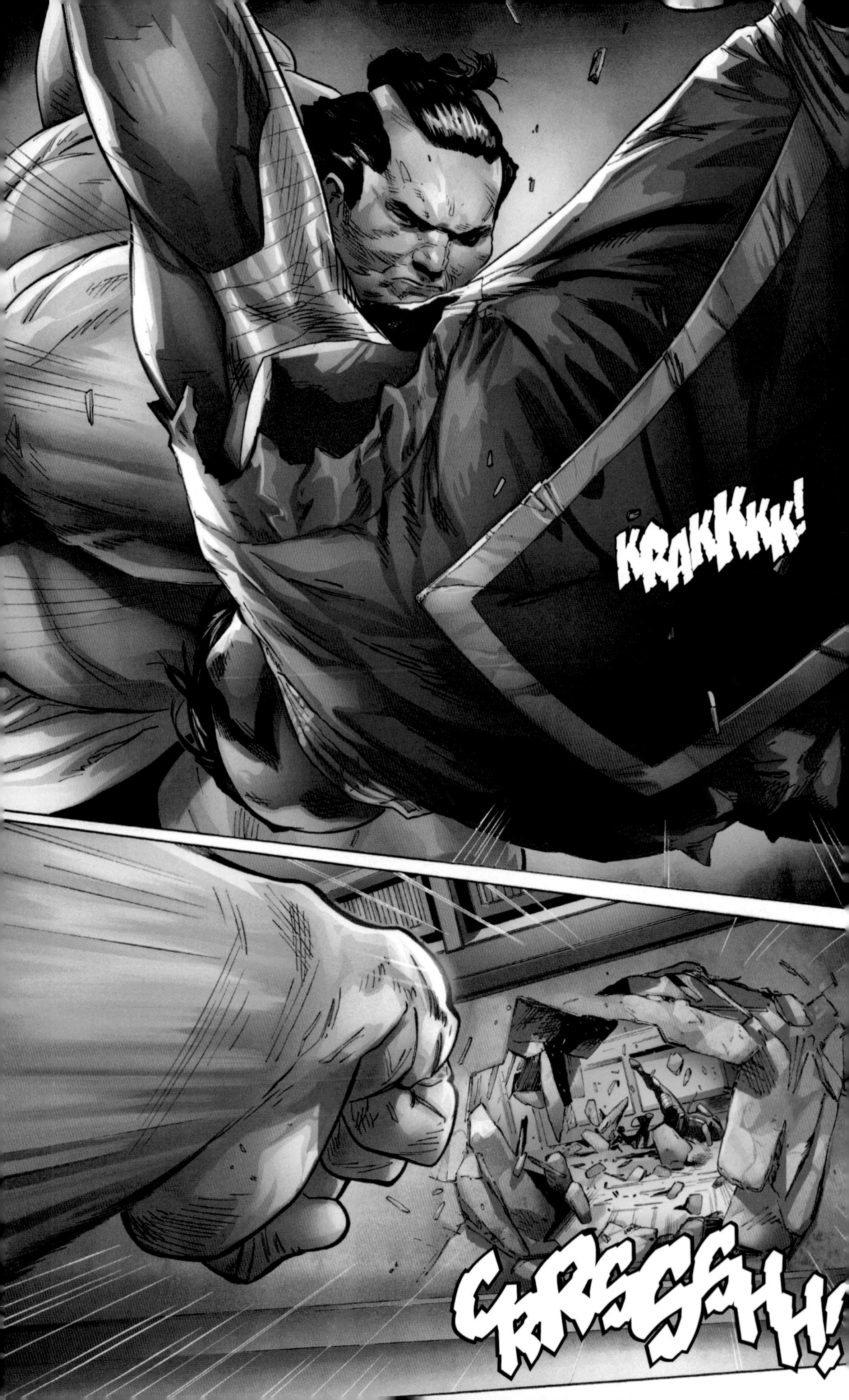
KRAKKKK!
CRRSSSHH!

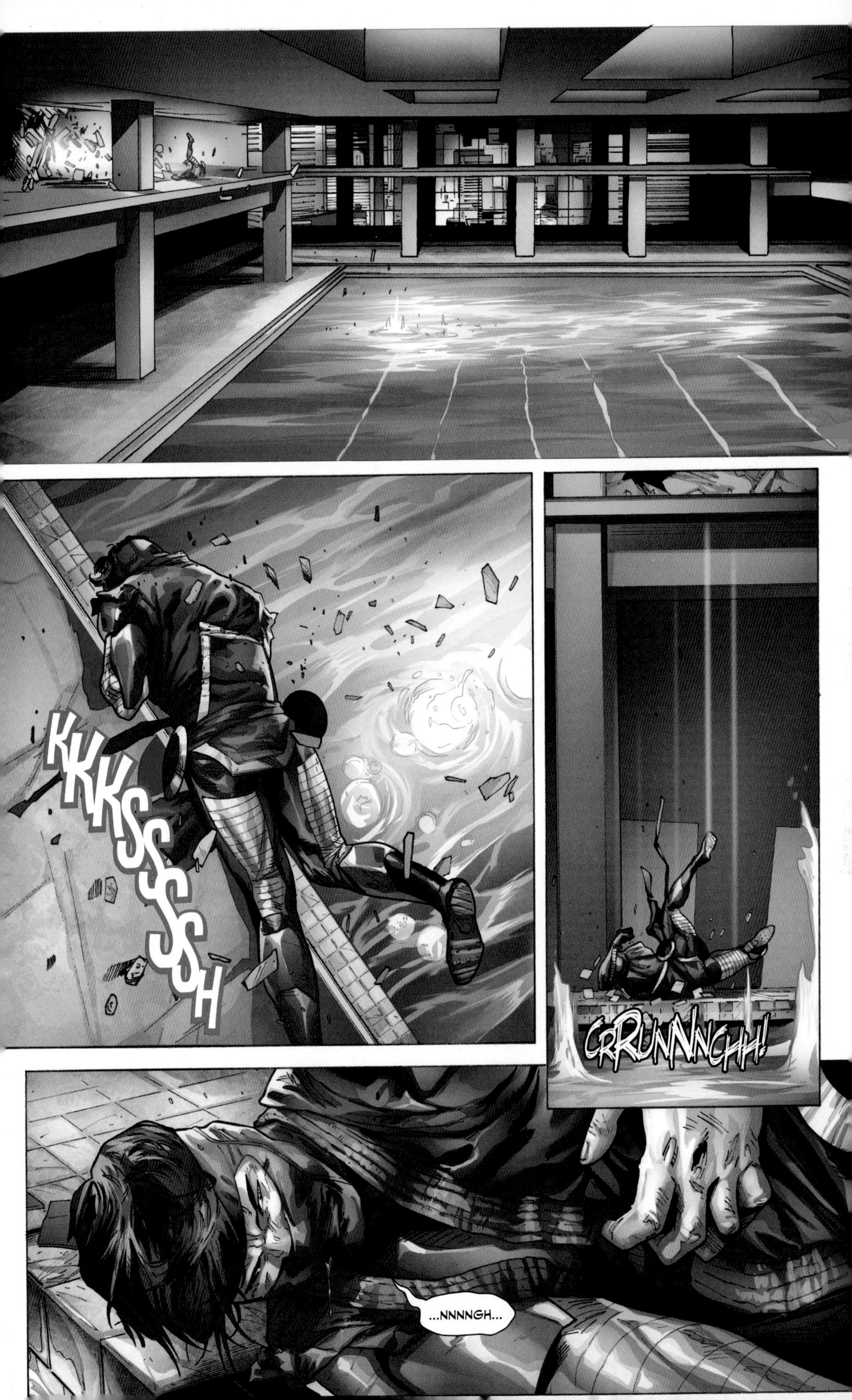

KKKSSSSSH
CRRUNNNCHH!
...NNNNGH...

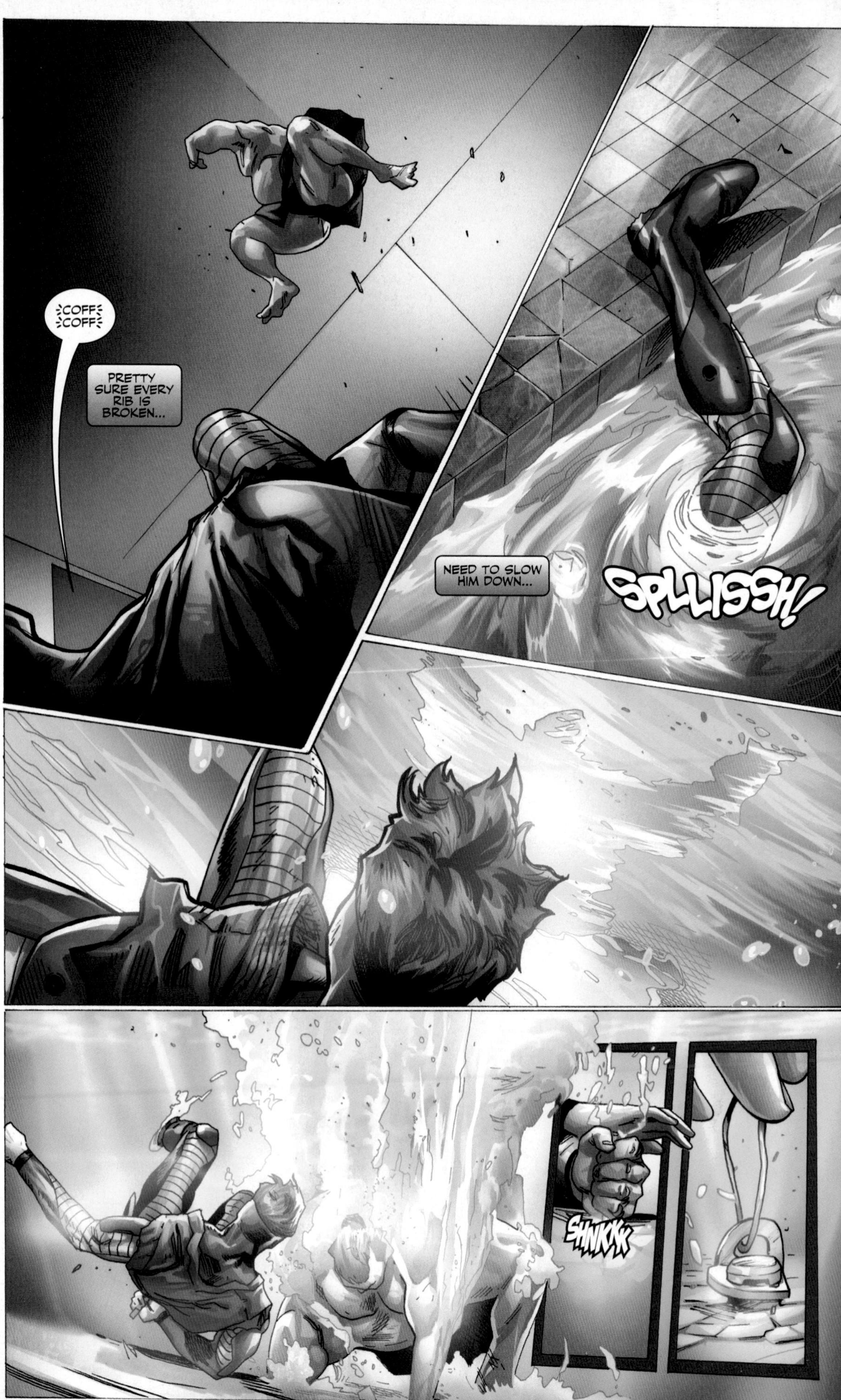
COFF COFF
PRETTY SURE EVERY RIB IS BROKEN...
NEED TO SLOW HIM DOWN...
SPLLISSH!
SHNKKK

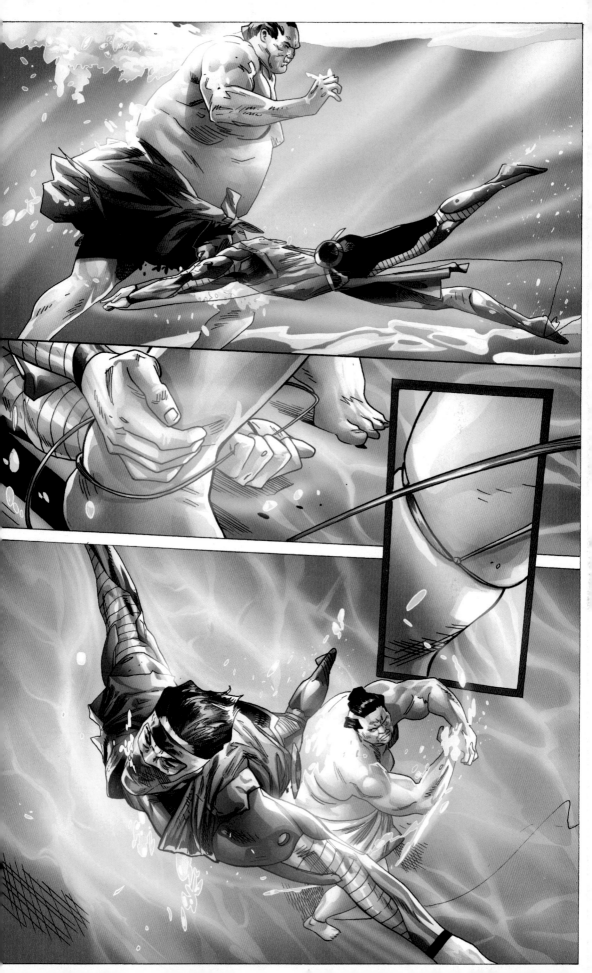

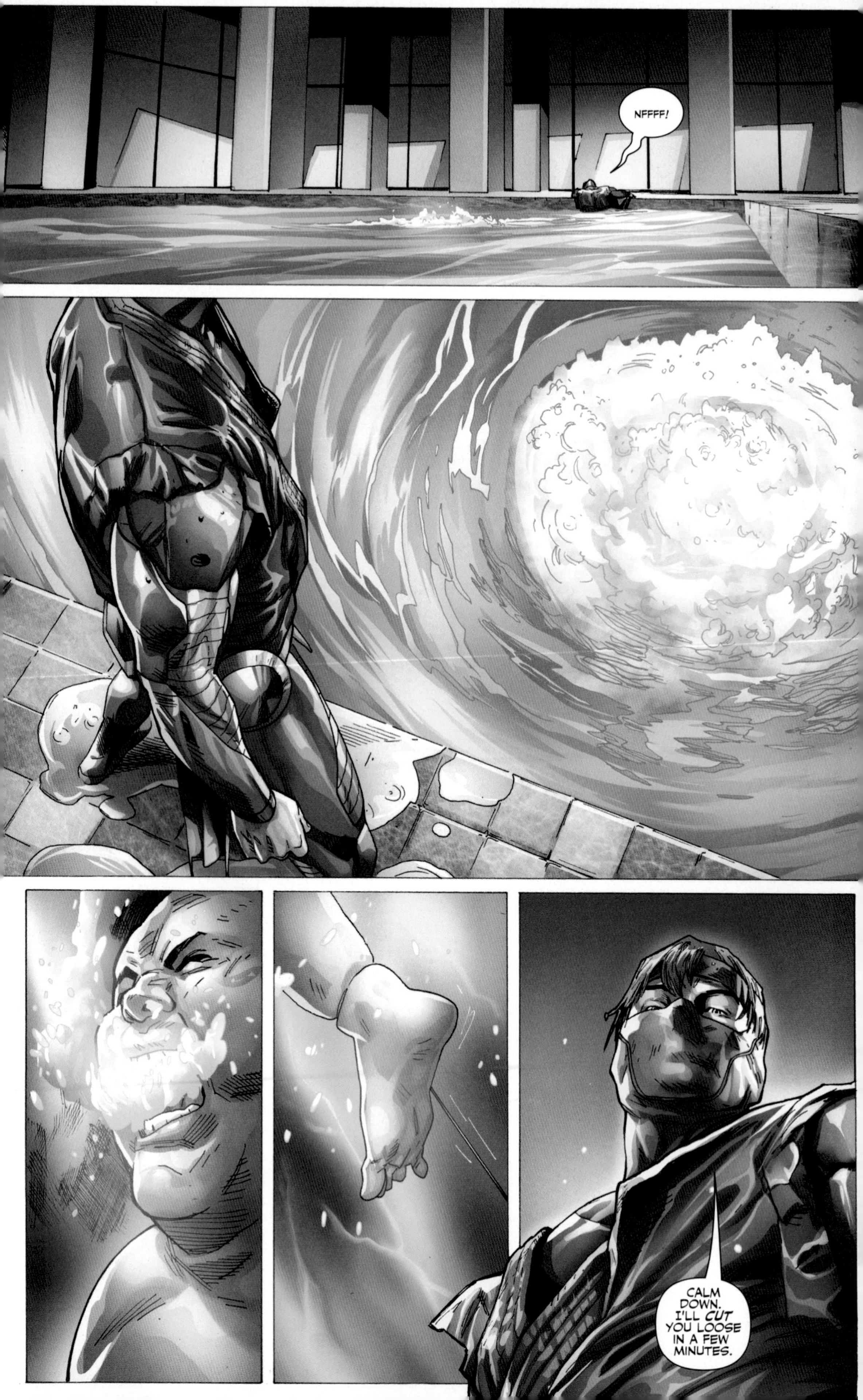
NFFFF!
CALM DOWN. I'LL *CUT* YOU LOOSE IN A FEW MINUTES.

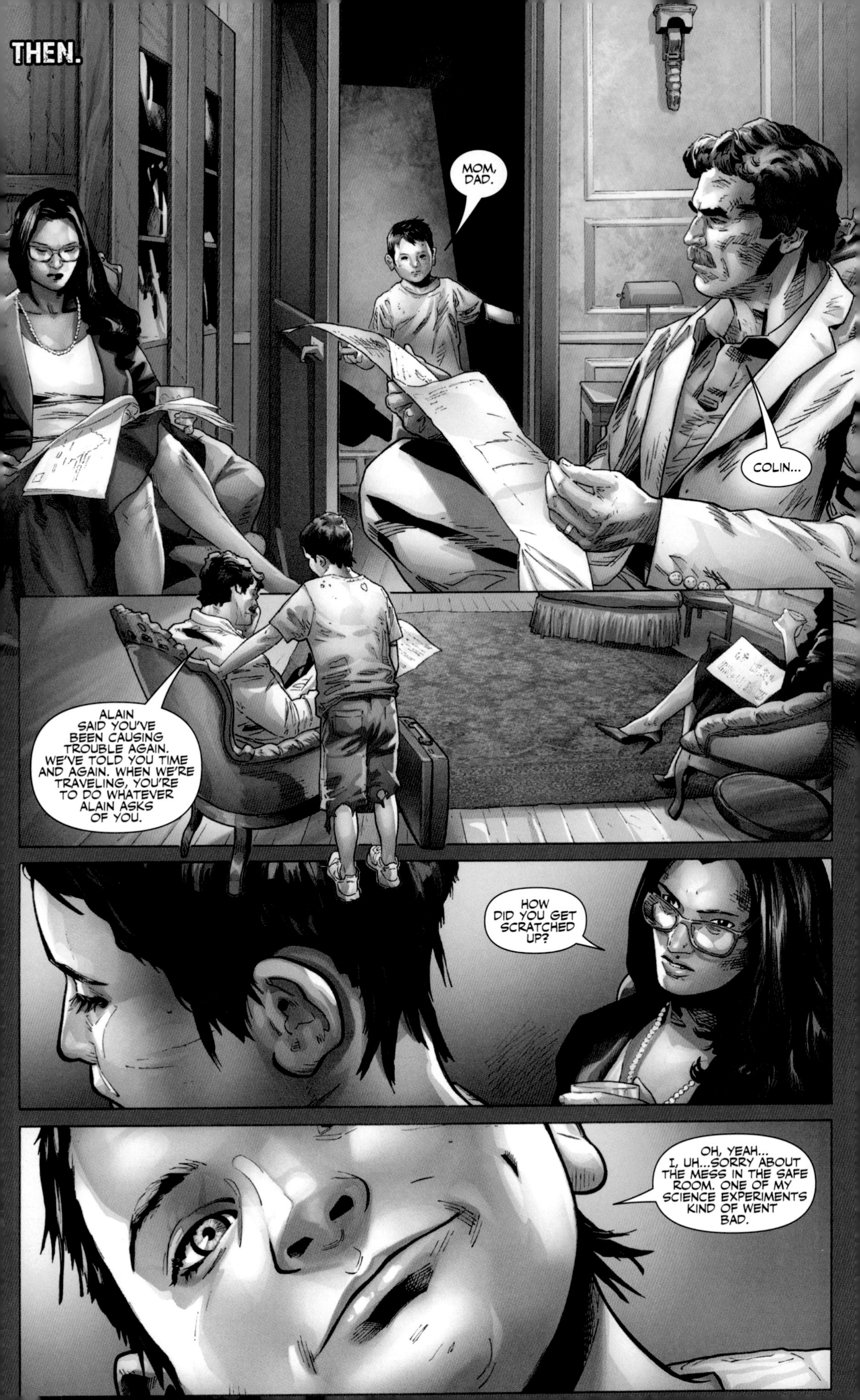
THEN.
MOM, DAD.
COLIN...
ALAIN SAID YOU'VE BEEN CAUSING TROUBLE AGAIN. WE'VE TOLD YOU TIME AND AGAIN. WHEN WE'RE TRAVELING, YOU'RE TO DO WHATEVER ALAIN ASKS OF YOU.
HOW DID YOU GET SCRATCHED UP?
OH, YEAH... I, UH...SORRY ABOUT THE MESS IN THE SAFE ROOM. ONE OF MY SCIENCE EXPERIMENTS KIND OF WENT BAD.

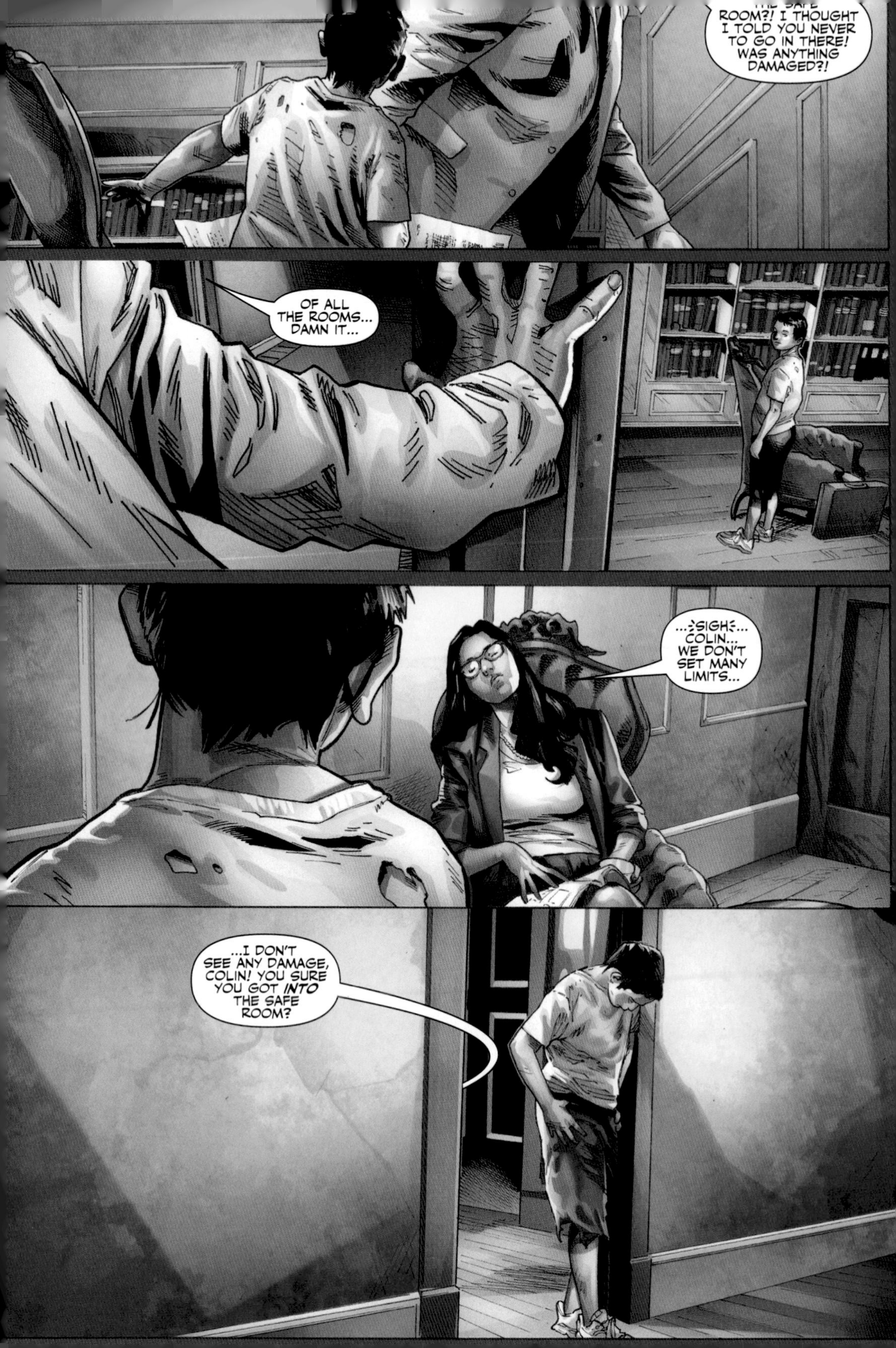
ROOM?! I THOUGHT I TOLD YOU NEVER TO GO IN THERE! WAS ANYTHING DAMAGED?!
OF ALL THE ROOMS... DAMN IT...
...SIGH... COLIN... WE DON'T SET MANY LIMITS...
...I DON'T SEE ANY DAMAGE, COLIN! YOU SURE YOU GOT INTO THE SAFE ROOM?

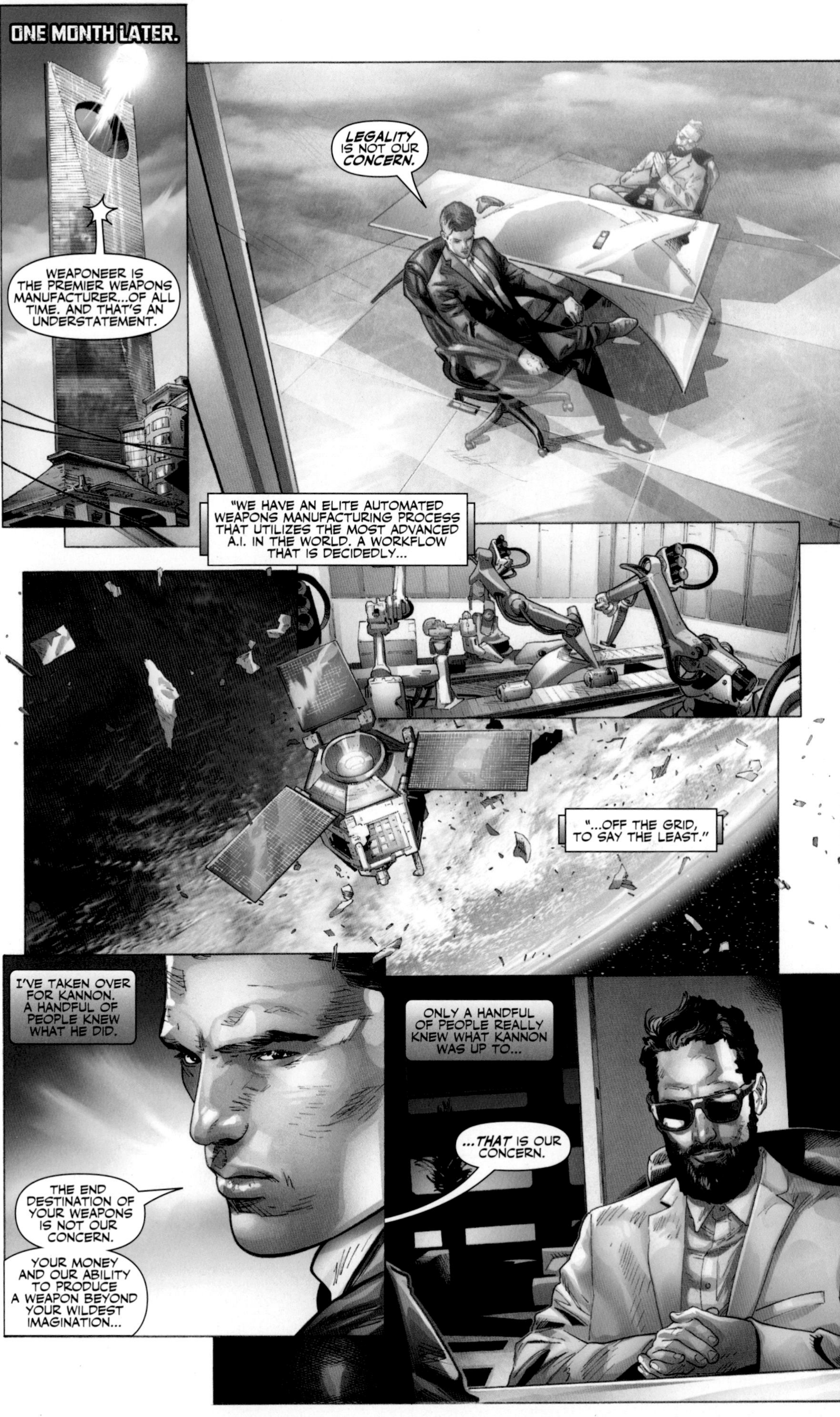
ONE MONTH LATER.
WEAPONEER IS THE PREMIER WEAPONS MANUFACTURER...OF ALL TIME. AND THAT'S AN UNDERSTATEMENT.
LEGALITY IS NOT OUR CONCERN.
"WE HAVE AN ELITE AUTOMATED WEAPONS MANUFACTURING PROCESS THAT UTILIZES THE MOST ADVANCED A.I. IN THE WORLD. A WORKFLOW THAT IS DECIDEDLY...
"...OFF THE GRID, TO SAY THE LEAST."
I'VE TAKEN OVER FOR KANNON. A HANDFUL OF PEOPLE KNEW WHAT HE DID.
THE END DESTINATION OF YOUR WEAPONS IS NOT OUR CONCERN.
YOUR MONEY AND OUR ABILITY TO PRODUCE A WEAPON BEYOND YOUR WILDEST IMAGINATION...
ONLY A HANDFUL OF PEOPLE REALLY KNEW WHAT KANNON WAS UP TO...
...THAT IS OUR CONCERN.

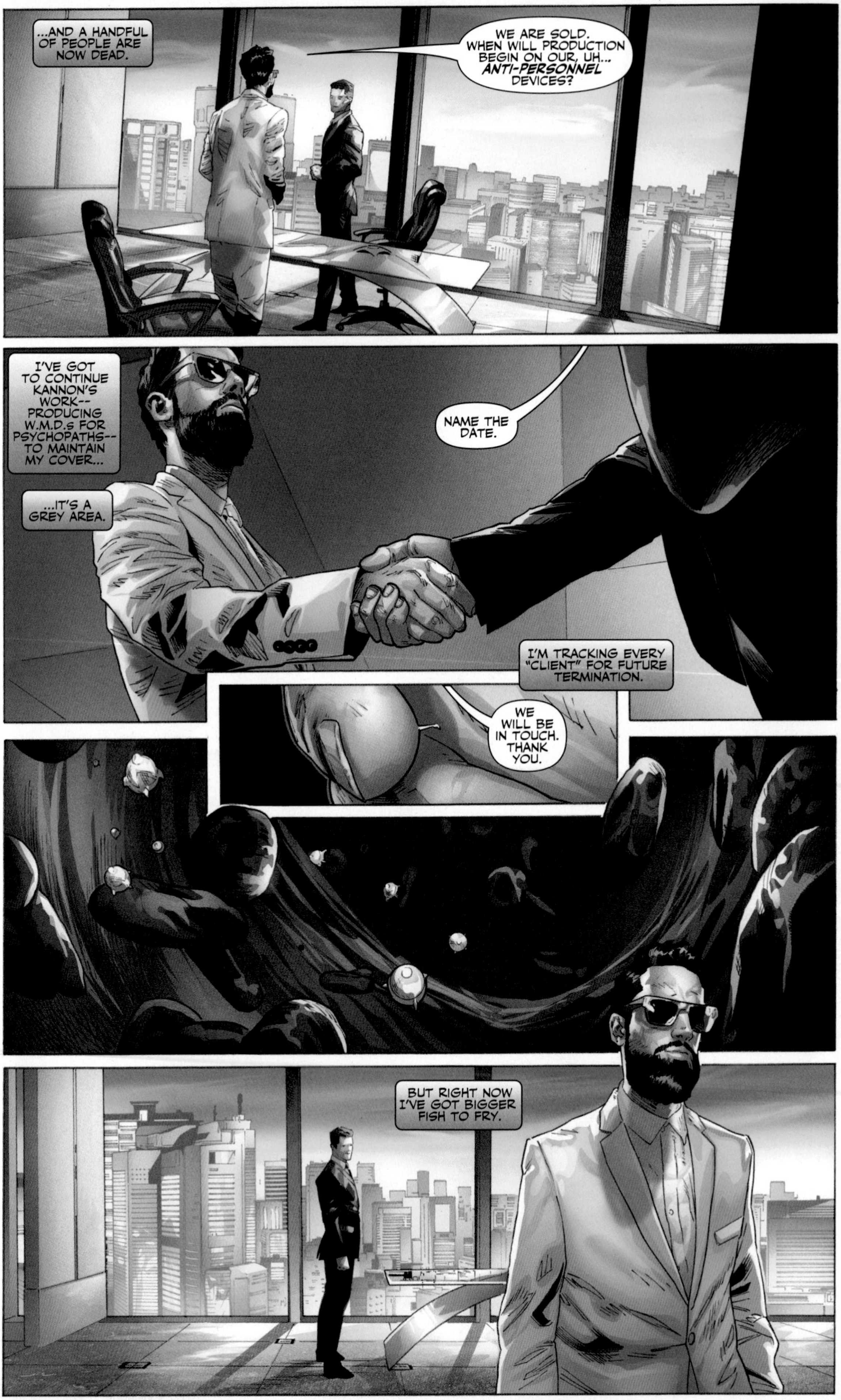
...AND A HANDFUL OF PEOPLE ARE NOW DEAD.
WE ARE SOLD. WHEN WILL PRODUCTION BEGIN ON OUR, UH... ANTI-PERSONNEL DEVICES?
I'VE GOT TO CONTINUE KANNON'S WORK-- PRODUCING W.M.D.s FOR PSYCHOPATHS-- TO MAINTAIN MY COVER...
...IT'S A GREY AREA.
NAME THE DATE.
I'M TRACKING EVERY "CLIENT" FOR FUTURE TERMINATION.
WE WILL BE IN TOUCH. THANK YOU.
BUT RIGHT NOW I'VE GOT BIGGER FISH TO FRY.

KANNON WAS JUST THE TIP OF THE ICEBERG. *ONE OF SEVEN* RUMORED OPERATIVES WHO FORM THE INFRASTRUCTURE OF WEAPONEER. I'VE NEVER BEEN THIS CLOSE TO GETTING THEM.

I'VE TRAINED MY ENTIRE CAREER TO TRACK DOWN THIS *SHADOW SEVEN.*

NOTHING IS GOING TO STOP ME NOW.

NEVILLE SET ME LOOSE.

AND I WON'T BE LEASHED.

NOT UNTIL THE JOB IS DONE.

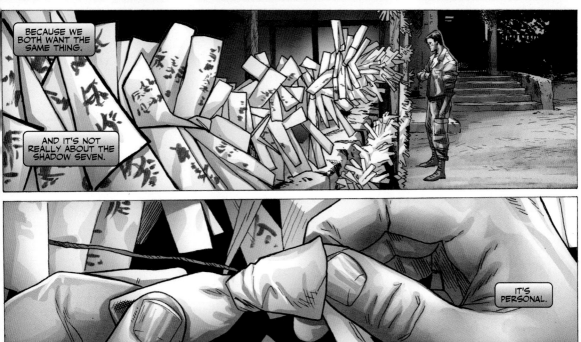

BECAUSE WE BOTH WANT THE SAME THING.

AND IT'S NOT REALLY ABOUT THE SHADOW SEVEN.

IT'S PERSONAL.

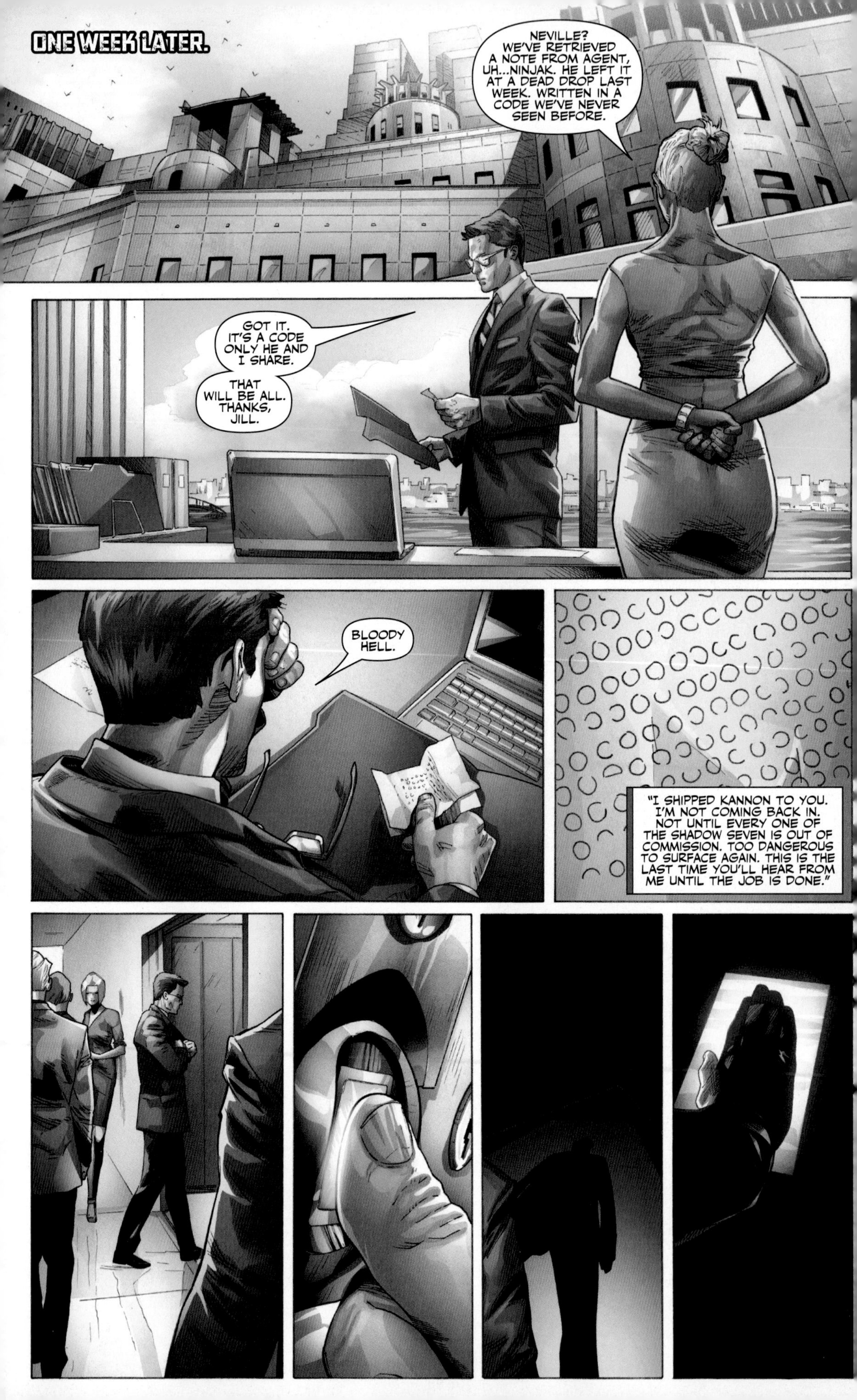
ONE WEEK LATER.
NEVILLE? WE'VE RETRIEVED A NOTE FROM AGENT, UH...NINJAK. HE LEFT IT AT A DEAD DROP LAST WEEK. WRITTEN IN A CODE WE'VE NEVER SEEN BEFORE.
GOT IT. IT'S A CODE ONLY HE AND I SHARE.
THAT WILL BE ALL. THANKS, JILL.
BLOODY HELL.
"I SHIPPED KANNON TO YOU. I'M NOT COMING BACK IN. NOT UNTIL EVERY ONE OF THE SHADOW SEVEN IS OUT OF COMMISSION. TOO DANGEROUS TO SURFACE AGAIN. THIS IS THE LAST TIME YOU'LL HEAR FROM ME UNTIL THE JOB IS DONE."

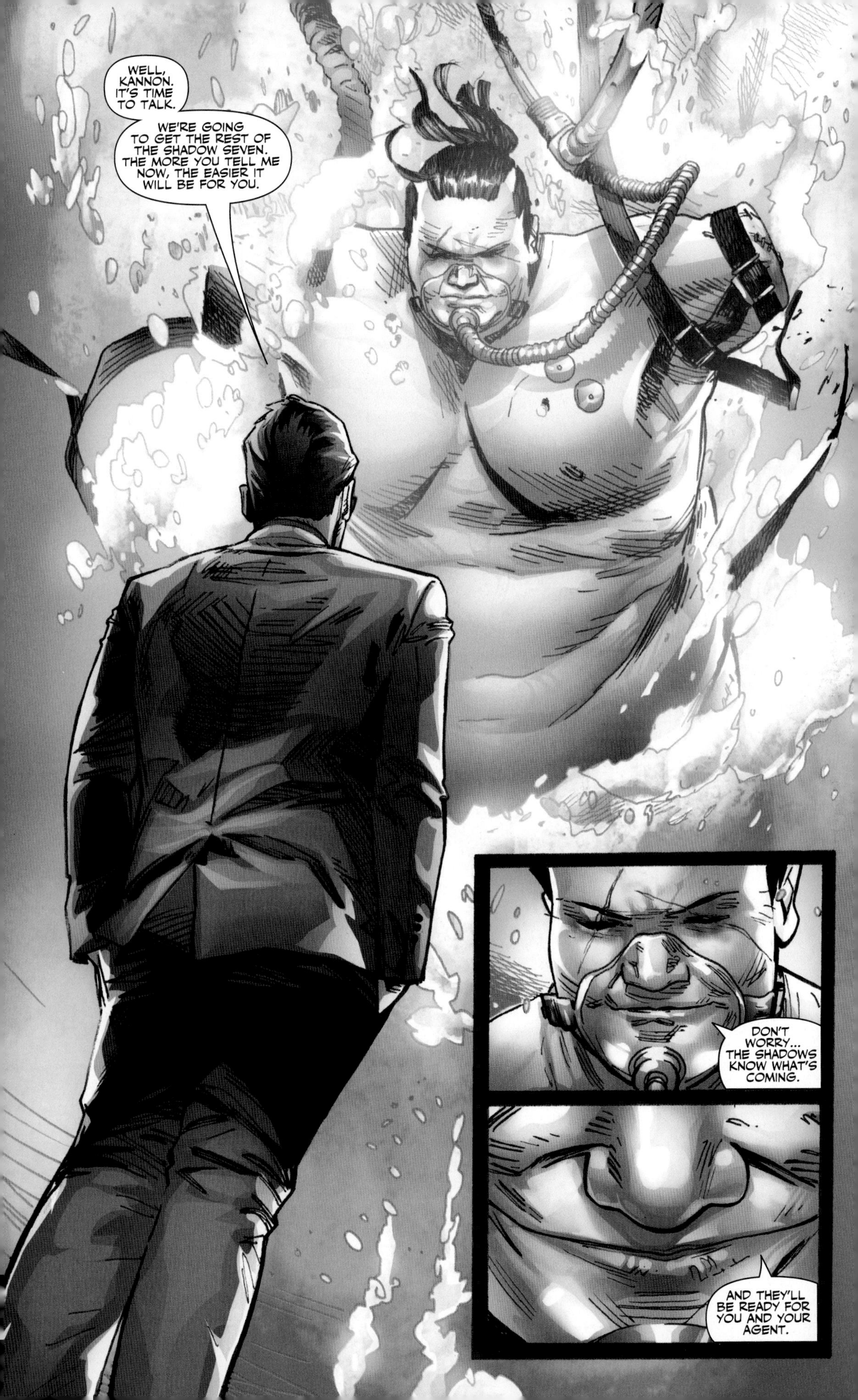
WELL, KANNON. IT'S TIME TO TALK.
WE'RE GOING TO GET THE REST OF THE SHADOW SEVEN. THE MORE YOU TELL ME NOW, THE EASIER IT WILL BE FOR YOU.
DON'T WORRY... THE SHADOWS KNOW WHAT'S COMING.
AND THEY'LL BE READY FOR YOU AND YOUR AGENT.

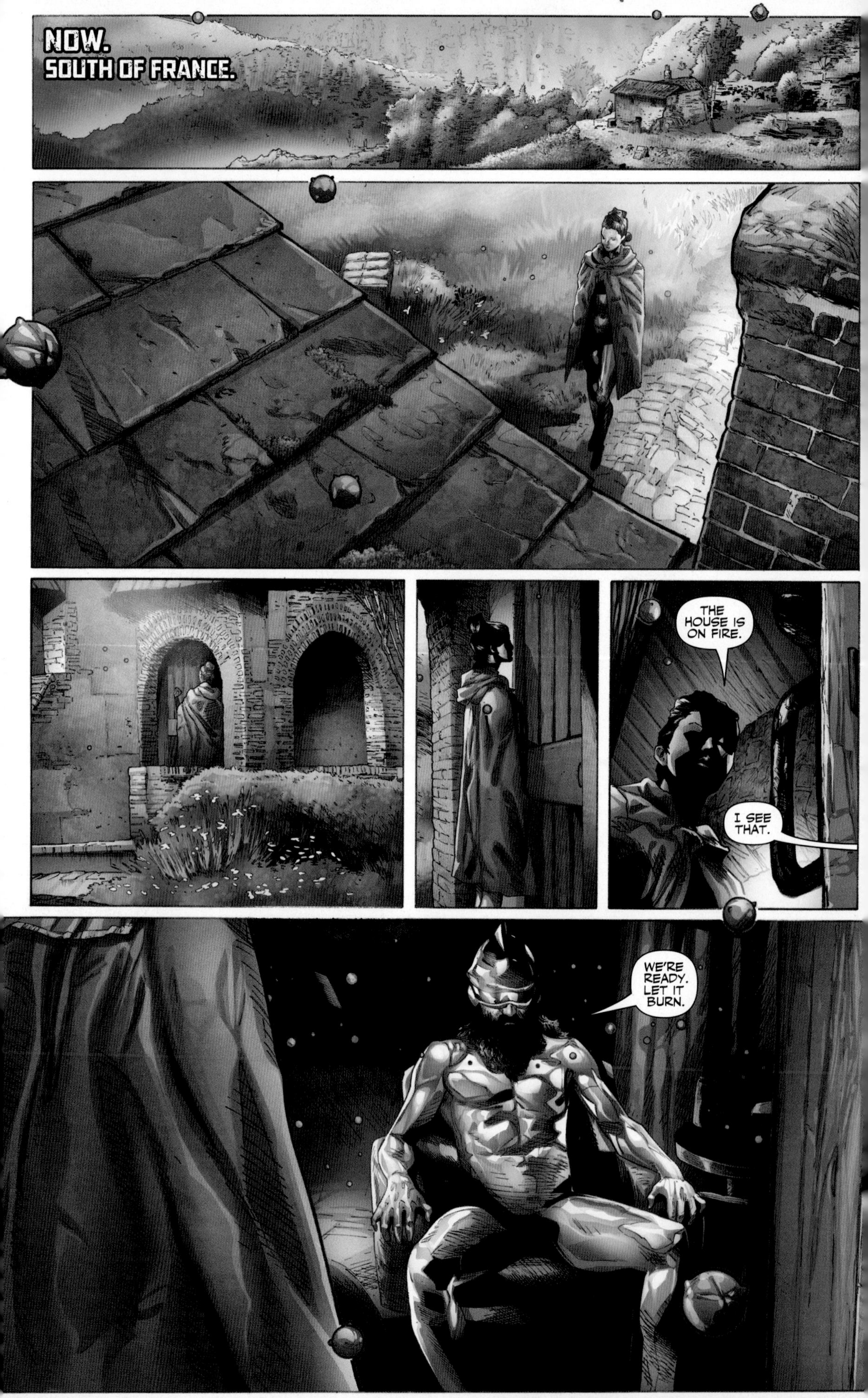
NOW.
SOUTH OF FRANCE.
THE HOUSE IS ON FIRE.
I SEE THAT.
WE'RE READY. LET IT BURN.

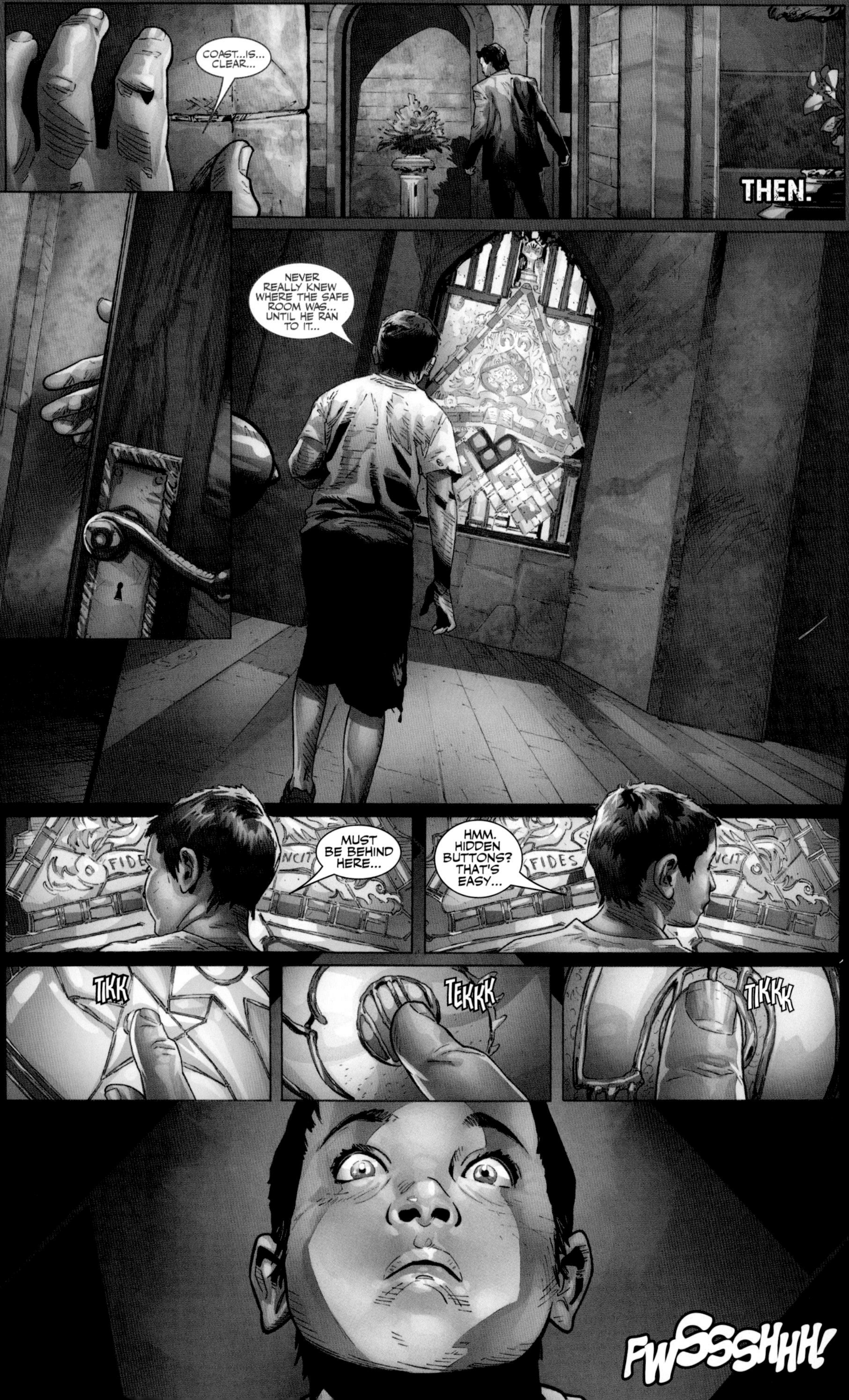
COAST...IS... CLEAR...
THEN.
NEVER REALLY KNEW WHERE THE SAFE ROOM WAS... UNTIL HE RAN TO IT...
MUST BE BEHIND HERE...
HMM. HIDDEN BUTTONS? THAT'S EASY...
TIKK
TEKKK
TIKKK
FWSSSHHH!

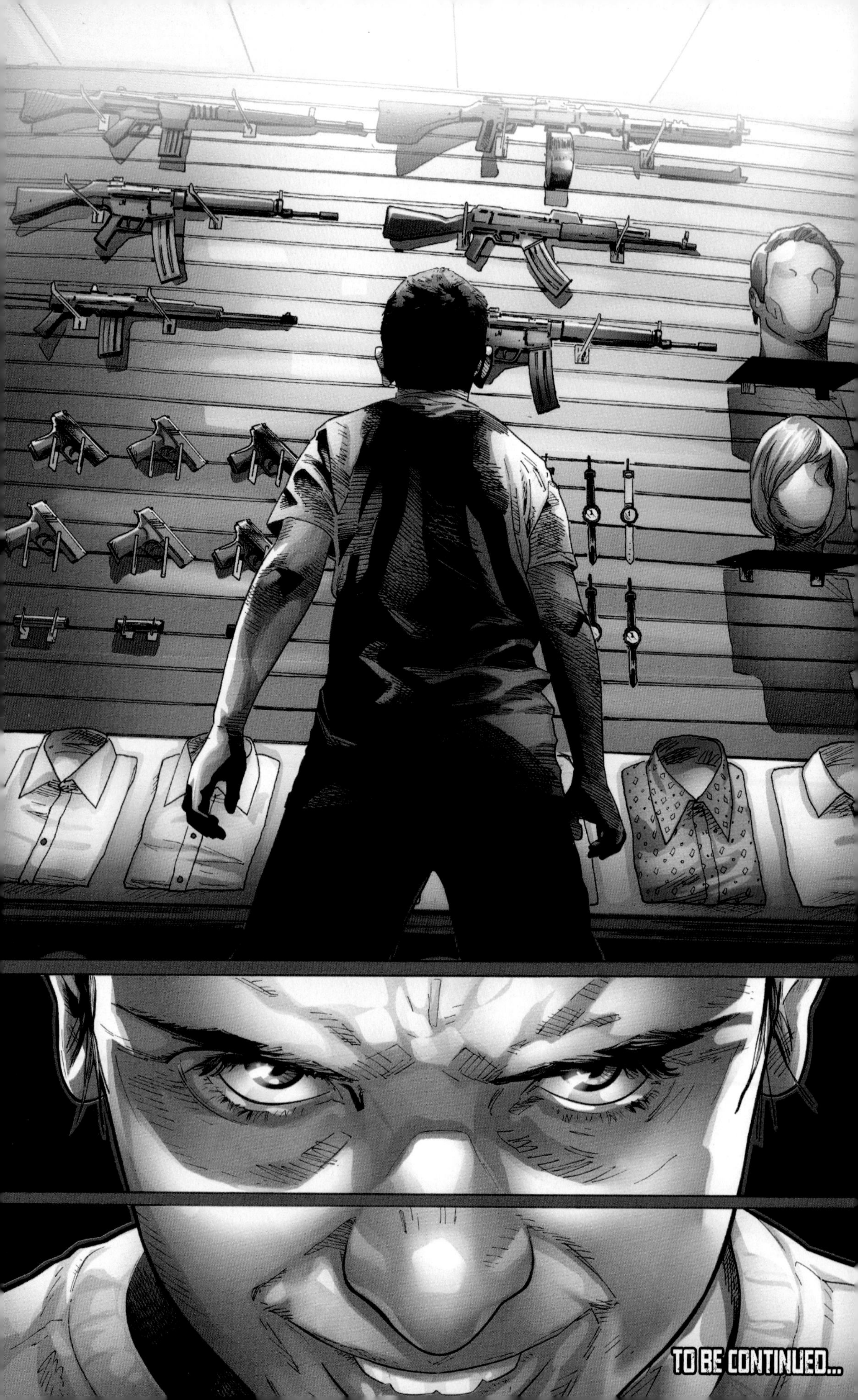
TO BE CONTINUED...

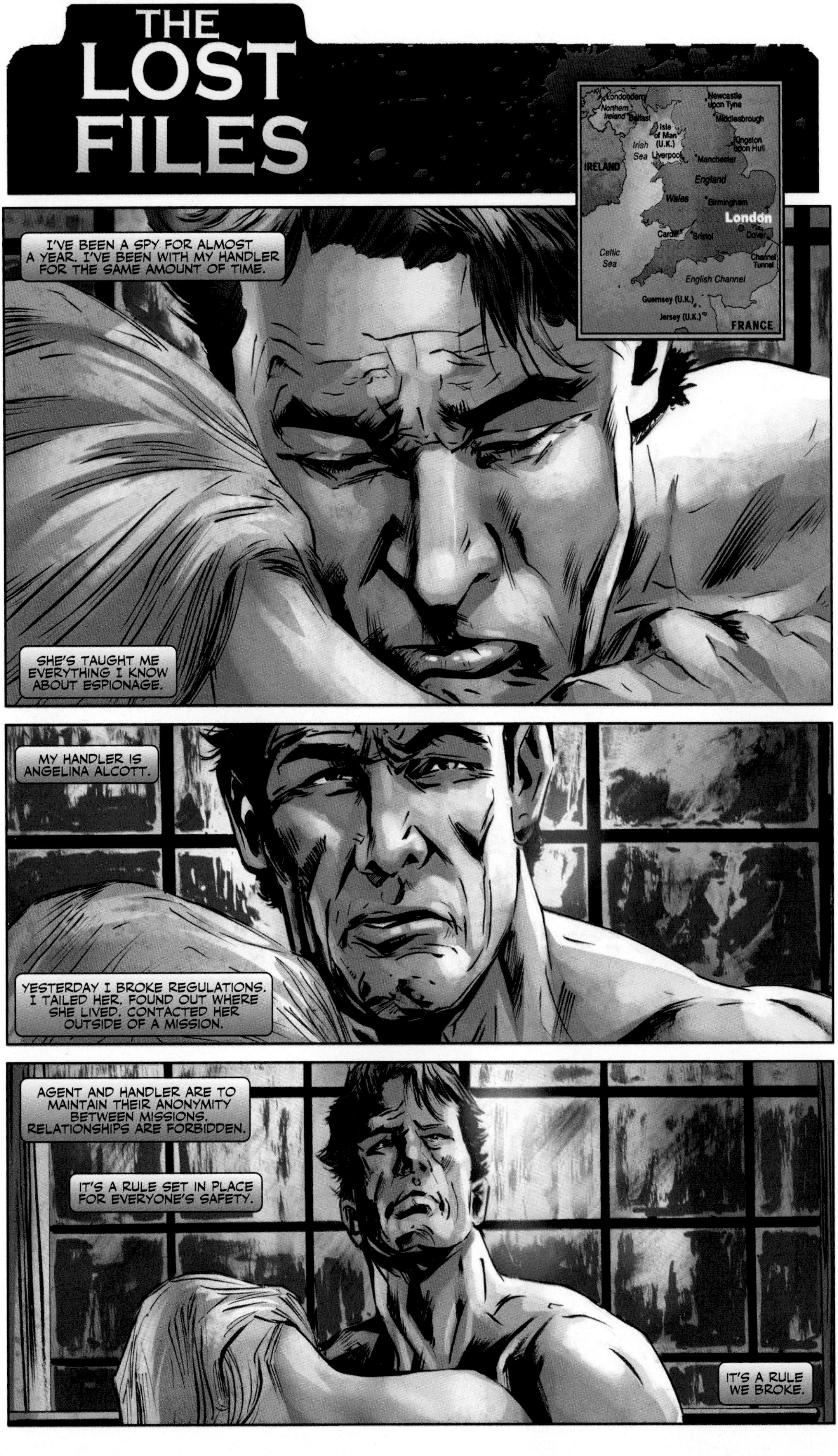
THE LOST FILES
Londonderry
Northern Ireland
Belfast
Newcastle upon Tyne
Middlesbrough
Isle of Man (U.K.)
Irish Sea
Kingston upon Hull
Liverpool
Manchester
IRELAND
England
Wales
Birmingham
London
Cardiff
Bristol
Dover
Celtic Sea
Channel Tunnel
English Channel
Guernsey (U.K.)
Jersey (U.K.)
FRANCE
I'VE BEEN A SPY FOR ALMOST A YEAR. I'VE BEEN WITH MY HANDLER FOR THE SAME AMOUNT OF TIME.
SHE'S TAUGHT ME EVERYTHING I KNOW ABOUT ESPIONAGE.
MY HANDLER IS ANGELINA ALCOTT.
YESTERDAY I BROKE REGULATIONS. I TAILED HER. FOUND OUT WHERE SHE LIVED. CONTACTED HER OUTSIDE OF A MISSION.
AGENT AND HANDLER ARE TO MAINTAIN THEIR ANONYMITY BETWEEN MISSIONS. RELATIONSHIPS ARE FORBIDDEN.
IT'S A RULE SET IN PLACE FOR EVERYONE'S SAFETY.
IT'S A RULE WE BROKE.

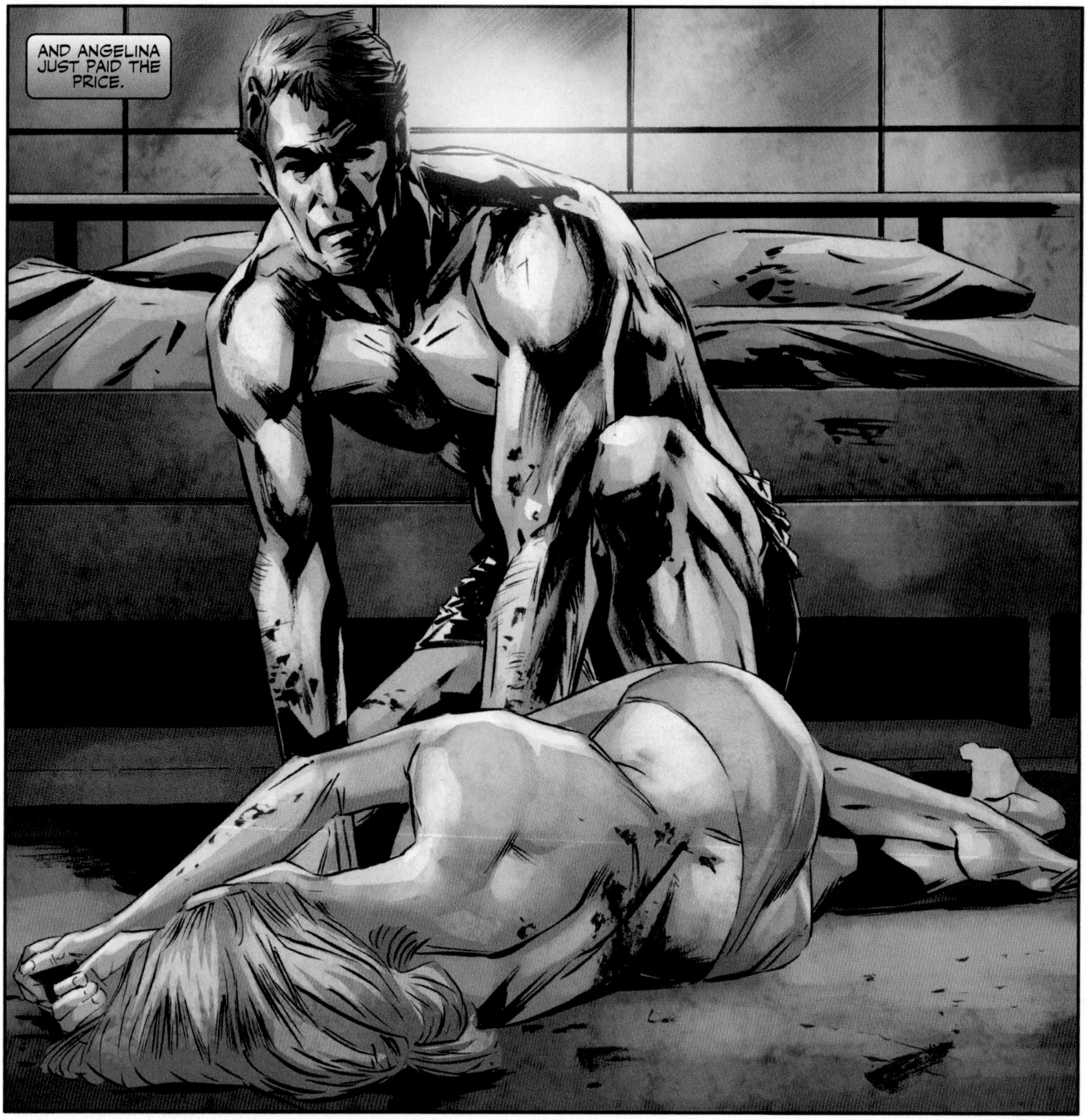
AND ANGELINA JUST PAID THE PRICE.

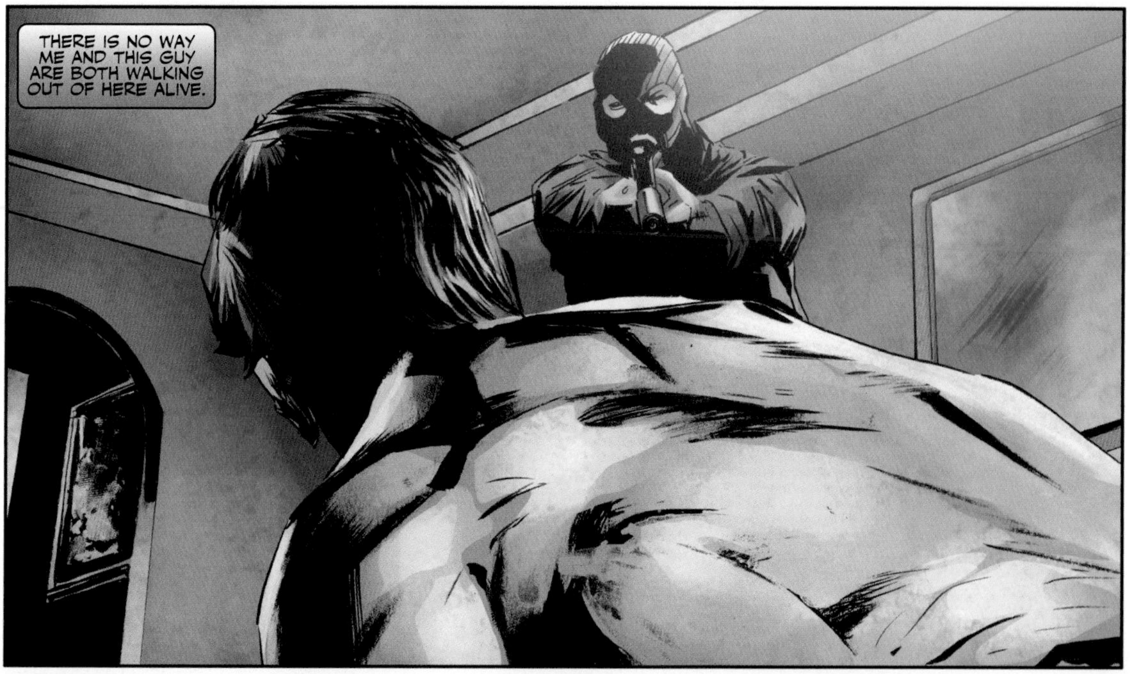
THERE IS NO WAY ME AND THIS GUY ARE BOTH WALKING OUT OF HERE ALIVE.

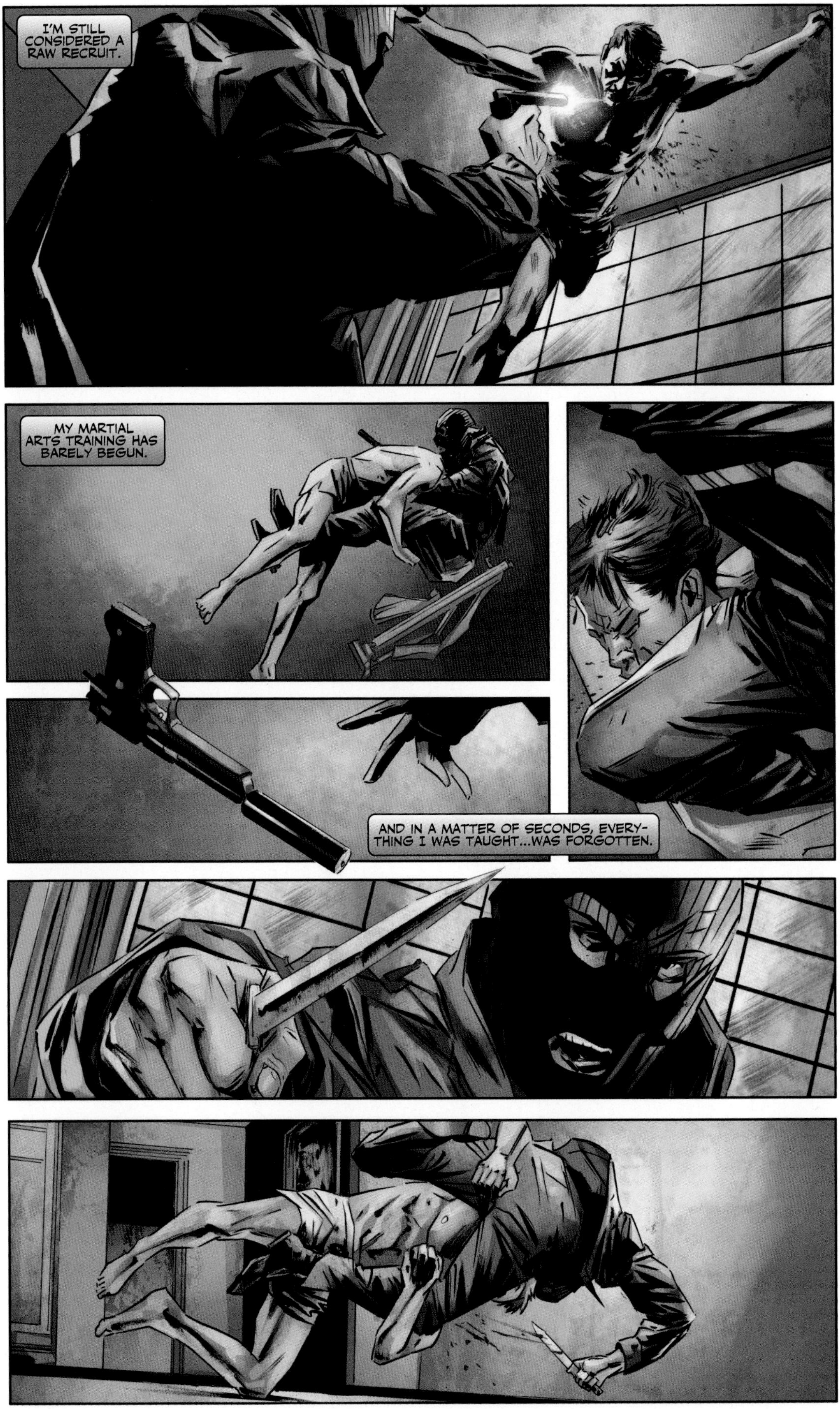
I'M STILL CONSIDERED A RAW RECRUIT.
MY MARTIAL ARTS TRAINING HAS BARELY BEGUN.
AND IN A MATTER OF SECONDS, EVERY-THING I WAS TAUGHT...WAS FORGOTTEN.

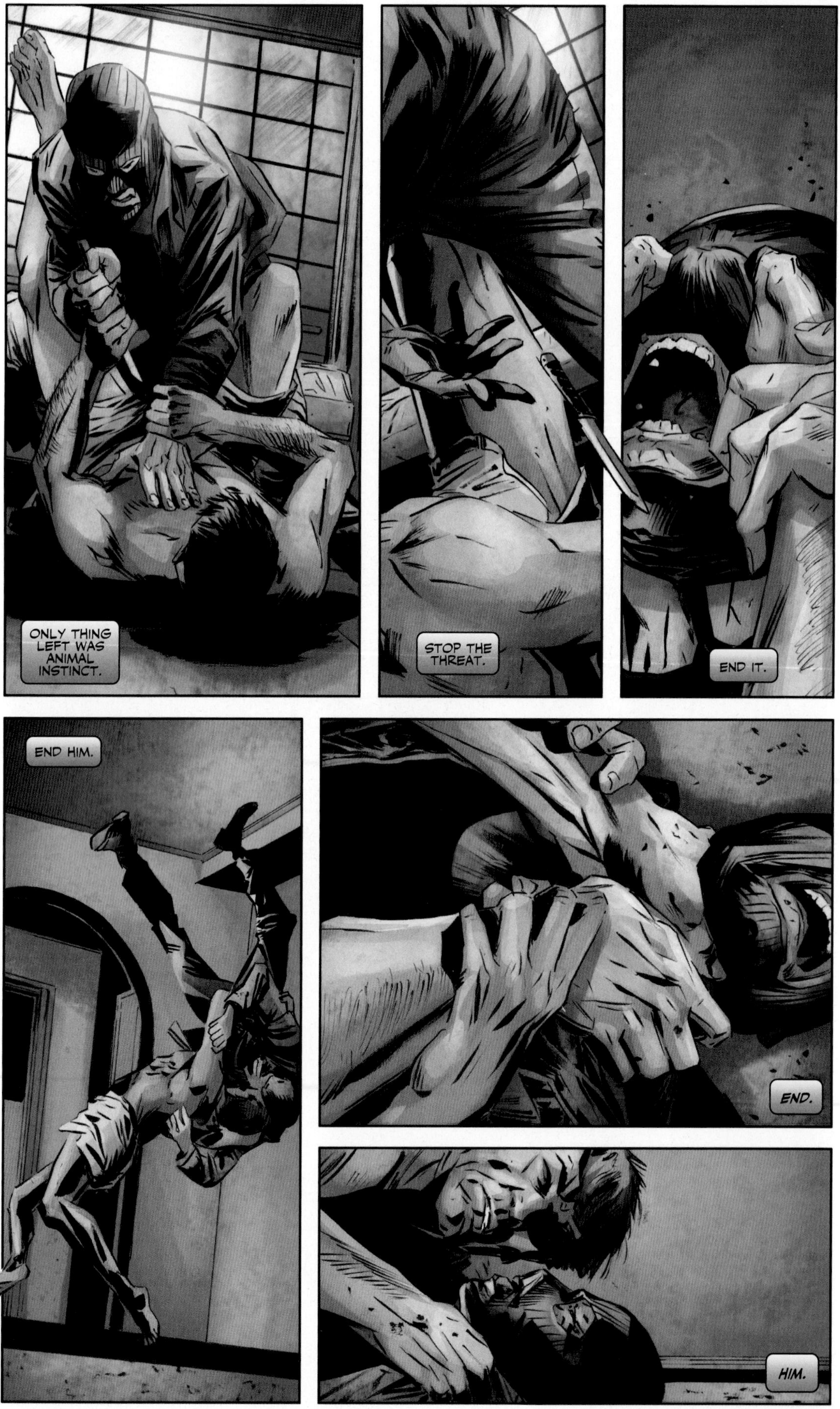
ONLY THING LEFT WAS ANIMAL INSTINCT.
STOP THE THREAT.
END IT.
END HIM.
END.
HIM.

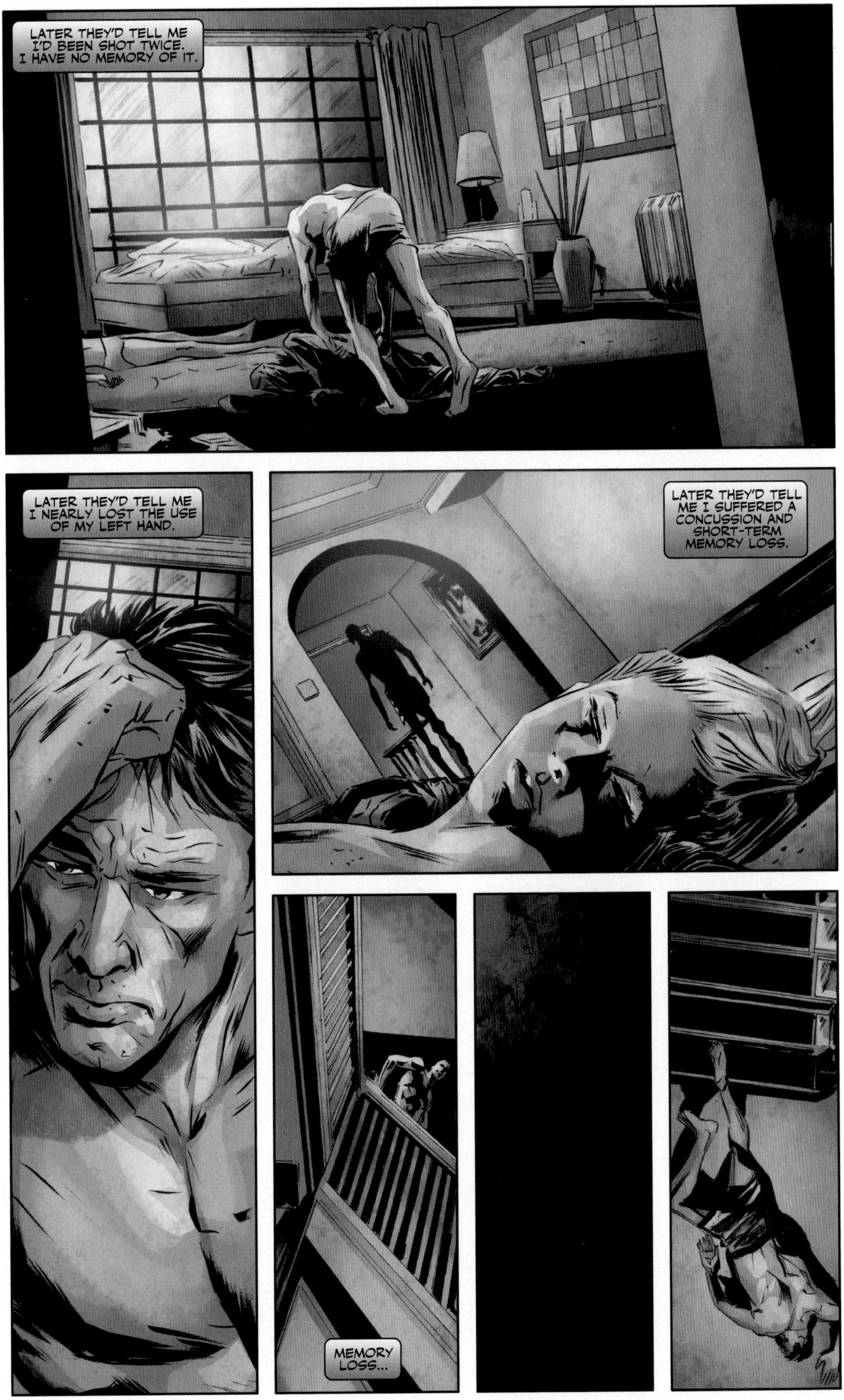
LATER THEY'D TELL ME I'D BEEN SHOT TWICE. I HAVE NO MEMORY OF IT.
LATER THEY'D TELL ME I NEARLY LOST THE USE OF MY LEFT HAND.
LATER THEY'D TELL ME I SUFFERED A CONCUSSION AND SHORT-TERM MEMORY LOSS.
MEMORY LOSS...

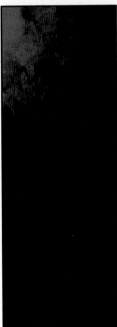

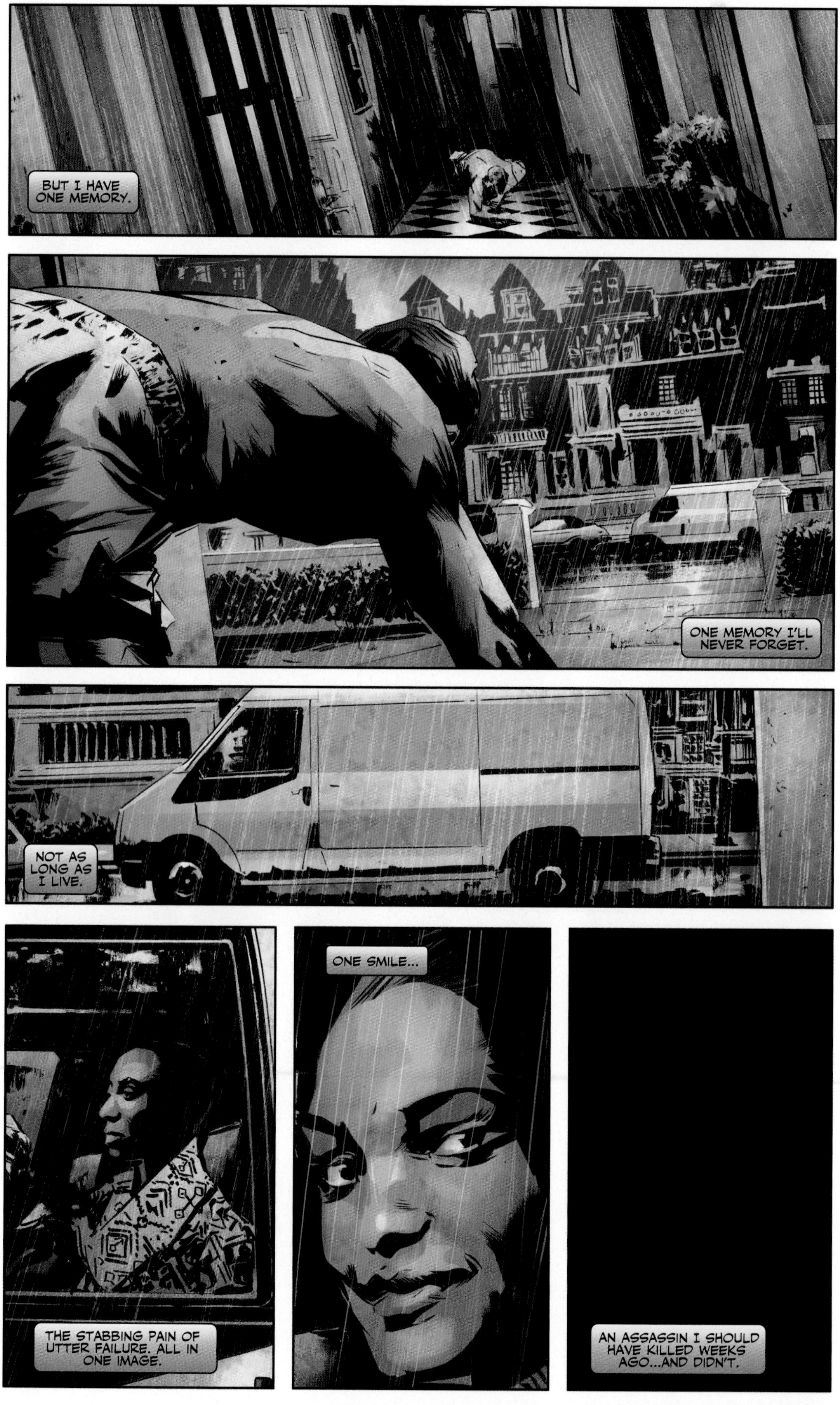
BUT I HAVE ONE MEMORY.
ONE MEMORY I'LL NEVER FORGET.
NOT AS LONG AS I LIVE.
THE STABBING PAIN OF UTTER FAILURE. ALL IN ONE IMAGE.
ONE SMILE...
AN ASSASSIN I SHOULD HAVE KILLED WEEKS AGO...AND DIDN'T.

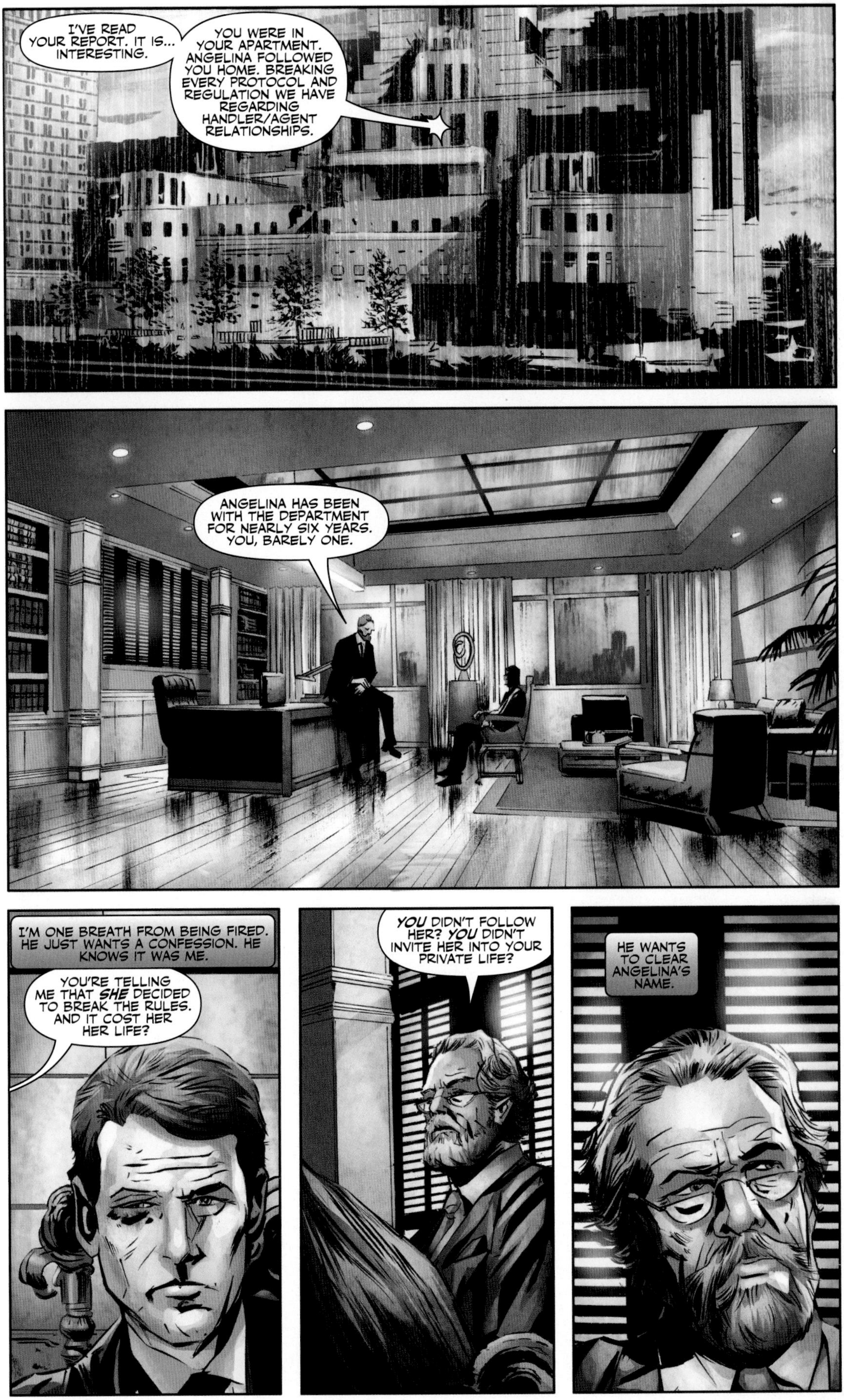
I'VE READ YOUR REPORT. IT IS... INTERESTING.
YOU WERE IN YOUR APARTMENT. ANGELINA FOLLOWED YOU HOME. BREAKING EVERY PROTOCOL AND REGULATION WE HAVE REGARDING HANDLER/AGENT RELATIONSHIPS.
ANGELINA HAS BEEN WITH THE DEPARTMENT FOR NEARLY SIX YEARS. YOU, BARELY ONE.
I'M ONE BREATH FROM BEING FIRED. HE JUST WANTS A CONFESSION. HE KNOWS IT WAS ME.
YOU'RE TELLING ME THAT SHE DECIDED TO BREAK THE RULES. AND IT COST HER HER LIFE?
YOU DIDN'T FOLLOW HER? YOU DIDN'T INVITE HER INTO YOUR PRIVATE LIFE?
HE WANTS TO CLEAR ANGELINA'S NAME.

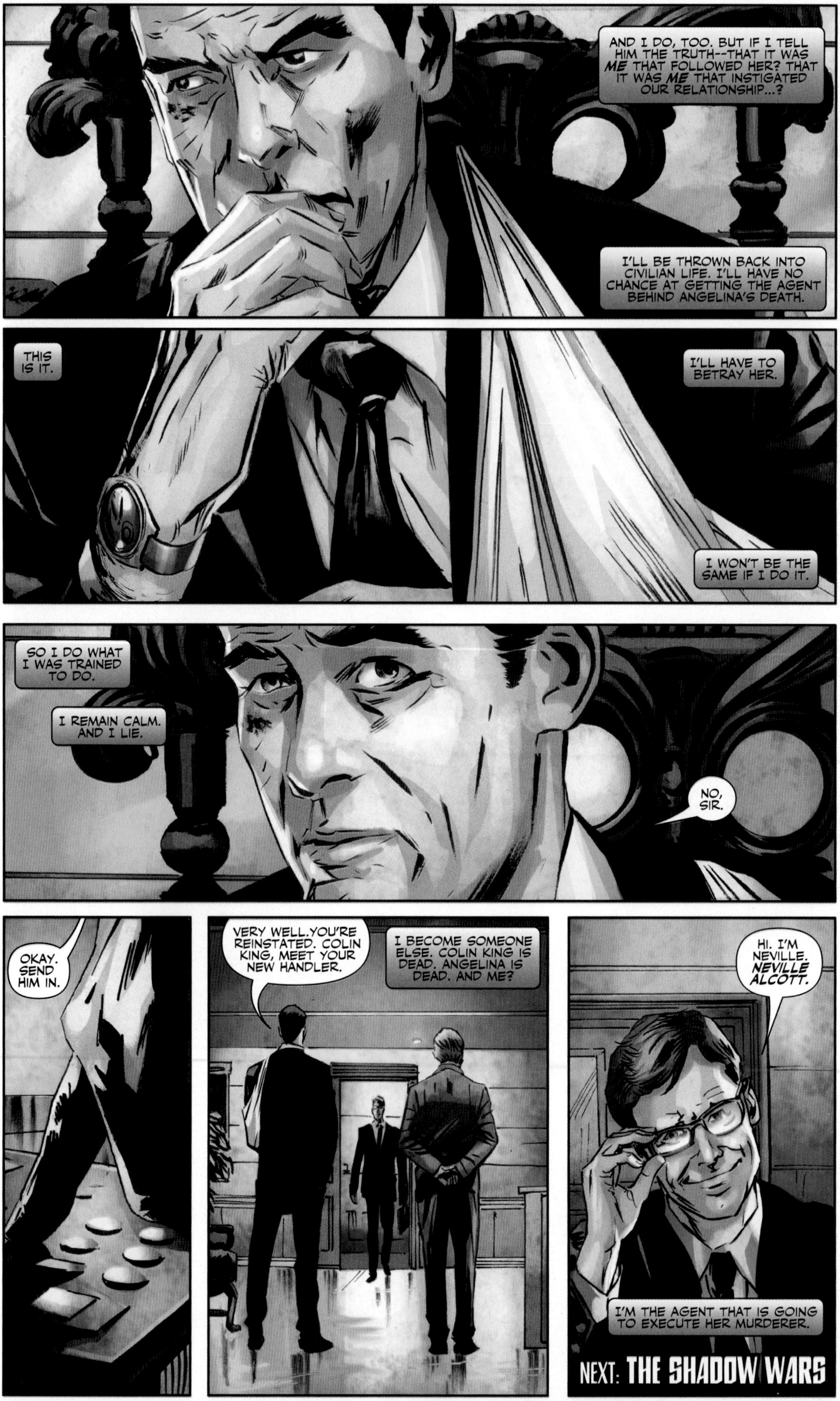
AND I DO, TOO. BUT IF I TELL HIM THE TRUTH--THAT IT WAS *ME* THAT FOLLOWED HER? THAT IT WAS *ME* THAT INSTIGATED OUR RELATIONSHIP...?
I'LL BE THROWN BACK INTO CIVILIAN LIFE. I'LL HAVE NO CHANCE AT GETTING THE AGENT BEHIND ANGELINA'S DEATH.
THIS IS IT.
I'LL HAVE TO BETRAY HER.
I WON'T BE THE SAME IF I DO IT.
SO I DO WHAT I WAS TRAINED TO DO.
I REMAIN CALM. AND I LIE.
NO, SIR.
OKAY. SEND HIM IN.
VERY WELL.YOU'RE REINSTATED. COLIN KING, MEET YOUR NEW HANDLER.
I BECOME SOMEONE ELSE. COLIN KING IS DEAD. ANGELINA IS DEAD. AND ME?
HI. I'M NEVILLE. *NEVILLE ALCOTT.*
I'M THE AGENT THAT IS GOING TO EXECUTE HER MURDERER.
NEXT: THE SHADOW WARS

GALLERY

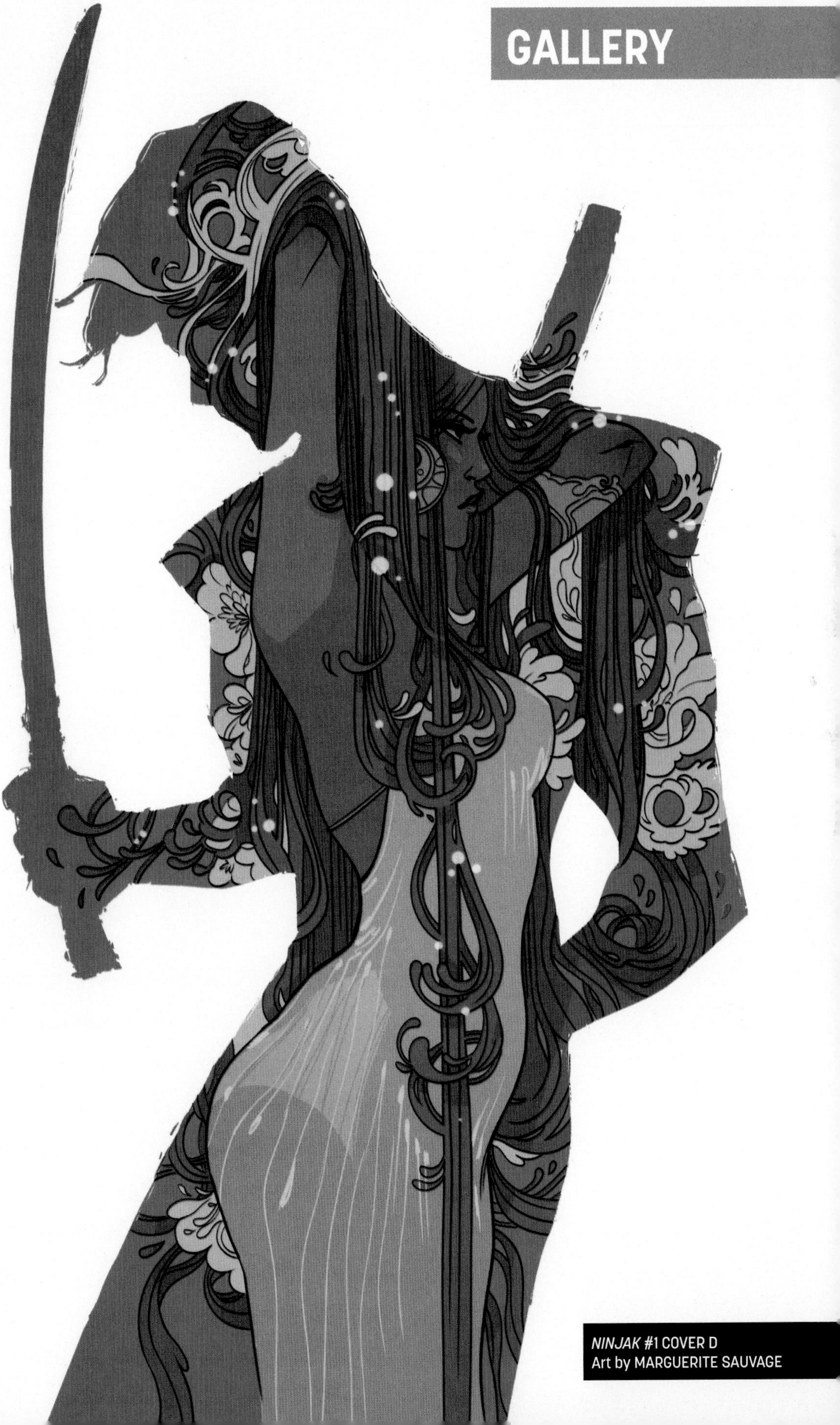

NINJAK #1 COVER D
Art by MARGUERITE SAUVAGE

NINJAK #2 COVER C
Art by PIA GUERRA

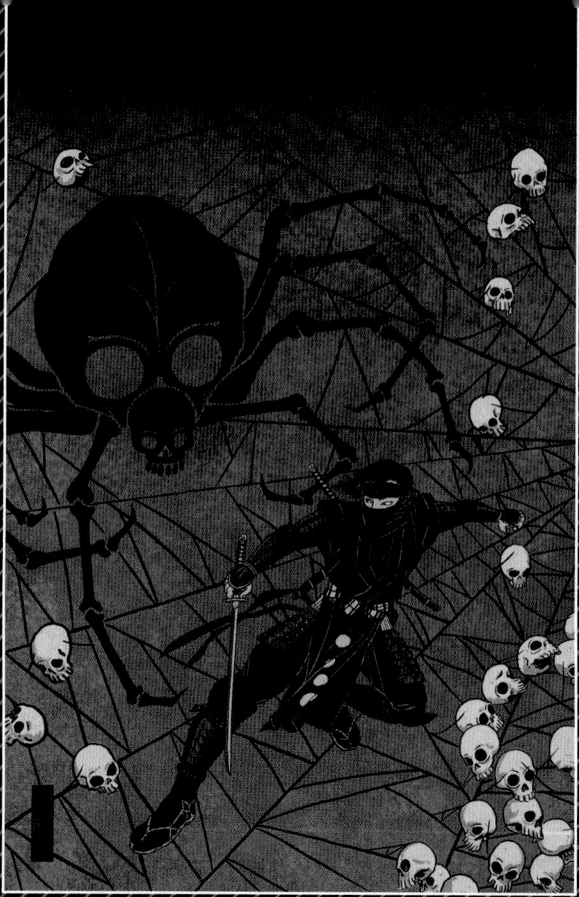

NINJAK #3 COVER B
Art by DAVE JOHNSON

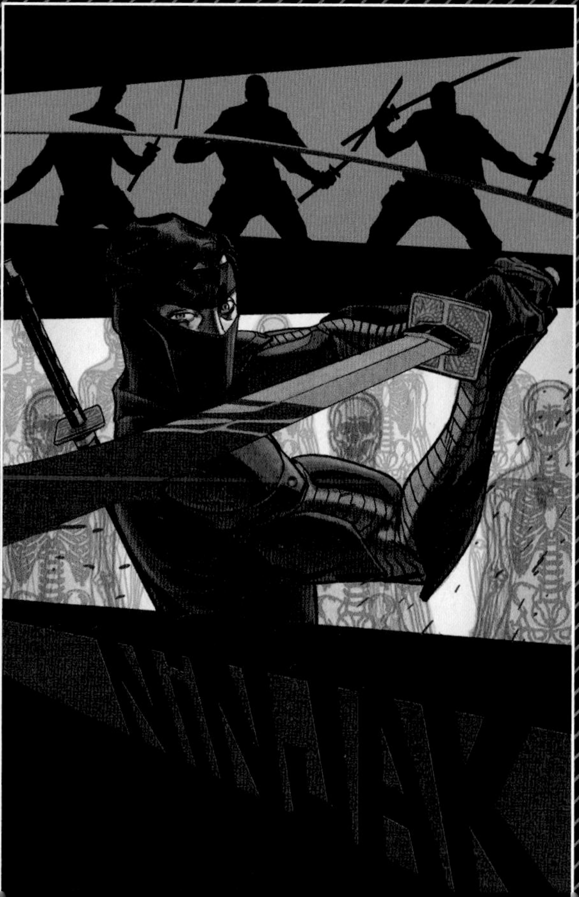
NINJAK

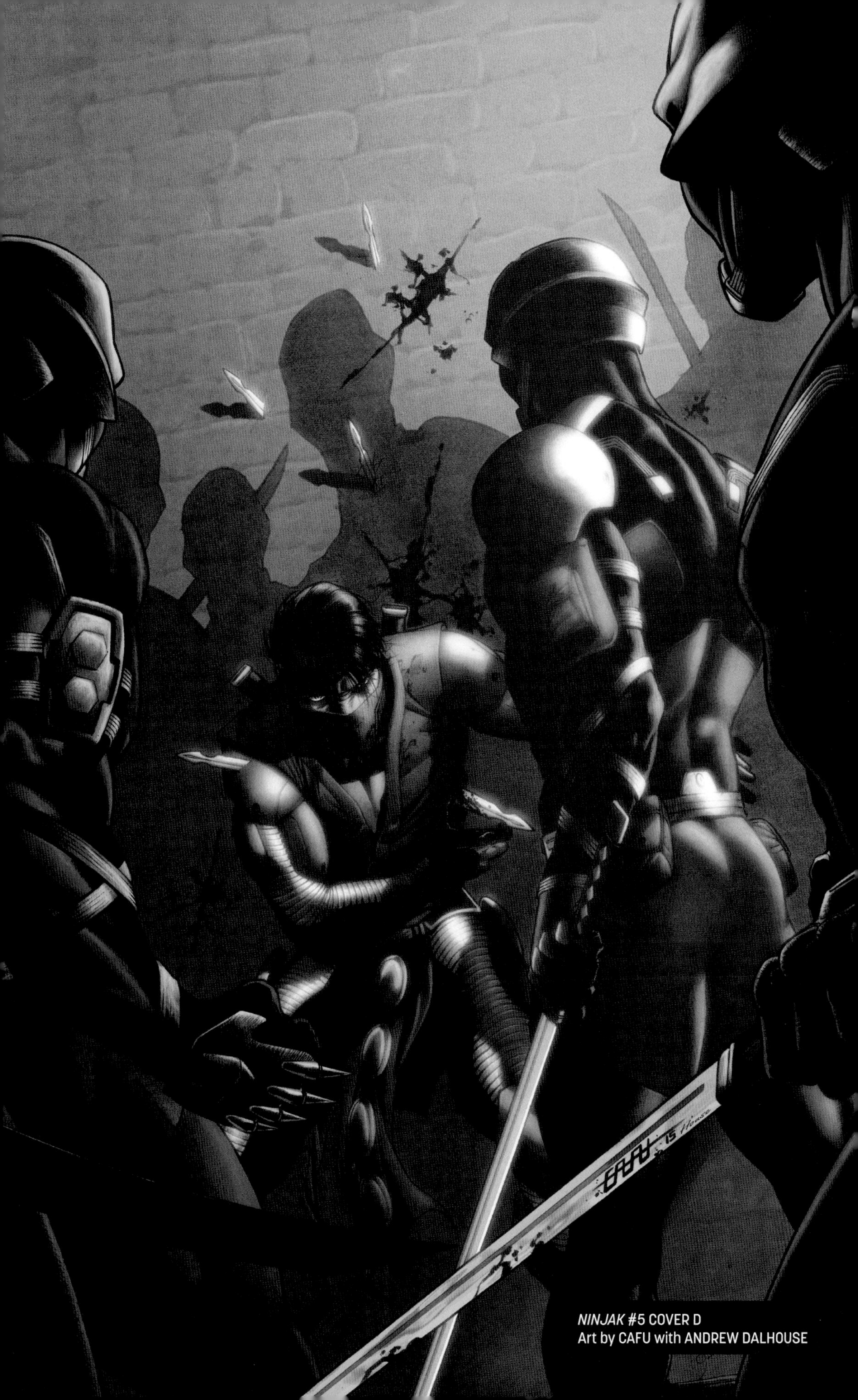

NINJAK #5 COVER D
Art by CAFU with ANDREW DALHOUSE

NINJAK #2, p.5
Pencils by CLAY MANN
Inks by SETH MANN

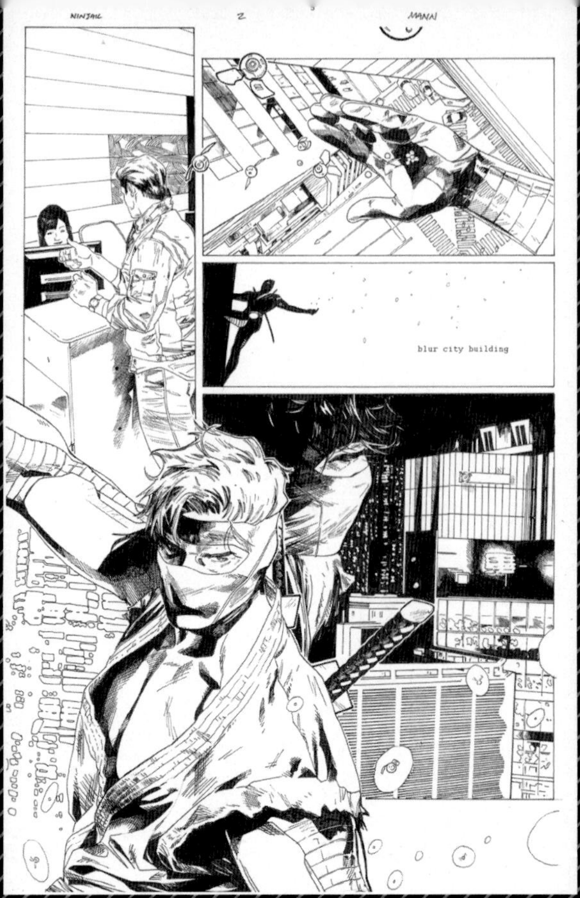
blur city building

NINJAK #2, p.22
Pencils by CLAY MANN
Inks by SETH MANN

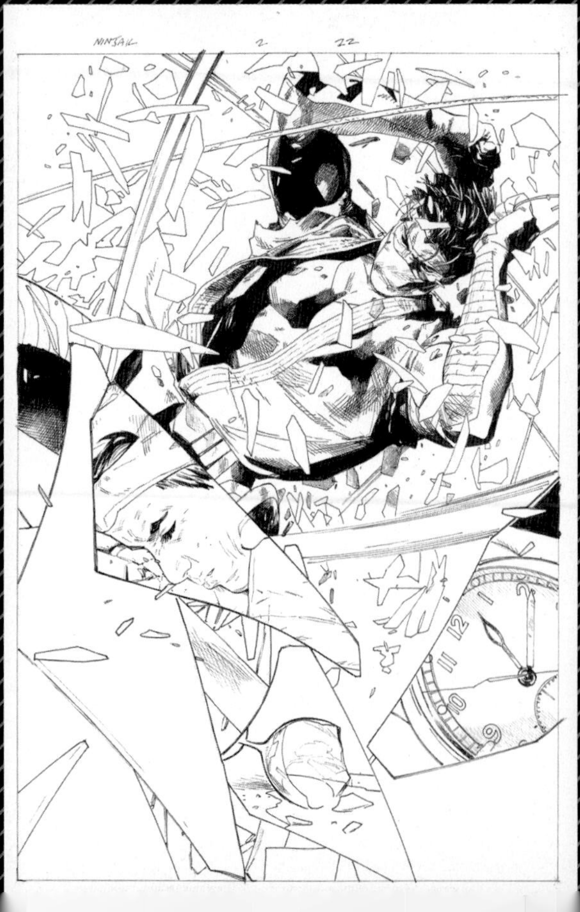

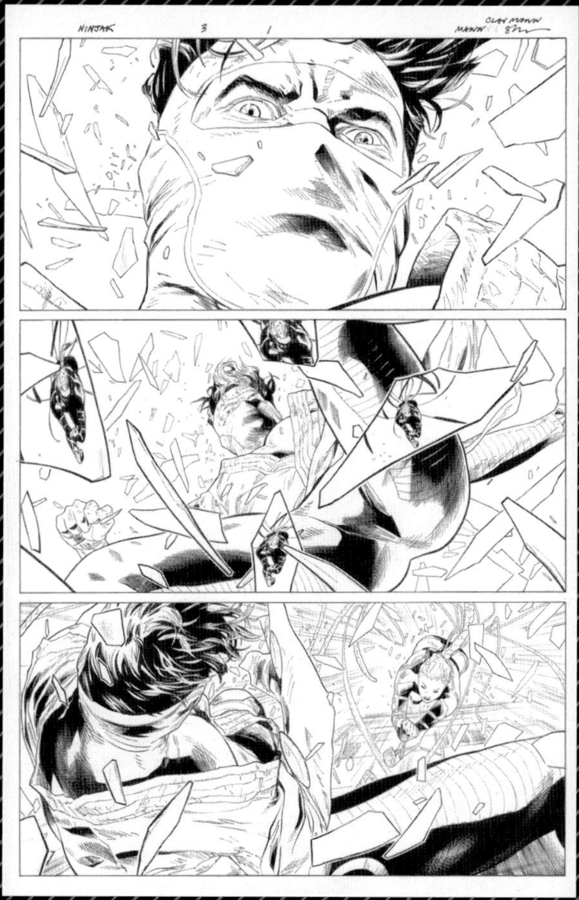
NINJAK
3
1
CLAY MANN
MANN

NINJAK #3, p.1
Pencils by CLAY MANN
Inks by SETH MANN

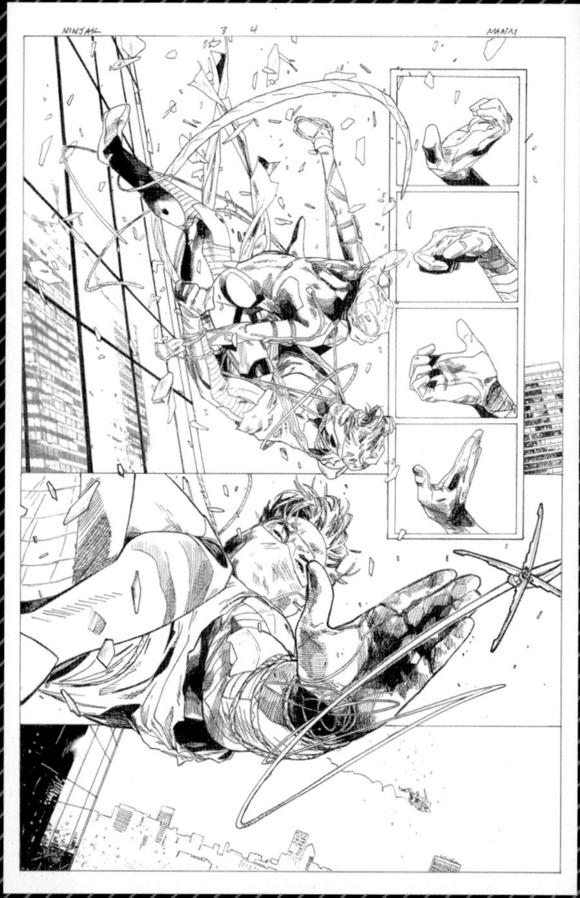
NINJAK
3
4
MANN

NINJAK #3, p.4
Pencils by CLAY MANN
Inks by SETH MANN

NINJAK #4, p.6
Art by JUAN JOSÉ RYP

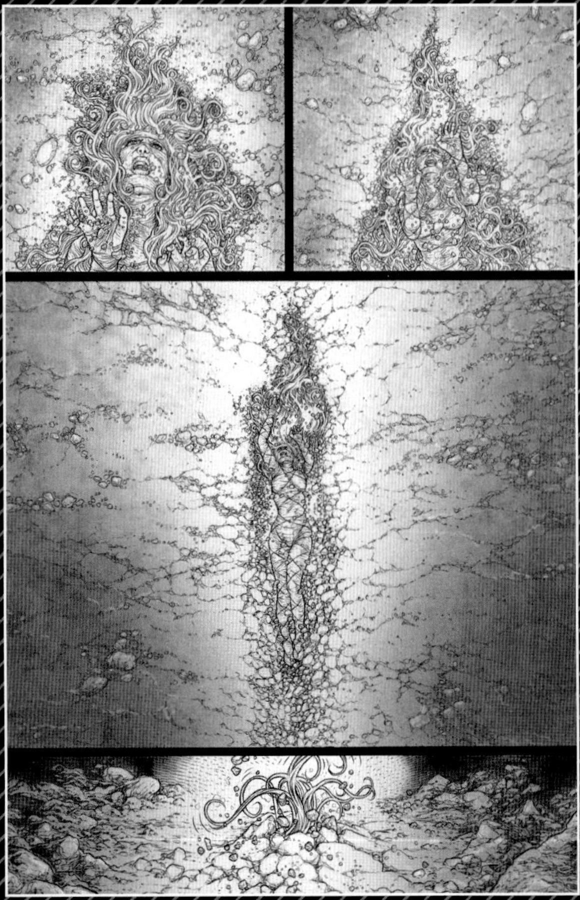

NINJAK #4, p.9
Art by JUAN JOSÉ RYP

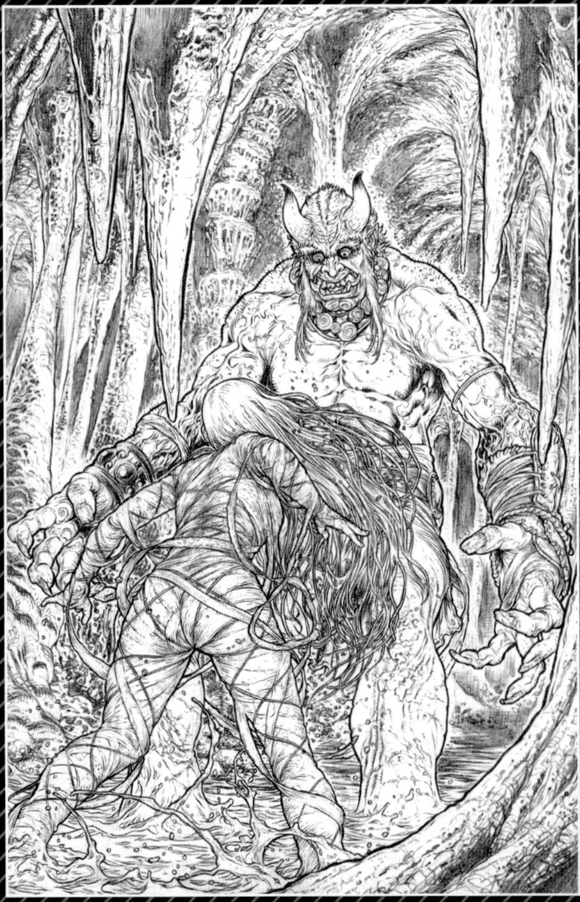

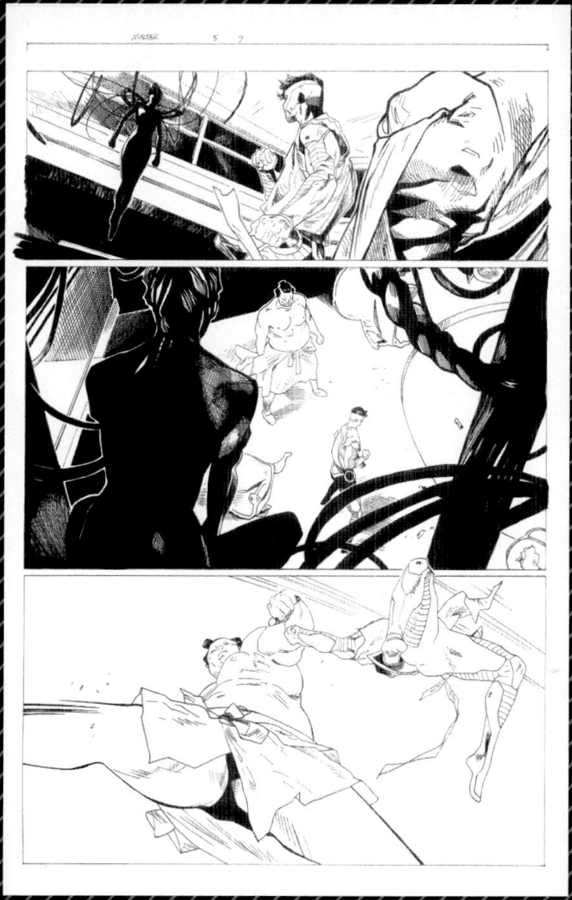
NINJAK 5 7

NINJAK #5, p.7
Pencils by CLAY MANN
Inks by SETH MANN

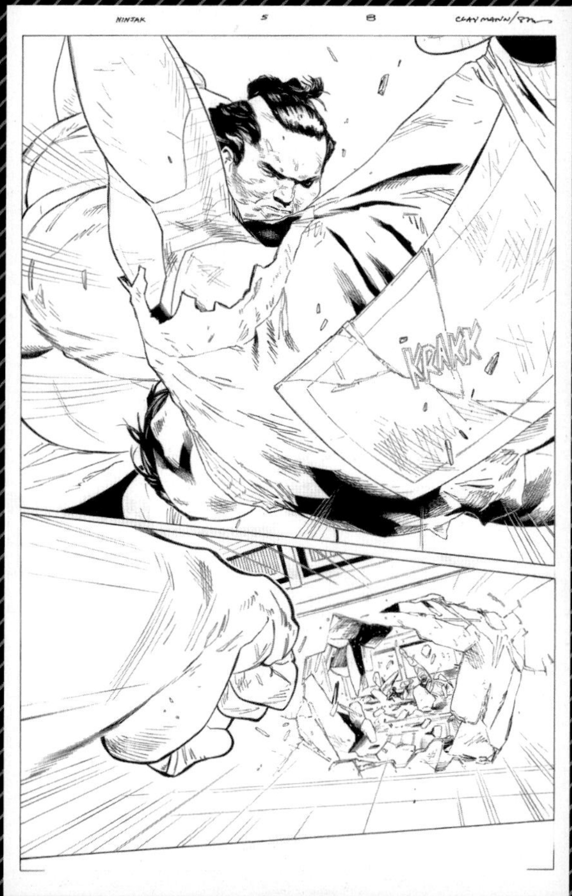
NINJAK 5 8
KRAKK

NINJAK #5, p.8
Pencils by CLAY MANN
Inks by SETH MANN

EXPLORE THE VALIANT UNIVERSE

VALIANT
THE MICHELANGELO CODE
ARCHER & ARMSTRONG

VALIANT
SETTING THE WORLD ON FIRE

VALIANT
OMEGA RISING
HARBINGER

VALIANT
BY THE SWORD
X-O MANOWAR

VALIANT
THE WORLD'S WORST SUPERHERO TEAM
QUANTUM AND WOODY!

ARCHER & ARMSTRONG

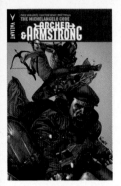

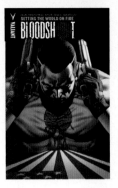

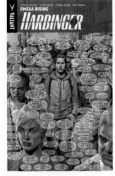

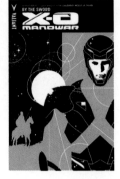

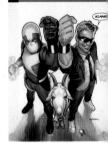

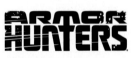

Volume 1: The Michelangelo Code
ISBN: 9780979640988

Volume 2: Wrath of the Eternal Warrior
ISBN: 9781939346049

Volume 3: Far Faraway
ISBN: 9781939346148

Volume 4: Sect Civil War
ISBN: 9781939346254

Volume 5: Mission: Improbable
ISBN: 9781939346353

Volume 6: American Wasteland
ISBN: 9781939346421

Volume 7: The One Percent and Other Tales
ISBN: 9781939346537

ARMOR HUNTERS

Armor Hunters
ISBN: 9781939346452

Armor Hunters: Bloodshot
ISBN: 9781939346469

Armor Hunters: Harbinger
ISBN: 9781939346506

Unity Vol. 3: Armor Hunters
ISBN: 9781939346445

X-O Manowar Vol. 7: Armor Hunters
ISBN: 9781939346476

BLOODSHOT

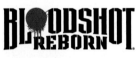

Volume 1: Setting the World on Fire
ISBN: 9780979640964

Volume 2: The Rise and the Fall
ISBN: 9781939346032

Volume 3: Harbinger Wars
ISBN: 9781939346124

Volume 4: H.A.R.D. Corps
ISBN: 9781939346193

Volume 5: Get Some!
ISBN: 9781939346315

Volume 6: The Glitch and Other Tales
ISBN: 9781939346711

BLOODSHOT REBORN

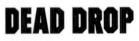

Volume 1: Colorado
ISBN: 9781939346674

DEAD DROP

Dead Drop
ISBN: 9781939346858

THE DEATH-DEFYING DOCTOR MIRAGE

The Death-Defying Dr. Mirage
ISBN: 9781939346490

THE DELINQUENTS

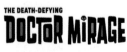

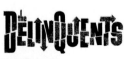

The Delinquents
ISBN: 9781939346513

DIVINITY

DIVINITY
ISBN: 9781939346766

ETERNAL WARRIOR

Volume 1: Sword of the Wild
ISBN: 9781939346209

Volume 2: Eternal Emperor
ISBN: 9781939346292

Volume 3: Days of Steel
ISBN: 9781939346742

HARBINGER

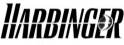

Volume 1: Omega Rising
ISBN: 9780979640957

Volume 2: Renegades
ISBN: 9781939346025

Volume 3: Harbinger Wars
ISBN: 9781939346117

Volume 4: Perfect Day
ISBN: 9781939346155

Volume 5: Death of a Renegade
ISBN: 9781939346339

Volume 6: Omegas
ISBN: 9781939346384

HARBINGER WARS

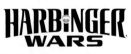

Harbinger Wars
ISBN: 9781939346094

Bloodshot Vol. 3: Harbinger Wars
ISBN: 9781939346124

Harbinger Vol. 3: Harbinger Wars
ISBN: 9781939346117

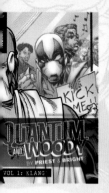

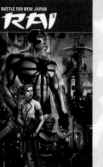

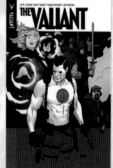

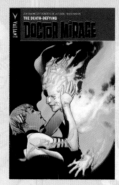

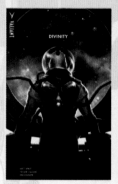

EXPLORE THE VALIANT UNIVERSE

KICK ME
QUANTUM AND WOODY
BY PRIEST & BRIGHT
VOL 1: KLANG

VALIANT
BATTLE FOR NEW JAPAN
RAI

VALIANT
THE VALIANT

VALIANT
THE DEATH-DEFYING
DOCTOR MIRAGE

VALIANT
DIVINITY

インペリアム MPERIUM

lume 1: Collecting Monsters
BN: 9781939346759

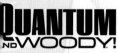

NINJAK

lume 1: Weaponeer
BN: 9781939346667

QUANTUM AND WOODY!

lume 1: The World's Worst Superhero Team
BN: 9781939346186

lume 2: In Security
BN: 9781939346230

lume 3: Crooked Pasts, Present Tense
BN: 9781939346391

lume 4: Quantum and Woody Must Die!
BN: 9781939346629

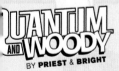

QUANTUM AND WOODY BY PRIEST & BRIGHT

ume 1: Klang
N: 9781939346780

ume 2: Switch
N: 9781939346803

ume 3: And So...
N: 9781939346865

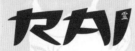

RAI

Volume 1: Welcome to New Japan
ISBN: 9781939346414

Volume 2: Battle for New Japan
ISBN: 9781939346612

Volume 3: The Orphan
ISBN: 9781939346841

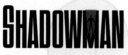

SHADOWMAN

Volume 1: Birth Rites
ISBN: 9781939346001

Volume 2: Darque Reckoning
ISBN: 9781939346056

Volume 3: Deadside Blues
ISBN: 9781939346162

Volume 4: Fear, Blood, And Shadows
ISBN: 9781939346278

Volume 5: End Times
ISBN: 9781939346377

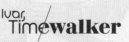

Ivar, Timewalker

Volume 1: Making History
ISBN: 9781939346636

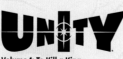

UNITY

Volume 1: To Kill a King
ISBN: 9781939346261

Volume 2: Trapped by Webnet
ISBN: 9781939346346

Volume 3: Armor Hunters
ISBN: 9781939346445

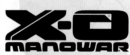

UNITY (Continued)

Volume 4: The United
ISBN: 9781939346544

Volume 5: Homefront
ISBN: 9781939346797

THE VALIANT

The Valiant
ISBN: 9781939346605

VALIANT ZEROES AND ORIGINS

Valiant: Zeroes and Origins
ISBN: 9781939346582

X-O MANOWAR

Volume 1: By the Sword
ISBN: 9780979640940

Volume 2: Enter Ninjak
ISBN: 9780979640995

Volume 3: Planet Death
ISBN: 9781939346087

Volume 4: Homecoming
ISBN: 9781939346179

Volume 5: At War With Unity
ISBN: 9781939346247

Volume 6: Prelude to Armor Hunters
ISBN: 9781939346407

Volume 7: Armor Hunters
ISBN: 9781939346476

Volume 8: Enter: Armorines
ISBN: 9781939346551

Volume 9: Dead Hand
ISBN: 9781939346650

VALIANT
HARBINGER
DELUXE EDITION 2

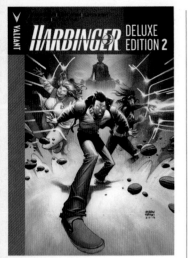

OMNIBUSES

Archer & Armstrong: The Complete Classic Omnibus
ISBN: 9781939346872
Collecting ARCHER & ARMSTRONG (1992) #0-26, ETERNAL WARRIOR (1992) #25 along with ARCHER & ARMSTRONG: THE FORMATION OF THE SECT.

Quantum and Woody: The Complete Classic Omnibus
ISBN: 9781939346360
Collecting QUANTUM AND WOODY (1997) #0, 1-21 and #32, THE GOAT: H.A.E.D.U.S. #1, and X-O MANOWAR (1996) #16

X-O Manowar Classic Omnibus Vol. 1
ISBN: 9781939346308
Collecting X-O MANOWAR (1992) #0-30, ARMORINES #0, X-O DATABASE #1, as well as material from SECRETS OF THE VALIANT UNIVERSE #1

DELUXE EDITIONS

Archer & Armstrong Deluxe Edition Book 1
ISBN: 9781939346223
Collecting ARCHER & ARMSTRONG #0-13

VALIANT
ARMOR HUNTERS
DELUXE EDITION

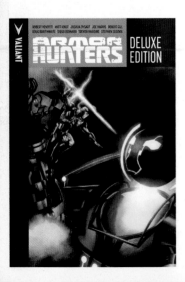

Armor Hunters Deluxe Edition
ISBN: 9781939346728
Collecting ARMOR HUNTERS #1-4, ARMOR HUNTERS: AFTERMATH #1, ARMOR HUNTERS: BLOODSHOT #1-3, ARMOR HUNTERS: HARBINGER #1-3, UNITY #8-11 and X-O MANOWAR #23-29

Bloodshot Deluxe Edition Book 1
ISBN: 9781939346216
Collecting BLOODSHOT #1-13

Harbinger Deluxe Edition Book 1
ISBN: 9781939346131
Collecting HARBINGER #0-14

Harbinger Deluxe Edition Book 2
ISBN: 9781939346773
Collecting HARBINGER #15-25, HARBINGER: OMEGAS #1-3, and HARBINGER: BLEEDING MONK #0

Harbinger Wars Deluxe Edition
ISBN: 9781939346322
Collecting HARBINGER WARS #1-4, HARBINGER #11-14, and BLOODSHOT #10-13

Quantum and Woody Deluxe Edition Book 1
ISBN: 9781939346681
Collecting QUANTUM AND WOODY #1-12 and QUANTUM AND WOODY: THE GOAT #0

Q2: The Return of Quantum and Woody Deluxe Edition
ISBN: 9781939346568
Collecting Q2: THE RETURN OF QUANTUM AND WOODY #1-5

VALIANT
JAMES ASMUS TOM FOWLER MING DOYLE
KANO JORDIE BELLAIRE DAVE LANPHEAR
QUANTUM AND WOODY!
DELUXE EDITION 1
MEH!

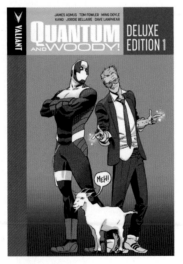

Shadowman Deluxe Edition Book 1
ISBN: 9781939346438
Collecting SHADOWMAN #0-10

Unity Deluxe Edition Book 1
ISBN: 9781939346575
Collecting UNITY #0-14

X-O Manowar Deluxe Edition Book 1
ISBN: 9781939346100
Collecting X-O MANOWAR #1-14

X-O Manowar Deluxe Edition Book 2
ISBN: 9781939346520
Collecting X-O MANOWAR #15-22, and UNITY #1-4

VALIANT
JIM SHOOTER DAVID LAPHAM
CHILDREN OF THE EIGHTH DAY
HARBINGER
VALIANT MASTERS
LB-AGIN

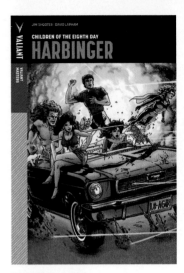

VALIANT MASTERS

Bloodshot Vol. 1 - Blood of the Machine
ISBN: 9780979640933

H.A.R.D. Corps Vol. 1 - Search and Destroy
ISBN: 9781939346285

Harbinger Vol. 1 - Children of the Eighth Day
ISBN: 9781939346483

Ninjak Vol. 1 - Black Water
ISBN: 9780979640971

Rai Vol. 1 - From Honor to Strength
ISBN: 9781939346070

Shadowman Vol. 1 - Spirits Within
ISBN: 9781939346018

VALIANT
KEVIN VANHOOK | DON PERLIN
BLOOD OF THE MACHINE
BLOODSHOT
VALIANT MASTERS

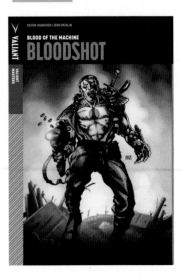

VALIANT
MATT KINDT | CLAY MANN | BUTCH GUICE | JUAN JOSÉ RYP
WEAPONEER
NINJAK

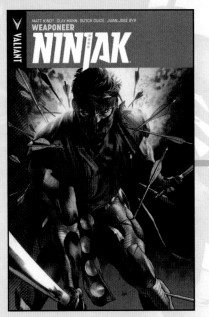

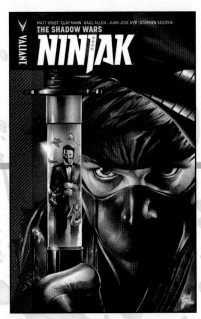

Ninjak Vol. 1: Weaponeer

VALIANT
MATT KINDT | CLAY MANN | RAÚL ALLEN | JUAN JOSÉ RYP | STEPHEN SEGOVIA
THE SHADOW WARS
NINJAK

Ninjak Vol. 2: The Shadow Wars

Read the smash-hit debut and earliest adventures of the Valiant Universe's deadliest master spy!

VALIANT
ENTER: NINJAK
X-O MANOWAR

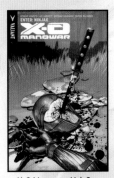

X-O Manowar Vol. 2: Enter Ninjak

VALIANT
TO KILL A KING
UNITY
NOMINATED FOR THREE 2014 HARVEY AWARDS

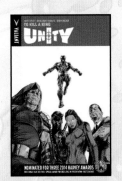

Unity Vol. 1: To Kill a King

VALIANT
TRAPPED BY WEBNET
UNITY

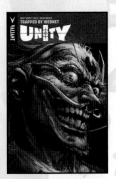

Unity Vol. 2: Trapped by Webnet

VALIANT
ARMOR HUNTERS
UNITY
MULTIPLE HARVEY AWARD NOMINEE

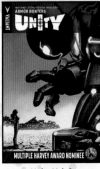

Unity Vol. 3: Armor Hunters

VALIANT
THE UNITED
UNITY
MULTIPLE HARVEY AWARD NOMINEE

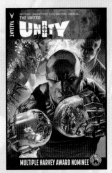

Unity Vol. 4: The United

VALIANT
HOMEFRONT
UNITY
MULTIPLE HARVEY AWARD NOMINEE

Unity Vol. 5: Homefront

VALIANT
THE VALIANT

The Valiant

VALIANT
DIVINITY
THE BEST NEW SUPERHERO OF 2015

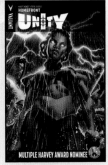

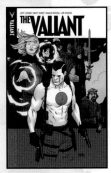

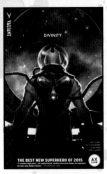

Divinity

VALIANT®

NINJAK®

VOLUME TWO: THE SHADOW WARS

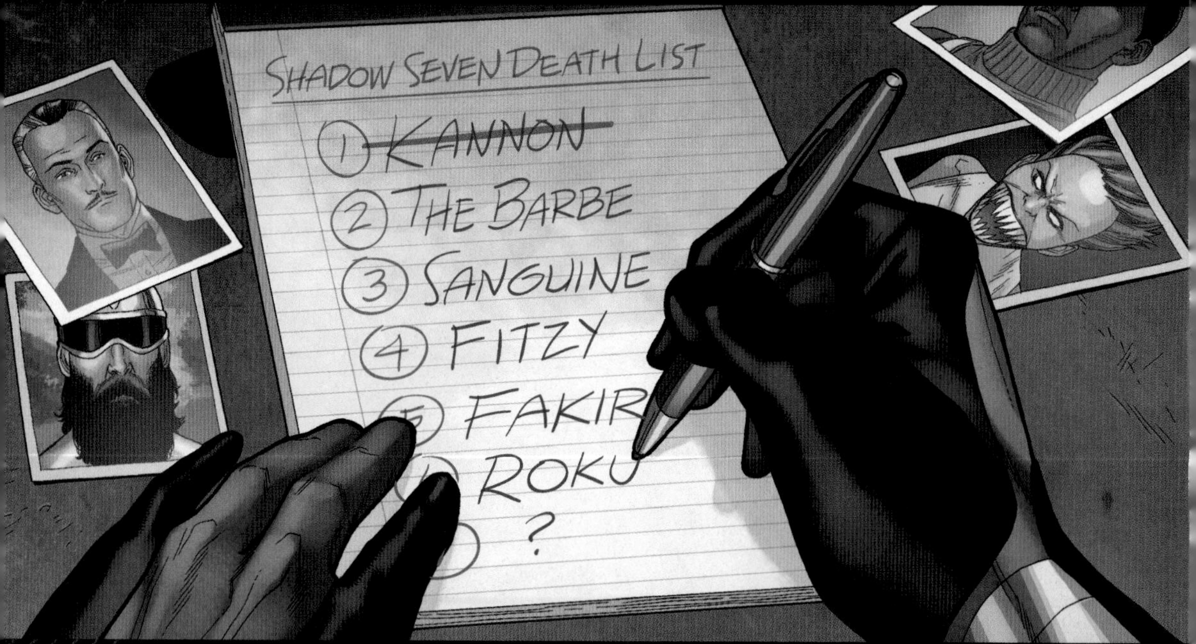
SHADOW SEVEN DEATH LIST
1 KANNON
2 THE BARBE
3 SANGUINE
4 FITZY
5 FAKIR
ROKU
?

WHO ARE THE SHADOW SEVEN?

That's the question Ninjak was sent to answer when he was dispatched to destroy terrorist organization Weaponeer from the inside out. As these mysterious new enemies make their move, Ninjak goes on a globe-spanning race against time to stop their machinations. Plus: discover how Colin King and Neville Alcott first met - and the deadly secret Neville has kept from Colin - as NINJAK: THE LOST FILES continues.

Start reading here as New York Times best-selling writer Matt Kindt (DIVINITY, *Mind MGMT*) and red-hot artists Clay Mann (*X-Men: Legacy*), Raúl Allén (BLOODSHOT REBORN), Juan José Ryp (*Clone*), and Stephen Segovia (*Superior Carnage*) begin a pivotal new chapter of the year's smash-hit new series! Collecting NINJAK #6-9.

TRADE PAPERBACK
ISBN: 978-1-939346-94-0

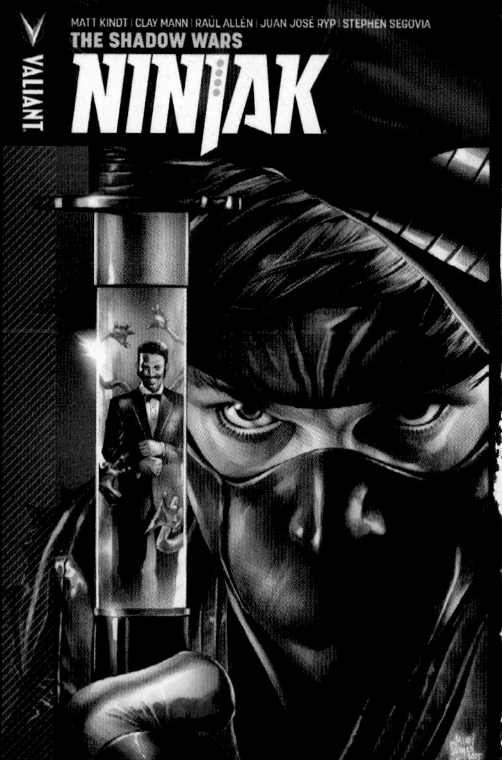
VALIANT
MATT KINDT | CLAY MANN | RAÚL ALLÉN | JUAN JOSÉ RYP | STEPHEN SEGOVIA
THE SHADOW WARS
NINJAK